THE BETRAYED

Reine Arcache Melvin

THE BETRAYED

Europa
editions

Europa Editions
27 Union Square West, Suite 302
New York, NY 10003
www.europaeditions.com
info@europaeditions.com

Copyright © Reine Arcache Melvin, 2018
Published by arrangement with Agence littéraire Astier-Pécher.
All Rights Reserved
First Publication 2022 by Europa Editions

Library of Congress Cataloging in Publication Data is available
ISBN 978-1-60945-773-0

Melvin, Reine Arcache
The Betrayed

Art direction by Emanuele Ragnisco
instagram.com/emanueleragnisco

Cover illustration by Ginevra Rapisardi

Prepress by Grafica Punto Print –Rome

Printed in Canada

CONTENTS

For Greg Brillantes
For Kassia and Oona

Chapter One
Now That I Am Dead

A life gathers into a face before us,
and starts to close its eyes.

—Ricardo M. de Ungria, "Continuing Love"

PILAR

In their exile they knew that nothing could last, yet the family tried to feel at home in the new country. The sisters' father played poker late into the night with other Filipino dissidents who had sought refuge in San Francisco, while their mother pawned her jewelry and threw dancing parties every other weekend.

To prop up their lives, they fabricated rituals. After Mass every Sunday, Lali, Pilar, and their father bundled up in heavy sweaters and marched a few blocks to the beach, where bare-chested young men played Frisbee and women in shorts ran along the shore. Men and women eyed the sisters, who were in their early twenties, with long black hair and Eurasian faces that were striking and intense and nothing like each other. Lali smiled and held the gaze of every man who pleased her, while Pilar lowered her head and stumbled closer to her father. Gregorio didn't notice the men, but he knew his daughters. He wrapped an arm around each woman's waist, reining in Lali with one arm and reassuring Pilar with the other, as he had all their lives.

Every Sunday, the aging dissident and his daughters strolled down that long stretch of sand, past bonfires and surfers, watching the gray waves roll in and thinking but not speaking of the country on the other side of that ocean. After eight years of political exile, the family was beginning to live as though a life away from Manila were possible.

At the moment that life ended, in the middle of a sunny afternoon, Pilar stood near the wall of the living room and listened to Lali and her boyfriend make love. Arturo's voice, thick and harsh. *Faster*, he said. Pilar hurried across the room, turned up the volume of the radio. The chatter of DJs, ad jingles, pop-rock music. She pushed the small dining table against the wall, unfolded a plastic tablecloth, and smoothed it over the table. She tore open foil packets and shook peanuts into wooden bowls.

Lali's voice, crying out. No words. The apartment was too dark, too small. Pilar pressed her hands over her ears. When was her mother coming home? And her father was out again, wandering the streets or visiting people, pretending life in this country had rhythms and reasons that could distract them from everything they had lost.

More cries. Lali wouldn't stop. She had no shame. Their father had spent his life fighting the General, and Lali was in bed with the General's godson.

Static on the radio. Pilar arranged decks of cards and poker chips on a folding table. She began humming the refrain of a song she had heard on the radio that morning, trying to displace the sounds on the other side of the wall.

Another cry. In the bedroom the sisters shared, Lali was performing. She had no right. She knew Pilar could hear her. She wanted Pilar to hear her. Arturo's voice again. *Beautiful*, he said. There was nothing beautiful in his voice.

Where was her father?

Pilar entered the windowless, pink-tiled bathroom, locked the door, and turned on the faucet. She pulled open the plastic curtains and twisted the shower knobs. The rushing water drowned their voices.

She switched off the light, undressed, stepped into the shower. Not looking at her body, not wanting to feel her hands on her flesh, she rubbed soap into a washcloth and the cloth against her skin. She increased the water pressure, lifted her face to the warmth and pounding water, shut her eyes until she could feel and hear nothing else.

She was combing her wet hair when someone banged on the bathroom door.

"Pilar!" Lali cried.

Something in her older sister's voice made Pilar set the comb on the shelf. She unlocked the door.

Lali in a white bathrobe, hair disheveled. "Get your coat," Lali said. "There's been a shooting. Papa's in the hospital."

Pilar's hair dripped water down the back of her blouse. From a distance she watched herself, seeing a slow dance unfolding underwater, where neither her father nor her sister could join her.

"Hurry up," Lali said. "You have to go to Papa."

Their mother entered the bathroom, wearing her camel coat and clutching her decades-old Dior handbag. Tension as thick as seawater pressed down on them. Pilar struggled against the weight, as she had in the summers of her childhood when she had raced Lali in knee-high water near the shore, her calves straining against the heavy tide.

She turned to her mother. For one bright, lonely instant she hoped the older woman would take her in her arms and tell her that everything would be all right. But her mother sat on the edge of the bathtub, set her handbag on the floor, covered her face with her hands.

In the emergency room, the staff told Pilar that her father was being operated on to remove the bullets in his chest and shoulders. For hours, in the waiting room under fluorescent lights, she sat alone on a chair. At some point, a man in green scrubs sat beside her.

"We'll be transferring him to his room in an hour," he said

carefully. "I have to be honest. He'll probably be unconscious for some time."

Pilar walked to the pay phone and called home.

"My God. Why haven't you called?" Lali asked. "How is he?"

"Not good."

"I know. The police were here. People have been calling. Everyone knows." Lali started talking so rapidly Pilar could only pick up scattered phrases: *The General's men. Finish him off.* And then: *Even here, no one's safe.*

Pilar pressed the receiver against her ear and tried to understand. The lights, the white hallway, the receiver in her hand—everything seemed close yet unreachable, angelfish and water behind glass.

"Mama called her friends in Manila," Lali said. "They're getting a psychic healer to try to save Papa. They can do it, you know—through long-distance healing. But he has to put up a fight."

"He's unconscious, Lali. He can't fight."

"Then we have to fight for him. That's what the healer said. Apparently, he's a very good healer. Lots of people in Manila have gone to him. There was that high school classmate of mine, Maribel. Do you remember her? She went into a coma after giving birth, and everyone said she would die. But her parents went to this healer, and he did something. He said he saw the thread of life like a light rising from her body, and he made it strong again. He gave some of his life to her."

Pilar twisted the cord of the pay phone. Nurses and doctors strode out of doors and back inside. Several of them looked Filipino.

"Do you believe that?" Pilar asked Lali. "Does Arturo?" Suddenly, Pilar was furious at her sister, at her sister's boyfriend and all he represented. Arturo and his family had flourished under military rule, building homes and businesses in Manila and San Francisco, profiting from the contracts and commissions the General had tossed their way.

"Arturo's here," Lali said crisply. "He's very concerned."

"I'm sure he is."

"Don't start! He had nothing to do with this."

Pilar breathed in deeply.

"He's the one handling everything," Lali said. "He's talking to the police. He's calling people."

Pilar's fingers tightened around the receiver. "Aren't you coming here?" she whispered.

"Someone has to be with Mama."

In a flash, Pilar understood the dispensation in her family. She would always be called on to keep vigil over the dying, while her sister arranged matters for the survivors.

She hung up without saying goodbye.

At a street corner near the hospital, Pilar waved down a taxi. She told the driver to take her as far from the hospital as possible, to circle the streets for an hour, then bring her back to where he had found her.

She pressed against the back seat, closing her eyes. Another taxi, another night. She was five years old and crying on her father's lap, her body blistered by an overturned pot of scalding tea. On parts of her cheek and chest, the top layer of skin had peeled off, like the surface of a tomato plunged into boiling water. Her father's arms tightened around her as she struggled against the wet sheets he had wrapped around her body.

"My brother burned himself like that when he was a kid," the taxi driver had told her father. "He still has scars all over his face. It looks horrible, but at least he's a man. What's a girl going to do, with scars like that?"

"It doesn't matter whether she's a girl or not." Her father's anger, bright and hard, beamed into her pain. And he had cradled her even closer to him, whispering words she couldn't understand.

In the weeks that followed, he drove her to the hospital every few days to have the burnt skin removed, so that new skin could form without scarring. She screamed as he held down her body and white-robed men treated the damaged skin. One day, her mother and Lali went with them. They watched the men strap her down. Lali pressed her hands over her ears and stared at her younger sister. Then her mother took Lali's hand and led her out of the room. They never returned.

Only Pilar's father remained constant. Each time the dark wave of pain began, he said: "Be brave, my little one. You're strong, *hija*. You'll survive." To please him, to seem brave, she had stopped the cries at her throat.

She had forgotten all this. Pain had done its silent, insidious work, effacing all traces of itself. Until this night, when her father was no longer there beside her, and she remembered all she no longer wished to know.

When Pilar saw her father, bandaged and motionless, punctured by tubes, she couldn't feel anything. She looked at the young doctor beside her. He had Chinese-Filipino features and a Filipino-sounding name—Jose Antonio Chua—but he talked and moved like an American. He was standing too close to her, the way men often did. She crossed her arms over her breasts.

"What can I do?" she asked, glancing at the motionless man on the white bed. "I can't just sit here."

The man on the bed was not her father. He had always smiled when he saw his daughters. She touched the railing along the edge of the bed, rested her hand on the cold metal.

"You can talk to him," the doctor said. "It helps, sometimes."

Her stomach muscles contracted, and she almost doubled over. "I haven't eaten," she murmured. "I should go home and get something to eat."

"Sometimes," the doctor said gently, "when people are unconscious, it helps—it's been known to help—to hear the voice of someone they love."

Her fingers curled around the railing.

"Once, we had a child in here who almost drowned," he said. "She was in a coma. Her parents talked to her constantly, trying to pull her back to life. Even when they went home to sleep, they left a tape of their voices speaking to her, so she would never be without their presence."

"A tape," Pilar repeated. "Could you get me a tape?"

A pause. He scanned her face. "I'm sure we can arrange something for you."

He left her alone with the man who had been her father. She dragged a chair next to the bed, wanting to touch him, but afraid of dislodging the tubes. She felt no grief, only a distance as cool as the metal along his bed.

Bandages covered his chest, arm, and part of his face. The features she could see—a closed eyelid, a sunken cheek— seemed paper-thin, bruised. She lowered her gaze. His finger- nails were misshapen and thick, with scars around the base. They had been damaged in prison. He never talked about those years in prison.

"Papa," she said, feeling like a fraud. She kept repeating the word, the intonation changing each time, until it was more a question than a plea. She shut her eyes, seeing the holes in his chest beneath the bandages.

The doctor returned with a cassette recorder. He knelt and plugged it into a socket near the bed.

She stared at the doctor's hands, remembering the white- robed men who had plucked at her skin. "And that child in the coma," she said, "the one who almost drowned, what hap- pened to her?"

The doctor's gaze flicked away. "To be honest, I don't remember."

He left the room. Because she couldn't look at her father, she sat on the floor beside the tape recorder and pressed the button. She watched the tape turn. "Papa," she said slowly. "It's Pilar. I'm thinking of you." She felt as if she were memorizing texts for a class. "Papa," she said again, then could think of nothing to say. Fearful of the silence, of gaps in the recording, she began to talk rapidly. "Lali and Mama aren't here, but they love you. Even after all the things Mama said. She was just scared. She just wanted a normal marriage, like all of us, and a big house in Manila, and money, like all her friends. It was hard for her here. It was hard for all of us."

Again, she stopped, but stopping meant thinking and she didn't want to think. She wanted only to find words to fill the tape so she could go home and sleep.

"Remember when Lali and I were small, Papa?" she said, but at that moment all she could remember from her childhood were the Frank Sinatra records he used to play every night. So she began to sing. She sang "Strangers in the Night" and "My Way," then switched to the nursery rhymes he had sung to her when she was a child: "London Bridge," "Mary Had a Little Lamb," "Bahay Kubo." The words and the rhythms of his voice came back to her as she sang. "Even now you're speaking for me, Papa," she told the recorder. "I can feel you speaking to me."

Pilar continued to chatter into the tape, reciting snatches of her childhood, repeating phrases other people had used. She heard the sound of her thoughts, unrestricted by any listener's response. She watched the flow of words, surprised by the voices pouring out of her. She wouldn't break the flow by going silent. If she hesitated, she knew she wouldn't be able to speak again.

Pilar glanced at the tape. It had stopped turning. She realized she had been talking into the void for a long time.

She left the room without looking at the man on the bed. As she walked down the hallways, she imagined him strolling beside her, a tall gaunt man with fine-boned features and the feverish, dreamy eyes of a revolutionary who had always expected other people to attend to the details of his life.

Her body began to shake. She pressed it into a phone booth and called home.

"Pilar," Arturo said, rounding the syllables of her name, his voice infused with that intimacy and concern that disarmed even those who despised him. "What's happening?"

"Have you heard from the psychic healer?" she whispered, afraid that voicing her hope might jeopardize it, even attract its opposite. Lali, not she, was the superstitious one, but this calamity showed how superficial her skepticism was, how easily it could be stripped away. She would believe anything now, if it would save her father.

Arturo hesitated. He had always mocked the healers and fortune-tellers that wielded such influence in Manila. Even through the phone line, Pilar sensed the struggle within him. Then he seemed to make a decision.

"Your mother's friends called from Manila," he said. "They said the healer went into a trance."

"And what did he see?"

Another pause. "He said the thread of light was still connected to your father's body. He said your father's going to be all right."

"Of course he's going to be all right," Pilar said quickly, remembering the phrases her father had used long ago as the men in white strapped her to the table. *You're strong, hija. You're brave.* To Arturo she said: "He's strong. He'll survive."

"Of course, Pilar," Arturo said, without inflection. Then, the warmth returning: "You're going to wear yourself out. Come home. There's food here. You need to rest."

In the kitchen, Pilar scooped a spoonful of rice directly from the rice-cooker. She chewed the grains over and over again. It was difficult to swallow. Arturo leaned against the kitchen counter. He watched her and didn't speak. Finally, he spooned rice into two bowls, moistened the grains with *adobo* sauce and bits of chicken, handed her a bowl. He began to eat, slowly and apparently without hunger. She realized he was eating only because he didn't want her to eat alone. She considered thanking him, telling him it wasn't necessary, but tears had been gathering behind her eyes since she had seen her father in the hospital, and she didn't trust herself to talk.

The phone rang, again and again. From her parents' bedroom came the muffled cadences of Lali's voice and, occasionally, a sharp exclamation from her mother.

She set the empty bowl in the sink, nodded at Arturo. He touched her shoulder. She made her way to the room she shared with Lali. Without removing her coat and shoes, she climbed into her bed, lay on her side, ran her finger back and forth over a crack in the wall.

Hours later, she returned to the hospital. She switched on the recording and sat beside her father's cot. She listened to her cracked voice singing songs whose words she had improvised. She listened to the poetry, the ramblings, the nursery rhymes, the pleas. She felt she was hearing herself for the first time, and she recognized nothing. For three days, she sat and slept beside her father's bed, listening to her voice. At some point, the police appeared. Arturo was there, too, helping her answer their questions. Lali came silently to visit, then left. At home, her mother remained under sedation.

On the third day, when the doctor entered the room, Pilar looked at him and spoke over her taped voice singing a lullaby: "I think if I hear myself five minutes more, I'll go crazy. Even when I turn it off, even when I sleep, I hear my voice singing. I don't see anything. I only hear this voice."

He stared at her.

"I don't want to make a scene," Pilar said quietly. "I just want to stop the singing."

His expression softened. He was looking at her the way Pilar's mother often looked at her daughters, the way his Filipino mother must have looked at him, caring and worried but afraid to intrude.

"Why don't you put on your coat?" he said. "My shift's over. We could have some coffee."

She followed him through white rooms and out into the brisk San Francisco afternoon. He led her into a coffee shop and ordered a blueberry muffin and black coffee. She asked for a glass of orange juice.

He grasped the edge of the table. He had delicate features and almond-shaped black eyes. "What really helped me in all this," he said, "was learning to detach. A doctor who can't detach gets shell-shocked right away." He eyed the blonde waitress as she placed the food and drinks on the table. "Once, when I was a resident, I was assisting in an operation. A nine-year-old girl."

Pilar noticed his teeth, even and white.

"She didn't make it," he said. "Something snapped, inside me."

In her mind she told him: Please stop talking.

"A friend tried to help me," he said. "He told me I had to learn not to get bothered."

She sipped her juice, watching his eyes. He looked away. She took a deep breath, trying to push back her distress. People didn't know what to say at times like this. He meant well. That's the problem, her father said—most people think they mean well, no matter what harm they do.

"My friend said I had to focus on my body, just my body," the doctor continued. "He said I had to let the thoughts go."

She broke off a piece of his muffin.

He pushed the plate to the center of the table and handed

her a knife. "He said our thoughts are like drunken monkeys, tumbling over each other, one after another, in the so-called temple of our minds. He said I had to dissociate what I was from what I thought."

She stared at his hands, strong and capable-looking, more masculine than his face. She wondered what it would be like to feel them on her skin. Her throat tightened.

"It helped me," he said. "I worked on it for months, and slowly I didn't get upset anymore. I could detach."

He offered her the last piece of muffin. She shook her head, reached for her purse.

He stared at her, his face sallow under the yellow light. "I'm sorry. I didn't mean to upset you—"

"Do you know what I think?" she asked. "I think it's over. I think my father's not there anymore."

He slid his chair back, crossed his arms over his chest. "You can't know that."

"There's a psychic in Manila trying to save him," she said. "And the psychic said he's going to be all right."

He hesitated. "You believe that?"

"In Manila, those things are possible. It's not the same here."

"What would happen if it didn't work?" he asked.

She clutched the edge of the Formica tabletop. She hadn't allowed herself to consider the possibility. Now, as she thought about it, her excitement frightened her. Without her father, there would be no need to remain in exile. They could finally move out of their cramped, lonely lives and return home—to their house, their friends, their maids, their parties. The anticipation nauseated her.

To end the conversation, she placed a five-dollar bill on the table. He tried to stand, but she shook her head and hurried out of the coffee shop. She turned a corner and strode up a narrow street, head bent, avoiding the eyes of strangers. She walked for hours, skirting the main roads, until night fell and the shadows cast by headlights flicked like tongues around her feet.

As Pilar rummaged through her purse for the keys to the apartment, Lali opened the door, her face blotched with tears. Pilar walked into the darkened hallway and shut the door behind her.

"When did it happen?" Pilar whispered.

"Three-thirty."

"He was alone?"

"We were looking for you," Lali said. "We thought you were with him."

"What happened with the healer?"

"Nothing," Lali said. Tears filled her eyes. "Nothing, nothing. He was wrong. He didn't know anything at all."

Shadows stretched across the ceiling and fell like ladders down the wall. Pilar examined the wall, wanting to see every shade of light and every change in the darkness.

"We should be with him," Pilar said at last.

Lali put on her coat in silence, and the sisters walked out of the apartment without speaking and without touching.

No one came to the wake. For six days and seven nights, taking shifts, Arturo, Lali, and Pilar sat next to the closed coffin in a chapel. They kept their mother under sedation at home. Every day they spread a table outside the chapel with Filipino food, but no one came, no one wanted to be seen with the family of the assassinated man. Their small community called and whispered their sadness, but they were afraid. On the sixth day, Pilar called the hospital and asked the doctor to attend the funeral. After a short pause, he accepted. On the seventh day, the corpse was buried in a Catholic ceremony attended by his widow and daughters, Arturo, the doctor, three American journalists, and a photographer. Pilar held her mother's hand and did not cry.

When the ceremony was over, Arturo invited the doctor to join the family for dinner. In the apartment they ate in silence, listening to the cries that erupted periodically from the widow's bedroom.

Over coffee, Lali said, "We're going back home."

Pilar stirred a sugar cube into the coffee.

The doctor, the only US-raised person in the group, was the only one who thought it necessary to respond. "Is it safe to go back?" he asked.

Lali and Arturo glanced at each other.

Pilar dropped another sugar cube into her coffee, smashed it against the bottom and sides of her cup.

"Lali and I are getting married," Arturo told the doctor. "I'm taking everyone back to Manila. They'll be safe there, as part of my family."

Pilar took one sip of the sweet coffee, then pushed the cup away from her. "Your family," she said. "Your family's *friend* killed my father. And now he'll watch over us?"

"*Por Dios*," Lali said, standing up.

Arturo reached for Lali's hand. "Pilar's upset," he told the doctor. "She hasn't really rested since all this happened."

"At least I'm not marrying the godson of the man who killed my father," Pilar said. "At least I'm not out to save my neck at all costs."

She left the room. The doctor hurried after her. In the hallway he asked her: "Do you want to have a drink somewhere? It might be good to talk."

She followed him down two blocks and slipped into the front seat of his car. He started the engine.

"Where do you want to go?" he asked.

She shook her head.

He glanced at her, then placed a thin arm around her shoulder. Because she couldn't speak, she pressed her body against his. She imagined he was somebody else, a man she didn't know. She wanted to feel desire, to go through it to the end, like pain, like death, but everywhere she touched him she kept hitting the walls of her narrow, frightened self. She looked at his closed eyes and half-parted lips and thought of all the women who let themselves be sucked and touched and bitten by men they didn't want. For the first time in her life, she was afraid she would become one of them.

She pulled away. He brushed back his damp hair with his fingers. She wanted to talk to him, to reassure him, but she could not. She couldn't look at his face again. She didn't want anyone's skin against her body again.

As she walked past rows of narrow houses and parked cars, she felt, for the first time since her father died, close to tears.

The plane glided to a stop on the runway. Minutes later, the family gathered their bags and stepped out the cabin door into the heat of Manila. Grasping her mother's elbow, Pilar followed Lali and Arturo down the metal staircase to the tarmac.

Pilar could hardly open her eyes in the light. The heat and sunshine seemed to flatten everything, casting all movements into a slow and stylized dance.

As her eyes adjusted to the brightness, she saw a sea of white flags waving from the roof deck of the terminal. White, she said to herself, and a moment later she understood: white, the color of the opposition. And then she began to hear. A brass band was playing her father's favorite songs: "Strangers in the Night," "My Way," "Bayan Ko." In her mind, she heard the tape of her broken voice improvise lyrics as her father lay unconscious on a hospital bed.

"My God," Lali said. "They're here for us."

"There could be trouble," Arturo whispered. He pointed at the military police barricading the crowds on the roof deck.

Slowly, they advanced across the bright hot pavement, the other passengers hurrying ahead of them. The band continued playing.

Pilar kept her eyes on the waving white flags. She recognized the banners: the public arm of the outlawed Communist Party, the extreme-right faction of the military, the religious left. All the fractious opposition groups had come together at the airport to welcome the family of the dead man. She saw the university students, housewives, clean-cut young soldiers, nuns, priests, and schoolchildren. They were all waving white flags as the band struggled through the refrains of "Bayan Ko."

Slowly, like the wind welling before a typhoon, a chant began. Then it grew louder, more penetrating, rumbling down from the rooftop and drowning out the music. They were chanting her father's name: *Gregorio, Gregorio*. With the back of her hand, Pilar's mother impatiently brushed away tears. She had grown very thin in the weeks since her husband's death, and often seemed disoriented by grief or tranquilizers. Now, she walked with her head high and back straight. Just before the plane landed, she had told her daughters: *We're going to walk out of here the way he would have.*

On the tarmac, a cortege of military police looped silently around them. Arturo lifted his face to the crowd on the roof deck and, like the politician's son that he was, smiled and began to wave. The chanting erupted into hisses.

"You're on the wrong side of all this," Pilar told him.

"Not anymore," Arturo said, his smile frozen as he surveyed the crowd. "He's my father-in-law now." He grasped Lali's hand, folded her fingers into a ball, and raised their fists high over their heads as they walked toward the terminal. The soldiers watched them warily.

"I've never seen anything like this," Arturo said as they entered the building, his fair-skinned, handsome face flushed with excitement.

One of his relatives rushed them through customs and escorted them to a waiting limousine. They drove through dusty crowded streets, past old men on bicycles and stray dogs limping beside street vendors. The sun was so bright Pilar couldn't talk. Her mother stared out the window.

"After all these years," Lali said. "If only Papa could have seen them."

"They're just using him," Arturo replied. He smiled and slipped his arm around his wife, as though to efface his words.

Later they looked back on that day as the beginning of the revolution that would drive Filipinos into the streets and the dictator into exile. In a barricaded house on the outskirts of Manila, Arturo's family lived through the year of turmoil in seclusion, waiting to see which side would win. Toward the end, Arturo, his mother, and her relatives transferred their support from the dictator to the opposition candidate. A week later, a US military jet spirited the dictator and his family out of the country. In the streets of Manila, people danced, hugged strangers, and shouted "Happy New Year!" although it was the middle of July.

Slowly, life returned to normal. Arturo spoke to old classmates and distant cousins in the new government and made the necessary adjustments. He was the dictator's godson, but Lali's father was a hero now, the symbol of the struggle against that same dictator. Arturo was also charming, well-connected, and a member of the country's landed elite, and every regime made room for people like him. Besides, Lali and Pilar were beautiful. For a few weeks, before the foreign journalists flew off to more newsworthy troubles in Asia, most of them tried, without success, to interview Gregorio's daughters.

Pilar's mother, lapsing deeper into grief, stayed in a shuttered room in Arturo and Lali's home. Pilar returned to her parents' two-story home in a once-fashionable district of Manila and lived alone among the toys and photographs of her childhood.

At night, she paced around the wooden house. Her father's favorite songs no longer played in her head. She watched black-and-white films on television and tucked striped sheets over her narrow bed. She had her life, her little jobs, and a dozen lunch companions, but nothing opened in her.

Late one afternoon, Lali called her. "We're giving a dinner party next Friday," Lali said brightly. "I want you to come. You haven't been anywhere in ages."

"That's not true," Pilar said, irritated with her sister. Lali was safe. She had her husband's home, her husband's family, her husband's money.

"And I want all colors," Lali was saying. "Parties are so boring. I told Arturo we have to do something different. I want lots of blues and greens and pinks. Green rice, purple fruit, blue roses. I want nothing to look like itself. Are you going to come or not, Pilar?"

Pilar imagined her sister at the other end of the line: the thin, chiseled face, the fragile body only slightly thickened by pregnancy.

"I always go to your parties," Pilar said.

"I think you stay alone too much. I think you should move out of that house."

Through the screen doors, she saw the night settle over the untended garden. The sisters said their goodbyes. Pilar turned on the radio, switching from station to station until she found dance music. She stretched her arms and legs in rhythm to the music, glancing at her image in a stained 19th-century mirror. Her body felt like an icon, dissociated from her. The body always met the world head-on, while the woman who was not her body remained one or two steps behind, watching the reactions. Always, there had been this sense of two selves: the body, which strangers desired, and then, darting behind it, the frightened rabbit's eyes.

To keep herself safe, she stayed alone. She didn't know how not to be alone. People who came too close made her rabbit's heart beat too rapidly. There was only this: the sense of a tiny crack inside her, where she was always afraid.

She climbed the stairs, unlocked her parents' bedroom, and entered it. On the floor near her father's desk, three large, sealed cartons held the letters, speeches, and documents they had shipped back from San Francisco. One day she and Lali would have to open them and deal with his papers, but she couldn't do that now.

Her parents' bed was still covered by the crocheted bedspread she remembered from her childhood. Suddenly, she was afraid to turn around, to look at the antique furniture and Ming vases her parents had collected. In Manila, no one wanted to live among the possessions of those who had died violently. People said those spirits kept returning to the persons and places they had known, seeking to establish contact with what they didn't know they had lost.

Pilar hiked up her skirt and knelt on her father's bed, then pressed her black hair against his pillow and said: *Papa, if you're here, show me something.*

She willed his presence with all her force. She stood and walked around the room, touching his things, calling upon him. But nothing happened. She remembered jumping up and down on her parents' bed and flinging herself into his arms, and her father whirling her around until they both collapsed, laughing on the bed. Now, there was nothing. No presence, no spirits, no sign of the life that had filled those rooms. She thought perhaps she should cry then, for the absence that kept him present in her life, but the moment for grief had passed. Life had returned to normal, eroding the significance of all that had happened before. No one talked of the past. No one wanted to return there.

On the evening of Lali's party, Pilar spread the country's top five newspapers on the dining table. She scanned the headlines and texts for mentions of her father, and the photos for a glimpse of his face. She cut out images and texts, arranged them in yellow and red folders. Occasionally, with a pencil, she wrote a few paragraphs in a spiral notebook. All this soothed her—the rustle of paper, the thickening folders, the words.

No one expected your death to lead to a revolution. No one, not even its leaders, expected the revolution to succeed.

She crossed this out.

Some people are already saying there was no revolution. Power simply changed hands, from one faction of the elite to another, leaving the country's structure and injustices intact. People say you would have been sad. I don't believe that. I believe you would say: This is only the beginning.

At the entrance to Lali and Arturo's home, Pilar hesitated. Torches illuminated the garden. She had expected seven or eight guests at a dinner table. Instead there were over a hundred people, not including the dozens of uniformed waiters, maids, and bartenders. People she had seen only in newspapers were eating and talking and drinking around a table laden with blue roses and colored dishes: fish spread with blue mayonnaise, green potato salad, brown bowls filled with steaming saffron rice, yellow bread rolls. Pale green lights on the ground outlined the swimming pool.

Lali walked through the crowds, her pregnancy almost invisible underneath a high-waisted cotton dress, her black hair curled around silk orchids.

"I thought you wouldn't come," she said, pressing a cool cheek against Pilar's flushed skin. Lali had become a politician's wife: her clothes elegant but not sensual, her makeup discreet, her smile professional.

"There are people here I'd like you to meet," Lali said breezily, as though she were talking to a stranger.

Pilar made the rounds with her, wandering from one cluster of guests to another. Under the mango trees, politicians mingled with bejeweled society matrons, hacienda owners, foreign diplomats, psychics, and journalists. She shook hands with the deposed dictator's defense minister, who had signed her father's arrest warrant and now headed the new government's military operations. Pilar scooped out a piece of blue fish next to the former cabinet members who had betrayed her father and, for a price, orchestrated their exile. The interior minister's eyes flicked over her. *Get the girls out of the country*, relatives had told her mother, when Gregorio was in prison. *If the military ever takes the girls in for questioning, God knows what will happen to them.*

The minister inclined his head, gave a brief, insinuating smile. To Pilar's dismay, she smiled back. Her hand trembled. She set the serving spoon on the table. These past months, power and allegiances had shifted repeatedly, the trials had begun, the Commission on Good Government was seizing back confiscated properties and redistributing them among the latest set of cronies, many of the high-level government officials in the garden were facing charges of corruption. And in the midst of all this, she was a young woman, and alone.

She walked away from the crowd and into the house. In the kitchen, Lali was supervising her maids and arranging slices of roast pork on a silver platter.

"I can't stay very long," Pilar said.

Lali looked up impatiently, her face older and harsher under the fluorescent light. "Don't start acting up again," she snapped. "Make an effort."

Pilar stared at her sister's belly, envying the fullness inside her, the bustle all around them. "How could you have invited all those people?" she asked. "When I smile at them, all I can think of is what they did to Papa."

"Then don't smile at them." Lali's black eyes met hers, and Pilar was afraid, as though she were a child again and confronted with her sister's sudden, violent tantrums.

Lali tucked a stray lock of hair behind an orchid. "I wouldn't be the one to judge," she said in a low voice, arranging parsley sprigs around the sliced pork. "I'm just trying to get on with my life."

"And our father's life?"

"Papa's dead," Lali said, her eyes as cold as the blue fish on the garden table. "I'm not."

Pilar walked out of the kitchen, down a corridor, took refuge in Arturo's study.

Lali got away with everything, even Arturo. Their father had never tried to stop her. Lali had met Arturo at one of those elegant Filipino-expatriate parties in San Francisco, where political beliefs mattered less than blood ties and the elite schools all the guests had attended. *The girls are growing up,* their mother had pleaded. *They need to meet people.* She didn't say *my people,* but Gregorio must have relented because once or twice a year, the sisters were allowed to meet a few of their mother's estranged relatives and their old convent-school classmates at those parties. When Lali started dating Arturo, Gregorio said nothing. When Lali brought Arturo home for dinner, Gregorio acted polite, even interested. But he refused to visit Arturo's house in Pacific Heights or to meet him outside the apartment. Exile frayed boundaries, Gregorio said, but unlike Lali, he had no intention of obliterating them.

Lali broke all the rules, but their father had always loved her best.

Hours later, Pilar returned to the party. In a corner of the garden, away from the noise and lights and conflicts, Arturo sat at a long table. He was waving his arms in the air, saying something that made everyone laugh.

She walked along the edges of the garden, in the shadows, hoping no one would notice her, making her way to Arturo's table. Without speaking, she pulled up a chair beside him.

He poured pink champagne into a flute and handed it to her. "My sister-in-law," he announced to the others. His arm curled around the back of her chair. He introduced the guests to her: a few government officials, two fashion models, the daughter of a sugar baron from the south and her German-filmmaker boyfriend, the French ambassador, and a tall, pale-skinned Chinese in an exquisitely tailored pin-striped suit. The Chinese was a Hong Kong real-estate broker, Arturo said, who also dabbled in Taoist magic.

Across the table, Pilar noticed a squat, dark-skinned man wearing a batik shirt and black rectangular sunglasses. Arturo didn't introduce him.

A belly dancer began to undulate around the crowded tables, to the hoots of drunken officials and business tycoons. As the people around her turned to watch, Pilar whispered to Arturo, "Who's the one with the sunglasses?"

"A psychic healer," Arturo murmured. "Supposedly the General's favorite. From Sumatra, I think. A Sufi."

She gave a faint smile. "I thought you didn't believe in these things."

"I don't. But the General wouldn't do anything without consulting him."

Pilar settled into her chair and listened to snatches of the conversations around her. She had long ago lost faith in any higher or lower powers, but tales of magic and supernatural grace continued to fascinate her.

"I don't charge for my interventions," the Chinese broker was saying. "For me, magic is a service."

A maid came and poured red water into their glasses.

"Can you help people?" Pilar asked.

"I do what I can," the Chinese broker said. He leaned closer to her, his lips curling under a thin mustache. "Last week, I got a call from one of the wealthiest families in Chinatown. Their eldest daughter had been in bed for months, unable to get up.

The doctors said there was nothing wrong with her. She was depressed, they said. Her father was desperate."

Arturo wiped the perspiration from his brow and glanced at the sky.

"As soon as I entered her room, I saw what was wrong. Beside her on the bed was the spirit of her dead lover, who had committed suicide because of her. I knew then that I couldn't take away her sickness. That was her destiny, to be tormented by the spirit she had hurt. I could do nothing. She had to be punished, to suffer, to work out that destiny. Only that could free her." He sipped the water. "It's a touchy thing to try to change people's destinies. Things go wrong. The forces are disturbed, and then they can rebound."

The psychic reached for a cigarette, his eyes invisible behind the opaque glasses. He turned to the Chinese broker. "But Taoists practice black magic as well," he said. "You tamper with the dead, don't you?"

A hot, sticky wind brushed Pilar's arms.

The Chinese lowered his fork and pushed aside the blue fish. "In Hong Kong, it's true, there are people who do things like that," he said. "They can conjure entities—spirits which aren't quite human—and attach them to people. I've never done it myself, but I know men who've brought dead children back to life. By diabolic means, evidently. It can be dangerous. Sometimes another spirit inhabits the child's body." Guests at the surrounding tables applauded raucously as the belly dancer finished her dance. "There are all these spirits around us, even here in the garden, hovering, waiting for a way back to life."

Pilar crossed her arms over her chest and pressed her knees together. In the end, they were just men—these psychics and spiritual masters, manipulators of the future and healers of the dead. She wondered about their lives, whether they were married, whether they were good to their wives, whether their children loved them. That was what mattered. The rest of it was a spiritual circus, diversions for people who had nothing left to believe in.

She glanced around her. A few guests lingered on the terrace. On the buffet table, blue roses drooped. Lali, barefoot and wan in her cotton dress, wandered through the cigarette-littered grass and settled into a chair beside Pilar.

"Isn't there a more practical way to use your magic?" a businessman asked the Chinese. "Can you use it on the lottery?"

"To some extent," he replied. "The other day, I was playing mah-jongg. Supposedly, it's a game of chance. The blocks are distributed at random. But then, as the game went on, I saw that one man was on a winning streak. Nothing seemed able to stop him. I realized I had to interfere. I had to confuse the energies."

Pilar lifted a spoonful of yellow rice, now lukewarm, to her lips.

"So what did you do?" Arturo said.

"I lied. I announced that I had won the round, even though it wasn't true. Of course, I had to show my hand, and people saw that I was bluffing. But by declaring that I had won, by lying, the energy got jumbled up. The winning streak was broken. The next round was played, and we all started out equal again. Equal in the sense that no one was favored to win. You have to do that in your life as well, or in other people's lives. Disturb the pattern, disturb the energies. Lie. Otherwise you're like a river condemned to flow always along the same bed. Block the flow, or divert it, and there can be new movements."

"But when do you stop?" Pilar said. "If someone asks you to do something—to save someone who's dying, for example—how do you know whether you should?"

She had spoken to the Chinese broker, but it was the psychic who twisted slowly in his seat and answered her. "This happens sometimes," he said, his voice low. "People come, blindly, they ask me to change their lives. Interfere in someone's destiny. Not long ago, a man was dying. His family told me they didn't want him to die."

Lali's eyes flicked edgily. In the man's black glasses, Pilar thought she saw her own distorted image: her neck elongated, one cheek flattened. A maid extinguished all the torches except for the one under the mango tree, which cast a web of shadows across the table.

"I tried to save him," the psychic said softly. "I entered into a trance. And there I saw the thread of light emanating from his body. And I strengthened the light, I strengthened the attachment of his spirit to the earth."

Arturo left his chair and stood behind Lali, his fingers gripping the edge of her chair. Pilar felt their tension lock into hers.

"Then, in a dream, the dying man came to me and said: Let me go, it's only you who holds me here. And I understood. He had seen the other side, and he wanted to go there. So I told him, in the dream, that I would withdraw my force, and we'd see what would happen. If his family wanted it badly enough, their desire would hold him to life. A few hours later, he died."

A warm wind swept through the garden, almost extinguishing the remaining torch flame. Lali, her eyes smudged by pale blue circles, turned to her sister.

"You're wrong," Pilar told the psychic, her voice cracking.

Lali reached under the table for Pilar's hand, then beamed a cold bright smile at the man in dark glasses. "Such stories," she said lightly. "And do you ever do anything that makes people happy? Do you ever manage to bring the dead back to life?"

"Not back to life, but back to rest," the psychic said placidly. "We encounter spirits all the time in our work, spirits who die violently, who haven't had the time to sever attachments." He smiled mirthlessly. "In China, there are stories of the dead walking at night through villages, traveling for miles and miles to return to the village where they were conceived. There the circle ends, and they can end their lives."

A weighted silence fell over the table.

"Do you feel it?" the psychic whispered. "Something's here."

The guests shifted nervously, searching for something no one could see. One of the women made the sign of the cross. Pilar closed her eyes, trying to feel whatever or whoever was there.

"Go in peace," the psychic said. "Go back to where you came from."

Pilar turned to Lali. Her sister, still forcing a smile, had tears in her eyes.

Arturo gave a small, tight laugh and said, "Well, I guess that ends our party."

Pilar strode through the windy garden and into the street. She kept sensing Lali's white face just over her shoulder, and she thought that if she turned around she would see her sister. But it was Arturo who appeared beside her.

"Don't mind them," he said. "It's the wind, the night, the drink. Don't believe what you felt in there."

The first fat raindrops splattered on her skin.

"Hurry," Arturo said. "It's going to rain hard." His cheek touched hers as he said goodbye.

Inside the car, she revved the engine impatiently, wanting to flee. The car lurched forward, then stalled. She turned the key and pressed repeatedly on the accelerator, but the car wouldn't start. Rain broke, so heavy and grey she couldn't see the road in front of her. She clutched the wheel, turning the key, still pressing on the accelerator. Then she stopped trying.

Rain strummed the metal roof, pushing her deeper and deeper into herself. She sat inside the car, in the black night, and the narrow world she had built broke open with the rain. Everything was still there: the presences all around her, the past she had shut away, her father's being, her father's death. For the first time since he died, Pilar began to cry. She cried for the presences she felt and could never speak to. She cried not for having lost him, but for having him still. She cried not because he had died, but because he hadn't died enough. His presence was all around her, and nothing could take that presence away.

She bent over the wheel, wanting to be contained within the small metal box, within herself, but instead she felt the surfaces of her life collapsing. She pressed her face against the wheel, unable to bear what she had glimpsed: the immensity, the littleness, the permeability of her self.

From beyond the rain, she heard an insistent tapping. She looked up. A pale face floated behind the rain-streaked glass. It was Lali, holding an umbrella, her white dress stained with dark circles of rain. Pilar unlocked the door, and Lali stepped into the car.

"Did you feel it, what happened in the garden?" Pilar whispered.

Her sister lowered her gaze.

"Was he there?" Pilar asked. "I couldn't feel him."

Lali gave a gallant smile. "Come inside," she said. "You can't go anywhere in this rain."

They held the umbrella close to their heads as they ran through the rain to Arturo's house.

In the living room, Lali kicked off her shoes and sat cross-legged on the leather couch. The branches of a banana tree lashed the windows.

Pilar searched through the stack of records next to the stereo. She pulled out a scratched Frank Sinatra record that had belonged to her father. As the man's voice crooned above the rain, Lali said: "Do you really want to listen to that? I haven't been able to, ever since."

The sisters sat in silence, listening to the music. Then, with a reckless smile, Lali pulled Pilar to her feet and draped her arms around her. Clumsily, Pilar returned the embrace. She hadn't held anyone in a long time, and the warmth of Lali's body unsettled her. Pilar felt her heavy breasts press against Lali's fragile body and, beneath her breasts, the pressure of Lali's pregnant belly. In that way, their bodies locked into each other.

Lali's hips began to sway, and Pilar tried to absorb the rhythm. The sisters danced slowly in place, their bodies tentatively embraced and explored, as though they hadn't known each other before.

The two women laughed.

Pilar felt a flutter against her stomach, where Lali's belly protruded onto hers. She held Lali closer. Again the flutter, which sent waves through her. She felt it was happening inside her.

"You feel it?" Lali said triumphantly. "It's been doing that for a week now."

Pilar felt the child moving between them.

"Quickly," Lali said. "Make a wish."

"A wish?"

"Yes. At the moment you first feel it. You have to give it something."

Pilar closed her eyes, hearing the rain. Then she said: "What can you give someone, Lali? A life? An ordinary life."

Lali backed away. "No," she said. "Not that." She pursed her lips and blew out air, as though to disperse the thought. "Don't be morbid! An ordinary life, that doesn't exist. No one notices a life when it's ordinary. Again, quickly, something else. I want something good."

Pilar lowered her face against her sister's hair. She realized it was right that Lali, who had always despised weakness, should carry new life within her. And she, Pilar, who had spent more than a year grieving and seeking a phantom, in the end had become what she was looking for—she had become his ghost.

Pilar knew then what she wanted to give the child: Gregorio's vision, but also a life as strong and ruthless as Lali's. Was it possible to be both merciless and honorable? It had to be. She needed someone to help her honor her father and stay true to him, to resist the relentless march of a country that was leaving him, his dreams, and people's memories of both behind.

She couldn't tell any of this to Lali—the wish was a gift for the child, not the mother.

A strong hand cupped her shoulder.

"Sinatra?" Arturo asked, laughing. He separated the sisters, made room for himself between them. He wrapped his arms around their waists, and the sisters did the same, forming a small circle in the middle of the room. Without speaking, Pilar held her sister and Arturo close to her. The pressure of their bodies comforted her. Arturo's fingers dug into Pilar's waist, and almost imperceptibly she tilted her hip toward him. A tremor went through her. His grip tightened. Awkwardly, the sisters and Arturo swayed across the darkened room, to the rhythms of music the dead man had loved.

CHAPTER TWO

THE ECLIPSE

The waves tell of beauty that comes unbidden,
approaching as a lover walks through a door,
each time familiar yet heart-stopping.

—ANGELA NARCISO TORRES, "Postcards from Bohol"

ARTURO

Six months after the revolution, Arturo awoke at dawn in his mother's home to find that Lali was gone. He sat up in bed, as abruptly as he had awakened. Lali had never disappeared like this, without a word. He glanced at the bedside table next to where she should have lain, folded over her rounding belly. The tabletop was cluttered with vitamins and calcium supplements, a jar of honey for her morning sickness, and a pencil and notebook for her dreams. He didn't open the notebook. He didn't open the closets to see whether her soft summer dresses were still there. He wouldn't seek evidence of betrayal. He loved her too well.

In the maids' kitchen, the plump cook sat, fanning herself beside a basket of glistening milkfish.

"*Manang*, did Lali have breakfast before she left?" Arturo asked, careful to sound disinterested.

Filomena shrugged. "I don't know," she said, leaning over to brush a fly away from the milkfish. Her upper arms sagged.

The family's driver walked into the kitchen, carrying two wicker baskets filled with white doves.

Arturo turned to him, shoulders tensed. "What are you doing with that?"

"They're for the president's rally this afternoon," the driver murmured. "She wants us to let them fly right after the eclipse."

The cook pried out a milkfish from the basket, wrapped it in a sheet of newsprint, limped toward the sink. A scapular of the Virgin bounced against her wide back. Wedged between the wicker cages, the driver sprinkled grains of raw rice over the doves. Arturo watched the fluttering birds, thinking of Lali's white dress lifting in the breeze during the new president's inauguration.

The ceremony had taken place stealthily at a country club near the military camp. The guests, culled from the country's most powerful families and the international press, listened to military jets flying overhead. Outside, the fighting raged.

Lali had pressed her shoulders against him, tense, her long manicured fingers digging into the palm of his hand. He had felt her fear. They had been back in Manila for more than a year, but she still thought the dictator's men would find her, the way they had found her father in an obscure side street in San Francisco. "It's over now," he told her, as a cardinal swore in the new president.

Suddenly, a white dove flew into the room and perched on the president's shoulder. The crowd at the country club inhaled collectively. They were deeply Catholic, and even more deeply superstitious.

"This is it," Arturo whispered to his wife. "This is all the president needed."

"It's a miracle," exclaimed a stylish matron beside them. She made the sign of the cross and fell to her knees. The new president lifted her face to the window. She wore the purple dress that had carried her like a banner throughout the upheavals and her campaign. The white dove clung stubbornly to her shoulder.

Lali looked up at Arturo. "Oh not again," she had said. "We don't need any more miracles."

Now Lali was gone, and Arturo sat in the kitchen with his hands clenched over the wooden table. Filomena patted the cleaned and headless milkfish on a kitchen towel. He stared at the belly protruding through her dress. The president had risen to power on people like these: the common people, the shirtless drivers and plump cooks, the beggar children mutilated by their parents. These were the believers. They would throng to the victory rally that afternoon. They would dance during the eclipse. They would unleash ten thousand white doves, hoping one would land on their beloved president's shoulder. They all needed another sign of grace.

Filomena washed her hands and arranged his favorite confection on a silver tray: glutinous rice steeped in coconut milk and sugar, then steamed in banana leaves. Arturo reached for a rice cake but withdrew his hand before he touched the tray. A pounding began somewhere in the back of his head.

Lali had clung to him at night during the fighting, her pale, pointed breasts flattened against his arm and chest. "Why did we come back to this?" she said. "We should have stayed in San Francisco."

He didn't answer her. He had never thought she might need an answer. Comfort, money, attention—he had given her everything else.

He walked out the back door. The air was cool. Wide, shallow aluminum basins held the day's wash. There was no one to call. Lali had no real friends. Afraid to provoke the wrath of the General, people had ostracized her family for years. Arturo understood their fear. Lali never forgave them.

In the deep blue light of dawn, on wires strung between coconut trees, the previous day's wash swayed damply in the breeze. He ducked between two rows of clothes, seeking her presence. Satin nightgowns and lacy underwear, tucked between stretch pants and striped maternity blouses—strangely inglorious memories of the woman who had chosen them.

He fingered the blouses, then brushed his unshaven cheek against a nightgown. He inhaled deeply. Her smell was masked by the odor of detergents and dyes. He glanced quickly around him to see if someone was watching. Air-conditioners whirred above him, their bulky frames protruding out of the walls and dripping into mud puddles on the ground. The second-floor windows were shuttered.

The sun had begun its ascent over the gray stone walls. He stared at the brightening sky. He imagined Lali alone in a dark room somewhere, staring at an eclipsed sun, and though he refused to fear for himself, he was afraid for her.

She had told him: "My father was killed. My mother and sister need to think I'm strong. Most of the family hasn't spoken to us in eight years."

He had brought her back. In the golden sun, he watched her grow pallid and fearful. He had watched the play of light across her skin. He was intoxicated with her body: the curve of her slender limbs, the black hair pulled back from her white face, the eyes made lucid by years of resentment. He had found her, loved her, married her.

Down a pebbled path he walked, cautiously, not wanting to think. Along the walls, nailed to makeshift boards, stood rusted cages from the days when his father bred fighting cocks. Only one rooster remained: an old, scraggly creature that crowed in the middle of the afternoon. Lali refused to have it killed.

He followed the path to the servants' quarters and entered a room beside the river. The smell of marine life and iodine wafted in. In a corner sat an old woman, her body shrunken beneath the red and yellow flowers of her summer dress. She looked up at him and smiled.

"Did Lali come here this morning?" he asked.

She clasped her wrinkled hands. "Lali comes once in a while. I'm an old woman."

He waited, watching the photographs she had tacked to the wall. Lali as a child, on a forgotten beach in the south, laughing, her face radiant, her skinny legs wide apart beneath the petticoat of her bathing suit. A younger girl with dark skin and thick black hair—Pilar—sat cross-legged on the sand, her face in shadow.

"Lali comes once in a while," her nursemaid said. "She forgets."

A barge plodded down the gray river. On the opposite bank, where graceful tree-lined mansions had stood in his childhood, a row of factories released clouds of white smoke. He watched the barge until it disappeared.

"Lali loved fish," the old nanny said suddenly. "When she was a little girl in the province, in the summer, we would sit by a river with a net, trying to catch wounded fish. She wanted wounded fish that we could make well again." The woman laughed soundlessly. "We caught a fish once. She thought she saw blood on its side. She made me put a bandage on the fish before returning it to the river. She loved animals, that girl. No one could tell her what to do."

He had heard the stories before, but today as he listened, he grasped the edge of the old woman's bed, and his knuckles whitened.

"There's an eclipse of the sun today," he told her. "Did you know that?"

"An eclipse?" She stared out the window. "But we can't see the sun."

The sky over the gray river was white with clouds. He glanced at his watch. Ten past seven. "Maybe it will come out later."

A six-year-old girl, the child of one of the maids, peeped into the room. "Sir, your mother's looking for you," she whispered. "She wants you to have breakfast with her."

He lit a cigarette and turned to the child. For a moment, he saw in her black eyes the child forming within Lali's pale belly.

"There's something about black eyes," Lali had told him when they first met. She had stood too close to him, her four-inch heels tipping her frail body forward. "Pale blue eyes, when you stare at them, you get taken into the paleness. You see infinity. But you can't enter into black eyes. You get yourself thrown back at you. That's why the best hypnotists and sorcerers have black eyes."

He blew cigarette smoke out the window. "Tell my mother I'm coming," he told the girl.

She scrambled away, her thin legs flashing under her skirt.

He touched the nursemaid's shoulder, tried to hide his concern. "Lali didn't tell you anything?"

She clicked her tongue. "She's too much like her father. Even when she was small, no one could make her do anything. She doesn't understand you have to make sacrifices in this life. She does what she wants."

He recoiled from the bitterness in her voice.

"And what's she doing, a pregnant woman, going out in the streets today?" she asked. "It's not safe. Women get miscarriages during an eclipse. In the province, there was a baby born with black spots on its body because the mother was outside during an eclipse. She should be in bed, with a black umbrella over her stomach, and garlic cloves on her navel, to protect the baby from evil spirits. What's wrong with her? She never cares."

A pulse spread slowly down the back of his head. He imagined this woman's hands caressing the Lali he did not know, the child Lali. He saw the child's small arms embrace her nanny without reserve, without resistance. Lali could no longer embrace anyone that way.

"Don't talk that way about her," he said.

As he rushed out of the room, a plump brown hen flapped into the air. He hurried down the pebbled path, past cages emptied of fighting cocks. In the laundry area, he eyed his wife's lingerie on the clothesline. He was disturbed at having her so exposed, so vulnerable. He unhooked and gathered up the pieces of cloth. Suddenly, he was angry at her for not being more discreet, for not telling the maids that certain things must not be hung carelessly in public. And the public were everywhere, squatting outside the kitchen or sitting in the driveway, playing cards and smoking cigarettes: the maids, their visiting sisters and brothers and children, the boyfriends they passed off as cousins.

The screen door of the kitchen had rusted. He pushed it open with his heel, his arms laden with lace brassieres and satin nightdresses. He carried them as if they were his wife's limp body.

In the kitchen, the cook stood hastily. "I'll take those," she said.

He lowered the clothing into her arms.

"Arturo?" a voice called tentatively.

His mother stood at the entrance to the dining room, hands on her wide hips, surrounded by cages of white doves.

"Aren't they wonderful?" She laughed. "Whatever else they may say about our president, she's no fool. Imagine the gall! A victory rally two weeks after the latest coup attempt! And she orders everyone to release white doves during the prayer of peace!" She knelt down beside the cage and poked a manicured finger into a hole in the wicker binding. The doves' wings fluttered in panic. "Four coup attempts in six months, and she asks us to pray for peace!"

"Then why are you going to her rally?"

"You love the one you're with, darling. We have to be there. It won't look good if we aren't." She tossed back her hair. "And where's Lali?"

"Don't tell me you haven't heard."

She smiled ingenuously. "Heard what? Nobody talks in this house."

The maids, he knew, told her everything.

Marilou tugged down her white T-shirt over her black

stretch pants. On the shirt, swelling across her large breasts, was a brown-and-white picture of herself—prettier and younger than she had been at the time, but recognizable all the same. Beneath the image she had emblazoned the slogan: "Vote for Marilou. She knows how to love you." They had printed thousands of those T-shirts when his mother ran for governor. Despite the huge political machine they had oiled over the years, despite the range of favors and money that had changed hands, she had lost, and badly, to a faith-healer who claimed to be inspired by God.

His mother had recovered from the humiliation by pretending it hadn't happened. She wore the campaign T-shirt casually around the house, and Arturo winced every time he saw it. They had lost a great deal of money on that election. Not much was left over for his own campaign, though his mother intended him to win.

His mother's powdered-blue eyelids shimmered in the daylight. "Give these birds some water," she told the cook. "We don't want them to die before the rally."

She swept into the dining room and sat at the head of the long mahogany table. Maids brought in warm *pan de sal*, coffee, and a basket filled with golden mangoes and thumb-sized bananas.

She rapped the empty plate before him with her fork. "Hurry and eat your breakfast. I want you to come with me to church." A faint tremor went through her face. "It's the last day of our novena," she said. She leaned toward him, and he caught a scent of her perfumed female body. He pressed against the hard back of his chair.

"You don't know?" she said. "You don't know what's supposed to happen today?"

His chair scraped against the marble floor. He had a vision of his mother in tight white slacks, the T-shirt with her young face stretched across her chest, singing and dancing the cha-cha for a provincial crowd at a campaign rally.

Her black eyes glittered. "The eclipse," she said, "is going to be the beginning of three days of darkness."

"Oh, Ma." He smiled. He slumped against his chair.

"But it's true," she said. "Why do you think the president scheduled her rally today? She may be naive, but she's not stupid. She wants to give people something else to think about. Throw them cakes! She was married to a politician for thirty years, remember."

"Ma, relax."

She waved her jeweled fingers. "People have been saying that the eclipse is a bad omen. It's God's warning against sinners, his punishment for the revolution. It's prophesied somewhere in the Bible."

He edged out of his chair. The cook poked her head through the doorway. He knew she had been listening. "Bring me a beer," he called out.

The head disappeared.

"Before church?" His mother laughed. "Oh, you're like your father." She spread softened butter over a bread roll. "And the whole week, the supermarkets have been full of people. Hoarding food. As if there was a revolution again. Everyone's panicking."

"You believe this?"

"The three days of darkness? I'm not taking any chances. People are saying that everything will close down. So I made Filomena buy ten sacks of rice at the market, and fish to put in the freezer. We can survive a month of darkness."

The young girl—the one whose black eyes had stared at him in the old nanny's room—placed a foaming mug of beer before him. In his mind he saw Lali stumbling through the darkness, across narrow winding streets to a black-curtained room.

"You'll come with me to the novena, Arturo?"

The foam dissolved around his lips. "Do you think it will help?"

"It might help you find Lali," she said curtly. Her fingers lay motionless on his forearm.

He didn't mean to slam the beer mug on the table.

She withdrew her hands and began patting her dyed black hair. "Arturo, these things *happen*. I never trusted that woman."

He watched her. Years of conversations that said nothing stretched like a river between them. Lali was the one strangeness in the suffocating familiarity of his life.

In the mirrored closet over his mother's shoulder, the first trace of the sun emerged from behind heavy clouds. He feared for it suddenly, as he feared for his wife. He thought of his unborn child, lost in streets filled with women fearing punishment, wandering through rooms packed with old people chanting against doom.

"I have something important to show you," his mother said.

He followed her down the hallway. In her sitting room, she sat before her dressing table and rummaged through a drawer. Carefully, she unwrapped tissue paper from a crude brass object. A triangular amulet: the double eye.

"To help you see what's behind you," she said. "It's a good thing to wear in a crowd."

She dabbed on holy water from a plastic bottle shaped like the Virgin Mary, which she had bought at a souvenir shop in Lourdes. He stared at the amulets—the pagan eye in her hand, the Christian icons on her dresser. The whole country was obsessed with outwitting disaster. He, too, had lived his life like that—warding off catastrophe, crossing himself for luck, holding Lali's frail, pregnant body at night.

"You'll need this today," his mother said, offering him the holy water.

He believed her, but he was revolted by her saints and her prayers, by the discrepancy between her fasting and her heavy breasts. Beside her, Lali was a waif, a child. If Lali didn't eat, it was for another reason altogether. Lali was the one being of lightness in that house. She was his amulet against catastrophe, the double eye his mother strung around her lined neck.

His mother was watching him in the mirror. She penciled on eyebrows with a brown liner. "That wife of yours will turn up. I never understood what you saw in that woman."

"Lali's the best thing that ever happened to me."

His mother laughed drily. He looked out the window. Through that glass they had watched military helicopters carry in ammunition for the revolution and the coups d'état, never knowing when or where the bombs would fall.

"If it weren't for Lali," he said, "we wouldn't have been allowed back into this country. You know that. Most of the General's men had to leave the country with him."

"If it weren't for Lali's father dying in front of a porno theater in San Francisco, you mean," his mother said. "That's exactly the kind of hero this country deserves." She spread red lipstick across her mouth, irritably. "And show some respect! The General is still your godfather. He was always very good to us."

He left the room.

The curtains were drawn in his bedroom, the blue-and-white striped sheets crumpled at the foot of his bed. He flung open the closets. Lali's red summer dresses and crisp white linen suits were hung neatly over a row of sandals and pumps. He rummaged through purses, pockets, folders, hating himself for it. He removed a piece of paper from a bag and unfolded it. He recognized her handwriting, but before he allowed himself to read her words, he tore the sheet into pieces and tossed the bits into the wastebasket.

He pressed his head against the door. The wood, still cool from a night of air-conditioning, soothed his skin. He remembered her hand, her touch, her black eyes watching him from the distance she had created between them.

He walked across the room, breathing in the odors of the musky creams he rubbed each night into her belly. He had pressed his head against that soft, pungent skin, listening for sounds of another life, a life so different from the darkness that enshrouded his own, from the loss and dishonor and uncertainty that had plagued him since the revolution. And his wife, with her long pale fingers stubbornly bare of jewelry, had stroked his hair.

The night before, a life before, he had fallen asleep with his arms around her, satisfied with himself, with her, with the grace she had brought into his life.

He opened the notebook on her side table. A photograph slipped from the pages. Pilar's stiff white smile, her hair pulled back from her face. Next to her stood Lali: arms flung around her sister's neck, long black hair, red lips, as unselfconsciously sensual as Pilar was reserved. He ran a finger over Lali's mouth, remembering her laughter.

He hadn't told her about the difficulties at work, the unanswered phone calls, the averted faces at the Rotary. He had friends. He had acquaintances who acted like friends. Many hadn't forgiven his family's closeness to the General. Many of those who now condemned him had tried, and failed, to be close to the General themselves.

He entered the bathroom and twisted open the faucet.

He leaned over the sink and splashed cool water over his face and neck. He pulled his head away, shaking off the drops that clung to his hair.

He backed his car out of the garage. The asphalt was gray and wet under the white sky. Eight o'clock.

His mother walked toward the car, waving at him. He pressed a button to roll down the tinted window.

"Can you drop me off at the church?" she called out.

She plumped down beside him and crossed her legs. A

houseboy opened the gates. The car edged toward the military checkpoint at the entrance to the highway. They slowed to a stop. Armed soldiers pressed their faces against the tinted glass. His mother lowered the window and dangled three fifty-peso bills over the glass. The soldiers' faces softened. They smiled.

"Buy yourselves some beer," she said gaily.

They waved the car away, young boys grinning in their military fatigues. His mother raised one penciled eyebrow, then threw back her head and laughed. The skin tightened under her jaw.

"Ma." He smiled as they sped off. "You're not supposed to bribe the military anymore. This is a new government."

She exhaled sharply. "One revolution isn't going to change anybody."

The highway was lined with abandoned tanks, shattered glass, and condominiums strafed during the last coup attempt. Buses and jeepneys were packed with colorfully dressed people carrying baskets of white doves.

At a stoplight, three children besieged their car. They held out rosaries with the president's face stamped on every bead. A boy who looked about five waved a plastic bag filled with black sunglasses. He brandished a hand-lettered flyer: "Eclipse-proof viewers."

Vehicles lined the highway as far as Arturo could see.

"I've never seen traffic like this," he said, "even in Manila."

His mother smiled vaguely at the sunglasses outside her window. "They all want to be at the rally before noon," she said. "The whole crowd will see the city turn dark, then the sun will return. That's what she wants them to see. No three days of darkness. Then they'll release the white doves, and everyone will say she worked another miracle."

"I thought you were prepared for a month of darkness."

"I don't take chances, darling."

He tucked the car into a side street, edging past sidewalk stalls and vendors selling young, green coconuts. He slammed his hand against the horn as a man on a bicycle cut in front of him.

No one in the streets could tell him where she was. Not the women in their shapeless dresses, not the children in tattered clothes, not the men sitting on benches in front of stores and smoking filterless cigarettes.

He jammed a cassette into the slot.

They turned into a square facing the church. A year before, during the revolution, students had been massacred in the square; the new president had quickly re-christened it the Square of Peace. It now resembled a bazaar. On makeshift bamboo tables, vendors had stacked religious memorabilia and remedies: statues of bloodied saints, rosaries, oils and herbs from the shamans in the mountains, charms for sorcery.

On another morning, he had walked through that square with Lali, taking photographs of her. She had sat beside street children and talked to them, allowing them to tug at her long pearl necklace. Then the rains had come and ruined their morning, and they ended up drinking coffee in a five-star hotel overlooking the bay. She held his hand all throughout break-fast, rubbing a bare foot against his ankle. They had laughed at the oil smears on the bay, swore never to eat seafood again, and agreed that despite all the difficulties of life in this city, it was good to be home.

He hadn't known she was pregnant.

Now the church's devotees jostled around him: old women dressed in black and clutching their missals, younger couples carrying garlands of *ylang-ylang* to string around stat-ues of their patron saints. Many of these devotees had been there the day after the revolution. The square had been full of people dancing and singing songs of freedom and lust. The drinking grew raucous after midnight, and the mob—the squatters, soldiers, fishmongers, and servants—thronged into the palace abandoned by the dictator. They tore paintings from the walls and stole everything they could carry away.

The same people were in the church today, praying for forgiveness, fearing the darkness that threatened to fall upon them. From inside the church a long keening began.

His mother's double-eye flashed beneath her neck. "How will you get home?" he asked her.

"My driver's coming."

People stared at them—the well-dressed society matron and her pale-skinned son. Beggar-children began tugging at their clothes.

"Give them something," his mother said irritably, as she disengaged the fingers from her pants.

He distributed coins.

"Listen," she said. "I know you don't want to tell your mother anything, but don't worry about that wife of yours. She'll turn up. Don't kill yourself looking for her."

"I never said she was gone."

"Oh," she said, distracted. "Did you try her sister's house?"

She entered the church. He made his way across the square. The slippers of beggar-children brushed against his laced leather shoes. He smiled at the children. They held out their hands for money and pointed at their mouths. On one bamboo table, eighteen Jesuses stared up at the white sky.

It will rain, it will rain, he heard people saying. Vendors tacked hard plastic sheets over their booths. An old woman huddled behind her oils and herbs. He needed Lali, the line of her body as she walked through those streets. In a country gone mad with revolutions and miracles and midday moons, she had brought a center of order to his inner world. He wanted only to return there, to the space and the self that had existed in her presence.

He moved blindly across the crowded square, guided more by instinct than by sight, to his car. Inside, he squinted and surveyed the sky. No sun. The first heavy raindrops strummed the metal roof. He navigated the car past booths and children and old women, and fiddled with the dials of the radio until he found a disc jockey rapping the news.

"About 100,000 people have been gathering at Camp Crame since early morning, carrying cages of white doves they will release after the eclipse. The president asks us to warn all of you not to look directly at the sun."

Rain streamed down the windshield.

"Mothers, take care of your children! The sun can burn their eyes. Only when the sun is totally shadowed by the moon will it be safe to look directly at the eclipse."

Lightning flashed. The car inched along wet streets. He had nowhere to go. He searched the face, the body, of every passerby. He wanted to talk to someone, but Lali and he had formed a world that excluded friendships.

He drove through the rain to a quiet residential compound sealed off by barbed wire. He nodded curtly at the old man reading a newspaper inside the guardhouse. After some shuffling of paper, the guard lowered his stooped body from the stool and stepped into the rain. He unlocked the gate.

Arturo drove down a driveway lined with mango trees to a house built just after the Second World War. He parked the car. The screen door was ajar. He walked into a cool, wood-paneled room, which opened to a verandah and untended garden. No one was there. Silently, he climbed the narrow staircase, the banister smooth under his hand.

Across the upstairs living room, in a space made light by translucent mother-of-pearl windows, Pilar sat on the floor, her back to him. Her dress was hiked over thin brown thighs. Outside, the rain steadied to a quiet drumming. Her back curved as she held a piece of glass over a candle flame. The muscles on her upper arm tightened. Without speaking, he watched her.

He lit a cigarette.

She turned around. After a moment, she said: "Arturo."

She lay the smoked glass carefully on the floor beside her and stood to meet him. The low-cut dress clung to her breasts.

He took one puff of the cigarette, then crushed it on the glass ashtray.

"What are you doing here," she said as she leaned over to press her cheek against his. He smelled her perfume—Saint Laurent's Rive Gauche, Lali's favorite—and stepped back before her skin could touch his.

"I'm looking for Lali."

"She's not here." She paused, fingering an ivory button on the bodice of her dress. "Why did you think she'd be here?"

"You're the only friend she has."

"I'm her sister. That doesn't mean we're friends." She smiled, parting her wide lips. "Why, did you have a fight?"

He shook his head.

"I wouldn't worry," she said. "Lali can take care of herself."

His wife's sister walked across the room, chest first, her legs long under the sheer cotton. He had never understood Lali's attachment to this woman, who was so unlike her.

She bent to pick up the glass. He glimpsed the full, brown breasts beneath the neckline of her dress. She sat cross-legged on the floor. Glancing at him, she tugged the hem of her dress over her knees.

"It smells horrible here." He smiled to soften his words. "Can't you stop burning that thing?"

"It's for the eclipse," she said. "Do you think we'll still have an eclipse?"

"I hope so."

The rain had slowed to a drizzle.

"Sit beside me," she said.

He sat on the floor next to her. She held the darkened glass over the flickering candle flame. "They say this is one of the best ways to watch an eclipse," she told him. "You hold a smoked glass against the sun. Only a dim image of the sun comes through, but at least you don't hurt your eyes. They say the best thing of all is to use welder's goggles or X-ray film, but I forgot to get some. I heard a lot of people are going to burn their retinas." The candlelight cast a faint sheen on her inner arms. "Are you going to the president's rally?"

He shook his head. He was scared to press, to ask questions, to disturb the surfaces that concealed them.

She stared at him. He had never noticed the color of her eyes. They were black, where he could see nothing, and so where all things were possible. He reached across for her hands and forced them to the floor beside her. The tips of her nipples were visible against the thin fabric of her dress. She looked down. He saw his lips sucking the taut brown breasts, so different from Lali's thin, pale body. He edged toward her and pressed his face against the side of her neck. She inhaled sharply. His mouth moved up her neck and brushed against the coarse strands of her hair. Awkwardly, she pressed her body against him.

He pulled away and stood up. He gathered the pack of cigarettes he had left on the table. When he turned to her again, she was twisting the top button of her dress.

"Do you want me to help you find her?" she asked, her voice meek.

He couldn't look at her. Outside the house, a car sloshed through rain in the driveway.

In the past years, his outer life, professional and political, had been fractured by upheavals. Only his personal life had seemed immune to disaster: his marriage, his love for Lali, the family he waited for in her. Now even Lali couldn't save him. For the first time that day, he knew what he wanted, and what he wanted was another woman's breasts against his skin. What he wanted was to betray Lali.

"I made a mistake," he told her sister. "I was looking for Lali."

He crushed the pack of cigarettes into his pocket. As he hurried down the stairs, she said: "Lali knows how to take care of herself. Why do you think she married you?"

He hesitated, then swung around and stared at her. "What are you talking about?"

From the top of the stairs she smiled coldly down at him. The light behind her silhouetted her long legs.

"You know what I'm talking about," she said. "We were with the opposition. You had friends in all the right places. Why shouldn't she have married you? We had nothing else."

He turned and walked down the stairs, measuring his steps.

Outside the rain had stopped. A glitter of sunlight fell on the puddles. She leaned out the mother-of-pearl window, no longer smiling, watching him as he got into the car.

"Wait," she said.

He thrust the key into the ignition and started the car. Through wet, crowded streets he drove, past stacks of garbage and shanties. Jeepneys stalled in front of him, pouring out their load of women, children, and caged white doves. Inch by inch, he measured his way home. He counted the shoes and legs and faces he passed, the cars lined bumper to bumper ahead of him in the flooded streets.

When he turned into the highway, he accelerated abruptly. He switched on the radio, imagining the contours of Pilar's body beneath her dress, her neck, her hair against his cheek. He began to hum to the music.

Then he saw Pilar smile mockingly at him from the top of the stairs, and he remembered what she had said. He stopped humming. He turned the radio on full-blast and forced her out of his mind.

He paused at the military checkpoint before entering into his mother's neighborhood. Recognizing him, the young guards waved him through.

On bougainvillea-lined streets he pushed forward. Eleven-thirty. The freak storm had passed. Sunlight poured over the stain of raindrops on his windshield. He blew the horn in front of the high gates. The car's wheels screeched as he turned into the driveway.

In the living room his mother sat, still tucked into her black stretch pants. "Finally," she said. "Can you help the maids load the doves into your car?"

"I'm not going to the rally."

"Please," she said. "We have to get there before the eclipse. We have barely an hour left."

"You'll never get there in time. The traffic's terrible."

In the garden behind her, a solitary sparrow hopped over the puddles.

"Where are the doves?" he said.

"They're already in the garage."

He entered the kitchen. At the wooden table, the cook and Lali's nursemaid sat, peeling garlic cloves. They glanced at him briefly, then at each other. He reached for a butcher's knife lying on the table.

He rushed toward the garage, two steps at a time. The soft cooing of dozens of doves suffused the dark shed. He unlocked the doors and dragged the cages out to the damp pavement. The drivers and houseboys looked up from their cards and stared at him. Sunlight fell on the birds. He held the knife up to the light, then swiftly began to saw off the top of the wicker cages. The birds panicked beneath him, flapping their wings.

When a foot-wide hole had been sliced from the cage, he thrust his hands into the mass of fluttering feathers and lifted one dove. Its tiny heart pounded against his fingers.

He held it up to the white sky. The bird trembled in his hands.

"Fly," he said. He tossed the dove into the air. It flapped its wings helplessly and fell to the pavement. He thrust his hands back into the cage and tossed another dove into the air. White feathers floated around him. From inside their wire cages, dogs began to bark. The doves on the pavement hopped over each other in confusion. The pavement crawled with cooing birds.

"*Señorito*," a driver said, his eyes wide with fear. "They don't know how to fly. They've been in cages all their lives. Their wings have been clipped."

"How could you buy doves that can't fly?" Arturo shouted, the vein pulsing in his throat. "How dare you buy us doves that don't fly?"

His mother appeared at the entrance to the garage. "What's all the screaming?" she shouted. When she saw the doves hopping over the pavement, she pressed her hands into her stomach. "Get out of there," she shouted at the drivers and her son. "Get those birds back into their cages."

She rushed toward Arturo and heaved her strong, solid body against him. "Get out of here. Leave them alone."

Arturo began to laugh. After a moment, warily, his mother laughed, too. "I really don't know," she said, patting back her hair. "They were supposed to be for her miracle."

She grasped his elbow and steered him back inside the house. The chairs stood scratched and abandoned around the kitchen table, where the cook had left her chopping board, two heads of garlic, and peelings.

"Arturo," his mother said carefully. "Lali's back. I saw her at church."

He cupped his hand against the edge of the table and brushed translucent shavings of garlic into it. He tossed the scraps into the wastebasket.

"Shall we go see her?" his mother said.

He washed his hands over the sink, rubbing detergent onto

his fingers. In his mind he heard the song he had listened to on his way home from Pilar.

He entered their bedroom. Black sheets tacked over the window obscured almost all light. His wife lay naked in bed, eyes closed, a white blanket covering the curve of her breasts. Two old women hovered over her. The nursemaid pulled down the blanket and arranged five cloves of garlic in a star pattern over Lali's navel. Her nipples, enlarged and darkened by pregnancy, faced the ceiling.

His mother strode through the darkness and held her hand. "Lali," she said. "Arturo's here."

The cook spread her massive body across the edge of the bed, a sea-wall separating him from Lali. His wife opened her eyes. Her vulnerable, rounded body, already flushed with the effort of sustaining life, pressed back into the bed and into the solicitations of the women around her. She glanced at him, then at his mother. She smiled.

He wanted to hit her. He took two steps toward her. Lali's black eyes flicked toward him. He recoiled.

"I'm sorry about all this," Lali said, gesturing at the garlic cloves in a sunburst around her navel. "But you know what they say about eclipses and pregnant women. They want to protect the baby."

"It's all nonsense," his mother said quickly. "But it won't do any harm, Arturo."

"I want to talk to Lali, alone."

"After the eclipse," his mother said.

"No."

Arturo sat on the darkened bed next to his wife. A folded black umbrella with a wooden handle rested against the side table.

"Where were you?" he whispered.

She lowered her eyes. "I went to church, Arturo."

"You never go to church."

"I do." Her pale fingers began to stroke her belly. "Today I needed to."

He reached for the umbrella and twisted it slowly in his hands. "Stop lying to me."

"I keep having these dreams. Papa holding his hands out to me, and I can't see his face—"

She tried to meet his eyes. He turned away.

"I'm sorry." Her voice was defiant. "I told him I was sorry. But I didn't want to end up like him. Can you understand that?"

Why shouldn't she have married you? Pilar had asked. *We had nothing else.*

Lali motioned for him to come closer. "People keep saying—"

He had always told himself: nothing and no one would endanger his marriage, his love for her. Now he didn't care.

"But they're wrong," Lali whispered. "It wasn't my being with you that allowed them to get to him."

Her hair lay disheveled on the pillow. He wanted to take the long black strands and wrap them one by one around her fragile white neck, but he did nothing.

His mother told Lali: "You see, I told him not to worry. You should have seen how worried he was."

He walked to the window.

The nursemaid crawled over his pillow and pressed her hand on Lali's belly. The three old women leaned over his wife, and she smiled at them. He felt like an intruder, blown to waves by their silences, their condescension. They had insinuated their way into his wife's pregnancy, as they would into the lives of his children. And Lali, by her femaleness and secret resentments, belonged more to them than to him.

He couldn't penetrate the old women around her.

Panicking, still hoping to contain the wreckage, he said: "I want to watch the eclipse. Lali, come with me to the garden. We'll watch it together."

She turned away.

"Arturo," his mother said. "Please."

He knew then what he had to do. He walked back across the room, past old women in black, and leaned over the bed to kiss his wife. As her lips brushed against his, he felt distaste. He knew that from then on he would stay with her because of the child, because of the people around them, because he had nothing better to do. He was alone again, and the thought exhilarated him.

The nursemaid glanced at her watch and said: "Only four minutes left."

The cook spread the blanket over Lali, unfurled the black umbrella and held it over his wife's swollen belly. Lali closed her eyes, as though to seek darkness more profound than the black-curtained room.

In the garden, Arturo held a wide aluminum basin of water to the sun. He tipped it from side to side, trying to capture the sun's reflection. When the sun had settled into the center of the water, he carefully lowered the basin to the damp grass and sat beside it.

The water was perfectly still. The reflection gradually faded. The garden turned deep blue, and a yellow haze appeared over the walls. In the water, the shadow of the moon slipped between the sun and the earth.

House and street lamps began to glow. In the sudden dusk, roosters crowed, dogs howled, neighbors applauded. A spattering of firecrackers illuminated the sky. Bewildered by the midday darkness, birds swooped through the garden, singing nocturnal songs and looking for refuge.

He lifted his eyes from the water, not yet daring to search for the shadowed sun. Just above the horizon, four bright stars flickered. Raising his vision tentatively, he thought he recognized Venus and Jupiter. The temperature dropped several degrees. A sudden breeze—the eclipse wind—cooled his bare arms and rustled the leaves of mango trees.

He remembered the warnings. Looking at the sun could cause permanent eye damage: a recurring afterimage, a blind spot, the perception of dancing clouds or rainbow colors. Encouraged by these possibilities, he stared directly into the eclipse.

The only visible light was the rim of the sun's corona surrounding the silhouette of the moon. In the violet sky, the rim of light seemed as fragile and feathery as wings. For three minutes during the eclipse, as his world plunged into darkness, the sun wavered above him like a white dove.

CHAPTER THREE

THE FISH

In our mythologies all women
who gaze too long at the moon
on water are overcome
by water.

—MA. LUISA A. IGLORIA, "Riversong"

LALI

Near the house were watchtowers, which Lali's great-grandparents and their servants climbed twice a year to watch the galleons sail in from Acapulco. When Lali was a child, her mother said: Never go up there. Even seeing the ocean is dangerous—pirate winds carry Moros from the south, and they never became Christian.

Bad people, bad ghosts, they were all around her. And still Lali played in the towers, secretly, when her mother was away. She invented songs about typhoon winds, trade winds, eclipse winds, pirate winds. She imagined living in a time of gold and galleons and pirates. She pretended she looked like the portrait of her Chinese-Spanish great-grandmother, with her slanted eyes and long neck, her white gloves and black-lace fan. Mexican trade had made her family wealthy. Not Spanish, they said—Mexican. Later they told her: we were the colony of a colony. Not even Spanish. We said we were Spanish, but no one was Spanish. When we went to Madrid, no one could understand what we were saying. And they warned her again: crazy women, vampires, dead Japanese prisoners from the war still dragging their chains, and the warnings fed her songs.

At night, in the room of Arturo's childhood, Lali turned her back to him and pulled off her satin nightgown. From behind, he would see only a woman's body, curved and wanting. No trace of the pregnancy that had disfigured her.

She lay beside him. He closed his eyes and ran his fingers over her thighs. A hollowing in the room, in her chest. There was a distance in his touch, a coldness, that she had never felt before. She became very still, aware of his hand on her skin, her skin under his hand. She was alert to the slightest shifts in pressure, to changes in his breathing, even to the vibrations in the air between them.

Eyes shut, he stroked her, his gestures mechanical. She looked at his face and feared for herself. Her marriage, her safety, depended on his wanting her.

She guided his hand to her belly, then to her breasts. Perhaps it was the pregnancy. Some men couldn't deal with it. And Arturo liked thin women. Maybe he was imagining she was someone else, pretending he had never touched her before. She sat up and lifted his hands over his head, crossed them at the wrist, rested them on the pillow. She began to caress him, in ways she knew he liked, in ways he had taught her at the beginning and now rarely dared to ask. And all the time her thoughts rushed backward and forward, skipping between images and phrases, trying to understand. It's nothing, she told herself. It's probably nothing. She knew he loved her. He had had flirtations, perhaps other women. None of them had mattered.

She tried. Movements, sounds, reactions. She feigned pleasure even as she panicked. He didn't open his eyes. When he started to come, she stopped trying and watched him.

Later, she lay on her side, facing him. He was on his back, breath still ragged, one arm bent over his head. Except for the chest and belly, he looked so much like her. Narrow hips and long legs, pale skin, high cheekbones, wide-set eyes. They looked so much alike that people sometimes thought they were brother and sister, and at times she wondered whether he had married her so he could imagine making love to himself.

She was afraid to speak. Maybe his distance was just a mood. He so rarely had moods. Arturo's amiability was one of the things she liked best and understood least about him. He walked into a party and seemed delighted to see everybody there. One or two nights a week, he came to this house, where he had grown up and his mother still lived, because he missed the people in the household, the cook and maids and drivers who had taken care of him for years. He sat with them in the kitchen, ate with his hands, teased them about their love lives. All the servants, even the grouchy old gardener, brightened when they saw him.

It will pass, she told herself. Leave him alone. Instead she edged toward him, close enough to smell his skin. A trace of lavender soap, deodorant, and those other odors, musky and male, that she recognized but couldn't name. Then the faint smells of the river came to her, too, the iodine and salt and sewage, slipping through the cracks in the walls and window frames of the large colonial house that had belonged to his family for generations. She and Arturo had grown up along the banks of this river, in different parts of Manila, at a time when the river smelled almost clean. That was a resemblance, too, as striking to her as that of their bodies, and for some reason this reassured her—the river, their appearance, these accidents of resemblance. She shut her eyes, imagining the South China Sea flowing into Manila's harbor and narrowing into this river, and sea water moving sluggishly past shantytowns and the presidential palace and Spanish-era mansions, gathering the city's waste as it made its way to an inland lake so vast young children thought it was the sea.

People from the same side of the river should never marry, her father had told her. She had been a child then, sitting with him by the banks of the Pasig. She watched a dark shape, almost as wide as the river, waiting beneath the surface of the water.

The people who lived here, her father said, were called the Taga-Ilogs—those who live by the river. At the time, he told her, and in different places, the river was aquamarine, blue, and yellow, and in the shallows almost transparent.

Papa, she replied, trying not to blink because she knew the shadow would disappear if she closed her eyes. There's an enormous fish there, at the bottom of the river. I see it every day when I come here. Can you see it?

No one, her father had said, has ever seen a monster fish at the bottom of this river.

Now she held her breath as she lay next to Arturo and knew that most of her life she had been seeking someone just like him, like herself, a lover from her side of the river. She had loved her father but hated the life he had imposed on her, the exile and dissidents and poverty, the long years of political struggle that had taught her not idealism but distrust, convinced her that almost no one and nothing were what they seemed, that her safety depended on an ability to detect the lies, secrets, and capacity for betrayal that hid behind words and smiles. Her family's safety, too, depended on her. None of them could sense the danger in other people.

Arturo wasn't dangerous. And he wanted things to be simple. In time, she believed, a life with him would wash away the worst of what had happened to her, and her life would one day appear simple, too.

But her father wouldn't leave her in peace. She tried not to think of him. He's dead, she told herself, each time an image or memory or that unspeakable pain surfaced. She couldn't imagine him on that sidewalk, after the shooting. She hadn't sensed the danger, and she was supposed to know better than everyone else. At night, he came back to her, in her dreams, a bloodied face, and at times, and this was worse, no face at all, no body, just a sense of him, a darkness, in distress. He was dead. And she hadn't saved him. How could she have saved him? He hadn't wanted to save himself. And the more the baby grew within her, taking up space inside her belly, the more her father filled her dreams. Sometimes when the dreams became too much, when she woke up with her chest so tight and painful she felt she couldn't breathe—she had never realized a heart really could ache, that the pain was physical and not figurative—when this happened, she slipped away from the house and drove to the musty old cathedral he had visited for novenas and penitence. She walked toward the statue of the Virgin Mary, with its slanted eyes and long neck and white hands like those in the portrait of her great-grandmother. She knelt at a wooden pew and prayed to her father, to the saints, to whomever might be out there. She prayed for him to leave her alone.

Arturo's room carried little trace of the boy who had lived there. Framed on the wall was a child's copy of a Picasso painting, a blue-toned old man curled around a guitar, which Arturo had painted in a remarkably sure hand when he was seven. Near the bed, a glass case displayed one of his early model ships. A galleon, with full sails, about two feet long and two feet high—she couldn't tell whether it was Spanish or

French, although Arturo had tried to explain the differences. He still constructed one or two galleons every year, spending months on each one, sewing the sails and nailing the planks with a delicacy and deftness that moved her.

She pressed her cheek against his bare shoulder. He nudged her away. The baby, she thought. Whatever's happening, if something is happening, he won't do anything to hurt the baby.

He switched on the lamp.

She sat up and pinched her nipples. A drop of yellow liquid pearled over each tip.

He tucked his hands under his head, elbows pointing toward the walls. "I had a dream the other night," he said.

She licked the liquid from her fingertips, trying to remember the last time he had really spoken to her. "Tell me about it," she said evenly.

"It was a silly dream, a dream of vampires. They were all around me, in your sister's house."

Her back straightened. "Pilar?"

He smiled. He had good teeth, even and white. "It was just a dream, La."

He turned his head to look at her, the smile shifting into that reckless, bad-boy grin she still found irresistible. "They were crawling in through the window. Beautiful. And these horrible red and black robes. Probably polyester. But the women were gorgeous, bending over me, breasts spilling out. They were about to bite off my feet when I woke up."

She gazed at him with wary tenderness. The expensive haircut, the body pummeled into shape by weights and sports, the high-bridged nose. Arturo always looked as if he had just stepped out of the shower, even after a night of hard partying or hours of sex. In the past months, no matter the strains and irritations that surfaced between them, his skin and smell had brought her back to him. She loved what he felt like. Memories came to her, from the beginning, the way he turned to kiss her in the cinema whenever on-screen lovers began to kiss or make love, the way he combed her hair after a shower, patted the strands dry, rubbed them between his fingers. The way he slept with his arms and legs around hers, seeking her even in sleep. Each time, she had been surprised and touched, but she had never told him that, never wanted him to know how much he meant to her. Not a bad man. That was what she had told her parents, when she started dating him in San Francisco. Despite everything, a good heart. Good hearts turn up in the most unlikely places, her father had responded drily. But her father had never tried to stop her. She knew what people said. A smart marriage. A brilliant move. But how could she live with it—how could she betray her father's memory this way?

"What's the matter?" Arturo asked. "You don't like vampires?"

No one, not even her father, understood this: the real betrayal wasn't marrying Arturo, but loving him.

"Don't look at me like that," he said. "It was only a dream."

She knew these sons of privilege. Men like him needed distractions, novelty, excitement.

"I used to see things, too," she said.

"Vampires?"

"No. Of course not. A fish. And it wasn't a dream—I really saw it."

The corner of his mouth lifted, but his eyes remained distant. Again she feared for herself. She had to bring him back to her.

"You saw a fish?" he asked.

"Don't make fun of me. An enormous black one, at the bottom of the Pasig. Next to the house we lived in when I was small. Every time I looked at it, it got bigger, and I was sure that one day it would be too big for the river. I was sure that one day, when the floods came, it would swim out of the river and break into our house, and then it would swim up the stairs and eat me."

He circled her wrist and rubbed his thumb against her skin, as he used to do, in the beginning, whenever she became upset. She leaned back against the pillows, distressed by the memory of their love.

"What do you do," he asked, "with dreams like that?"

Maybe she was mistaken—maybe nothing was wrong. Or maybe everything was, and he was trying only to keep the surfaces smooth, hoping she wouldn't notice.

She wanted to say: Tell me how the dream ended. Tell me whom you were thinking about when we made love. Tell me what she looks like, how you imagined her when you were inside me.

Instead she said: "One night, it was raining so hard, I was sure the fish was there, waiting for me to sleep. I saw its black tail banging against the window. Bigger than the window, really, but my father said it was just the giant leaves of the banana tree, hitting the glass."

"I don't want our baby to dream like that," he said.

"It wasn't a dream."

On that night, so long ago, rain had been pounding the roof, water dripping through holes that Japanese bullets had made during the war. She had jumped from bed and gathered her red plastic tea set, then made her father sit on the floor beside her. Hurriedly, she arranged the small plastic saucers, forks, and knives in front of them. "We have to eat it quickly, before it kills us," she told him. With a knife and fork she cut the invisible fish into many pieces and spread them across her tea set. Then they ate every morsel, even the eyes, which were bigger than her head, and when they finished eating, her father asked her sleepily: "Is it gone now? Have we killed that fish?" And she knew they had. She never saw it again, and the shadow disappeared from the bottom of the river.

Now Arturo turned to her in bed and said: "He was always a little strange, wasn't he, your father? Even before the politics."

Nothing she said could make him see the father she had loved. Gregorio's self-doubt and idealism had no resonance in Arturo's universe, where power and privilege were all that mattered.

Gregorio wasn't practical, her mother had said when Lali was growing up. He couldn't make money, didn't know how to build a life. But he had seen how big the world was, how full of colors and magic. Lali and Pilar had been thrilled by his stories, the people on the same banks who couldn't marry each other, the aquamarine, blue, and yellow rivers. Now that he was dead, Lali sought out the colors he had taught her to see. She arranged red and green sachets of potpourri in her closets, tucked colored buttons into the bottom of her handbags. A trade, she told him. I'll gather tokens of you, and they'll be my talismans against you.

A fluttering inside her. She pressed Arturo's hand against her stomach, where the baby was kicking. He kissed her on the cheek, his eyes withdrawing. Her chest tightened. Her inner sense, the barometer that had guided her through years of intrigue and exile, was broken. It had failed her with her father, and it was failing her now.

His fingertips touched the hollow of her cheek. He smiled again, tentatively, and a moment later she mirrored his smile. He said, seemingly at a loss for anything else: "Your face is getting so thin."

Perhaps everyone needs a surface life, to stay intact, she told herself. Maybe that's all it is. Not someone else.

He kissed her briefly on the lips and belly, as he did every night, then turned to his side, facing the lamplight. Arturo couldn't sleep in the dark. She grasped his shoulder, as she did every night, holding him until his breathing steadied and her touch eased him into sleep. When she was certain he was asleep, she pressed her parted lips against his shoulder.

In the morning, she was awakened by his arm against her chest. He was reaching over her to switch on the radio. Slowly, the news filtered in. A ship lost at sea, a storm in the middle of the night, thousands lost. One of the worst shipping disasters in the country's history, the newscaster said.

Arturo sat up, switched off the lamp, picked up the phone on his bedside table. He tapped a few digits, then pressed the receiver against his ear, holding it up with his shoulder as he tore out a sheet of paper and scribbled on it. Without looking at her, he said: "It's one of our ships."

Again the stirring inside her.

No one knows exactly how many people were on board, the radio announcer said. *We have the ship's manifest, but it seems there were many more passengers than the ship was authorized to carry. There are reports of 2,000, even 3,000 passengers. Families have begun to hold vigil outside the main office of the shipping company.*

"There couldn't have been that many," Arturo said.

We've received an unconfirmed report that the captain was able to jump ship before it sank.

Arturo switched off the radio, walked naked into the bathroom. She watched him shave. Finally, she said, "I think we should cancel the party next week."

He leaned forward and inspected each cheek.

"I think we should cancel it," she said. "You should talk to your mother."

"We're not cancelling anything." He stepped out of the bathroom, opened the mirrored closet door. "Cancelling would make it look like we've done something wrong."

"You can launch the campaign in a few weeks. You shouldn't do it now."

"You know who's going to make a big stink about this, don't you?" He chose a pale pink shirt and pulled the sleeves over his arms. "A lot of people are out to get me. It has nothing to do with the ship." His voice was calm, but he was fumbling with the buttons of his shirt, unable to insert any of them into a buttonhole. She realized his hands were shaking. "Ships sink every goddamn month in this country," he said.

She left the bed and went to him. Carefully, she buttoned his shirt for him, one ivory-colored disk at a time, rubbing the skin behind the cloth so they could both pretend she was caressing instead of helping him. They didn't speak. When she was done, he squeezed her shoulders, but his face was tense and he looked over her head at the door.

After he was gone, she locked the door and sat on the bed. She thought of the ship, the passengers in the storm. She thought of Miguel, her old boyfriend, his green eyes and dark skin. He had died in another shipwreck, so long ago. She told herself: Arturo will take care of this. His family will take care of it. There must have been lifeboats. Everything will be okay.

She made the sign of the cross and prayed for this to be true.

Hours later, Lali entered a large open-space office. Ringing telephones and dozens of employees in white shirts hurrying from one cubicle to another. She recognized almost no one.

A tiny woman appeared beside her. "Very sorry, ma'am," she stammered, "but Sir heard you were coming. He's waiting for you."

Without knocking, Lali opened a door and entered Arturo's wood-paneled office. The curtains were drawn. The air-conditioning chilled her.

"You should keep your door open today," she said. "Act like you're accessible."

"Why did you come here?" He was sitting behind an antique mahogany desk, folders piled neatly on one corner. A sky-blue sweater partly covered his pink shirt. His phone began to ring. He picked it up, listened for a moment, then said: "Absolutely no one should be allowed into the building."

She watched the movements of his mouth and thought of the party next Saturday, the preparations that had been going on for weeks.

"And no comments to the press," he said.

As he spoke, he fidgeted with a drawer next to his desk, sliding it out a few inches and then shutting it, over and over again. The first time he had taken her to his childhood home by the Pasig, she had opened his bedside drawer while he was in the shower, after a night of lovemaking and little sleep. The outer face of the side panel, visible only when she slid out the drawer, was filled with drawings and scribbles. HELP, he had written, over and over again, in a boyish handwriting, in many shapes and sizes, shaded or outlined, inside stars or boats, in pencil and in red and blue ink. With the tip of a finger, she had traced the letters, wondering what his childhood had really been like. She had shut the drawer and never spoken to him about it.

Now he set the telephone on its stand. "What happened?" she asked.

"Stupidity. Corruption. Bad luck." He clicked on the remote control to switch on the television. "The Holy Trinity of disaster in this country."

The phone rang again. The voices of her husband and the newscasters overlapped and blended into each other: *There shouldn't have been so many people. There weren't enough lifeboats. Who smuggled all those people on board? Who's been feeding the details to the press?*

Restlessly, she glanced around the room. She rarely imagined Arturo's other life, this place where he spent his days. Behind his desk, the wall held framed photos of him, his father, and grandfather, shaking hands with a succession of the country's presidents. The other walls displayed paintings by Filipino masters and contemporary Asian artists, antique maps, and a collection of tribal spears and daggers. Everything was understated and elegant, but she wondered how much power Arturo really had. The most important business decisions were made in living rooms and coffee shops, where his mother, aunts, and uncles drank hot chocolate and spoke to each other in a mixture of Spanish, English, and Ilonggo. Arturo was the titular head of the family's group of companies, but the older generation didn't trust him with their wealth. He's still young, they said—he has to prove himself. Besides, the country's a mess. The dictatorship, then the revolution, wrecked the economy; even the very wealthy are panicking. But no one doubted that Arturo would eventually succeed, especially if he entered politics. Young men from powerful families almost always did well in business—they faced little or no competition, they were propped up by the sharpest minds they could hire, and they were related to or had gone to school with everyone who mattered.

The president's thin, patrician face appeared on the television. Square-rimmed glasses, a rosary around her neck. She asked for prayers, promised to investigate the accident. Justice will be served, she said, loudly but without emphasis, as though she were reading the words for the first time on a prompter. The scene shifted to Arturo's office building and the crowds around it. The camera zoomed in on a toddler clutching the blouse of its young mother.

"This can blow up in our faces," Lali said.

Arturo was whispering into the receiver, staring at the curtains. Monosyllabic answers, no expression on his face. His full lips almost touched the receiver. The mouth of a libertine, she had thought when she first met him.

He replaced the receiver. "Someone should go down south to investigate." His back pressed against the leather-upholstered chair. "The ship was full of families, La. Mothers, children, grandparents. Returning to Manila after the holidays."

"Are you sure?"

He gave a hollow smile. "Positive."

She wanted to comfort him, but she didn't know what he needed from her. She was afraid to do or say something that would push him further away.

"This is going to make me look very bad," he said, "just before the campaign." His voice was measured, but his eyes had a distress she had never seen before. With a start she realized he had no idea what to do.

Shouts and cries outside. They hurried to the window, parted the curtains, just wide enough to look through the glass. Beneath them, hundreds of heads tilted backwards, looking up. Arturo pointed to the horizon. A small figure was descending in a parachute, swaying over the crowd.

He shut the curtains. "We'll see it better on TV."

The television screen displayed a close-up of a man in military uniform. *It's Jimbo!* The commentator's voice cracked with excitement. In a lower, more collected voice, he added: *Jaime Montenegro, rebel leader of the right-wing faction of the military, has just jumped from a helicopter and is now parachuting over the families of the Doña Cristina victims.*

"He's just using this," Arturo muttered.

The crowd seemed to undulate, hundreds of figures in pastel colors swaying from side to side, opening and closing to create a clearing for his landing. But the wind carried the parachute to a field just beyond the crowd. Moments later, the television showed the man on the ground, grinning, arms lifted over his head.

Montenegro has been on the run since escaping from prison, where he was serving time for plotting the first two coup attempts.

Arturo turned off the sound. "In any other country, they'd arrest him."

"They'll never do that. Everyone knows who his backers are."

"They're treating him like a movie star!" Arturo said.

"At least he knows how to use the media."

"You think I don't know how to use the media?"

"I think you shouldn't be looking at the TV to see what's happening right outside your own building." Be careful, she told herself. But he had to understand how serious this was. "Look at him—he's talking to the people. Poor people, good Jimbo. Turn up the sound! Don't you want to hear what he's going to say about you? You think your PR people will take care of it?"

Anger cut across his face. Frightened by what she saw in his eyes, and by what she might say next, she walked out of the room. Employees stopped what they were doing and stared at her. No one spoke. She asked his secretary to make her coffee, then drank it alone, standing, in the windowless room that served as a cafeteria.

He's gone, she told herself. Something in him has left me. She sipped the coffee. Small hard grains of sugar coated her tongue. Life was a series of ruptures, her father had told her once. Most people didn't know that. They thought their lives were built or discovered gradually, but far more likely were the sudden changes that destroyed everything that happened before, and altered the course of a life. And ruptures, when they happened, were often small, easily overlooked—it was their consequences that were enormous. Most people recognized the ruptures only in retrospect—that moment, that action, that loss, that refusal to act. Those words, spoken or not. And by the time recognition came round, it was too late.

She returned to his office. Slouched on the leather couch, Arturo was watching a giant yellow-gray sun on the television. The phone kept ringing. Without turning his head, he said, "Don't pick it up."

"Why are they showing the sun?" she asked.

"They say it's dancing. They say it's a miracle." His head turned toward her. The lower part of his face had the amused, ironic expression she knew so well, but the distress in his eyes had deepened. Her heart went out to him.

On the screen, the rebel leader waved his arms in the air, cheered on by the crowd.

"Has he said anything?" she asked softly.

"Apparently, he wants to talk to me. He says he cares for

the people, he'll protect them from people like me who over-load ships and let families die."

"You have to go out there and *do* something," she said. "He'll turn them against you. You can't just sit here."

"I have a lot of people doing a lot of things at this very moment."

"I'll go myself, then."

She walked toward the door.

"Lali?"

She turned to him.

His face had softened. "You don't have to keep trying to save everyone."

It was his kindness that wounded her. She had spent so many years learning to act and interact on the surface, hiding all that really mattered, all that was vulnerable to attack. It had never occurred to her that Arturo could see into her, or that he, too, might be hiding.

"Someone has to go out there," she said uncertainly. She opened the door, hoping he would stop her. "It's not in Jimbo's interest to hurt us. He just wants the crowd's sympathy."

"My men are there. They'll be watching out for you."

In the hallway, his managers glanced at her, then averted their faces. She hurried down the stairs, past surprised security guards.

Just outside the building was the crowd. Next to the door-way, security guards watched her in alarm. She lifted her hand, signaling them to stay away. The crowd closed in on her. A woman was shouting at her, but Lali couldn't understand the words. She stood still, hands over her belly, head down. A few voices cried out in her defense. Slowly, the people in front of her began to push those behind them, creating a path for her.

As she made her way through the crowd, she thanked people for letting her pass. She whispered: "I just need to talk to him."

The sun pounded her head and arms.

"You're lucky you're pregnant," a woman cried.

It seemed to take hours to reach him.

He was smaller than she had expected, and he had pale skin and a sharp nose. His smile was broad and ingratiating, but didn't reach his eyes.

Jimbo led her up a makeshift podium. The crowd looked up at her. A microphone, cameras. No fear, only stillness inside her. In the distance, the office building. Was Arturo looking at her through a window? Was he watching her on television?

Jimbo lifted his right arm into the air. The crowd cheered. Talk to them, he mouthed. His eyes shone. In a flash, she realized she had played into his hands. There would be photos in the newspapers, videos on television: the right-wing military rebel sharing a platform with the daughter of the martyred national hero. She was validating him with her presence.

She tapped the microphone. She had no idea what to say. Women's faces, upturned, beneath her. They couldn't have been older than she, but their faces were creased, their cheeks sunken. None of you will be forgotten, she heard herself say. Her voice was steady, but her hands were trembling so much she could hardly hold the microphone. She tried to think of what her father would have said. Instead she remembered speeches by the General's wife, whom she had watched on television with her friends when she was a teenager. Now she repeated some of the phrases: Your children are my children. I'm a mother, too, and I know what suffering is. I pray to our Mother Mary, for you, for those you love, for all of us.

She told the crowd to leave their names and addresses, and the company would make amends to each of them. She told them her family would take care of their families. She said other things, the words coming out of her. There is hope. We can still believe. No one means to do wrong. My heart, she heard herself say, breaks for you.

In her mind another voice said: Anyone can say anything.

Then Jimbo was gripping her arm, helping her down the stairs and escorting her back to the building. The energy of the crowd seemed to carry her forward. Heat under her cheeks, behind her neck.

She reached the building, walked slowly up the stairs.

In his office, Arturo was sitting on the couch, watching images of her and Jimbo on television. Without looking at her, he said, "You were crazy to say all that." The only sign of anger was a muscle twitching in his cheek.

"Someone had to do something," she said.

He glanced at her. "Look at the state you're in."

"What did you think I was going to do?"

"Talk to him. Not grandstand like the General's wife in front of a crowd."

She didn't answer.

"You're shaking like a leaf," he said.

"I'm fine."

"You could have hurt the baby."

"You could have gone out there yourself!"

He flinched. She wished she could hold him.

He turned to the television. The camera panned the crowd, then zoomed in on individual men and women. An old woman prayed the rosary. Arturo picked up the remote control and switched off the television. His hand covered his eyes. "I love this country," he said. "But I wish to God we never came back."

At least 3,000 people missing. That was the latest estimate.

Officials took nearly a week to determine how many people were aboard, the radio announcer said. *This was a cargo ship and was not authorized to carry passengers.*

Lali shifted in her bed. She pressed her ear against the radio, the volume turned as low as possible so as not to awaken Arturo. He was on the far end of the bed, curled away from her. Early morning, and his bedside lamp was still lit. They had spent most of the week since the shipping accident in his mother's home, where high walls shielded them from the press and public.

Raining again. It was a bad day for a party.

The Coast Guard issued no warnings. The storm caught them by surprise.

Another man's voice on the radio, nervous and young: *I never saw the sea like that. And it was so dark. The lights had gone out. Then someone started saying the Hail Mary over the loudspeakers, and everybody prayed. We were leaning against each other.*

Only two children were recovered alive, so far. But there were other survivors, rescued from lifeboats or discovered on nearby islands.

Lali turned the volume slightly higher.

"You can't keep listening to this," said a drowsy voice beside her.

Arturo pushed away the sheets. She glanced at her exposed body. A dark brown line had appeared in the past few weeks, running from between her breasts to her pubis. She didn't want him to see her this way, in this light. She pulled a sheet over her stomach. Seven months pregnant. She couldn't get used to the way she looked, nor to the way she was looked at. Unexpectedly, and perversely, pregnancy had filled her with fantasies and longings, but men looked through her now, and their lack of interest disoriented her. She wondered how much other men's desire had stoked Arturo's.

The search for survivors has been called off. Fishermen from the nearby islands say the sea is infested with sharks.

"Will you please turn off that thing?" he asked.

She had hardly seen him, in the week since the accident. He came to bed after she fell asleep. Too much to do in the office, he said. Too many meetings. The relatives, the consultants, the lawyers, the backers. And today they would all be here for the party, the unofficial launch of his campaign.

Survivors say there weren't enough life jackets. Panicked crew members and passengers grabbed whatever they thought might float and jumped overboard.

"I can't listen to this." He leaned over her and switched off the radio.

She had to bring him back to her. She turned to him. Her mouth on his skin. She no longer wanted to do this.

"We don't have time," he murmured, but he didn't pull away.

Her mouth pressed down over his torso. He became very still. She knew what he needed. Years of hearing him tell her what to do, what to wear, how to move, when to stop moving. She knew now. And she could do this while thinking of other things, without feeling vulnerable or invaded by the relentless-ness of his desire. It came to her that she was breaking a personal taboo, separating sex from desire. Perhaps from now on, with him, with anyone else, it would be impossible to bring them back together.

Tension rising in him, his back arching. Where was he now? What was he imagining? Who was he imagining?

When it was over, she rested her cheek on his belly. His taste in her mouth. He didn't pull her to him, nor touch her hair.

He stood. Moments later, the shower began running. As she lay in bed, the baby gave a few kicks. She pressed her hand into the place where she had felt the movements. How could she feel close to something she couldn't even imagine?

It didn't matter. Soon this pregnancy would be over, and she would find a way to make him want her again.

Arturo's mother adjusted the knot of her white silk scarf. "This is my lucky scarf, darling," she told Lali. "Blessed by the archbishop himself. My fortune-teller told me I have to keep my neck covered throughout Arturo's campaign. She said there's a risk I might get beheaded, but this scarf will keep me 200 percent safe!"

They were sitting in the upstairs kitchen, used for the more pleasant aspects of cooking. The messier preparations of pork, fish, and chicken—the gutting, scaling, and beheadings—took place downstairs in the dirty kitchen, where the maids, house-boys, and drivers had their meals.

"Don't you think it's too hot for a scarf, Tita?" Lali asked.

"Hot? You know I never sweat! The Lord blessed me by not giving me sweat glands. When I went for my checkup in San Francisco last year, the doctors were so amazed. They had never seen anyone like me before!" A maid stood behind Marilou and began brushing her hair. "You're going to get your hair fixed before the guests start arriving, I hope? Anching can do it for you after she's done with me."

"I can do it myself," Lali said.

"My dear. Please. This is for Arturo!" Marilou looked disapprovingly at Lali's short white dress. "I want you to look nice."

Lali considered responding, but arguing with Marilou would only make things worse.

"And you should get yourself made up properly, too. The wife of a politician has to look beautiful. Look at what's-her-name—our dear president. No lipstick, no mascara, nothing! And she thinks she'll win votes that way?"

"Arturo's not running against her."

"He's running against her *cousin*. It's practically the same thing. Anyway, she's got no chance this time around."

"Then you don't need me." Lali tried to sound polite. "You'll win anyway."

"Of course we'll win! But some people—they talk. What idiots."

Lali curled her fingers around a cup of warm milk, aware of the heat from the stoves, the odors of fried onion, garlic, and meat.

"Yes, I'm close to the General," Marilou said, "but that doesn't mean I approve of him! Unlike many people in this country, my dear, I know what it means to be loyal!"

On the table, a wooden box held a dozen tubes of lipstick, several plastic containers of eye shadow, and three eyeliners.

"Why is Arturo taking so long?" Marilou asked. "That poor boy. All that agitation over the ship, as if he created a typhoon on purpose!" The maid patted powder over Marilou's face. No wrinkles on her forehead. That was the latest rage in Manila—collagen injections to fill out wrinkles. "It isn't easy, running for office the first time. Even if he knows politics. Not like his father—all *he* ever cared about was the hacienda. Sugar, sugar, sugar, and not an ounce of political sense! But Arturo takes after me. A pity I can't run myself this time."

Lali gazed at the mask-like face. Her mother-in-law had the pale skin and aquiline nose of a European, but her eyes were black and slanted, and her cheeks broad. She told people she was three-fourths Spanish and Portuguese, with only a touch of Filipino and Chinese, although Arturo laughed at this and said the only European in her family was a lusty Spanish friar in the last century.

"It's a woman's business to be beautiful, you know,"

Marilou said. "And to be a good mother. That's the role God gave us."

Lali reached for the box of makeup. "May I?"

Marilou gave a quick, distracted nod.

Lali selected a tube of crimson lipstick. With her finger and without a mirror, she spread it slowly over her lips. She faced her mother-in-law, crossed her bare legs, leaned forward to reveal the cleavage she had for the first time in her life because of the pregnancy. Small shifts in gesture, posture, expression, and she felt herself switch from compliant daughter-in-law to sexual being. The maid's eyes widened.

Marilou looked flustered. She seemed to sense that something had changed without understanding it. Finally, she said: "That dress is really too short! Anching, show Señorita Lali those dresses I told you to iron."

Lali turned her face to the sunlight. Marilou and the maid stared at her. Confusion and hurt in Marilou's eyes. Lali was suddenly ashamed. She leaned back against her chair, uncrossed her legs, removed the expression from her face. She hadn't been fair. Marilou wasn't a rival. She wasn't even an enemy.

Arturo walked into the kitchen, his damp black hair parted in the middle, his face puffy and dreamy, as though a part of him were still in their rumpled bed. She remembered his skin against hers, only an hour ago.

He bent over the stove and lifted the cover of a casserole. She imagined other women looking at him. The strong lines of his shoulders, the narrow waist, those arms. When had she stopped looking at him this way?

She had stopped so many things. She had shut down her grief for her father, the hollowing that a word like grief could never contain. You couldn't stop feeling in one part of you and be alive in the rest. Was that something her father had told her, too? In any case, she had stopped. What if Arturo had sensed what was happening inside her, and his distance was a response to her own? Sometimes, she thought there were underground rivers between people, flowing from one to another, and everything people felt and understood about each other, everything that mattered, came from these rivers. The exchange of information, the conversations, the chatter, everything that was part of the surface life, were only hints, signposts, and at times—and, in her case, almost always—diversions to prevent people from seeing into her.

"What time are the guests supposed to come?" Arturo asked.

"One o'clock. But they'll come whenever they want."

"I'm sick of campaigns," Arturo said.

"Then thank God I'm here to handle them for you," Marilou replied.

"I don't want your men in the province to start causing trouble."

"Don't act so superior. Even the Church supports vigilantes—and my men aren't vigilantes! Who else are going to fight the Communists?"

Lali rubbed the reddened skin around her wedding ring. She could no longer remove it—her fingers were too swollen. Two more months of this. And she would have to pretend to be satisfied. She would have to attend his political dinners, smile at his backers, speak to their wives, invoke her father's memory to legitimize his campaign.

Poor Papa. If he had lived, he would have disappointed everyone around him. He had always been a bookish and impractical man, too small for the dreams people had built around him. But death had replaced the person she had loved with someone grander and colder—a symbol, a hero. Marilou made sure that his name was mentioned in every piece of campaign literature and that Lali appeared smiling beside her and Arturo in newspaper photos. And Lali accepted this. She couldn't live in Manila without Marilou's money. She couldn't live like Pilar, in the ramshackle home with only one live-out maid, turning off the lights at night, sleeping without an air-conditioner to save on electricity bills.

"We can't sanction private armies," Arturo said.

"It's not the same thing," Marilou snapped.

"Ma, between the private armies of people like you—"

"People like *us*, darling. Your father and grandfather had no choice! Who would have protected their workers in the hacienda? The government?" She waved her hand in the air. "This is the kind of country we have. You want law and order? You want justice? Then you take it into your own hands! No one's going to do it for you!"

Arturo sat down at the table, across from Lali. When he was a child, she knew, he had been happiest in this kitchen, sitting beside the cook Filomena, doing his homework while she prepared his dinner.

A maid arranged the day's newspapers in front of him. He began to flip through the pages. "I don't want you talking like that in public, Mama," he said curtly, without looking up. "That massacre in the south last month—that was another vigilante group. I can't deal with another scandal."

Marilou shrugged. "People forget everything."

"Don't talk like that!"

"I'll talk any way I want! I'm your mother!" She picked up a folded newspaper and fanned herself vigorously with it. "Besides, the massacre was the governor's fault. Everyone knows he spends all his time with his mistress in Manila, instead of taking care of his province!"

"And the people who fled the village after the massacre?" Lali asked. "Weren't they killed in the refugee center?"

"Lali," Marilou said testily, "where do you get your information? From the newspapers? You have no idea what's going on outside Manila."

"Leave her alone, Ma."

From over his newspaper, Arturo glanced at Lali.

She smiled, grateful for the sympathy. He looked away.

"I'm saying—long live the vigilantes," Marilou said petulantly. "The public loves them. The Church says . . . Arturo, what did that bishop say the other day? The public has a right to self-protection! And he's right!"

"You can't treat this like a provincial election, Ma. People in Manila won't stand for those things. Lali, what's wrong?"

"It's the smell—onions, garlic. My stomach's queasy."

"Then let's go to the dining room."

He carried the plates and newspapers out of the room. Lali followed Arturo into the main dining room, which was sprawled on a terrace across one wing of the house. The far end of the room overlooked the river; one side perched over the garden, with its swimming pool, mango and papaya trees, red bougainvillea, and hibiscus. The dining table, carved from the trunk of a single tree, could seat forty guests.

Arturo sat at the head of the table, Lali by his side. The sky was slate gray.

"Marilou will throw a fit." He pointed to an article in the newspaper. "President Peachy is beginning to sound like her. Listen to this: 'If there's any group that should be dismantled, it's the Communists, not the vigilantes.'"

Lali pushed the glass of milk away from her.

He said: "Look what she says here: 'Nothing will intimidate this president.' Whenever there's a problem in this country, her only answer is more police action, more military action. That's all she knows. Forget social and economic reform—she doesn't know what that means."

He was silent again as he turned the pages. She recognized many of the people in the photographs. Some had held high positions under the General. She had gone to school or on dates with several of them. The same faces, the same family names. This was a country where clans mattered. In one family she knew, the eldest brother had fled with the General to exile in the United States, while a younger brother had been appointed labor minister under the new president. The idea was to link one member of the family to each political faction, make sure the family businesses thrived, no matter who was in power. Family above friends, and both above country. Her father was one of the few who never sold out. But then, he had little to lose.

"Do they say anything about the ship?" she asked.

A pause. "They say a lot about the ship," he said gently. "What do you want to know?"

She didn't answer.

"Are you thinking about that guy you used to go out with?"

The underground river again. People sensed things without knowing that they did. He thought she was upset about Miguel.

"No," she said quietly.

She told herself: Don't get drawn into this.

The baby kicked inside her. She returned to her milk, forced pieces of toast into her mouth.

"More coffee?" he asked.

The light, filtered by clouds, softened his face. She nodded. He poured coffee and stirred two teaspoonfuls of sugar into her cup. She watched his fingers, comforted by the gesture, by the small intimacies that still bound them.

The coffee stung her lips. She set the cup on the table and dipped her finger into the hot liquid, remembering something else her father had told her: pain existed at the point of transition between two opposing sensations. Her finger hurt only where it registered both the heat of the liquid and the coolness of the air. She wondered whether this was true. She wondered when she had stopped believing everything her father told her.

When Miguel died, years ago, in that other shipwreck, she

had driven out of the city. Two hours later, she stood in front of white-crested waves. She walked along the beach, thinking of that kindhearted, young man, in another part of that sea, wondering what he had done and felt in those moments. Later she wrote a card of sympathy to his wife and parents. They never found his body. She hadn't expected to feel so upset. He had been her lover for only a summer, but she appreciated him most after his death.

His ghost never came to her. She had thought it would, at least in her dreams. She was sensitive to spirits. She would have felt him, the way she sometimes felt her father.

"Do you hear that?" Arturo asked.

A woman's voice, crying out. Then louder shouts. The sounds seemed to be coming from the servants' kitchen beneath them. Lali couldn't make out the words. Then Marilou's sharp voice, the maids' high-pitched exclamations.

"Let's go." Arturo hurried out of the dining room and down the narrow staircase. Lali followed him.

At the entrance to the servants' kitchen, Lali leaned against the doorframe. A dank, low-ceiling room. Oversized pans on the floor, baskets full of market produce on the dirt floor. The house had been built centuries ago, during Spanish times, for a governor general. Some of its rooms, like this one, seemed to be cracking everywhere.

On a stool in the middle of the room, the cook sat in silence, facing the wall. She wore rubber sandals and a loose beige housedress, her body thick under the cloth. Marilou and Arturo stood on each side of her. The maids, most of them in their teens, huddled in a corner of the room, staring at the meter-long fish on the kitchen table. From the opposite corner, houseboys and drivers watched.

"What's happening?" Lali asked.

Arturo lifted his head. "She won't touch it."

Lali walked across the room, arms crossed in front of her

belly, self-conscious in her short, tight dress in front of the drivers and houseboys. She touched the cook's shoulder. "*Manang*, what's wrong?"

Filomena made the sign of the cross.

"*Manang*," Arturo said. "I am *asking* you to open that fish. You know we have guests coming."

He gripped the edge of the table. Lali had an image of him as a young schoolboy, sitting alone in the dining room every morning, in his khaki pants, white shirt, and black school tie, facing the clouds and river, while Filomena—a teenager then—fussed over him. He said Filomena was kinder to him than his mother had ever been.

The cook clicked her tongue. "No one is buying fish."

"It's just ignorant people talking!" Marilou said angrily. "Apparently, the fish vendors in the market are practically giving away their fish. No one wants to buy any."

The cook twisted her head toward Arturo. "I told your mother we can't buy fish today, and she said we had to have fish. I do what I'm told, Señorito. I buy the fish, I take out the scales, but I'm not going to open it. You open it if you want. God is against this. I'm not going to be the one to find those things!"

"What things?" Lali asked.

The cook shook her head.

Lali crouched in front of her. "*Manang*, tell me. What don't you want to find?"

"Señorita, you understand. You don't have to ask me."

"I'm asking you."

Filomena wiped her face with her apron. "The neighbor's cook—she opened a fish, and she found a man inside. God forgive us! When she cut it open to clean it."

"A man?" Arturo gave a quick, false laugh. "*Manang*, you know you can't fit a man into that fish."

The cook leaned toward Lali. "A man's *thing*, Señorita."

The young maids tittered. Filomena glared at them. "And in the market, they say they've been finding children's fingers and human teeth, in the fish. They found only a few bodies in the ocean, but 3,000 people died! Señorita, no one is buying fish in the market! We can't eat fish."

"That's ridiculous," Arturo said.

"Fish are eating people, Señorito! It's that ship. They couldn't find the bodies. And now they're finding parts of bodies inside all the fish in the market!"

"That's just gossip!" Marilou cried, but she retreated to a corner of the room, near the maids.

"It's true, Señora."

"We need that fish!" Marilou said. "We can't just serve chicken and pork!"

"Ma, if that's the story going around, no one will eat it."

"Fish don't eat rotting bodies!" Marilou said. "I heard it on the radio this morning. The president was on Channel 2—she told everyone not to panic. She said the bodies sank too deep for fish to eat. And even if they didn't sink so deep, the health minister says it's safe to eat fish again—fish won't touch bodies that have been dead a week." Marilou's face was turning pink. "This country," she said, lifting the collar of her blouse up and down rapidly, to cool herself. "I tell you, it's going to the dogs."

"Ma—"

"Don't contradict me. Under the General, no matter how poor people were, they could at least afford to eat fish! Now we have a new president, and fish are eating people!"

Lali gestured at the fish, which was spread out on newspapers, a fillet knife next to it. "It's okay, *manang*. You can throw it away. We'll serve something else."

"Don't listen to her!" Marilou bellowed at the cook. "I'm the one who pays your salary!"

The maids and houseboys watched them, tense and titillated by the possibility of a fight.

"That's enough." Arturo picked up the knife, turned it around so that the handle faced Filomena, and offered it to her. She averted her face. "Open the fish." His voice was kind. "Please, *manang*. It's ridiculous, what they say in the markets. I promise you, there's nothing inside it."

"This country will starve to death if we can't eat fish!" Marilou said.

"Señorito." Filomena looked sternly into Arturo's eyes, as though he were a child again. "God have pity on you."

He set the knife on the table.

A familiar scent. Yves Saint Laurent's Rive Gauche. Pilar was standing at the doorway, wearing Lali's perfume.

"They told me you were all here," Pilar whispered. The agitated faces of Marilou and Filomena turned to her. "I'm sorry. I didn't mean to disturb you."

Pilar had dressed up for the lunch—a long, white linen skirt and a sleeveless white blouse that set off her golden-brown skin. Black hair in a ponytail, no makeup. Her eyebrows were thick and dark, heightening the intensity in her eyes. The expression on the rest of her face was polite and guarded.

"How pretty you look," Lali said. "White suits you."

"Everyone's saying we shouldn't be having the party."

"Pilar!" Arturo called out, as though he had just noticed her. He beamed a politician's smile at her.

Pilar lowered her eyes.

Arturo ambled across the room and kissed her on the cheek. He gripped her waist. Lali watched them. Pilar's full, strong body, against his. She remembered the three of them holding each other and circling the darkened room, while Sinatra sang and the rain fell. Pilar had blushed then, too.

It's not possible.

Lali's pulse began to race. She walked away from her husband and sister and picked up the fillet knife.

"What are you doing?" Marilou cried.

"Someone has to clean the fish."

It can't be Pilar.

"Arturo! Don't let her! She's never cleaned a fish in her life—she'll just make a mess."

"I've seen people do it," Lali said evenly. "Arturo, can you help me? I want everyone else out of the kitchen."

He hesitated, and Marilou protested, but everyone except Lali and Arturo quickly left the room. The couple stood alone in front of the fish. Flies gathered on window screens. From far away, Lali heard the bells of ice-cream vendors as they pushed their carts down muddy streets.

The fish lay on its side, one bright eye staring at them.

"Could you hold it down for me?" she asked.

Arturo pressed the head and tail against the newspapers. She took a breath, shoved the blade into the silver flesh and slit open the belly.

She was aware of Arturo's body beside her, his hands, the tension between them. For years, she had tried to calculate every word and gesture, measuring how much to give him without making herself vulnerable. Now, she was losing him. Perhaps he was already lost.

How can it be Pilar?

Again she plunged the knife into the belly. Breathing through her mouth so as not to smell the fish, she scraped out red and violet bits, then used a teaspoon to pry out the remaining organs. Finally, she wrapped the pieces in sheets of newsprint and threw the crumpled, bloodied paper into the garbage.

"Now, Filomena won't be scared to steam it," she said. And she would tell Filomena how to decorate it—a coating of mayonnaise, strips of minced vegetables. And the guests would eat the fish, and everything they imagined inside it.

Cramps, she told them. And they believed her. Pregnancy had its advantages. Even Marilou told her to stay in bed—*Join us later, when you feel better. Even just to say hello. Don't worry. They'll be here all afternoon.* Arturo looked skeptical, but said nothing.

Lali stayed in bed until mid-afternoon. When at last she stood and pulled back the curtains, a gray sky hung low over the garden. The rain had stopped.

She pulled leggings and a sheer white blouse over her, climbed the stairs, walked across creaking wooden floors to the dining room.

At the main dining table and smaller tables around it, dozens of guests were sipping coffee and cognac. The buffet held a dozen silver serving plates, the candles beneath them had been extinguished, and screen covers protected the dishes from flies. On a platter lay the giant milkfish, covered with green mayonnaise and alternating strips of minced carrots, red peppers, and sweet green pickles. No one had eaten the fish.

Marilou sat at the head of the table, flanked by Arturo and Pilar. A maid added a chair for Lali between Marilou and Arturo. As Lali approached the table, all the men stood. She gestured at them to sit down. They were looking at her now. Pregnancy had its advantages. She sat down and unfastened the top two buttons of her blouse. From where she was sitting, she could see the deep green leaves of the mango trees.

One of Arturo's uncles asked her, "Are you feeling better now?"

She arranged a bright smile on her face. "I'm sorry I missed the lunch."

"Please! In your condition, it's an honor you join us at all."

"We kept the food out for you," Marilou told her, disapproving, staring at Lali's nearly transparent blouse.

After a few solicitous remarks about her health, and some winking and joking about the future president in her belly, the guests returned to their discussions. A maid poured water into a red chalice, part of a set of forty-eight chalices that Marilou had bought on a trip to Venice.

A short, bald man said, "We ordered the police to round up 300 suspected Communists, a whole village."

Beside her, Arturo fidgeted with his napkin. "You know Tony, don't you, Lali?"

"Of course." She widened her smile and tried to remember who he was. It came to her—one of Arturo's distant cousins, a mayor in a small town in the south.

"We detained those Communists for thirty-six hours in a school." Reading glasses hung from a gold chain around his neck. "That's the legal limit. We had to act fast. We wanted everyone to know that those bastards weren't going to get away with killing two policemen. And not just killing. They slit their throats and—excuse me, ladies, you may not want to hear this—"

"Did you find the killers?" Arturo interrupted.

"Of course. We have a list. Developed for us by intelligence agents." He pulled out a piece of paper from his wallet, unfolded it, and put on his spectacles. "Mole on the chin—Communist lecturer," he began to read. "Mole on the center of the forehead—courier. A mole each on the left and right cheek, and one on the forehead—liquidator. Two moles on right cheek and one on left—a Communist general."

He wiped the perspiration from his forehead, folded the paper. No one spoke. Arturo tipped back his chair and looked at the ceiling.

Finally, Marilou said: "That's such a coincidence! My grandmother used the same method! She said a woman born with a mole under her eye would cry a lot in her life. And a woman with moles on each side of the lips, like me"—she gave a coquettish smile—"means she's good at kissing."

Several guests laughed uneasily.

"Did you use that list to identify the killers?" Pilar asked.

"Of course."

"That's barbaric," Pilar said.

The mayor removed his spectacles.

"Does anyone want more coffee?" Marilou asked.

"And what did you do to them?" Pilar asked him.

"Pilar, please," Lali said sharply.

The mayor straightened in his chair. "They're waiting for trial. What do you think? We follow the law. Not like some people we all know!"

Arturo shifted his gaze to Pilar. Their eyes met. Lali watched them.

Pilar grasped the chalice with both hands. She lifted the wine to her lips but didn't drink it. Arturo continued to look at Pilar. The mayor was speaking, but Pilar no longer responded.

Her knees shaking, Lali stood and walked toward the buffet, reached for a plate. She stood in front of the untouched fish. Its eye was dull now. The chopped pickles, red peppers, and carrots had sunk into the green mayonnaise. She scooped up a large portion of fish. Beneath the green, red, and orange toppings, its flesh was white and soft. She returned to the table. Almost every head turned toward her. She bit into the fish, aware of the silence in the room.

Arturo was staring at her mouth. And Pilar's flushed face, not knowing where to look.

Lali turned to her husband and offered him a forkful of fish. He hesitated. His lips parted. Slowly, she fed him, aware of everyone watching them. As she pulled out the fork, his lips closed around it. He began to chew. She watched his mouth, both attracted and repulsed by its movements. Now the fish was inside him, too. She offered him another forkful. He held her wrist, guided the fork inside his mouth. His eyes were bright. Taboos—the thrill of breaking them. She knew what he liked. She knew what excited him. Much later, when she looked back and tried to understand how things could have gone so wrong, she would remember this moment and regret all that it had set in motion, but now, she felt only relief. She had an idea. She had a plan. She knew what to do about Pilar, and how to bring Arturo back to her.

Chapter Four

The Gift

I do not know my own position.
Somewhere behind me is a structure
of masks and walls that have been my life
in plays with lives. Each four-cornered

room unknown to and unknowing of each other
contains me, knowing all, known
to all, and yet unknown. I have come
to a room of mirrors and am caught

by my selves.

—EMMANUEL LACABA, "Il Principe"

PILAR

A re you listening to me?" Lali's voice on the phone was insistent.

Pilar pressed her back against the wicker armchair. Screen doors opened to a lush, unkempt garden. The smell of rich earth, plants creeping up walls and over each other. She had long ago stopped trying to control that growth, that abundance always veering toward decay.

"I'll be there in two hours," Lali said. "Get dressed, okay? I'm taking you somewhere."

Outside, in the fading light, a gecko began its song.

"Where?" Pilar asked, resisting her sister but also intrigued by her.

"You'll see. It's a surprise."

Pilar switched on a small lamp next to her. Shadows stretched across the room, over tiled floors, to the threadbare beige sofa. Nothing in this house had changed since her childhood. Lali hadn't set foot here since they returned to Manila. It's like a mausoleum, she had told Pilar.

"I'll be ready," Pilar said.

They said their goodbyes. Pilar turned on the television. Black-and-white images floated across the screen—a romantic melodrama with Eurasian actors and actresses who had been popular after the war. Voices filled the room, chasing some of the fears that surfaced at the end of every afternoon. She had always thought of herself as solitary, but she had never lived alone and was unprepared for such loneliness.

She climbed the stairs, entered her parents' room. The carved mahogany bed, the crocheted bedspread, the pillows where her father had rested his head.

She strode across the room, opened the top drawer of his filing cabinet. At random, not giving herself time to think, she pulled out a brown folder and tucked it under her arm.

Near his desk, books crammed a wooden bookshelf, many of them piled horizontally on top of others until almost no space was left between planks. Almost every night during martial law, before his arrest, he would select a book from that shelf and read to his daughters. She remembered a Nick Joaquin story about May Day Eve, a young girl running down at midnight to stand in front of a mirror and whisper an incantation—*Mirror, mirror, show to me, him whose woman I will be*—and the face of the man she would marry appearing in the mirror. Pilar was about eleven or twelve when she first heard the story, and the words had thrilled and frightened her—the idea of growing up and marrying a man who would touch her and be with her for the rest of her life, the thought of lying next to a man who would make her his woman.

She pried out the book from a packed row of paperbacks, turned the pages until she found the story. Her father had penciled a vertical line along one passage: *He ached intensely to see her again—at once!—to touch her hands and her hair; to hear her harsh voice. He ran to the window and flung open the casements and the beauty of the night struck him back like a blow.*

Oh, Papa, she thought. The romantic, always. And hopeless—this was a story about a marriage gone bitterly wrong, and he had marked only the passage about falling in love.

She shut the book, returned it to the shelf. She eyed her father's closet door. Did she dare? No one had opened his closet since the morning after his arrest, when her mother had gathered the shirts and pants the soldiers had thrown on the floor. Fiercely, her mother hung up his clothes one by one, the suits and *barong tagalogs* and short-sleeved shirts. Next, she gathered the folders and papers scattered on the floor. She wouldn't let anyone help her. Lali and Pilar sat cross-legged on the bed, watching her, pressing their shoulders together and clutching each other's hands, frightened by their mother's anger but also comforted by it, because it left no space for anything else. When the room was tidy again, their mother moved into the guest bedroom. She never returned to the bedroom she had shared with her husband. For two years after that, they had no direct contact with Gregorio, no letters, no calls, only cryptic official updates and rumors. Then came the messages, the late-night meetings, the car that came for them at dawn, the safe houses, the terrifying nights and days that followed.

Pilar stared at the closet door, imagining what it would be like to touch his clothes, to smell him again. Her stomach contracted.

She returned to the dining room, set the file on the mahogany table, next to red and yellow folders filled with the newspaper clippings and magazine articles she had been collecting since the General fled. Beside them she had arranged a large spiral notebook, scissors and glue, and several books that had appeared in the months after the General left—rushed collections of articles from the opposition and underground publications, memoirs, day-by-day accounts of the events leading to the General's ouster. Soon she would have to make sense of all this, go through them and arrange them into a book, or two books, or even a few articles. She had no idea how to do this, but she would learn.

She picked up the brown folder from his filing cabinet, flipped through the sheets, pulled out a poem typed on yellowing paper: "Il Principe," with a name below the title,

Emmanuel Lacaba. Someone, probably her father, had circled these lines:

I do not know my own position.
Somewhere behind me is a structure
of masks and walls that have been my life
in plays with lives.

Did all his files, even those in the sealed cartons, contain poems and stories? What stirs the heart *is* subversive, her father had told her. But the soldiers weren't trained for that— they had ransacked his files and left almost everything on the floor. That's why the dictatorship, the new society the General tried to create, couldn't work. It was too literal, he said. People need to dream.

He also said: Keep records, Pilar. Write things down. Not to remember them, but to make them exist.

She would write his story, starting with what was happening right now and going backwards, to the weeks after the General left, the revolution that ousted him, her father's death, his life. In this way, she could start with the clippings that were easiest to read and work her way gradually to the most painful. She wasn't ready to open those cartons from San Francisco, to read his letters and journals and speeches. She wasn't ready to know what he had still hoped to be. She was afraid to see his handwriting on a page, or his clothes on a hanger—these were too physical, too real.

In the mirror over the bathroom sink, she spread gloss over her lips. She remembered Arturo's mouth, the shock of feeling him against her.

She hadn't kissed anyone since the doctor in San Francisco and Arturo on the day of the eclipse. She had kissed the doctor because she was upset about Lali, and Arturo had probably kissed her for the same reason. Both were mistakes. With Arturo, it was also wrong. She and he acted like it had never happened.

Arturo needed to charm—men, women, children, animals, it made no difference. He stood too close to people, gazed into their eyes, switched on the warmth and sympathy, as though nothing or no one else existed at that moment. She told herself that a charming man could also be heartless. She had to stop falling for it, imagining she mattered to him.

For years, when she was growing up, people had glanced at her and looked away. During recreation in school, she sat alone. The scars faded as she grew older, but her shyness did not. She wanted to be left alone. When people told her she was becoming pretty, she smiled and turned away. One day, when she was about seventeen, she looked into the mirror and saw that it was true—all that remained was a coin-sized patch on her cheek, and another just over her breast. Her heart had lifted then, and for a time she believed her life, her whole self, would change.

Lali parked her black Mercedes on the driveway. Through the open window, she smiled up at Pilar. Arched eyebrows, violet powder around her eyes, bright red lips against pale skin.

"Don't you want to come in for a bit?" Pilar asked.

"We don't have time." Lali patted the seat next to her. "Come on."

Pilar entered the car. They drove out of the compound. The night sky, without stars, domed the city. Lali's Mercedes, air-conditioned and with tinted windows, swerved through side streets into the other, rougher Manila, past tiny convenience stores and wooden homes.

Lali leaned forward. Her short, sleeveless red dress hugged her belly and exposed toned legs and arms. Even pregnant, she had a way of dressing that made people imagine her naked.

"Did you enjoy the lunch yesterday?" Lali asked casually.

Pilar remembered Arturo walking toward her in the servants' kitchen, the look in his eyes.

Lali gripped the steering wheel. "Do you know what he told me after the lunch? He said: 'I never noticed how different you and Pilar are.' He's known us both for years, and he never noticed how different we are?"

Pilar's heart began to thump. Impossible to know what was real, what Lali knew, what Arturo had told her. Perhaps there was nothing. The kiss, his arms, his eyes—all of it, nothing.

"I shouldn't have come," Pilar said.

"Don't be silly. It's normal that he notices you." Lali slipped a hand under her dress and rubbed her shoulder, revealing the strap of a red bra. "Don't you think so? Everyone thinks it's a shame you stay home so much. And you're so nice, you know? Everyone says you're so nice. And Papa always said you're the real beauty in the family."

"Take me home," Pilar said.

Lali shook her head.

They were entering a part of Manila Pilar had never seen before. Narrow streets, the darkness broken only by the headlights, an occasional bare bulb or kerosene lamp flickering through an open window.

"What do you think of when you sit alone in that house all night?" Lali asked. "Do you watch television?"

"Where are you taking me?"

"I told you. It's a surprise." The car swerved into an alley so gutted by potholes the Mercedes could hardly outpace a skeletal dog running beside it.

Pilar copied Lali's smile and said, "I enjoyed the lunch very much."

"Stop lying to me."

"What do you expect me to say?" Pilar whispered. "You know I don't like politics. I don't like those people you and

Arturo have to make deals with. The way they talk about the ship sinking, as though it's all about *them*—"

"I'm not talking about the ship today. Okay? One day. A break." Lali glanced at her. "We're doing all we can for the families."

"I keep thinking about what Papa would say, if he were alive to see you."

"Stop using Papa to justify what you think!"

"You know he fought against so many of those people."

"You think he was a saint?" Lali asked.

"Don't you dare."

"Don't I dare what? Say that Papa played politics, too? That he tried to make deals, too? Everyone made deals, Pilar!"

"Not in that way. Not him."

"Maybe what happened to him in San Francisco was a mistake, not a choice. Maybe he screwed up. Maybe he would have preferred to *live*. Did you ever think of that?"

"What's wrong with you?"

"I think you still can't forgive me for marrying Arturo."

"It's not Arturo." Pilar's voice caught.

"Then what is it? You can't forgive me for being married? For being pregnant?" Her tone softened. "Pilar, you're my *sister*. Don't hate me."

The headlights, yellow over the road, deepened the shadows between houses.

"I don't want us to fight," Lali said.

"I don't know how you can keep going out"—Pilar's throat hurt—"and doing all the same things, after the shipwreck, after Papa, after everything that's happened. Do you know what people are saying?"

"It's over. I'm not going to talk about it."

Pilar scanned her sister's profile, wondering what was happening inside her. She didn't ask. It was easier to argue with Lali than to be moved by her.

"Please, Pilar. We only have each other."

"There's Mama."

Lali shook her head. "All she does is sit in that dark room and take tranquilizers."

"We tried—"

"And that Indian food she orders, and her medicines—"

There's Arturo, too, Pilar wanted to say. But only for Lali. She felt again as she had as a teenager, when Lali's life—Lali's adventures and boyfriends—had seemed more vivid and real than her own.

The car turned into a road bordered by trees and wooden houses, which were partly visible behind low walls and iron gates. Many of the homes were almost in ruins, with tin roofs warped by sun and rain. This was old Manila, and so little of it remained. Pilar knew there were pockets like this in the city—small neighborhoods or streets that had somehow escaped the American bombs and Japanese fires that had destroyed most of the city at the end of the war.

Lali's voice, probing and wary, interrupted her thoughts. "You look exhausted. Are you sleeping okay?"

"I have to take pills."

"Sleeping pills? Every night?"

"Since Papa died."

"You have to stop. That's so bad for you."

Not every night, and only to stop the dreams. In the weeks following his death, Pilar had dreamt of her father—the moments after the shooting, that gaunt, dignified man on the sidewalk. Had he known he was dying? Had he felt pain? The pills killed the dreams. Everything that people said about the dead—the afterlife, the ghosts, the messages—was a lie. He was gone. The dead left no trace, at least not for her. She had called for him, again and again, and he hadn't come.

Lali squeezed her hand. "Promise me you'll take care of yourself."

"I'm fine," Pilar said.

A 20-foot-high brick wall, the top lined with shards of broken glass. Lali blew the horn—three short blasts, followed by a long one. On one side of the iron gates, a small door opened. A teenaged houseboy peered out, then shut the door. Slowly, the high gates opened toward the inside. An asphalt driveway led to a 19th-century Spanish colonial mansion, with a wooden balcony overlooking the driveway, mother-of-pearl windows and ornaments, stone pillars on the ground floor. The house was flanked on one side by an eight-car garage and, on the other, by an overgrown garden so dense with trees and shrubs Pilar couldn't see how far it extended.

Lali parked the car in the garage. From the arched doorway of the house, an overweight, pear-shaped man ambled toward them. He seemed to be in his late thirties, with a small bald head, elfin features, and smiling, upturned eyes.

He hugged Lali. "Darling, I didn't realize how pregnant you are!"

Lali gave her cocktail-party laugh and patted her stomach. Pilar steeled herself.

"And you're Pilar?" His arm circled her waist. "Lali's told me so much about you. I'm Nico." He wrapped his other arm around Lali's waist and pulled both women close to him. Pilar tensed. "I'm a lucky man tonight! Lali, you should have only daughters. A whole tribe of gorgeous girls who'll break every heart in Manila!"

"Tell that to Arturo." The cheerfulness in Lali's voice was as brittle as her smile. "My husband wants a son. Someone to carry his name. An *heir*."

"How you ended up with someone so predictable is beyond me. What do you do when you need something kinky?"

Their laughter was loud and, to Pilar's ears, displeasing.

Nico eyed her. "Let's go inside?"

The houseboy stood at the doorway, his long black hair pulled into a ponytail. He was wearing well-pressed khaki shorts, a fake Lacoste shirt, and rubber slippers. Nico handed him some bills. "You're off for the night, Fred," he said.

He led the sisters into a spacious living room. Marble floors, carved wooden furniture, paintings by second-tier Filipino artists.

"Why is it so quiet?" Lali asked.

"I sent everyone away. It's better that way, isn't it?"

"I don't like it." Lali rubbed her hands together. There was a nervousness about her that began to make Pilar nervous, too.

They climbed a grand staircase to the second floor, across another living room and into his bedroom. Soft lamplight, red cushions on the floor, a low round table with a copper-plated top. On the walls hung black-and-white photographs of aging socialites and bare-chested young men. In an alcove at the far end of the room, red silk curtains framed a king-size bed.

Nico sat on a floor cushion, gestured at Pilar to sit next to him. He asked Lali, "Have you explained to her what we're going to do?"

Lali shook her head. She was standing near the door, tiny and fragile in the cavernous room. From some angles, Pilar thought, she doesn't even look pregnant. But she *was* pregnant, with Arturo's baby. Pilar imagined him leaning toward Lali, as he had toward her.

She had to stop.

Lali inspected the photographs on the wall. Pilar watched her, as she had most of her life. While other teenage girls stared at their reflections, scrutinizing their faces and bodies, Pilar had avoided mirrors and looked at Lali instead. She knew her sister's body—small-boned, elongated, almost without curves—better than she did her own. A few times, in her dreams, she looked like Lali.

Lali lifted herself on her toes to examine a photograph.

Pilar remembered another night in Manila, years ago, in another room, and Lali again on her toes, her arms in the air. Pilar must have been about fourteen, Lali a year older—it was after the General had declared martial law but before he imprisoned their father. The room was filled with the teenage sons and daughters of the country's elite; at the time, people from opposing political camps still spoke easily to each other, and families were only beginning to send their children to schools in the United States and European countries, to protect them from kidnappings and blackmail at home. At the party, a young man told Lali that she looked like a lollipop, with her round face and straight body. "A lollipop?" Lali repeated, laughing, slightly drunk. She asked it again, more loudly. A few teenagers turned to look. Lali pulled her dress over her head, draped it over a chair, and clambered onto a table. Everyone stopped talking and stared. In her lacy white underwear and stiletto-heeled sandals, she pirouetted like a ballerina, hands high over her head, pink nipples visible beneath her bra. "Do I look like a lollipop now?" she called out gaily. Pilar stood against the wall, acutely conscious of her own body. She was too tall, arms and thighs muscled from years of swimming. She watched her nymphlike, dancing, half-naked sister and thought: I can never be like her. Lali stepped down from the table, wriggled into her dress, and cheerfully accepted two flutes of champagne, one for each hand. Only Lali got away with that. Young men flocked around her, but no one tried to lure Pilar out of her corner. "You better not tell Papa and Mama," Lali had muttered on the way home, her legs lifted and spread apart, feet resting on the backrest in front of her, while the driver glanced nervously into the rearview mirror.

Their father, like all men, had never been able to say no to Lali.

Pilar became aware of Nico's puzzled, monk-like face, a few inches away from hers. "Are you feeling okay?" His voice was kind. "Maybe you need some fresh air? Do you want to visit my garden?"

"Don't, Nico," Lali said. "We have to go there later, anyway."

"You can stay here if you don't want to come. You know where the goodies are."

"Nico, I'm *pregnant*."

"They're one hundred-percent natural."

"I'd like to go outside," Pilar said.

He led her out of the room. In the dimness of the garden, they walked along a narrow path. Branches and leaves almost obscured the night sky. In some areas, soft light from the house penetrated the garden.

"Do you like it?" Nico asked.

"I've never seen anything like it. It's like a jungle."

He laughed. "It *is* a jungle. I had tribesmen from the mountains come down here for months to build it. They had tents all over the downstairs living room. I wanted my own jungle in the middle of the city." He pressed his hand against her back. She started. Afraid to offend him, she didn't step away. "And they built me a wall—you can't see it from here. It's fabulous. No cement, just stones laid one on top of the other in the old way. They still know how to do these things in the mountains. They say it's completely resistant to earthquakes. And I have artificial mist pumped in when it's very hot—it's never hot in this garden. You'd think you were in the mountains."

His fingers pressed into her spine.

"And the animals," he said. "I'll try to find you some. We have monkeys here, and the most fabulous birds, every color—you can't imagine how beautiful they are. And peacocks, and a lion."

"A lion?"

"Come."

He gripped her hand, as awkwardly as a boy would. His fingers were smaller than hers. For some reason, this reassured her.

Hand in hand, they wound their way to a far corner of the garden, less dense and slightly more luminous. He stopped. At the foot of a mango tree, a long, bulky shadow lay on the ground. As they approached it, the shape grew more distinct. She recognized what she was seeing. A mangy lion, emaciated, like one of those circus creatures that had distressed her when she was a girl.

"Don't worry," Nico said. "He won't bite. We tranquilize him."

"He's not even tied up!"

"He's not dangerous. He can't stand. And come, look at our monkeys." He tugged at her hand. Another winding path, another bamboo grove, then a cage, several meters wide and as tall as Nico. Several small, sad-eyed creatures huddled on a ledge, staring back at her.

"What do you think?" he asked.

"I feel sorry for them."

"I'll tell you a secret—they feel sorry for us, too."

The odors of the cage mingled with the smells of wet earth.

"Each one of these animals is my teacher," he said.

"You tranquilize your teachers?"

"Nico?" Lali's clear voice rang through the garden.

"We're here, darling, next to the monkeys."

"I can't see a thing."

Twigs crackled as she approached them. Lali emerged from the shadows, holding her red dress higher up her thighs.

"I thought you didn't want to see the garden," Nico said.

"I don't. But your house spooks me." The edginess had returned to her voice. "I don't like it here. Come back inside."

"You have no idea how lucky you are," Nico told Lali. "Try growing up in the province."

They were sitting on the cushions on his bedroom floor.

Lali rested her hands on her belly. She laughed. "You had everything you wanted in the province."

"I was bored to death." He sat like a pyramid on the floor, large hips and crossed legs at the base, his body narrowing upwards, culminating in the small oval of his head. He faced Pilar, eyes and lips upturned. "My family has an hacienda in the south. Have you ever spent a long time in an hacienda?"

She shook her head.

"There's nothing to do," he said. "Nothing to think. We'd go from one house to another and lie down on beds and talk and eat. And eat and talk. In my circle, if you knew the price of sugar on the world market, you were considered an intellectual."

"Will you do the massage now?" Lali asked. To Pilar, she said: "He does the best massages in Manila. Do you want to go first?"

"I don't like massages."

"He won't touch you. It's not that kind of massage. Explain to her, Nico."

"I do a magnetic massage." Lali unzipped her dress.

"I run my hands over your body," Nico told Pilar, "but no touching. Your boyfriend will have nothing to complain about."

"Pilar doesn't need a boyfriend." Lali stepped out of her dress and unhooked her red bra. "She's strong. Self-sufficient. Unlike me." Her pale breasts were free now, the nipples staring at Pilar.

"Your tits look fabulous," Nico said.

"That's what I think. It's the only nice thing about being pregnant. Arturo, of course, doesn't agree. You know what he told me? Only cows have tits."

"Well, then he's not as predictable as I thought."

She strode around the room wearing only red lace panties, her legs slim and muscled under the round belly. Pilar felt a flush spread over her cheeks.

"Take off your clothes," Lali told her. "You'll see. He's marvelous."

Pilar gripped the edges of the cushion. Lali knew how self-conscious she was about her body.

"Oh, come on," Lali said cheerfully. "Don't be afraid. I'll turn off the lights."

Nico squatted in front of Pilar and looked into her eyes. "You have to enter your fear. It's the only way."

"Don't tell me what to do."

"You know what you're afraid of, don't you? It's not being naked—it's being seen. We like our excuses. We like to stay weak. It's harder to act—"

Lali poked his upper arm. "Nico, don't force her."

"I'm not going to force her." He turned to Pilar. "But if you can face your fear, if you can get undressed in front of us—"

"Leave her alone, Nico. She said she doesn't want to!"

Lali began to light candles on the low table.

"I'm not afraid of how I look," Pilar told him.

"Of course not."

"What about me?" Lali asked playfully. "What about my massage?"

Nico and Pilar exchanged glances. She thought she saw compassion in his eyes. Maybe he, too, was upset by Lali.

Lali lay on a mattress on the floor. Nico knelt beside her. His hands hovered a few inches above her forehead, palms flat, facing downward. Very slowly, without touching Lali, his fingers moved over her face and neck, then over each shoulder and arm, pausing a minute or two over each area. He continued over her breasts and belly, then down over her thighs, knees, calves, and feet. Pilar imagined Arturo looking at Lali like this, wanting her.

Pleasure on Lali's face. Her brow furrowed, her mouth opened a crack. "The baby's getting excited," Lali said.

Pilar thought she saw a faint pulsing in her sister's belly. Arturo's baby. She had no right to want a man who was having a baby. To have wanted, she told herself.

She wished she could be Lali even for a moment, so she could feel a presence inside her, a child inside her. To know, even for a few hours, what it was like to have a life as full and as safe as her sister's.

Lali lay without moving, black hair spread around her face, lips and legs parted. Lali needed pleasure, not love. Intense, reckless, animal pleasure. Pilar had spent her whole life looking at Lali and had never been able to understand that need.

Did Arturo love Lali? When he wrapped his arms around this body, did he love the woman, too?

She had to stop thinking about him.

But people got sidetracked. Even her father must have understood that. He had circled the poet's words: *a structure of masks and walls that have been my life—*

And he had marked the surging: *He ached intensely to see her again—at once!—to touch her hands and her hair—*

He must have known this.

Lying on the floor, Lali crossed her arms over her head. Her breasts were fuller than they had ever been. "A real massage now," she told Nico. "You promised me. *With* touching."

"Lie on your side," Nico replied gruffly.

"Help me take off my panties first." Lali was provoking him, with that flirtatiousness Pilar knew too well. "Come on, Nico. I'll feel more relaxed that way."

Roughly, he tugged the panties down her legs and tossed them aside. Her sex was smooth, hairless. Lali rolled to her side, her back to them. Black hair fell over pale shoulders to the mattress. Her torso tapered down to narrow hips and

small, firm buttocks. From behind, the only hint of pregnancy
was a thickened waistline.

"Help me," Nico told Pilar, his voice faltering.

She didn't answer.

"Touch her," he whispered.

"I can't."

"You'll be my hands." He mouthed the words: *I can't touch
her.* Out loud he said, "You have to do it for me."

"I don't know how to," Pilar said.

"I'll put my hands over yours, and I'll guide you. You just
have to follow me."

In a flash it came to her that he, too, was afraid. "Tell me
what to do," she told him.

"I don't care who does it," Lali said. "But do it."

Pilar knelt next to him and slipped her fingers under his.
The back of her hands touched his palms. Gently, he pushed
down on her hands, until they touched Lali's lower back. Lali
sighed, rolled forward as far as her belly would allow her,
exposing most of her back. Keeping her hands under his,
guided by shifts in pressure or direction, Pilar massaged the
length of Lali's back, moving upwards. Her sister's skin was
soft, pliant.

She thought: This is what Arturo feels when he touches her.

She cupped Lali's shoulders. With Nico's hands pressing on
hers, she moved down Lali's back again, feeling the curve on
each side of the spinal column, and continued further down,
over the hollow at the base of her spine, to her buttocks.

This was what he felt.

She wanted to turn Lali around and feel her belly, but
Nico's hands weighed down on hers, radiating a warmth and
energy that seemed to pass through her to Lali. She allowed
him to guide her further down, to the inside of Lali's thighs,
over slender calves to her toes, pretending her hands were
Arturo's.

Her own body began to respond. No way to ignore it.

Nico's head twisted toward her. "That's enough," he snapped.

He withdrew his hands and rested them on his lap. Reluctantly, she lifted her hands from Lali. Her sister rolled over and lay on her back.

"Fantastic," Lali said. "You could have gone on forever." She cupped her breasts. "Kiss me, Nico."

He lowered his eyes.

She pinched the tips of her nipples. "Kiss me."

"Stop it," Nico growled.

She was laughing. "It's all right. You can pretend I'm a boy."

"Why are you doing this?" Nico asked.

"It's all right." Lali was ingesting air, trying to stop the laughter. "These days I can't get anyone to want me." She sat up, black hair falling over blue-veined breasts. Another deep breath. Her face was solemn now, though her eyes sparkled. "That was marvelous. Thank you."

Nico leaned over a candle and lit a cigarette.

"You shouldn't smoke near me. I'm pregnant, you know."

He inhaled, then stubbed the cigarette.

"Pilar," she said, "you should change your mind. He's really good."

"It's enough for one night," he said sullenly. "And Pilar doesn't want it."

"You're so difficult, both of you!" Lali stood, gestured at her shaved pubis. "You like it? Arturo likes it. He wants to pretend I'm a little girl. Don't I look like a little girl? With my stomach out of the picture, of course." She held a cushion over her stomach.

Nico's lips tightened. "Let me do something for you," he told Pilar.

"No massage."

"I understood that," he said.

"Read her fortune," Lali told him.

"Would you like that, Pilar?"

Pilar shook her head. Lali trotted around the room, blowing at the candles but not managing to extinguish any of them. Her red lips curved upwards. "I need to be touched by someone who actually *wants* me."

"Okay," Pilar told Nico. "Read my fortune."

Nico returned with a white bathrobe and a small bundle wrapped in a red scarf. He untied the scarf to reveal a stack of gold-bordered tarot cards. A reproduction, he told them, of a very special set of 15th-century Italian tarot cards. The devil card had been missing from that deck—no one knew why, or what it looked like; another devil card, from a more recent set, replaced it.

Pilar shuffled the deck and selected ten cards, handing each one to him. The backs of the cards were deeply creased, the edges uneven. He arranged the cards facedown on the floor, in the shape of a cross, then turned them over one by one. The devil, reversed, a frightening, bare-chested man with a demon child on each side of him—cherubic blond children with horns on their heads. The lovers, joined by their right hands, with a blindfolded, naked young boy standing on a fountain between them. The wheel of fortune. The Emperor. And other cards she couldn't identify.

"I can read this," Lali said. She pointed at the cards and spoke in a theatrical whisper: "There's a man, Pilar. Finally. But you have to be careful. He's with someone else."

"That's ridiculous," Nico said. "That's not what the cards say."

"She knows what I'm talking about," Lali said.

Pilar stared at the cards. The shapes and colors blurred into each other. She told herself: *Lali's playing with you. She wants you to say something about Arturo, and if you do she'll never forgive you.*

"I know what's happening," Lali told her, "and it doesn't matter. Does that help?"

Nico grabbed the cards, patted them together, and tied the scarf around them. "You shouldn't do that," he told Lali. "Those are my cards. No one else is supposed to read them."

Pilar told herself: *You haven't done anything wrong.*

"You know that saying, Pilar? That the worst thing you can do for someone is a favor?" Lali, still naked, crouched beside her. "Well, this is my gift. God knows you need one."

"What are you talking about?" Nico asked.

"She knows. Don't you, Pilar?"

He looked from one sister to another, as though trying to understand what was going on. "What's wrong with a favor?"

"It puts you in debt to the other person. It creates *resentment*. Doesn't it, Pilar?"

Nico draped the bathrobe over Lali's shoulders.

"A gift," Lali told her sister. "See what happens." Her voice carried traces of something darker—melancholy, perhaps, or fear. Pilar didn't know what was happening, but she knew Lali well enough to know she was up to something.

"It's late," Nico said briskly. "We're not finished. Do you want to continue?"

Lali slipped into the bathrobe and tied the belt. "Of course!"

"Where are we going?" Pilar asked.

"To the garden."

"I'm going home," Pilar said.

"You can't," Lali told her. Then, more gently: "Please. This is the surprise."

Nico slung a large knapsack over his shoulder. They hurried down the staircase and out to the garden. From between black clouds, the moon slid into view. Nico grasped Pilar's waist and steered her forward, along a path she slowly began to see. She held her hands in front of her face, palms facing outward, shielding herself from dangling branches and vines. Lali walked behind them.

A small clearing, encircled by trees. In the middle of it, a hole had been dug into the ground, several feet deep and wide enough for two people, surrounded by piles of earth and a stack of wooden planks.

Lali pointed at the hole. "That's for a burial."

Nico laughed. "It's just a teaching," he told Pilar. "Don't worry."

"A ritual." Lali tapped the edge of the hole with her shoe. "Bonding with mother earth, and all that."

Nico knelt next to the hole, opened his knapsack, and removed folded plastic sheets, like those used by painters to protect floors and furniture. Pilar peered into the hole. Wooden planks lined the sides and bottom. Nico removed his shoes, sat at the edge of the hole, pushed himself into it. When he stood, only his shoulders and head rose over the ground. He unfolded the sheets and spread them over the planks, flattening them with his feet. When two layers of plastic covered the wood, he climbed out, using footholds that had been driven into one wall. "It's ready," he said. "You can go in."

Lali set a rectangle of folded plastic on the edge of the hole, sat on it, and pushed herself forward, into the hole.

"Pilar, come in with me!" Lali was sitting at the bottom, looking up. The white bathrobe spread around her like a misshapen flower.

Pilar hesitated. She sat on the plastic sheet, dangled her legs over the side.

Lali grasped her ankles. "Come on."

Pilar inched forward on her hips and let herself drop. She landed on her feet, the plastic sheets crinkling beneath her. Lali tugged at Pilar's hands, gesturing at her to lie down beside her.

The sisters lay on their backs, legs bent, facing the sky. Above them, a few stars pierced the darkness. Pilar's head and her feet almost touched the walls of the hole.

"It's not so bad, is it?" Lali asked.

"What going to happen?"

Nico peered over the edge. "Are you girls okay in there? Can I start?"

"It's perfect," Lali said.

He set a long wooden board across the top of the hole, several feet above them. He arranged another board beside it, then another, until the planks covered the hole like a roof.

In the darkness, Lali squeezed Pilar's hand. Their shoulders touched. "Close your eyes," Lali said.

Pilar heard soft thuds. She tried to sit up.

Gently, Lali held her down. "It's okay," she whispered. "He's just adding another layer of wood over the first. So that we're really covered."

"How long do we have to stay here? I can't see anything."

"One night," Lali said.

"No!"

"We're not chained here. All you have to do is stand up and push the boards and you can get out."

"How can we breathe?"

"Don't talk so loud. He'll put some tubes down. There'll be lots of holes—don't worry. He's done this hundreds of times. Close your eyes. It's easier."

"I can't breathe well."

"You can get out if you want to. Just stand up."

Pilar didn't answer.

Lali turned and wrapped an arm around her. "It's all right. Nothing will happen. I promise."

Pilar couldn't see her sister, but Lali's touch reassured her. She felt like a child again, when she had believed nothing bad could happen to her, as long as Lali was beside her.

She tried to focus on her breathing. The darkness seemed to magnify every sensation.

"Don't go to sleep," Lali said. "Listen to me. This is important."

The smell of damp soil, through the planks.

"Arturo's going to need somebody," Lali said.

"I can't stay here."

"And I rather it be someone I trust. You have until the baby is born. Do you understand?"

Pilar couldn't speak. Her heart was pounding so much she thought Lali could hear it.

"This is my gift," Lali said. "For now. But I'll want him back." Her mouth touched Pilar's ear. "I can show you what he likes."

Pilar pulled her head away.

"You'll be helping me," Lali said.

"You don't know what you're saying."

"It's okay," Lali said sadly. She cradled Pilar's head against her shoulder. "It's not your fault. Some men just can't take pregnant women."

Just before dawn, the sisters hurried across the garden and out into the driveway. Pilar glanced at the sky. No stars, no moon. The darkness seemed almost luminous to her. She reached for Lali's hand, as she had when they were children.

Lali turned to her. Her eyes were pained and raw, as though some protective layer had been stripped away. "Be careful," Lali said. "He's not what you imagine."

They drove through the old city. Pilar pressed her forehead against the window, watching the shapes and lights along the quiet streets, thinking of how her father had smiled at his daughters and told them he loved them, and of what he would say if he knew what she was about to do.

Chapter Five

Love Released Like Lepers

A religion permeated with bodily images (witness such doctrines as the Incarnation and the Resurrection of the Body), Christianity's history is marked by a deep-seated tension arising from a double vision of the body as locus of sin and medium of the divine . . .

Filipinos reinterpreted and selectively adopted elements of the new religion. . . . While missionaries stressed the virtues of asceticism, Catholicism's strongest appeals proved to be the sensuous rituals and colorful pageantry that accompanied religious feasts (fiestas), expansive events that nourished the body in ways the missionaries could not quite control.

—Resil B. Mojares, "Catechisms of the Body"

Arturo

Arturo walked toward the island's only bar, a dirt-floor shack by the pier. A few meters away, waves swept over a gray beach. He glanced at the sky. No clouds, no threat of a storm. He imagined Lali and the baby inside her, in a small plane over the sea. His chest tightened.

He entered the bar. White plastic tables and chairs, a counter lined with earthen pots. His men slouched around tables, drinking beer. No other customers. He dragged a chair and table to a far corner of the room, sat with his back to the wall. Always sit where you can see every person and every entrance, his mother told him. You don't want to get ambushed.

A teenage waitress walked toward him, so petite he thought at first she was a child. The tips of her small breasts pushed against her T-shirt. She had a round face, flat nose, and broad cheekbones, but youth had arranged her features into a sturdy prettiness that on this day, in this town, he was happy to consider attractive.

"Can I help you, sir?" she murmured, looking at the ground.

He leaned forward and turned his head, meeting her gaze from below. She blushed. He sat up, noting her long black hair, the mole over her lip, her scents of soap and shampoo. How did she manage to smell so clean in this heat and squalor? He imagined her crouching every morning in a corner of a one-room shack, pouring cold water over her body and rubbing soap into her skin.

"A beer," he told her, trying to sound casual.

"With ice, sir?"

He nodded. He gestured at his men, asked her to bring them anything they wanted. She walked away. Small waist, tight body. At the counter, she cracked ice with a pick. A muscle flexed in her upper arm. He told himself: Don't be an idiot.

Behind the cash register, a garland of twinkling lights framed a poster of the Sacred Heart of Jesus. White face, blue eyes gazing upward, pink cheeks, honey-blond hair flowing to his shoulders. Did you notice, Lali had asked him once, how Jesus always looks American in this country?

Again he imagined the small plane, somewhere in those blue skies.

Why were they so late?

The waitress set his beer on the table. She refused to look at him. There was a softness about her, a sweetness. She hurried away. Don't be scared of me, he thought.

In first-year high school, he started going to parties with girls. He stood at one end of the room and chatted with his classmates from the all-boys Jesuit school that all the men in his family had attended, but what he really wanted was to sit with the convent-school girls, to smell them and stare at them. The slender, sassy ones were his favorites. He loved their hair, the little curves in their bodies, the giggles, the bare arms and legs that looked so smooth and forbidding. Later, when he began to date, their talk baffled him—all that dissecting of experience. Lali wasn't like them. She was the most feminine of them all, and she had no patience with women. She approached sex like a man. She didn't need foreplay. She didn't want cuddling. She asked him not to talk to her during sex—the effort of listening to him diminished her pleasure.

But Lali's directness had misled him. She was more complicated than anyone he knew, suspicious of everything people said and did, an expert at hiding her own feelings.

Arturo's driver tapped him on the shoulder. "They're arriving, sir. The plane already landed."

Arturo thanked him and walked out of the bar. In the distance, a white van bounced down the road. Dust clouds billowed behind it. Arturo forced his lips into a smile, bracing himself for the encounter with Lali.

The van stopped. The driver opened the back door. One long slender leg appeared, then another. For an instant, Arturo didn't see his wife, the accumulation of tensions and resentments that Lali had become. He saw only the legs of a woman, and he was taken aback by their beauty.

"Arturo?" she asked hesitantly.

The smile felt stuck to his face. A rush of relief, which he mistook for pleasure.

"Where's Lali?" he asked.

"She couldn't come. Didn't she call you?"

Pilar's yellow dress had coffee-colored stains, her hair needed brushing, her eyes squinted in the sunlight. To his mind, she had never looked so beautiful.

"She wasn't feeling well," Pilar said. "She asked me to take her place."

He stared at her lips.

"Why didn't she tell me?" he asked. "You didn't have to come."

Her mouth tightened. "That's what I told her, but she insisted. She was supposed to call you." Pilar seemed anxious, evasive. "She kept saying it's such a big rally, it's important to have a woman from the family."

"She didn't call me."

Pilar glanced over his shoulder. He followed her gaze. At the doorway, the waitress stared at them, wide-eyed.

"Well, I'm sorry," Pilar said.

The strong lines of her body, under her dress.

"Can we go to wherever we're staying?" she asked. "I have to change."

"What happened?"

"Turbulence. I spilled the coffee."

"There's a toilet in the bar."

The driver brought her a small leather bag, and she hurried into the shack. A moment later, she stepped out. "I can't change in there. Did you see the toilet?"

He laughed. Her face softened. It wouldn't be hard, he thought. But he wasn't going to do anything. One kiss, Pilar, he told her silently. That's all it was.

"There's a so-called department store up the road," he said. "They should have a changing room." He told himself he had no time for complications. Not the waitress, not Pilar, not Lali.

She slung the bag over her shoulder and marched up the road. Her yellow dress clung to her thighs.

He leaned against a wall of the bar, in the shade. Across the street, his airbrushed face smiled back at him, next to a campaign poster of his opponent—a plump, handsome man called Carlos C. Benedicto III who had been born in the province and assigned there after the General fled. Everyone knew Benedicto was both corrupt and incompetent, but he was good-natured and a distant cousin of the president, and everyone in the region had heard of him.

Arturo smoked one cigarette.

An aide approached him. "The mayor's waiting for us at the rally, sir. The others are there *na*, he said."

Arturo crushed the cigarette into the sand. "Okay. I'll go tell Miss Pilar."

The sandy street wound away from the pier and up into the village. No one in sight. The sun beat down on him. He wondered where everybody was. He had been traveling for more than two weeks now, one campaign stop after another. All these island towns were beginning to look the same: the ramshackle pier, the dusty main road lined with nipa huts and sparsely stocked stores, one or two funeral homes, a gas station.

The heat weighed on him, slowing his movements. He imagined hostile eyes peeking at him from windows. He wondered how many people were going to show up at the rally. But the organization had been thorough, and more than enough money had changed hands. A part of him still wanted everyone to like him, and the viciousness of a political campaign wounded him in ways he would never admit to his advisors and family.

In the department store, sparrow-like shop girls leaned over counters, chatting and fanning themselves. They looked up when he entered. He wandered through narrow aisles, past packages featuring fair-skinned women and fat babies who looked like no one on this island.

At the far end of the room, bare golden-brown shoulders and black hair appeared over the door of the dressing stall.

He strode toward her.

"Sir!" a shop girl cried. "Please, sir! It's for women only!"

He reached the stall, stood on his toes, and looked inside. Wearing only white panties and a bra, Pilar stood in front of a full-length mirror, her back to him. Their eyes met in the mirror.

She turned around. He expected protest, a scramble to cover herself. Instead, she stood in front of him, arms at her sides. Tall and wide-boned, breasts rounding over the cups of her bra. She looked nothing like Lali, yet there was a resemblance—a certain bearing, a fierceness in her eyes—that made her seem both the opposite and double of her sister.

"Please go," she whispered.

Suddenly he understood her expression. It wasn't embarrassment. She was offering the sight of her body to him, and she was terrified.

Lali had told him about Pilar's dislike of undressing, about the burn and scarring when she was a child.

"I'm sorry," he said, meaning it.

She lowered her head, rummaged for the clothes on the floor, held them against her. She lifted her head. Tears in her eyes.

Be careful, he told himself.

"Please," she said. He could hardly hear her.

He turned away, walked into an aisle, and stood in front of a rack.

The lettering and images on packages blurred into each other.

She came to him. She had changed into a sleeveless pink dress.

He touched her elbow. "I didn't mean—"

She withdrew her arm. "You mean everything," she said lightly.

Her eyes remained fearful.

He followed her out of the store, tracking the body beneath the dress. As they strolled down the road toward the pier, she said, "I haven't been to a place like this in so long." She seemed to be forcing herself to sound cheerful, almost flirtatious. "I forget this country has places like this. You know, whenever we leave the city for the province, we always end up going to resorts or to friends' houses at the beach or in the countryside, and it's nothing at all like this. How can people live here?"

"Most of the country is like this," he mumbled.

"It makes me feel sad."

Here we go, he thought. Now, she would talk about her feelings, shift his attention from the body he had seen in the dressing room. Suddenly he missed Lali, her impatience with sentimentality. Really good sex makes you sleep, she said. It doesn't make you cuddle and talk. As a teenager, Lali told him, she used to send her driver to buy *Playboy* and *Penthouse* for her—she enjoyed photos of naked women, and she studied their poses and facial expressions for clues to men's fantasies.

Pilar was still speaking. He listened only for cues in her intonations, quick to nod or smile whenever it seemed required.

By the time they reached the sandy yard in front of the bar, Pilar's face was flushed. Her earnestness alarmed him. Did she imagine herself in love with him, or he with her? Because he had kissed her on the day of the eclipse? Because he had just seen her in her panties and bra?

He wanted to tell her: We're here to campaign. That's all.

He entered the bar. Under the poster of the Sacred Heart, the soft-eyed waitress watched him. Again her sweetness moved him. He paid the bill, pressed a hundred-peso bill into her hand, tried to think of something to tell her. She lowered her gaze. He wished he could do something for her. He wished he could believe this election, any election, could help her.

In the air-conditioned, leather-upholstered van, Pilar waited for him. Jazz played over the speakers. An open bottle of Chanel No. 5 perfumed the air. He leaned against the headrest. He had sworn he would never end up like his parents. He had wanted a happy marriage. Maybe a few women on the side, but nothing to undermine his marriage. One day Lali had been his, curled into him at night, her face quickening when she saw him. Then it had ended. And here was Pilar. He sensed, behind her reserve, a passion as intense as Lali's. He wondered what it would be like to release it. Months ago, on a holiday in a mountain town, the three of them had walked along the souvenir stands in Mines Park, looking at the pornographic wood carvings and tribal cloth. The sisters were so lovely that people stopped them and asked if they could take their pictures. Both of them, he thought.

Pilar crossed one slender tanned leg over the other, toward

him. Forget it, he told himself. There were a million other women, more available, more experienced, and none of them related to Lali.

At the far end of the town's main square, on a wooden stage, he sat with the other candidates and faced the crowd. In normal times, the square served as a basketball court. Now it was packed with families, food vendors, bodyguards, children, and beggars. The mayor had lured the crowd with peso bills and the promise of entertainment—music, dances, a beauty contest. Politics was show business. On television, the week before, Harvard-trained technocrats danced the cha-cha to a cheering studio audience, and movie stars without high-school degrees promised economic transformation.

A nightclub singer from Manila, reportedly one of the mayor's mistresses, ambled to center stage. The crowd whooped as she stood before them in a skintight, low-cut evening gown. The local band hit a few notes, and she began to sing: *People, people who need people.*

In an elevated section of the square, near the stage and cordoned off by security men, Pilar and some candidates' wives sat inside a VIP box. Unlike the rest of the crowd, the women had chairs and lace fans. Pilar bowed her head. Black hair fell over the sides of her face. Arturo stared at her, willing her to look at him.

The song ended. The crowd applauded and whistled. The mayor, wearing elevator shoes, strutted across the stage. A short, balding man in his sixties, he kissed the singer on both cheeks. The crowd hooted. "Our thanks to the beauteous Miss Nora Capiri, the famous star from Manila!" the mayor announced into the microphone. "And now, a few words from our vice-mayor!"

A slight man with thick eyeglasses walked hesitantly toward the microphone. "Good afternoon, ladies and gentlemen," he mumbled. He cleared his throat. "We thank you all for being here. We also thank Mr. Arturo Mariano, for honoring our town with his presence."

Arturo stood and waved to the crowd, a smile pasted on his face. The politicians onstage clapped politely. Moments later, the crowd returned a feeble applause.

"It is not by accident," the vice-mayor continued, "that God has given us our new president, after years of suffering and evil. Mother Mary has heard our prayers, and she has given us a saint for president." Arturo studied his fingernails. The president was a bumbling fool to Manila's elite, but she had become Joan of Arc to the masses. Her handlers knew what they were doing. Call on divine order. Bestow spiritual meaning on every misfortune, mishap, and disaster. He had forged an uneasy alliance with her—what else could he do? She had God and saintliness on her side, and he needed her support to win the election. But she was playing with him, refused to endorse him as her candidate. "I will not oppose you," she had told him coyly the last time he visited the palace. He inclined his head. She inclined her head. They shook hands. They both knew he was waiting for her to fall. Four coups d'état in six months, two of them secretly backed by Arturo's allies.

"This government rules by divine right!" The vice-mayor removed his glasses and rubbed his eyes. "I was in Manila when the revolution happened. I was in church, with my family, with thousands of people. We prayed hard, all night, all day, for a good government. Everyone was scared the church would be attacked. We prayed that President Peachy would win. And God heard us!"

Arturo clapped. There had been no revolution. The country was still run by the five dozens of families that had controlled it for generations. The General was gone, President Peachy was in, and her brother Ricky was taking over everything the General's cronies had left behind. And almost everyone who mattered still met at the Polo Club for *merienda* every Sunday.

The vice mayor returned to his seat. On the edges of the square, vendors hawked barbecued pork, grilled corn, and soft drinks. The mayor marched to the microphone. "And now, for the long-awaited moment of this rally—the crowning of Miss Ilapat! Our five finalists are waiting to present themselves to us, and our special guest, Mr. Arturo Mariano, will do us the immense honor of choosing the loveliest of the loveliest."

The speakers played an instrumental version of "There She Is, Miss America." Five young women in blue swimsuits, opaque beige pantyhose, and stiff hairdos climbed the stairs to the stage. Their nervous, red-lipsticked smiles seemed painted on their faces. Heavy makeup made them look much older than they were. He thought of the young waitress in the bar, her small breasts under her T-shirt, her gentleness. These girls were probably as gentle, behind these masks.

Each girl stepped up to the microphone and said her name. In the square, supporters clapped and shouted. The girls stood in a line in front of Arturo and the other candidates, facing the crowd. Drums rolled. The girls pulled back their shoulders and began to do quarter turns. A hush over the square.

Arturo glanced at his watch. He knew whom he had to choose. The mayor had whispered the name of his candidate— a girl whose father probably had contributed significantly to one of the mayor's projects. He shut his eyes. The shouting began again. He waited. Harsh cries now, from different parts of the square. He opened his eyes. The girls turned their heads from side to side. The band stopped playing. Screams punctuated the chaos. At the edges of the crowd, people were pushing and running away. Those stuck in the middle shoved each other, trying to break free. No shots, Arturo told himself. No one is shooting. Now the beauty contestants were scrambling in their high heels down the stairs. At the far end of the square, several dozen people in tattered brown robes wended their way into the crowd. Their movements were slow and graceful, in contrast to the panic around them. The crowd seemed to part around them. Policemen and the candidates' bodyguards ran across the stage, guns drawn. Arturo's bodyguard grabbed him and hurried him through a back door.

"Where's Miss Pilar?" Arturo yelled.

"Dinggoy went to her—don't worry, sir! They'll meet us at the van, sir."

They ran through a gravel path, Arturo's heart thumping, past shacks and trees, until they reached the bulletproof van. Another bodyguard murmured into a walkie-talkie. Arturo didn't understand what he was saying.

When he hung up, Arturo said, "What's happening?"

"Somebody released lepers into the square, sir. They brought them in by bus."

"Lepers?" To his dismay, he almost laughed. He suppressed it.

The bodyguard watched him doubtfully. "There's a leper colony in the next village, sir."

"Where's Miss Pilar?"

"Dinggoy's with her, sir. There's no more danger. She said she wants to stay a little longer."

Arturo returned to the square. It was deserted except for a few dozen lepers, squatting in the shade cast by the wooden stage. Hoods partially concealed their faces; coarse brown robes covered their arms and legs. On one side of the square, abandoned barbecue stands released black smoke, filling the air with the smell of burned pork and charred corn. Arturo saw Pilar's bright pink dress and black hair. She was talking to a leper.

When he reached her, she gave him a quizzical smile. The leper next to her was bent over, his face in shadow beneath the hood. The lesions on his hands were dark around the edges, with pale, discolored centers. Arturo averted his gaze.

"Come on," he told Pilar.

"I was just talking to him."

Gently, he held her upper arm and began to lead her away.

She stepped away. She thanked the leper for talking to her, then marched tensely beside Arturo toward the van. Banana and papaya trees lined the road, casting giant shadows on the ground. Behind the trees, the vegetation was so thick Arturo couldn't see through it. Two minutes from the main square, and the jungle was already eating into the city.

"So what are we going to do?" she asked quietly.

"Get out of here."

"They won't organize another rally?"

"No one will come back after the lepers."

After a moment, she said: "That man I was talking to. He told me there's a dead woman in a church near here. He said she performs miracles. Her name's Lola Bea. Can we go see her?"

He asked her how she could have stood so close to the leper, looked at those sores on his hands and face.

She paused. "Marks on bodies don't bother me."

He remembered what Lali had said about her scars. "I'm sorry. I didn't mean—"

"You always *mean*."

Inside the van, she tugged the seatbelt over her. "You know what he told me? Today is one of the feast days of St. Lazarus. You know what he died of?"

"Leprosy, and he's wrong—his feast day's in December."

"Apparently, he has several feast days." Her voice had that odd, forced flirtatiousness again. "That's what they say here. When he was born, when he died, when he was born again."

In the front seat, the bodyguard looked at them over his shoulder. "Where do you want to go, sir?"

"Take us to the mayor."

Pilar said: "He told me Lazarus's disease enters into water

on his feast days. Anyone who takes a bath or goes swimming today might catch some horrible skin disease."

The air-conditioning began to cool the van.

"Come on," she said. "Please." Her playfulness surprised him. "Let's go see Lola Bea? It won't take long. They say she'll purify me."

She uncrossed her legs, tugged the hem of her pink dress over her thighs. Okay, why not, he thought, forcing his eyes away from her legs. The day's ruined anyway.

"Say thank you," he told her, teasing.

She tipped back her head and laughed, and her pleasure excited him. He laughed, too, watching her wide mouth.

Through the car window, he stared at the landscape, aware of her next to him. Sugar fields on all sides, water buffaloes standing in mud, naked children splashing in stagnant ponds. Young men were working the fields, their perspiration-drenched T-shirts rolled over their nipples.

He slumped against the seat. He disliked the dead time of travel—airplanes, cars, helicopters, all the places where he was stuck between where he was going and where he had come from, with nothing to divert him from his own thoughts. The rush of daily life, his political career, the family businesses, the flirtations with new women—none of these could save him from a vague, disorienting sense of his own solitude.

Pilar stared out the window. He wanted to break her silence.

"He'll pay for breaking up the rally," Arturo said. He meant to sound forceful, but he was distracted by her bare arms and legs, the curve of her breasts.

She started. "Who?"

"Benedicto."

"You think it was Benedicto?"

"Who else would do that?"

"Still." She smiled. "You have to hand it to him. Sending lepers into the square like that."

"You think it's funny?"

"I don't think anything," she said evenly. "I just want to see Lola Bea."

She turned back to the window. In the rearview mirror, the driver's dark eyes glanced at Arturo. A good friend had been ambushed up north during another election campaign; his own bodyguard, paid off by opponents, had betrayed him. No way of knowing who was on your side. Allegiances shifted, life was cheap, poverty or power could corrupt any-one. Filipinos were such a warm, loving people, people said—the nicest in Asia. The happiest, too. And among the most brutal. The week before, a hacendero's private army had raided the home of a labor leader in a southern village. They slashed open the stomach of his pregnant wife. Trust only your own blood, his mother had said. At this moment, Arturo felt threatened by everything else—his wife, her sister, his bodyguards, this country with its irrationality, its reli-giousness, its violence.

The van bounced along for several kilometers, past small villages near the sea, then continued inland. At the end of the road, a footpath curved up a slope to a stone chapel.

Pilar unlocked her door.

"Wait," Arturo said. "Let Dinggoy go first and see if some-one's there."

The bodyguard ran up the sandy path to the church. Minutes later, an old priest shuffled toward the van, lifting the hem of his brown robe. From a distance, he looked as small and frail as a girl.

Arturo rolled down the window. "Good morning, Father! We've come to visit Lola Bea."

"She's at the cemetery." The priest was wheezing as he reached the car. He seemed to be in his eighties, with sharp, birdlike features and bright eyes. "The bishop won't allow us to keep her in the church."

Under the hot sun they followed him, along another path to the graveyard behind the church. In single file they walked down the main alley, past the tombs. Then into a narrower alley, overgrown by weeds and lined with wooden crosses, to a nipa hut in a far corner of the cemetery.

The priest knocked on the door. "Tony! Visitors for Lola Bea!"

A scrawny young man appeared at the doorway. His jeans hung low on his hips. One eye, smaller than the other, narrowed into a slit when he smiled.

They removed their shoes and entered the hut. A rattan couch covered with plastic sheets, a Formica table, a statue of the Virgin Mary over the television. On a wall, a faded portrait of the deposed General and his wife, both looking more energetic and more Caucasian than they ever had in their lives.

Tony made a sweeping gesture. "Please, have your seats."

Arturo and Pilar sat on the couch, the plastic crinkling beneath them. The young man brought out four bottles of Coke, plastic straws, a tin of saltine crackers.

Tony bowed. "I'll go tell Grandma that she has visitors." He disappeared into a doorway curtained by strings of seashells.

Arturo ate five crackers in quick succession, pushed the tin away from him. "Why can't you keep her in the church, Father?"

The priest's dainty fingers curled around a bottle of Coke. "The bishop says it will take years before the Church conducts its investigation. He says this may be the work of the devil. And we have so many people coming, from all over. We can't control it."

Pilar reached for a cracker. "Control what, Father?"

"The miracles! That's why you're here, no? Lola Bea is still taking care of the sick and the dying." He chortled. "You wait. You'll see her. She's been dead for decades, and she looks like she's sleeping. How can you explain that?"

Pilar brushed crumbs from her lap.

"Tony's a tricycle driver, but he used to be the village drunk." The priest lowered his voice. "A gambler. And a thief. Maybe worse. Everyone knew that." His eyes flicked toward the doorway. "One day, it must have been in August, he decided he wanted a new table. So he visited the cemetery that night—there were marble slabs over some of the graves. He thought it would be *bongga* to have a marble tabletop. But God works in mysterious ways. The last person Jesus forgave was a thief, remember." The priest laughed, cupping a hand over his mouth. "Tony was removing the marble slab, and he accidentally broke the glass over the casket. He looked inside—and there was our Grandma. Her dress all in shreds, but her body and her face—perfectly preserved! And she still had the scapular of the Sacred Heart around her neck!"

Pilar looked at Arturo. He gave a brief smile. You wanted this, he mouthed.

"Tony was transformed. He stopped drinking. He spent the whole day sitting in the cemetery, by Grandma's grave, talking to people who came to see her. And then something incredible happened. A liquid—it looked like Coca-Cola—began to form in a corner of the casket. It smells like herbal oil—you'll see. And when Tony rubs a little of that oil on people, they get cured. Blind people see again, infertile women have babies. It's miraculous." The priest stuffed a cracker into his mouth and crunched into it. "But the bishop doesn't want to believe."

The shell curtain rustled. Tony stepped through it. "She's waiting. Father, will you pray now?"

With some difficulty, the priest lowered himself to his knees on the bamboo floor. "The bishop says I'm not supposed to do this," he said cheerfully. "But I have to follow my heart. I can't believe the devil would do so much good." He gestured at the others to kneel beside him and hold hands, then led them through a lilting version of Our Father. Pilar's eyes were closed and her lips moving, but Arturo couldn't hear her.

Tony led them through the curtains, down a short corridor and into a windowless room, so dark they could see nothing at first. The smells overwhelmed Arturo—medicinal herbs, incense, rotting flowers. Tony lit a candle. Against the back wall, four stools held up a wooden casket. Tony hurried toward it, leaned over, and began to murmur. He straightened and told Pilar, "She says she wants to see you."

Pilar flinched. Arturo pressed his hand into the small of her back and steered her forward. They stood over the casket. The dead woman's face and arms had turned almost to bone, except for a thin layer of brown flesh that looked as dry and fragile as onionskin. The lids were shut, the eyes sunken into their sockets. Matted white hair cradled the skeletal face. Death seemed to have astonished her: her mouth was open, revealing two rows of small yellow teeth.

"Isn't she beautiful?" Tony lifted the corpse's arm and bent it at the elbow.

Bile rose up Arturo's throat.

The priest chuckled. "You see? Her arms and legs are still pliable. And she's been dead for almost thirty years!"

Tony held out the arm. "You want to bend it?"

Pilar shook her head. She looked away, crossed her arms.

Bracing himself, Arturo forced a smile. "Sure," he said.

He told himself he was a politician, an expert at christenings, weddings, and wakes. He knew how to deal with the dead—he had looked into hundreds of caskets without really seeing a corpse. His mother had taught him the trick: Fill your mind with pleasant images, she told him, and never look a dead person in the face. Every time Arturo walked toward an open casket, he visualized the face and body of a beautiful friend or acquaintance. This time, as he glanced at the outside of Lola Bea's casket, he tried to imagine Pilar in the dressing room, but the image wouldn't hold.

He touched Lola Bea's arm. Cold. But the flesh was also soft, yielding under his hand. With a start he imagined his own body in this casket, decades after his death, mouth open, body shrunken and skeletal. A rush of nausea.

Pilar's fingers brushed his. The warmth of her skin jolted him.

"I need air," he muttered.

Her dark eyes focused on him. Candlelight softened her face.

He didn't want her to see him this way. With difficulty, trying to pronounce each syllable clearly, he said: "I'm going outside."

He stumbled toward the doorway. Strings of shells swung around him. In the living room, by the window, he told himself: Breathe. Through the mosquito screen, the sky was a cloudless blue.

A rustling behind him. Even before he heard a voice, he knew it was her.

"We can leave, Arturo, if you want."

"I'm fine." He turned to her. "It's just the smell. I've seen dead people. Massacred women, murders—"

She cut him off. "It's all right."

Why had he never noticed her voice? Kind, round, calming. It seemed incapable of malice or cruelty.

Her eyes held his. "We should leave."

"I'm fine. Let's go back in."

In the candlelit room, the priest and tricycle driver leaned over the casket. The priest beckoned at them: "Hurry! I have a surprise." He held a plastic sheet over Lola Bea's face. Moisture formed on the inner surface of the sheet.

"She's breathing," Tony whispered, stroking her hair. "Do you see?"

Arturo focused on the sheet that blurred Lola Bea's face, trying not to see the rest of the corpse.

The priest chuckled. "The municipal health officer came here. He said the moisture's a sign of decomposition, but where's the decomposition? Can you see it? Can you smell it? She's been here in the heat for months. Even the General's corpse needs a freezer, I told him. Is this a freezer?"

Tony asked Pilar: "Do you have something to tell her? She told me she's waiting for you."

"I was speaking to lepers today."

"I know—Lola Bea told me. She told me you need to be cleansed." Tony dipped his fingers into a corner of the casket, held out his hand.

A dark, sticky-looking liquid clung to his fingertips. That's the stench, Arturo thought. To avoid it, he inhaled through his mouth.

Tony wiggled his fingers. "There's always more, no matter how much I use."

The priest made the sign of the cross over the liquid. "Please, get on your knees," he told Pilar. "You have to ask God to forgive your sins. You have to be worthy of Lola Bea's blessing."

Pilar closed her eyes. In his mind, Arturo told her: Don't fall for this.

She knelt and lowered her head. Tony dabbed the liquid on her forehead, neck, and palms.

Stop praying to that monster, Arturo thought. Lola Bea had nothing to do with goodness. The only miraculous thing about her was that she still had a body. Miracles were no guarantee of goodness. In school, the priests had said the spirit had to break free of the body, but people were always scheming to manipulate God through their bodies, or through the remains of other people's. Flagellations, fasting, relics, amulets—it was all the same thing. Faced with a preserved corpse, even a skeptic like Pilar wouldn't take chances.

She was standing next to him. Shadows cut into her cheek-bones and deepened the hollows around her eyes. "I'm done. Do you want to go next?"

He managed a smile. "It's okay. Lola Bea's done enough for today."

As they entered the living room, the priest said: "If you want to thank Grandma, there's a box by the television." He pointed to a wooden box with a large sign over it: "Donations." Arturo slipped a hundred-peso bill and two campaign leaflets into the slit.

The priest sat down and took a large gulp of Coke. He wiped his lips with the back of his hand. "I've been doing research about her. Preparing for the Church's investigations. She was a good woman, everyone says. She took care of all the sick and dying in the village. I heard that once, when she was taking care of someone, she even licked their wounds."

Arturo glanced sideways at Pilar. She kept her eyes on the priest.

"Jesus came to her. He asked her to drink the blood from his hands, from where they put the nails. After that, she stopped eating. She fasted for months, but she gained weight."

Tony nodded. "She was a saint," he said solemnly.

"And she had visits from Jesus every night. There's a niece of hers, an old woman now, but still alive. She says Jesus came to Lola Bea, embraced her. That's the reason she never lost weight."

There it was again, Arturo thought. The physical was the spiritual. The touch of God wasn't a metaphor.

"Arturo?"

Her eyes were luminous and calm. He recognized that look in a woman. Confidence, even power. She knew he wanted her.

"It's hot," he said. "Let's look for a place to swim."

They said their goodbyes, promised to return. Halfway down the cemetery path, they turned to wave. In front of the hut, the stooped priest and lanky ex-thief swung their arms in the air.

Pilar and Arturo sat on flat rocks jutting out to the sea. Foot-high waves broke beneath them. No one else around. He had sent the bodyguards away, instructed them to return at the end of the afternoon.

"I don't think you can swim here," she said. "Do you see the currents?"

With one casual gesture, he shifted his position so that his hip almost touched hers. He waited. She didn't move away. Carefully, monitoring her reaction, he asked: "How could you let him put that liquid on you?"

Her face, near his, shone with perspiration. "It smelled horrible, didn't it?"

The heat burrowed into his skin. In the distance, the sea was aquamarine. Sunlight glittered over the crests of waves. An image surfaced: the ship at night, lurching into the storm. Families still thronged outside his office, but they were docile now, lining up to get paid. The money, insignificant for his company, pacified them. Some seemed almost grateful. At Lali's insistence, they had met with every family. She wept at each encounter. Show business—she had the gift. The families warmed to her and barely looked at him, although it was he who had the nightmares, who needed a drink or a joint before and after each visit.

"When are we leaving this place?" Pilar asked.

"Tomorrow, around noon," he said. The pink dress clung to her thighs. "I need to talk to the mayor in the morning, find out what really happened at the rally. Don't worry about it."

"Please don't condescend to me," she said.

Sunlight over her face. A small white mark, slightly indented, was perceptible on her cheek.

"Okay," he said. "Tomorrow we have to visit Crisostomo."

"The faith healer who defeated your mom?"

"No, his son." She was so near him. He became aware of his heartbeat. "The father died in office, but he passed command to his eldest son. Three sons, and they're all called Boy—Boy One, Boy Two, and Boy Three. Boy One hates politics and faith healing—he wants to be a rock star—but he's in charge now. So we have to visit him, buy his music demos, see what he wants from us in exchange for his support."

She looked toward the waves, but didn't seem to see them.

He didn't know what else to say. If she were any other woman, he would kiss her.

At last she said: "It was bizarre to talk to that leper. I felt close to him. I know what it's like—in a small way, I'm not saying it's the same thing—to be like that. To be marked."

"To be like a leper? How can you say that?"

"That's not what I said." She wiped her neck. "It's so hot. I can't stand it anymore."

He stood and brushed the back of his pants. His head felt light, his knees weak. "There must be a river somewhere. There's always a river near these villages."

Trying to steady himself, he helped her to her feet. They took small, careful steps over moss-covered rocks, the sea murmuring behind them.

There was no transition. One moment they were in flat ground, the fields scorched ochre by the sun, then the jungle rose before them. They plunged into it. A sudden dampness, shadows, a carpet of tangled roots and fallen leaves. No birdsong, no rustling.

"Can you hear it?" he asked.

She tilted her head.

"Water," he told her.

Her lips parted. "I can't hear anything."

"I could always find water, when I was a boy," he said, suddenly shy. "People used to make fun of me."

Immediately, he regretted telling her this. But Pilar nodded and said: "There was someone like that, when I was small, in my grandparents' house in the province. You could put her into a field, anywhere, and she would point and say, 'There's water here.'"

He wondered why he had disliked this woman.

"And she was always right," Pilar said.

"I feel stupid talking about those things."

"It's okay. It's interesting." She hesitated. "You never really talked to me."

Through gaps in the canopy of leaves, sunlight fell like lace over her skin. Her face in profile. From this angle, she was flawless. But she wasn't the woman he had known for years. His wife's younger sister—dark, watchful, introverted. Nothing like Lali. He felt no more desire, only an awareness of the distance between them. Perhaps he didn't know her at all. Perhaps he had never known any of his women.

She tilted back her head, exposing her neck. Her eyes were black, expectant. "Now I hear it."

The kindness in her voice, again. He began to notice the colors around him—blue-green patches between leaves, red flowers peeking between roots. She stood beside him like one of the *diwatas* the maids had whispered about in his childhood—beautiful fairies always touched by evil.

She asked, "Are you okay?"

"I'm fine," he lied.

When he was a boy, in bed at night, he thought that if he needed his mother badly enough, she would feel it and come to him. He had never stopped believing she would come, every night for years as he fought off sleep, with only a lamp to comfort him and protect him from the darkness.

Pilar reached for his hand. "Let's find the water?"

He followed her. Her touch seemed to tether him to himself. Twigs and leaves crackled beneath their feet. In the distance, he heard the faint rush of water. As a child, on many days and for many reasons, he hadn't been allowed to bathe or go swimming. Not on Good Friday, not right after church, not under a rainbow or a full moon. And never on the feast of St. Lazarus. Dangerous, his nanny had told him. She was the old amah from Hong Kong, shaking her head. Disease gets into the water, people get sick and die. Magic is physical, it works only through things, don't give it a chance. And Lazarus is tricky, she whispered, you have to be careful. He has another feast, and most people don't know about the second one, the secret one. You mustn't enter water on that day, too.

They forced their way through a gap in the bushes and discovered the muddy, sloping banks of a river. Over black rocks, green water flowed.

"We found it," she said, childlike in her pleasure.

He touched the hollow at the base of her neck, between her collarbones. She didn't move. He had already kissed her, on the day of the eclipse. Neither of them had ever spoken about it. But the memory remained, a live wire between them. He had kissed her once. He could do it again.

She took two steps backward.

"My father," she told him, "used to say something about people from the same side of the river."

"I know. People from the same side should never marry."

A shadow crossed her face. "Lali tells you everything, doesn't she?"

Of course Lali had loved him. But something breaks in a marriage. He didn't know when it had happened, or how, but now he looked back and knew that what he had, what he thought he could not lose, what he had spent so much time running after and then settling into, the center, the anchor, the reason—all that, broken. And he didn't know why.

Pilar was speaking again. She told him about the burn, the scar, the fear of watching people watching her. He gazed at her earnest, lovely face. When she finished, he said, "You have no idea how people see you, do you? You're beautiful."

"Sometimes I wish I could feel myself," she replied. "Something solid, inside. Sometimes I think there's only this shell."

He pressed two fingers against her mouth. After a moment, she parted her lips. There was an awkwardness in her, a willingness to please, that frightened him.

She broke away. She crouched by the river and dipped her hand into the water. Long hair fell in front of her, exposing the back of her neck. He stripped, waded into the river, lowered himself into the cool water. She didn't look at him. He swam away from her but felt bound to her, suffused by her.

When he turned back, she was in the water, strong brown legs kicking behind her, swimming toward him. The pink dress slid over white panties. She lifted her head, black hair flattened against her skull.

She was standing beside him. In chest-high water, she moved closer.

He said, "We can't do this—"

Her shoulder touched his. Later, he would tell himself: she was the one who came to me. Now he wrapped his arms around her. Their mouths touched. He dipped his hand into the water. Hand under her dress, he unhooked her bra. She stopped moving. In the cool water, her breasts were soft and warm. She wasn't at all like Lali.

Her hips pressed against his.

He said, "Should we—"

"It's okay," she whispered.

Her skin against his, golden arms over green water. She closed her eyes; black lashes touched her skin. He held her waist. As he entered into her, he thought: Thank goodness she's not a virgin.

Afterwards, he remembered to look at her. Over the surface of the river, only her head was visible. She was staring at the banks, or the trees, or the sky, the haze of light. He wanted to speak to her, to say the right thing, the kind thing. The words wouldn't come. He felt depleted, exhausted. He wanted to lie down somewhere. He wanted her to go away.

Finally, he said, "I'm sorry if it was too quick."

She didn't move. Tears gathered in her eyes.

"It happens sometimes. The first time." You're babbling like a fool, he told himself. "When I want someone too much."

"What will you tell Lali?" she asked.

He touched her chin, lifted her head, tried to make her look at him. "Nothing. You know that."

What had he done? His wife's *sister*.

They swam to the shore and stretched out on a patch of dry grass. Around them, the ground was moist, spongy, smelling of decay. She tugged the hem of her dripping dress over her thighs, stretched her arms above her head. Her inner arms looked soft and damp, paler than the rest of her. Her dress began to dry unevenly, mottling into different shades of pink. Pinpricks of sunlight darted over the river and disappeared into moss-covered rocks. He contemplated her— nothing she did or said could distract him from the beauty of her face and skin.

They lay without speaking for a long time. A few meters away, trees he could not name huddled together. He thought of the campaign, the travels and meetings and speeches and exhaustion, but there was also this—the spaces between campaign events, the strange wayward beauty of these islands, this jungle and river, this woman beside him, all these places he had never seen.

He drifted in and out of sleep. At some point, more from solicitude than passion, he ran his hand along her inner thigh, then rested it between her legs. She tensed. He brought his finger to her lips. Cautiously, she licked it. To his surprise, she turned and pressed her mouth against his.

She pulled back her head, eyes closed. He kissed each of her eyelids.

Again he made love to her.

When it was over, she lay on the grass, passive beneath him, eyes open, unblinking, staring at something over his shoulder. He wanted to turn around, to see the sky, the light, whatever had captured her attention, taken her away from him.

He rested on her, mouth against her shoulder.

"You're heavy," she whispered.

He lifted himself.

"No." She was out of breath. "Stay there."

He allowed his weight to press onto her. On her neck, he smelled a trace of the oils from Lola Bea's casket, and in flashes of image and sensation he remembered the skeletal face and open mouth and this smell as he touched her, and the soft cold arm. He thought of all the wakes he had been to, and all he would have to attend, sometimes three, four wakes in an evening when he was campaigning. People expected it, votes were won at wakes, and you couldn't run for political office and not make the rounds of wakes. Weddings and baptisms needed invitations, but anyone could go to a wake; there were food and drinks and lots of people to talk to. He breathed rapidly through his mouth. I can't keep looking at dead bodies, he thought. It's going to get worse and worse.

The odor grew stronger, more pungent. He rolled off Pilar. A moment later, afraid that he had frightened her, he turned to his side and wrapped an arm around her waist. She turned her head away from him and faced the river.

He caressed her hip. Strong, compact, curved. The strangeness of her. This unsuspected body, beneath the familiar face.

In a dreamy voice, she asked, "What do you think he meant, my father?"

He kissed her shoulder. "About what?"

"People from the same side of the river."

The smell was gone. He smiled. "I can't think clearly right now."

People build lives again, he told himself. Maybe this was a beginning. Love, or the part of himself that had loved, his youth—something had to remain.

A meter away from her head, a yellow-green dragonfly hovered over a rock, its wings shimmering in the sun. He stared at it, mesmerized, as though he had never seen a dragonfly before. The heat and dampness on his skin, those fragile wings, the curve of her hip—every detail of the ordinary world seemed magical.

She said, "I think there's a reason for taboos like this."

"Like what?"

"Like not sleeping with your wife's sister."

He forced a laugh, but removed his arm from her waist.

"Because that's what it means, no? People from the same side of the river?"

A pause. "What do you want me to say, Pilar? That I'm sorry? I'm not sorry. I'm happy." But the sun was shrinking, the river receding. He became aware of an irritation on his skin, where his stomach had rubbed against hers.

"I read about it, before coming here," she said.

"*Read* about it?"

"Incest—"

"This isn't incest, for God's sake!" he said.

"So we know who belongs to whom, you know? So we don't get confused."

"What are you talking about?" His voice sounded hollow. He was furious at her for speaking, for puncturing his pleasure. "You want to know what I think? Why people on the same side of the river shouldn't marry? Because they get tired of each other. Because they're so used to seeing each other, smelling each other, hearing each other, that they don't want to make love to each other at all. That's what happens when you live with someone, Pilar. That's the real taboo."

Her eyes widened as he spoke. Long, unmanicured fingers circled her throat. When he stopped talking, she said, "You know this is wrong."

"Why? It's finished between Lali and me. You know that."

"She told me it was okay," Pilar said, wary, watching his face.

He sat up. "What are you saying?"

"She said I should come to you. She told me it was okay."

"She asked you to come to me?"

She didn't answer.

"Better you than someone else? Is that what she said?"

She bit her lip. Defiantly she told him, "She said you shouldn't be alone."

He stood. Anger pulsed from his head to his chest, then settled, tight and concentrated, in the pit of his stomach. He stared down at her. He wanted to spit. "She sent you here, knowing this would happen?"

She picked up her panties, slid them up her legs. Goosebumps marred her arms and thighs. She reached behind her, under her dress, to fasten her bra.

"I'm sorry," she said. "I shouldn't have said anything."

She was shaking. Even in his anger, his heart went out to her. He wanted to take her in his arms. Naked, hands on hips, he faced the sun. He wanted heat and water to pour through him, to wash away her words and face, to make him forget this had happened.

He heard movement. From behind, hesitantly, she wrapped her arms around him. Her breasts pressed against his back.

Nothing to say. He had gone too far. And she was needy, like every woman he had made love to for the first time. He untangled her arms from his waist and turned to her. Her beauty startled him. That golden skin, those black eyes. She crossed her arms over her chest.

He grasped her shoulders and pushed her to her knees. With one hand, he held the back of her head. She didn't resist. He tightened his grip.

Near the end of the war, his grandmother had told him, a Japanese officer had entered their house and told Arturo's mother, who was only fifteen at the time, to sew the button on his fly. He unbuttoned his pants—the Japanese used buttons, not zippers, his grandmother said—and removed them. His underwear looked like a diaper, and he had short legs. He told Marilou to kneel in front of him. The terrified maids called for his grandmother, who ran into the room, saw her teenage daughter kneeling, head bent, needle in her hand. The older woman grabbed the pants and knelt in front of the officer. I'll do it, she told him, trembling because the beheadings had already begun, those Japanese officers could get angry so quickly, and her daughter shouldn't stay in the room. They were lucky, she told Arturo—this Japanese was one of the good ones. He allowed Marilou to leave the room. Her mother knelt and sewed in her place. Decades later, when Marilou grew up and became a mother, she told Arturo: We wanted the Americans to win because we saw them swim in the river. They were tall and handsome, and the Japanese weren't. All the girls spied on them from the windows, and we prayed the Americans would win.

He released Pilar, knelt in front of her. Tears in her eyes again. He told her he was sorry. She touched his cheek. He didn't know what was happening. None of this made sense. He only knew that he wanted her, wanted above all to be good to her, but he didn't know if he was capable of goodness. He wanted to stretch her out on the grass and tell her stories about the boy he had been.

"Hold me," she said.

The urgency in her voice dismayed him.

She guided him to the ground beside her. Blades of prickly grass scratched his back. From between the blades, mud moistened his skin. She leaned over him, and he tightened his arms around her. They clung to each other, her cheek against his. They didn't move.

Later, when they were dressed, she said: "Don't tell Lali." The pink dress, crumpled and stained, but almost dry, stuck to her body.

"I thought she wanted this," he said.

"Promise me."

"You know I won't say anything."

"This isn't for Lali," she said.

They walked hand in hand through the jungle. They had nothing to say to each other. Late afternoon light slanted over the jungle, softening the heat. In bushes and branches, birds or beasts rustled and fluttered. Shadows swung across her face.

"Can you hear it?" he asked her.

The fading rush of the river, a bird's shrill cry.

He remembered her wet breasts beneath the pink dress, the moistness inside her, the sun and water warming, and then cooling, his naked body. Magic is physical—his old nanny was right. He felt a happiness that he wanted to believe was love. The feast of St. Lazarus, Pilar had told him, and anyone who touched water would catch a terrible disease. It's here, he thought, and suddenly he was a child again, the world immense and so full of mysteries he wanted only to lie down and hide from it in this woman's arms.

Chapter Six

A Man Without Consequences

I forgot how perfume cannot obliterate.

I forgot children softening harsh wool with thin fingers in exchange for broken rice kernels

I forgot discovering the limited utility of calm seas.

—Eileen R. Tabios, "Pilipinx"

LALI

The knife came down on the neck, partially severing the head. Lali slammed the blade down again. The swing started from her shoulders, not her wrists. You need the whole arm, Filomena told her. The cook was leaning against the sink, watching her.

Lali gripped the wooden handle. She needed to learn. No one had ever taught her these things. She struck down again. The knife missed the chicken's neck, and the edge of her hand sank into cold flesh.

"Enough, Señorita!" Filomena's warm hands pried the knife away.

From high windows, sunlight slanted into the room. Lali scanned the glass for a glimpse of the sun. Something was dangling from the ceiling. A garland of garlic, the small white heads threaded together like flowers, nailed to the ceiling just over the window.

Lali wiped her hands on a kitchen towel. "*Manang*, nothing will happen to my baby." She spoke with a confidence she didn't feel. Her own grandmother, each time she was pregnant, had worn a necklace of garlic to bed every night, afraid the winged torso of a *manananggal* would insert a needle into her stomach and suck out her baby while she slept.

"Better to be safe, Señorita," Filomena said. With several expert movements, she hacked the chicken into pieces. Cooking was her gift from God, she had told Lali. We all have a gift, but most people forget they have to use it for His glory, not our own. That's why people become sad, or don't succeed, or are unhappy even if they do. It's all for nothing if it isn't for Him.

Filomena washed the chicken pieces in the sink, folded a clean kitchen towel over them, and set the bundle on the counter. As she leaned over to sponge the table, her large belly touched the edge of the table. She was almost obese, but Lali didn't dare tell her. Instead she said, "You have such a pretty face, *manang*."

The cook's broad face softened with pleasure, as Lali knew it would. No one in her family was pretty, Filomena said. When her mother found out she was pregnant, she had cut out pictures of movie stars from magazines and taped the photos all over the walls. Elizabeth Taylor, Susan Roces, Marilyn Monroe—Filomena's mother gazed at them for hours every day, all throughout her pregnancy, to make her baby beautiful, in case it was a girl. The beauty in those photos entered her eyes and went down to her stomach and into the fetus, and that was how Filomena became pretty.

"It's good to be pretty," Lali told her now. "It's the best thing you can give a girl. Then all the men will want to marry you."

"No one wanted to marry me. I'm too dark! God made me pretty, but he wanted to make sure I didn't become conceited!"

Filomena began laughing, low-pitched peals that tumbled into the room. She sat at the table, shoulders shaking. Lali watched her, bewildered by the cook's merriment but also charmed by it. She began to laugh, too.

The kitchen door swung open. Marilou strode into the room, a bright yellow scarf around her neck. Filomena hurried to the sink. Lali sat down, crossed her arms. Her mother-in-law often complained that Lali didn't know how to keep a proper distance from the servants. All those years in the States, she had heard Marilou tell Arturo—how can you expect the maids to respect her? She drinks coffee with them every morning. She sits in the kitchen and *chats* with them.

Now, Marilou lifted one eyebrow and said, "Have you heard from Arturo?"

Lali hesitated. "He's still in the province."

"And Pilar is still with him?"

"I was the one who told her to go, *Tita*. I couldn't go myself."

Marilou waved a red-nailed finger in the air. "Filomena, you have to stop this garlic business. The whole house smells like garlic. Nothing is going to happen to Señorito Arturo's baby."

From behind, the cook's shoulders stiffened. "Have patience, ma'am."

Marilou shifted her gaze to Lali. "You intend to let Pilar continue campaigning with Arturo? People are going to start talking, you know."

Filomena scrubbed dishes in the sink. From the set of the cook's shoulders and the tilt of her head, Lali knew she was straining to listen.

"People always talk," Lali said. "I ignore them."

Marilou stared at Lali's belly, then at her shoes, her dress, her hair. Finally, in a softer voice, she said: "You need new clothes, *hija*. Take my card and go to Rustan's." She lowered herself into a chair across from Lali. When Marilou spoke again, she sounded kind and almost despondent. "A woman should never let herself go. Even if she's pregnant."

Marilou had been beautiful, Lali knew. The photos were everywhere. A tinted one from her debutante ball, a few years after the war, her layered, rose-colored silk gown spread like petals around her as she sat on the floor.

"You know how men are," Marilou said.

Black-and-white images of Marilou as a young bride, voluptuous in a tight bodice and full skirt. A portrait taken on a trip to the Vatican, early in her marriage, her sharp features framed by a black lace veil, eyebrows arched, lips full and soft-looking. Marilou had spent more than half her life learning to attract men. Those skills were worthless now. Every society imposed a limit on a woman's desirability. In Manila, the cut-off date came early. Lali reached for her mother-in-law's hand and squeezed it lightly, sorry for her, and afraid for herself.

After their wedding, Arturo bought them a glass and stone house in a leafy gated subdivision in the midst of Manila's business district, far from Marilou and the row of wooden colonial mansions by the river. Now Lali drove back to that house, stood on her toes in the white-tiled bathroom, and reached for Arturo's comb on a shelf. She ran the tip of a fingernail across the plastic teeth, trying to find a strand of his hair. Nothing. He scoffed at her stories about witchcraft and magic, but he had removed every trace of himself from his things. She returned the comb to the shelf.

In her early teens, she had been an expert at stealing hairs from boys' combs. At parties in a friend's beach house, late at night, the girls huddled in a shed in the garden, watching her wrap paper around the hair, strike a match, and bring the flame to the paper. As the hair frizzled and crackled, Lali recited spells to bring back one girl's straying boyfriend, or to help another capture the attention of the boy she wanted. She never recited spells for herself. Bad luck, she knew. A maid had tried to teach her the incantations, which sounded like a mix of Latin, English, and several local dialects, but Lali never remembered the words. So she invented her own. *Let his heart burn and founder. Let him be yours forever and ever.*

In the bathroom mirror, just under her neckline, a drop of chicken blood stained her dress. She poured a few drops of hydrogen peroxide into a wet towel, rubbed it into the stain. The blood dissolved into a faint pink smear. Suddenly, she sensed someone standing behind her, just over her shoulder. She swung around.

No one.

The window was closed, the door locked from the inside. The fine hairs stood on her arms.

Papa, she whispered, although she wasn't sure it was him. With spirits she was never sure. She took another breath. Ghosts needed to be reassured, or they would continue to linger. Don't worry about me, Papa, she told the spirit. I know what I'm doing. I won't lose any of this.

She knew what it was like to be poorer than any of her friends. Those long years in San Francisco, that cramped, frightened life. Even now—not often, but enough to disturb her—her life felt like a balloon that a word or an act could puncture.

I'm not stupid, Papa. Don't worry. Pilar is a means, not a threat. An infatuation. Arturo will get over it. Where would I go if I left him? To a little apartment in some shabby neighborhood somewhere, one of those places Mama's sisters whispered about, where women who tried to be free end up regretting everything they've lost?

The presence, hovering over her. She couldn't be certain it was him.

Go away, she said gently. You don't belong here anymore.

The dead lingered, some people said, because they were looking for a way back to life, a crack they could slip through to take the place of the living. Lali didn't believe this. Her ghosts usually had something to tell her—a message or an instruction, words of consolation or, more rarely, regret. Other ghosts didn't know they were dead. For as long as she could remember, she had been aware of spirits. They were as real, and as distant, as the pedestrians she glimpsed through the tinted windows of her car. As soon as she entered someone's house for the first time, she located the ghosts—they had their favorite spots, near antique burial jars converted to plant-holders, or in little-used nooks or a study at the end of a long corridor. But some ghosts joined the family for dinner, or sat in an armchair in the middle of the living room, or lay at the foot of the bed while the children watched cartoons on television. She never pointed them out. Most people didn't want to know who lived with them. Besides, she didn't actually see ghosts—only felt and heard them—so she never knew for sure who they were.

She raised her head, looked around. The presence had disappeared. She made the sign of the cross.

She returned to her bedroom, changed into her short white dress and high-heeled sandals, fastened pearl earrings and a pearl necklace. In the full-length mirror, she inspected herself. Her legs and arms still looked slender and toned, and pregnancy had released a radiance in her complexion. But no one noticed. Arturo didn't notice. For the first time that day, she tried to imagine him. Some forsaken island, a bedroom borrowed from one of his handlers, an old wooden bed.

She couldn't imagine Pilar.

She bent forward, hair falling over her face toward the floor. Starting from the scalp, she brushed her hair, over and over again, until her scalp stung.

Let him have Pilar. Let him have her completely, go through her, discard her. That was the only way for him to get over her. Pilar could never hold on to him. He would never fall in love with Pilar. Lali knew his type—dusky, pouting, paper-thin models, or those Australian girls with Amazon bodies and golden hair who sometimes appeared in magazine photos, seated a row or two behind Arturo, or standing at the edge of a group. Arturo's tastes were predictable. He liked women who made other men jealous.

And he had been proud of her. When they walked into a party, he watched other men look at her. My wife, he told them, both acknowledging and mocking their desire, as he did when he gave dinner guests a tour of the house, the tennis court, the swimming pool, the garage with his sports cars. Visitors struggled to seem unimpressed, and Arturo's self-deprecating commentary discouraged any compliments. Be careful, she told him. People won't forgive you. He laughed away her warnings.

In a dark, air-conditioned room, near the edge of a king-sized bed, Lali's mother lay under a blanket. Only her head was visible, white hair in wisps around her face. Outside, the sun was shining, but the curtains were drawn and lamplight carved shadows into her face. Next to the bed was a beige arm-chair. Across the room, on a matching armchair, a plump young nurse was sleeping, head bent to the side.

Lali sat on the bed and kissed her mother's forehead.

"*Hija*," the older woman whispered.

All that remained of her mother's beauty was the heart-shaped contour of her face, softened now around the edges, and the almond-slanted eyes. She spent her days in her bedroom—with the curtains always drawn—watching television, waiting for the brief visits from her daughters, Arturo, and the parish priest. Marilou never visited her—old people depressed her, Marilou said, although the two women were almost the same age.

Her mother gave Lali a weak smile. "How's my grandchild?" she asked.

"Kicking, Ma." Lali pressed her mother's hand against her stomach. She wanted to warm those bony fingers, rub some energy into them, some life.

Her mother withdrew her hand. "I had a dream last night."

"Tell me about it," Lali said kindly. She was thinking: How can she live like this? How can she stand it?

"A very powerful dream." Her mother's expression was guarded.

What was it about life, Lali thought, that made most people cling to it, even when all pleasure or possibility of pleasure was gone? Her mother numbed herself with tranquilizers. It was relatively early in the day—she wasn't slurring yet.

"It was a dream about Pilar," her mother said. "She was in a field. Flowers blooming all around her. And more flowers coming out of the ground. She lay down and was covered with petals."

Lali forced a smile.

"Why hasn't Pilar come to see me?" her mother asked plaintively.

"She's campaigning, Ma. I told you."

"It's dangerous in the province."

"You can't go on like this, Mama, without daylight. Staying in bed all the time. We have to open the curtains, let in some fresh air."

Her mother gestured at the armchair. "He's here, you know. Your father."

Lali lowered her eyes. She tried to feel his presence.

Ghosts were so personal. She couldn't feel her mother's ghosts, and her mother would never feel hers.

"And your dream," Lali said briskly. "What else was there?"

"He doesn't want me to tell you."

"Of course he does." Her smile hurt her cheeks. "Papa always told me everything. I'm the strong one, remember?"

"Pilar's life is opening. Finally. Everything is opening for her now. Something is blossoming inside her."

Lali stopped smiling. In a soft, tight voice she said, "I'm the one who's pregnant, Mama."

"She's opening inside, like a flower."

Lali stood up. "Why are you doing this?"

Her mother's eyes were hard. "You got what you wanted," she snapped.

"What are you talking about?" Lali asked, hurt and confused by her mother's hostility.

"The life you wanted."

"You should be grateful, Mama!"

Across the room, the nurse opened her eyes. She struggled out of the armchair. "Ma'am, ma'am," she told Lali. "Please don't upset your mother."

"You should be grateful you have a home here," Lali told her mother. "Arturo gave us a home. This room, your nurses, everything."

"I'm grateful! Is that enough?" Her mother reached for a glass of water on the bedside table. Her hand shook. The nurse sat beside her, brought the glass to her lips. "Don't you wake up at night, Lali, and ask yourself what your father would have wanted?"

"We both know what Papa wanted!"

"After everything he did for us."

"How about what *I* did for us, Mama? Do you ever think about that?"

"Please, ma'am," the nurse told Lali. "Please have pity. Her blood pressure will go up."

"Stay in your bed, then, Mama. But I'm warning you—people lose patience."

She wanted to run. Instead, she walked slowly out of the room. Her mother's eyes seared her back. Outside, she leaned against the wall of the corridor, until her heartbeat became almost imperceptible again. Did even her mother blame her for marrying Arturo? She told herself: Don't think of Mama, don't think of Arturo, forget Pilar. She repeated to herself something her father may have taught her, one of the many things she had attributed to him after his death, memories or fictions or platitudes constructed like walls to prevent her from feeling the extent of her loss: You're strong, Lali. You can afford to be generous.

She returned to her mother's bedroom, sat on the bed, faced the television. Without talking to each other, Lali, her mother, and the nurse watched soap-opera actresses gesturing and talking.

Maybe I was wrong, Lali thought. Maybe I miscalculated. But I won't let Pilar destroy my life.

Pilar's phone rang sixteen times, then disconnected. Lali dialed Arturo's private office number. His warm, polite voice on the answering machine. She dialed his number three more times, and each time hung up just before the end of his message.

Stop this, she told herself.

There was only one way to stop thinking about Arturo.

She had done it before, with other men.

She drove to an upscale shopping mall, knowing exactly what she was looking for. Inside, hundreds of people streamed through the aisles, talking and laughing. Few could afford the imported goods on display, but the air-conditioning and pop music were free, the shop windows interesting, the food stalls numerous and cheap. She scanned the crowds.

At last she saw him. Near the plastic palm tree in the center of an aisle, a head taller than anyone else, the odd Caucasian in a sea of Asians. He had long reddish hair tied in a ponytail, pale skin, slanted eyes beneath thick eyebrows. He wore clean jeans and a pressed blue T-shirt, yet he seemed gangly among the crowds of well-groomed Filipinos, most of whom were wearing local versions of the latest Western fashions. He appealed to her. He looked gentle and lost, so far from anything and anyone that resembled him. This could work, she thought. A stranger, a transient, a man without consequences.

He was walking away, a head floating above the crowd. She

hurried after him. When she reached him, she touched his shirtsleeve. "Excuse me, please?"

He turned to her. Beneath thin lashes, his eyes were a disconcerting black. The intelligence in his face pleased her. Several red hairs curled over the neckline of his T-shirt. He was very thin, with the slightly haunted look of a white man who had spent too many years traveling around Asia.

He glanced at her round stomach. "Sorry?"

She drew a breath. Long ago, for a month after a painful breakup, she had picked up men and slept with each of them once. Each stranger helped her erase the man she needed to forget. It had to be a stranger, someone she would never see again. You can do it, she told herself now. Out loud she said: "I have to ask you something. Do you mind? I know a place where we can have very good coffee."

A small vertical crease appeared between his eyebrows. He seemed taken aback by her forwardness, but also, perhaps, intrigued by it. It was lonely, she knew, to be a foreigner like him in Manila.

He smiled—a wide smile that illuminated his face. "A quick cup?"

Her heart lifted. He followed her up an escalator, then another, to the top floor. She sauntered slightly ahead of him through the crowd, past small restaurants and stands selling barbecued pork, hamburgers, sweet pizza, pastries. With shy, curious smiles, young women looked past her toward him.

At the coffee shop, two armed security guards framed the entrance. She gestured at a small, wrought-iron table. He sat down before she did, bending his long legs and turning them sideward. He seemed uncomfortable in a seat that had been designed for much shorter people. In silence they examined the menu. A young man wearing a black beret and a long black apron came and took their orders.

After the waiter left, she fixed a smile and held out her hand. "I'm Lali."

He clutched her hand and didn't let it go. "David."

Her hand tensed in his. He tightened his grip. Be careful, she told herself. "Are you visiting the country?" she asked, trying to keep her voice light.

His grip relaxed. "I've been here two years."

"That's long." She withdrew her hand. To her relief, he didn't try to hold on to it. "Are you working here?"

One side of his mouth curled upward. He had interesting eyes, thoughtful and probing. "To tell the truth, I don't know why I'm here. Fate, I suppose. Or laziness. I was in Malaysia for years. Penang. Have you been to Penang?"

She shook her head. He spoke softly, yet his accent and gestures seemed so loud, so American.

"The first time I traveled out of North America," he said, "it was to Penang. I was on a beach there. I had never seen anything so beautiful. I remember thinking: if this were a woman, I'd reach out and make love to her."

He didn't look like someone who reached out to women, much less made love to anyone on a beach. But there was an exoticism about him, and an intensity. She relaxed into her body, curious to know what she was feeling. Did he want her? If he did, there would be an answer inside her—some movement of repulsion, or attraction. She couldn't feel anything.

The waiter brought two cups of coffee, two cinnamon rolls and foil-wrapped rectangles of butter. He picked up a roll, buttered it. "What did you want to ask me?"

His gaze touched hers. A vulnerability in his eyes, cracking the surface. He made her feel vulnerable, too. Suddenly, she no longer wanted to flirt with him. She didn't want to lie.

"I think my husband's falling in love with my sister."

He looked embarrassed. "I'm sorry," he said at last.

"I'm joking." She felt mortified.

He didn't speak.

Finally, she asked, "What are you doing in Manila?"

He shifted in his seat, glanced at the exit. "I came here before the revolution," he said awkwardly. "Then I stayed to cover it. The other journalists left. I didn't. I became fascinated by the country. The psychic healers, for example."

"You have to be careful. There are a lot of fakes."

Almost imperceptibly, he recoiled.

I should leave, she thought. This is a mistake. The only one who can make me feel better about Arturo is Arturo.

He broke off a piece of cinnamon roll. He glanced at her stomach, and concern flicked across his face. "A newspaper editor in New York told me that no one wants to read about this country. It's not sexy anymore. The revolution's over. But I'm doing an article on paramilitary groups. I'm going down south one of these days. Have you heard of the massacre in that village?"

"There are so many massacres that I lose track."

"You lose *track*?" He set the knife on his empty plate. "Violence is so taken for granted in this country. I can't understand it."

"What don't you understand?"

"How nice people, people with such a strong mystic tradition, can be so brutal. Where does that come from?"

"It's just like that. Each reinforces the other." Reddish strands fell away from his ponytail and clung to his neck. She hoped no one she knew would see them. She was sorry she had told him about Arturo and Pilar. "I read that somewhere," she said, "or someone told me. I don't remember. People become spiritual because of the violence, and vice versa." She gave a half-smile. "You look very skeptical."

"I'm just tired." He told her he had come here amazed by what was happening. A bloodless revolution. People on the streets, nuns leading the crowds, young girls putting flowers into the barrels of soldiers' guns. It was extraordinary, he said. He should have left the next day. Or the next week. Later, it was too late.

She sipped her coffee, lukewarm now. He was just another foreigner, thinking he understood the country. She had met people like him at embassy parties—not the diplomats, but the outer fringes of the embassy guest list, the stringers and long-term expatriates. She missed Arturo, his irony and easy elegance.

"Then the revolution was over, and nothing had changed," David said. "The rich will never give up their hold on this country. Ninety percent of the people are just getting poorer."

She wished he would stop talking about politics. So many foreigners came here and talked about politics, the revolution, the dictator, her father. Politics tired her. She considered telling him she was more interested in the results of politics—money, power, a home no one could take away from her. But he would misinterpret that, too.

"You have to try to understand," she said. "Politics here is personal. People think of their families, their friends, their relationships. Those are the things that matter in a life. Very few people are willing to sacrifice that to some abstract cause."

"Some people did."

My father, for example, she thought, and look what happened to him. Look what happened to *us*. He isn't an example. Or only an example to do the contrary.

David leaned across the table. "Let me see your face. You look so familiar."

His hand, large and warm, cupped her cheek. Her blood seemed to rush to the surface, where his skin touched hers. Here we are, she thought. At last. With the slightest movement, she pressed her cheek into the curve of his fingers. A tremor went through her.

He tapped the mole on the side of her mouth. "You know

what they would do to you if they arrested you?" He reached into his back pocket, unfolded a newspaper clipping on the table. "I saw this in the paper. It's how the police identified members of the Communist Party, after they arrested half the village and locked them up in a schoolroom." He began to read: "*Mole on the chin—Communist lecturer.*"

Heat on her cheek, where his skin had touched hers. "I know," she said, flustered. "Everyone knows."

"You think people can be tried for crimes based on *moles*?"

"Of course not. But I don't find it ridiculous. Marks on bodies are important."

"They killed the ones with the wrong *marks*." He folded the article and inserted it into his pocket, asked for the bill. He pushed his chair away from the table, at an angle, and twisted his torso to the side, as though to put as much distance as possible between them without having to leave the table.

Her cheek still felt flushed. "What do you want to hear?" She tried to speak gently. "You foreign journalists are parachuted in here. You understand so little, but then you write your long articles, which the whole world believes."

"You should come with me, then."

"You don't recognize what you don't know."

"Come with me," he said.

"Where?"

"To the south. To see those people. The ones who survived the massacre."

"I can't do that."

The waiter set the bill on the table. David studied it, then counted out peso bills and coins for half the total. She opened her handbag and wallet, set a few bills on the table, surprised and humiliated that he hadn't offered to pay for her.

That wide smile again, transforming his face. He looked wonderful when he smiled. "Don't look at me like that," he said. "*You* invited me."

She gazed into his eyes, startling black against pale skin. "I could interpret for you," she said slowly. "If I go."

If she went away, maybe Arturo would worry about her again. Maybe he would miss her.

"You speak the dialect?" he asked.

"I'm not saying I'm going. But my mother's family is from there."

David was looking around the room, his attention ebbing. She had to bring him back to her. "Also someone I knew, long ago. An ex-boyfriend. Miguel. He disappeared near that village."

His eyes returned to her.

"A shipwreck. They never found his body. But some people think they've seen him."

"A ghost?"

"No. I don't know. Sometimes I like to think that maybe he just said—enough. That he didn't want to go back to Manila, the old life, all the stress and the business and his family. Sometimes I imagine that he lives in a hut by the sea and walks naked along the beach at night, when he thinks no one can see him. We used to do that."

He glanced at her lips.

"I've always thought I should go there," she said.

He had nice forearms. Too white for her taste, but lean and muscled, despite his thinness. Men didn't realize how attractive forearms could be. And those reddish hairs. Not many. Just enough. She had never slept with a redhead. She wondered what the rest of his body looked like. She imagined red hairs curling across his chest, across his lower belly. She imagined his thighs. Even men as thin as David sometimes had muscular thighs and buttocks. A man's body could be so surprising. Men who looked thin with their clothes on could be either flabby or muscled when they removed their shirts and trousers. Often, it was impossible to know what you would find.

"He was in love with you?"

"At one point," she said. "It's hard to know now. He got married. I know he loved his wife."

Miguel had called her in tears, the night before his wedding.

"And you loved him?"

"He was the kindest man I ever met. And one of the most beautiful. Green eyes, golden skin."

It was irresistible for a woman—a man's attention, like that. His pleasure in her presence. She had been so happy with him. Then it became suffocating.

She said: "He used to tell me—we were teenagers—that he wanted to spend the next ten years developing his sensibility, learning about himself. But you know how it is here. He had to take over his father's business. He said no one would ever give him money for wanting to become a good man."

With several brusque movements, he stood up. His thigh hit the table. "I have to hurry. I'm sorry." With a wry smile, he offered his hand.

Confused, she shook it.

"It was nice meeting you," he said.

He strode down the aisle and didn't turn back. She stared at the floor. Her thighs felt heavy and damp against the seat. She imagined herself pregnant for the rest of her life, until her hair turned white and no man ever wanted her again.

Large pale fingers, the lower segments flecked with red hairs, touched the table. He squatted until his eyes were almost level with hers. "Why don't you come?"

She didn't hide her pleasure.

"I'm meeting someone called Sister Esperanza," he said. "I've been tracking her for years. She's in Manila now."

"I try to avoid nuns. I spent twelve years in a convent school."

The dimple appeared again, illuminating his face. "She isn't really a nun. A psychic, very powerful. People say she sees everything that will happen. She sees inside people."

"How horrible."

He laughed, rocked back on his heels. She was aware that people were watching them. Young women stared openly at him. A white man, young, not unattractive, was always desirable. Yet he was lonely. She was certain. She couldn't feel a woman in him.

"You can come with me," he said.

She reached for her bag and stood. "Let's go," she said, with that wild swing of anticipation she hadn't expected to feel again.

He told her he needed to stop by his house, and directed her to a row of modest townhouses near the river. She locked her car, glanced up and down the dark, trash-strewn street. It seemed like a dead end. No moving shadows, no headlights. A few old cars hugged the curb.

They walked up a path and climbed several steps to the front door—these newer buildings along the river had been built several feet above the ground to protect them from flooding. He fumbled with the keys, pressed his shoulder against the door, shoved it open.

She stepped inside. A white room, almost empty. No ghosts. A vague odor of incense and mold floating over the smells of the river. A low-watt lightbulb dangled from the ceiling. On the floor, two batik-covered cushions and, tacked on the wall, a silk painting of a scene from the Mahabharata. A kitchenette had been built in a corner of the room: a white cabinet on the wall, a sink, a portable two-burner stove on top of a small fridge.

"There's almost nothing here," she said.

"I've been trying to give everything away. One by one, everything I own."

She sat on a cushion and stared up at him, imagining the

body beneath the clothes. Lean but not muscled, she decided. Not skinny, either. He would look better naked. Most men did.

"Do you want to take anything from here?" he asked.

"Not really."

Not even a bed. No women, then. She was right. But where did he sleep?

"I'm leaving. I've been in Asia too long." He sat on the floor, facing her. He bent his legs, pulled them toward his chest. "When everything's gone, I'll go back to the States, see my family."

"You have a family?" Unexpectedly, this hurt her.

"My parents, that's all."

He stretched his legs. The tip of a large, black-socked foot brushed against her ankle. Her small feet, strapped into high-heeled sandals, looked pale and fragile next to his. Fear lifted its cold head inside her. If anything happened, she would never be able to describe him. His features were too bland. A tall white man, handsome when he smiled. That was all. He would cut off the ponytail, dye the hair and eyebrows. They would never find him.

"Close your eyes," he said.

She told herself: Do whatever he wants. "What do you feel in this room?" he asked.

Even with her eyes closed, the room felt bare. He seemed to have drained all life from it. Usually, when she entered a man's room for the first time, the air felt charged with his smells and a particular masculine energy. Even a hotel room, after a few hours, became weighted with a man's presence, arousing her as she stepped through the doorway. But she couldn't feel a man in this room. Was that a sign of peace? Or absence? She knew nothing about him. That, too, was new. Here, in the city of her birth, everyone existed in context. She rarely met anyone who didn't know who she was, who her father was, who her husband was.

"Do you hear it?" he asked. "Someone's praying."

She waited.

"*Jesus, save me*—again and again," he said. "Listen well."

A tightening in her chest. Religious fanatics—they were the most dangerous. She glanced at the door, the windows, any possible escape from this room. "I heard it the first night I slept here," he said. "A woman's voice."

She counted the steps to the door, calculating how quickly she could get away from him.

What had she been thinking, coming here?

"*Make me a channel for your love*," he said. "I can't get it out of my head. Do you hear anything?"

She told herself she could handle this. She had spent so much of her adult life defusing intrigues and lies. He was only a man, eroded by heat and loneliness and the distance from anyone who understood him.

"You don't hear it, then." Humor had returned to his voice, calming her. "You don't believe me, do you?"

"Ghosts are so personal," she murmured.

He smiled. His nose was wide, his eyes slanted. He had been in Asia so long that, from some angles, he had even begun to look Asian.

"Let me show you something, Lali."

He led her to a small windowless room, not much larger than a walk-in closet. He switched on the light. Unframed photographs and newspaper clippings plastered the walls. In front of her, almost level with her head, a glossy black and white photograph showed an impassive young man with long hair and a headband. His torso was bare; tattoos snaked across his chest and arms. He held up a man's decapitated head.

Her stomach cramped.

"Vigilantes," David said, without inflection. "The Church condones them."

She touched her belly, thinking about what Filomena had

said—images entered through a pregnant woman's eyes and into her baby. She averted her gaze.

"You have to look." He pointed at another photograph. Two men with machetes, kneeling beside a shrouded figure stretched out on the ground, holding up the amulets around their necks. Again she looked away before she could see the details. "The Soldiers of Christ," David said. "That's what they call themselves."

"This is sick."

"They're running wild. Killing and slashing and wearing amulets to protect themselves. Politicians support them. Anti-Communist crusaders, they say. Look." He pointed to another photo, in color. She glimpsed bodies, ashen and bloodied, lying side by side. She forced her gaze away. Her head was hurting. "This was the massacre in that village," he said. "You know why it happened?"

She shook her head. She didn't want him to see how upset she was. Get out of here, she told herself. She couldn't move.

"The paramilitaries said the village was feeding rebels. So they set up checkpoints into the village, used armed patrols, intimidation. The village was terrorized. And one day, they went in, and most of the young men weren't around. They thought they had gone to the mountains to join the rebels. So they lined up those who remained and shot them. So many mystics in this country, and yet—"

"It's disgusting to put up photos like these."

"I'm trying to understand," he said. "The bishop says these people are just trying to protect themselves. He said these men—look at their faces, Lali—are helping to keep the peace. And the police superintendent in the nearest town—look, I have a picture."

"I don't want your pictures."

"Look." He gestured at another photograph. A large wooden desk, empty except for three telephones. On the wall behind it was a poster of the new president, hands on her lap, smiling. "That's the police superintendent's office. He wouldn't let me take his picture. He said vigilante groups should go forth and multiply. He said they're the only ones brave enough to fight off the Communist rebels. Even the president supports them. It's all part of your tradition of warlords and private armies."

"You can leave if you don't like it here. You can go back to the States."

"*Leave if you don't like it here*—that's what people always say when it's impossible to defend something." His voice softened. "I *will* leave. But first I want to see those people. A few survived. The men never came back. They'd be killed if they ever returned."

"There are a hundred things like that in the papers, every week."

"And you don't care?"

"Of course I do. But what am I supposed to do?"

"I want to understand," he said. "I see women like you, at parties—beautiful women, with expensive jewelry and convent-school accents and diplomas from Western universities. And champagne flowing, and your amazing homes in those so-called villages, and your maids in white aprons, and your well-mannered children. Everyone so charming, and so civilized. And no one seems to see. The other life, the killings, the mutilation, the poverty."

"We know it better than you do," she said.

"Explain it to me."

"Do you think displaying articles and photos like this will change anything? Do you think talking will change anything?"

"I stayed here because I wanted to understand what makes people do these things. This violence. I wanted to understand, from the inside." He began to raise his hand toward a group of images, then let it fall.

She watched his fingers. She was retreating from him, into herself. The smells of the river entered the room, bringing her back to the long afternoons of her childhood when she watched the river rising, and mornings when she awoke to find silver-gray water covering the garden and ground floor of their house. The water stayed there, for days or weeks. The house-boys paddled canoes through flooded streets to search for food. She and Pilar sat on the staircase and went fishing inside their house. Nothing else to do. No running water, no electricity, no school for weeks, everyone waiting for something to happen. He would never understand this. And later, the coups d'état. Early-morning phone calls, her mother ushering her, Pilar, and the maids into the pantry, locking the door, waiting for soldiers or rebels to break into the house. And in school, the nuns gathered the pretty young students and told them: If the rebels come into your home and try to touch you, it is God's will that you don't resist. It's not a sin to let them do what they want with you.

Survival trumped virtue—even the nuns understood this.

"Look at this," David said. "These women were hanged."

She had learned early not to see. She turned away from the children begging in the street, the front-page photos in tabloids, the shadows near the entrances to restaurants or five-star hotels.

"One of them was pregnant," David continued.

He touched the edge of the photograph. This time she looked at his finger, not the image.

"How do people rationalize that?" he asked. "People here are so loving, so kind."

Light kicks in her belly. Seven months. The baby could survive outside her now. She tried to imagine the fetus floating in her belly. But she couldn't imagine it at all. This was a punishment, she knew. Early in the pregnancy, she had wanted it to disappear—one long, bleak night when Arturo was away and

the wind and rain pounded the window. She lay in bed, nauseous, unable to sleep, perspiring despite the air-conditioner.
She couldn't stand to have her body vampirized by another
being, to allow that strangeness to take shape within her, alien-
ating Arturo. If she had to choose between Arturo and this
pregnancy, she would choose Arturo. For a few minutes, she
began to think about how to end the pregnancy. In the morning, she knelt beside her bed, pressed her forehead against the
mattress and prayed for forgiveness—or rather, for the absence
of punishment. She was horrified by her thoughts of the night
before, and terrified by the idea of a handicapped baby. The
murderous thoughts never came back, but all images of the
baby, good and bad, disappeared as well. She could feel it kick,
and that was all. No connection. That was her punishment.

"And there were nuns," David was saying. "Tortured for
days."

His photos excited her. The intensity of them. She couldn't
tell him this. It was possible to imagine killing. It was only a
narrowing of perspective, the shutting down of certain areas of
the mind and heart. The way one photo stops existing when
you look at another.

"The men thought they were Communist organizers," he
said. "When the nuns were released, their serenity amazed me.
They didn't break. I asked one of them about this, and she
said: 'I kept sending love, I kept praying for them. I knew they
were hurting themselves far more than they were hurting me.'"

"That's why they let them go," she whispered.

"What do you mean?"

"They couldn't break them, so what was the point of keeping them?"

That wariness in his eyes.

"We all have to move on," she said. "That's the main
thing—you move on, and you don't look back. You live for the
good things."

His large frame blocked the doorway. "And what do you call good?"

"The sun, a man's hand. Water over my body." He was shaking his head. She began to speak quickly, recklessly, determined to provoke him. "Food. Money. Beautiful houses, I don't know. Travel. Pretty clothes."

He was staring at her mouth again. "Come with me," he said. "We'll go down south together. You can look for that ex-boyfriend of yours."

"He's probably dead."

"You believe that?"

"I don't know. I suppose so. People say he comes to his wife in dreams." But he never came to her.

This is how you handle pain, Miguel had told her. You recognize you've hurt those who hurt you, so you don't get angry and you don't blame them. One fit of rage can destroy months, even years, of good intentions.

"Take something from here," David said. "It would be a favor—one less thing to keep me here."

Nothing kept him here. He could fly into this country and fly out, whenever he wanted.

"The woman I hear," he said, "the woman I imagine—she told me once that there's only one question we have to ask ourselves, in any situation: Am I loving? Then I come into this room and look at these photos, and the things I would like to believe in—that people are basically good, that there is some kind of God, or at least some spiritual order—all that falls apart. Yet somehow I think if I look deeply enough, if I keep looking, it will all come back together."

He gave an embarrassed smile. Their eyes met. She felt no desire for or from him. Shyly, he wrapped his arms around her. His embrace wasn't sexual. He was all angles and imperfections, but he had strong arms. A comforting body. Arturo and her other lovers worked out so hard that even naked they seemed clothed by muscle. But David was both bony and soft. He wasn't her type. This reassured her.

Only pain makes people permeable, Miguel had told her. Happiness is tight and hidden—it pulls us inside ourselves.

David's gentle hands on her lower back. How long had it been since anyone held her this way, with affection and no desire?

David looked down at her. She didn't want him to be her lover, and she didn't believe a man could be her friend, but his eyes were kind. No demands. No judgment. As though it were the most natural thing in the world for a pregnant stranger to be in this room, in his arms.

She pulled away. "Don't you have a girlfriend?"

A smile touched his lips. "People here think it's abnormal to live alone."

"No girlfriend, then?" He shook his head.

"No boyfriend, either?"

"I'm alone, Lali."

"You have that woman. The one you hear."

"She's only a voice."

She wanted to ask more questions, but stopped herself.

She followed him into the main room, which had the dangling lightbulb and batik cushions. The smells of the river floated toward her again. And from somewhere, a trace of kerosene.

In the kitchenette, he filled a kettle with water, set it over a burner, and turned the knob. He flicked a cigarette lighter and brought it to the burner. Blue flames cradled the base of the kettle. From the wall cabinet, he removed two white mugs. He had reduced his world to a few objects—two burners, a cabinet, a sink and small fridge, two floor cushions, a painting, photos taped to the walls. She had never met anyone who wanted so little. But emptiness was dangerous, she wanted to tell him—all this space for presences to fill.

The kettle whistled. He switched off the flame, poured hot water into the mugs and set them on the counter. It occurred to her that he had been sterilizing water, not making tea.

"Your turn," he said. "Talk to me."

She wondered what it would be like to knock down, one by one, the props of her own life, to follow this man to the south, to look for traces of Miguel, for the images David wanted to see. She had built her life on solidity—her body, Arturo's body, everything they owned or were capable of acquiring. Impossible to imagine a life without these, yet when she looked at David, he seemed peaceful.

No passion, though. And she couldn't imagine a life without passion.

"Are you okay?" he asked. She saw the concern in his eyes again, and imagined he was thinking about her pregnancy, perhaps even about what she had said, about her husband falling in love with her sister.

She should never have sent Pilar to Arturo. She should never have taken that risk.

"That nun you told me about," she said. "Will you take me to her?"

At the curb, she felt inside her bag for the car keys.
"We should walk," he told her. "It's not that far. We can't show up there in your Mercedes."

She unfastened her pearl necklace and earrings, tucked them into the bottom of her handbag, next to the colored buttons.

The street was dark, without sidewalks. In her heels, she tottered along the curb, past potholes and piles of garbage. She pressed one hand against her belly. At times the baby moved her, despite everything. The way it stopped kicking when she walked, the way it sensed movement through all those layers of flesh and fluid. She hoped it would be happy. She hoped it would always feel safe.

She felt the presence again, just behind her. She twisted her head to the side and glimpsed something—a face, perhaps, but half of it was missing or so scarred or bloodied she couldn't tell who or what it was.

"What's the matter?" he asked.

She shook her head. The face disappeared. She blew into the air.

"It's nothing," she said.

He led her to a busy avenue lined with hotels and restaurants. Cars with yellow headlights were stalled in traffic. Several meters ahead, under a street lamp, about a dozen adults and children squatted on newspapers on the pavement. Behind them, several women and two boys huddled over a trash can. Scavengers. They were all over the city now, rummaging through garbage cans in front of office buildings, restaurants, and department stores. Manila already had millions of residents, many of them in shantytowns, and thousands were arriving every week from the provinces.

She clutched her bag with both hands.

He stopped walking.

The livelihood program, she told him. Another government program gone wrong. Manila had too many scavengers and too much garbage, so the president's brother decided to put the two together—to use the scavengers for garbage collection. Large-scale recycling, the newspapers called it: scavengers would sift through garbage and collect cans, bottles, cartons, paper, and anything else that could be recycled, then sell them to the city government. This would reduce the capital's garbage volume by 40 percent, according to the president's brother, and provide livelihood for slum residents. Brilliant man, people said—who cares if he dropped out of university? Except his plan wasn't working. Garbage collectors—the official ones—wanted to earn extra money, too. They had started moonlighting as scavengers, competing with the slum residents, threatening them. Several scavengers had already been killed, the newspapers said.

Light and shadows flickered across David's face. "Human lives are so cheap here. There's no outrage."

"Like what happened with that ship," she said, watching his face for a reaction.

"Exactly. They should put the owners of that ship in prison."

"It was one of ours," she said.

His gaze remained on the road. "You own the Five Star Shipping Lines?"

"Not me. My husband. His family."

A tense silence. "Arturo Mariano? You're his wife?"

She nodded.

"The daughter of . . ."

She waited.

"Jesus," he said finally. "I used to wonder about you." The tone of his voice had changed. More careful, more guarded. This often happened when people understood who her father was. She was sorry she had told him.

"I admired your father," he said.

"Many people did."

His eyes were bright, curious.

"I'm nothing like my father," she said.

He nodded. She sensed a tenuous agreement between them—she wouldn't ask him about his past, and he, at least for now, wouldn't probe into hers.

They crossed the avenue and made their way down a side road. Behind locked iron gates, dogs barked. She followed him down a dark alley, where trees stood like sentries in front of modest two-story wooden homes. He stopped in front of a black gate.

"This is it." His fingertip wavered an inch away from the doorbell. He turned to her with a small, apologetic smile. There was new respect in his eyes, but it had nothing to do with her. "I've wanted this for so long," he said.

"It's just a doorbell, David." She brushed the bell with a fingertip. "Do you want *me* to ring it?"

"Not yet."

She stood on the tips of her sandals, trying to peep over the gate. A mango tree, curtained windows. No lights, no movement.

"No one's home," she told him.

He leaned against the gate and said that wasn't possible. He had been trying to find Sister Esperanza for years, followed leads, travelled to places where she was supposed to be, and she had never been there. He had spent three months in a village high in the mountains, where she was rumored to be living with an ex-priest and the child she had given birth to when she was sixty-four, but he had found no trace of the priest or the child or her. But now, he said, he was certain she had returned to Manila, and that she was inside this house.

Lali's heels touched the ground. "She had a child at sixty-four?"

"People said it was a miracle. And they said if it could happen to anyone, it would happen to her."

"And you believe this?"

"They say the child's special—she sees spirits, the other worlds."

She wanted to tell him: Be quiet. Speaking about spirits attracts them, and the spirits here aren't good ones. People like him traveled through Asia as though it were a spiritual supermarket. They forced things to happen, insisting on what they wanted, and had no idea of the consequences.

"The child speaks to dwarves," he said. "What do you want from Sister Esperanza?"

"People say she sees through you. Immediately." The apologetic smile again. "And they say she saw God."

"David, can I tell you something?"

He looked at her, expectant.

"I think you really should pack up what's left of your life here and go back to the States."

He watched her.

"You've been here too long. I've seen foreigners get lost."

"I'm not a foreigner. My grandmother was born here. My mother, too. She's half-Filipina—"

"That's not possible."

A pained smile. "Which makes me one quarter."

"How can you be Filipino? You don't look it at all. You don't *sound* it." But that explains the eyes and nose, she thought. That odd mix of features. She said, "No one would ever guess you had Asian blood."

He winced. Be kind to him, she told herself. He didn't harass you about your father, or your husband. She searched his face for traces of mixed blood, intrigued by this new layer of ambiguity. He no longer fit into her box for foreigners. He thought he belonged here. Here was his wound. She no longer wanted to charm or tease or do any of the things she usually did to escape discomfort and distress.

Footsteps crunched the gravel. The gates creaked and began to part. A short, small-boned girl, barely out of puberty, peeked out at them. Her white hair was twisted into braids and coiled over her ears; her eyebrows and lashes were white, as well. Her face, almost without angles, had a purity that made her seem almost simple-minded. Her long-sleeved yellow dress, dotted with printed strawberries, reached from her neckline to below her knees.

"Come, please," she said with a bright smile. "My mother's waiting for you."

Woven mats on the floor, candles, a wooden table surrounded by four chairs. On the table was some kind of package, about three feet high and two feet wide, wrapped in white muslin. In front of it sat an old woman, shrunken and hunched in a black dress. She seemed barely five feet tall and no more than eighty pounds. Her thinning grey hair had been pulled into a bun on top of her head. Wrinkles crisscrossed her forehead, cheeks, and neck.

She motioned for Lali and David to sit down. "Let's do this quickly." Her voice was much younger than her face. She stared straight ahead, not looking at them. "How long have you been trying to find me?" Without waiting for an answer, she caressed the object on the table, then unwound layer after layer of cloth. Slowly, a shape became visible. A small oval on top, apparently a head, and what seemed to be a beam on the shoulders. Some kind of statue, Lali guessed, probably one of those wooden saints that adorned churches or altars in people's homes. When a single layer of cloth remained, the old woman rubbed her hands over it, then unveiled a copy of the Black Nazarene—the dark-skinned Christ, half-kneeling and carrying a cross, worshipped by Lali's mother, aunts, the maids, and just about every other person she knew. The original statue, life-sized and made of wood, was displayed in a cathedral in Manila. Thousands flocked to it every Friday. In the 17th century, people said, a galleon had transported the statue across the Pacific—Jesus was white when he left Acapulco and black when he arrived on these islands. A miracle, people said. Others claimed a fire in the ship had charred the wood.

Now Sister Esperanza kissed the edge of his maroon robe, murmuring to herself. Beneath a crown of thorns and a diadem with three rays, the Nazarene's face and eyes were tense with suffering.

Sister Esperanza tilted her head toward David. "I can't do anything for you."

He opened his mouth to speak.

"What happened to you," she continued, "you're not going to solve it here." She whispered something to the statue, then pressed her ear against its chest, nodding or shaking her head from time to time. Minutes later, she said: "This thing you want to know, this thing that troubles you—our Lord tells me you have to run to it, not away from it. It will help you grow. But you keep running away. You don't want to learn from it. So other things keep coming into your life, as bad or worse than this thing that frightens you."

"I keep hearing a voice," he protested feebly.

"Do you know what it wants from you?"

"No."

The old woman flattened her ear against the statue again.

Years before, Lali had seen the original Black Nazarene,

removed from the cathedral and carried in a procession through streets jammed with devotees, creating stampedes as people pushed others aside to try to touch it. Many threw pieces of cloth at the men carrying the statue, imploring them to wipe the statue with their cloth and throw it back to them.

Sister Esperanza's hands curled around the base of the statue. "Our Lord tells me you have to ask yourself—what's the lesson in my suffering? Patience? Humility? Acceptance? Forgiveness? Whenever we go through hard times, there's always a lesson, and we have to learn it. Then we won't be suffering anymore." Her voice was weary. "But most people, all they want is to feel better. It doesn't work. If you refuse to face your suffering, to understand what it means for your soul, then it will keep chasing you, getting bigger and bigger." She coughed, a wracking sound. "I keep telling this to people. But nobody really listens. People want to be saved, but they don't want to change. They don't want to become humble. They don't want to accept. They certainly don't want to forgive. I'm tired of this work. I want to go back to the mountains, but He won't let me." Her cloudy, unfocused gaze swept over Lali's face, then over the wall, without any shift in expression, as though there were no difference between the two. With a start, Lali realized the woman was blind.

Sister Esperanza pressed her ear against the Black Nazarene's chest. Then she told David: "Young man, he wants me to tell you—this thing that troubles you, this thing that brought you to me. You see it as a tragedy, but it's only a lesson. You couldn't do anything for that woman. It's arrogance to think we can intervene in another person's life. That was her destiny. Yours is learning to deal with it."

David bit into his nail. All those years of searching, Lali thought, and he ends up with this.

Sister Esperanza was staring at an area just over David's head. "Any questions?"

He hesitated. "No, Sister."

"It's not what you wanted to hear, I know." She turned to the side of the table where Lali was sitting. "And you? You want me to tell you anything?"

"It's up to you, Sister."

Sister Esperanza's fingers ran up and down the statue. "There's a spirit attached to you. Do you know that?"

Lali started. "Do you see him?"

"So you know it's a man. Yes, I see him. But half of his face is gone, or covered in scars. Or blood. I can't tell you who he is. Whom have you lost?"

Lali glanced at David. "My father."

"It's not an older man," Sister Esperanza replied impatiently. "A boyfriend? In any case, you've made him suffer. You have to make amends. Otherwise he'll stay beside you."

Lali rubbed her bare feet against the floor. "I thought it was my father."

"I told you—it's not an older man. If you want him to stop coming to you, then you have to go to him. To the place where he disappeared, so he won't need to keep seeking you out."

Lali and David exchanged glances.

"Pray for him," the old woman continued. "Make amends. Some spirits become more desperate, more persistent, until you appease them."

"And then he'll go away?"

"Maybe—rituals have meaning. But that's not what's going to free you." She stroked the Nazarene's maroon robe. "You're caught in a world of fear, desire, power. Listen to this now. You people have to listen so I can stop talking. I'm tired. You don't realize how tiring you are. We're made ill not by what's done to us, but by what we desire. Every time you make love with a man, you absorb his energy. You're changed by him. It's not a game. Each one leaves a mark, and those marks stay with you forever."

The white-haired girl tiptoed into the room. Sister Esperanza twisted her head toward her, alert and tense. When the girl touched her shoulder, the older woman's face relaxed. She told Lali: "You love a man, but he's not the one you think. And it's your family that needs you now."

Lali clasped her hands tightly on her lap.

"You have to listen," Sister Esperanza said. "I'm not saying the family is the answer to anything. No family helps any of us. We're in them to make amends for the damage we created in the past. But there's no alternative. You can't just reject yours because you don't like who they are, or who you become when you're with them. With family, too, you have to ask yourself: Why am I with these people? What are the lessons?"

The girl bent down and kissed her mother's cheek, white hair against gray.

"I can say one more thing." Sister Esperanza's voice was hoarse. "People think they should be afraid of God, but what they should really fear is God's law. God's law is very precise. You can't avoid it. Every thought, every word, every action has a precise and inescapable consequence. When you hurt someone, that suffering comes back to you, increased and magnified. Fortunately, the same is true for goodness."

David's black-socked foot tapped against the floor.

"People tell me: Sister Esperanza, we're only human, we can't escape our weaknesses. The law says the price of being human is suffering, but we aren't *only* human. There's another power inside us. We can tap into it. We can ask God to work through us." She began to wind the muslin around the statue, kissing each part of its body as she covered it. With difficulty, she stood. Her daughter slipped an arm around her waist. "I have nothing more to tell you. You'll see a donation box by the door, but I don't want you to put anything inside."

"We'll be happy to make an offering, Sister," Lali said.

"Do you understand what I said? This isn't an exchange. I

want no debts toward you." Her voice was harsh, but her clouded eyes seemed illuminated, and she touched David's shoulder as she hobbled past him toward the doorway.

The warm, sticky night wrapped itself around them. Under his armpits and across his stomach, patches of sweat stained David's shirt.

Just outside the gate, Lali asked: "Did you believe any of that?"

He didn't answer. All those years of searching, she thought, and it came to this.

They walked without speaking through alleys and across avenues, assaulted by horns, neon lights, the stench of garbage and exhaust. Pedestrians jostled for space on narrow, uneven strips of pavement. She held her bag against her chest and crossed an arm over it.

The noise and lights of the avenue gave way to a dimly lit neighborhood of shanties and narrow streets. In the distance, the silhouettes of skyscrapers cut into the violet sky.

They began to cross a footbridge over a narrow canal. He stopped, leaned over the low railing, stared at the muddy bank and water several feet below them.

"Do something," he said. "One true thing. Something you've never done before."

A pause. "That's hard."

His black eyes found hers. Her pulse began to race. There it was again—the wild anticipation.

"Try it," he said.

Slowly, she unzipped her bag, fingered the pearl necklace, calculating how much it was worth. The pearls were fake, but it was a designer brand, expensive. She patted the bottom of her bag until she found the earrings, clasped into each other. Also fake, in a gold-plated setting, and easily replaceable. He wouldn't know the difference.

She held up the earrings. He glanced at them. She leaned over the railing, tossed them into the black water. They hit the surface with a small plop.

"You're cheating," he said.

"I am *not*."

He laughed. A moment later, she laughed, too.

"A *true* thing," he said.

She rummaged inside her bag, then dangled the pearl necklace in front of his face. In one quick movement, she launched it into the canal. As soon as the necklace hit the water, she knew she had made a mistake.

She unbuckled the straps of her high-heeled sandals and stepped out of them. She walked to the end of the footbridge, placed one hand under her belly to support it, and took a few steps down to the bank. Spongy earth seeped between her toes.

He hurried after her. "Are you okay?" he asked. "You shouldn't do that!"

"I have to get it back."

"You can't."

In the distance, the reflections of a few lights from squatter homes broke the blackness of the water.

He wiped his hands on his jeans, glanced at the footbridge behind them. "I'll do it. You get back on the bridge."

He led her along the bank and up to the footbridge. She glanced at her mud-stained feet, trying not to imagine what she had walked on. The baby started kicking. He returned to the bank. At the edge of the water, he turned and looked up at her. She gave a small wave. He removed his shoes and socks, stripped to his boxer shorts, rolled his clothes into a bundle and set them on the ground, over a pile of empty bottles. In the moonlight his body was elongated and pale, hairless except for tufts of hair on his forearms and upper chest. His thighs and upper arms were thin, not muscled. He walked into the water, a strange and luminous figure plodding through the darkness, ponytail hanging down his back, arms held out to the side for balance. Her heart went out to him. She turned away. When she looked at him again, he was sloshing through muddy water over his ankles, trudging toward the spot where her necklace had hit the water.

She couldn't watch him moving through that filth. It doesn't matter, she called out to him, but he ignored her. She rubbed her feet against the ground, trying to remove some of the mud, then wiped away what she could with the tissue paper and baby cologne she carried in her bag. She strapped on her sandals. She glanced at him in the water. His back to her. He wouldn't see what she was about to do. She walked as quickly as she could manage in high heels, away from the footbridge, the water, him.

On an avenue, she flagged down a taxi, directed the driver to David's townhouse.

No lights in his windows. She paid the taxi driver and hurried to her car. Inside, she locked the doors, started the engine, switched on the air-conditioner. The smell of garbage on her clothes, her skin. A stickiness between her toes. There's nothing, she told herself. Your ghosts are nothing. This night is nothing. What you feel with David means nothing. Sister Esperanza is a diversion. You've made a mistake. You need to find Arturo.

At home, she soaped and rinsed herself three times. When at last she felt clean, she stopped the shower, patted the drops of water on her arms and legs, wrapped a towel around her waist.

She curled up in her bed, under the blankets, her skin cool and scented.

When she opened her eyes, night filled the room. Far away, a baby was crying. Instinctively, she touched her belly. The cries were faint. She slipped into a bathrobe, tiptoed out of her bedroom.

No light, no sound. Everyone in the household seemed to be sleeping. Quietly, without turning on the lights, she walked down the long corridor, following her feet, allowing them to take her where they wanted.

The door to the nursery was ajar. The cries had stopped. Inside, a shadow leaned over the empty crib. Her heart skipped. She couldn't see the face, but she knew who it was—the ghost, the presence, that had hovered over her shoulders.

She wanted to run away. Instead she made the sign of the cross and, heart pounding, walked into the room.

The shadow turned to her. A face without features, almost transparent.

Her eyes focused. She asked, "What are you doing here?"

"I have a meeting tomorrow." He switched on a lamp. "Don't worry. I'll be gone by evening."

Her body, soft and heavy with sleep, seemed to belong to another woman. She took a step toward him.

"Don't come near me," Arturo said.

The lines of his shoulders, that mouth.

"Where's Pilar?" she asked.

"In the province."

They eyed each other.

"It's late," she said at last. "Come to bed."

He pointed at the nanny's cot. "I'll sleep here."

"Don't be ridiculous." She had meant to sound matter-of-fact, but her voice cracked. He had never refused to sleep with her.

He gestured at the room. "I like what you've done here—I can almost feel the baby in here."

The warmth in his voice wounded her. She walked to the dresser and removed a stack of neatly folded baby clothes.

You did this to us, she wanted to tell him. After the eclipse, with Pilar, or with someone else, how can I know, but something happened. Something closed, something made you turn away from me, and you never told me. Maybe you don't know yourself. Maybe—is this possible?—you're not even aware of how serious this is.

He reached for the white pajamas on the top of the pile, pinched the shoulders, and held them up. "I can't believe anything can fit into this," he said.

For the first time, she could see the baby. Wearing those pajamas, its small head against his chest, his strong hands cradling its head and buttocks. It came to her that Arturo would be a good father. He would adore the baby. For some reason, the thought distressed her. He would have more claim to it than she did, because she still felt almost nothing for it—no warmth, no curiosity, no affection. She had read that maternal feelings sometimes come only after birth—that people end up loving what they have to care for. She wished she could believe this. For months, she had been pretending to be pleased, but she had no patience with the tasks and rituals and preparations for a baby. What she wanted was to feel connected to this being inside her, and she couldn't talk to anyone about how difficult that was.

With the neat, precise gestures he used to construct model ships, Arturo folded the sleeves and legs of the pajamas, then returned them to the pile. Another image, more distinct than the first, came to her: Arturo was holding a daughter. That was why he would be a wonderful father—the child would be a girl. Arturo loved girls. Lali saw him in the garden. He was carrying a pretty toddler with red silk ribbons in her black hair, both of them laughing. Arturo and their daughter would be happy together. They wouldn't miss her.

A frightening thought: Maybe Arturo could love and she couldn't.

That wasn't true.

"I'm tired, Lali."

She remembered his naked torso in bed, his face over hers, his arms. Arturo knew how to touch a woman. Very few men did. He gave pleasure with his hands, his mouth, his eyes. He was interested in every part of her body. He knew so many ways of making love to her, ways she had never known before, never imagined. She wondered how many women he had slept with to know so much about her body.

He lifted the pile of baby clothes and returned them to the dresser.

"I was thinking of going away for a while," she said carefully. "To visit my uncle, down south."

"Now?"

"After the baby's born."

"You want to visit your uncle, or you want to go away?"

She didn't answer. Again she was taken aback by the possibility that he knew her better than she had thought.

"How will you afford it?" His gaze was dark and steady. "Lali," he continued, not unkindly. "I've never known any woman in your situation who's managed to change her life." He sat on the narrow bed and began to unlace his shoes. "Too much to lose. Don't you think so?"

He unbuttoned his shirt. He stood, his back to her, removed his trousers and underwear. Years ago, they had taken photos of themselves making love. Two slender young bodies in the grass, similar to each other, the orange-gold sunlight of late afternoon slanting over their skin.

On the cot, he lay on his side, facing the wall, an arm folded over his head.

She sat on the bed and touched his thigh. His back and shoulders tensed. Tentatively, sensitive to any sign of resistance, she held his thigh and shoulder, then pulled him toward her. He lay on his back, eyes closed. She bent over and kissed his belly.

Abruptly, without speaking, he propped himself up on an elbow and nudged her head away. He looked as sad as she felt.

She stood and left the room. She staggered down the corridor, unable to see in the darkness, her hand sliding against the wall. Don't be a fool, she told herself. He loved you, and now it's over. For now it's over. That happens. People lose each other. You've lost him.

And with him, the safety she had longed for all those years in San Francisco.

But she would always be the mother of his child. He wouldn't abandon her.

She needed to go away. Not to her uncle, not to another man, but away from what she had become. She longed for people who didn't know her, a life that held no memories, no expectations, no weight.

5

I n front of David's townhouse, she locked the car, surveyed both sides of the dark street. She rarely visited this kind of neighborhood alone, and never at night. In places like this, people could open their front door in the morning and find a mutilated corpse at their feet. *Salvaged*, people said. She didn't understand why that word was used to describe these particular killings. People disappeared in the city, night and day. Hours or days later, in empty fields or dark alleys, bodies appeared, discolored, barely recognizable, often bearing signs of torture. Rumor had it that the military and police orchestrated most of the kidnappings and killings. The problem was that you never knew where they would deposit a body, and you didn't want to see what they had done to it.

She rang David's doorbell several times. Finally, the door swung open. He was wearing white boxer shorts. A small belly curved over the waistband. Reddish-brown hair, loose and wavy, tumbled over his shoulders.

"You washed your hair?" she asked.

His face was puffy with sleep. "I do occasionally, yes."

"My goodness. It's beautiful. You look like a different person." She lifted her hand toward his hair. "It softens your face. You should never wear a ponytail again."

She squeezed past him to enter the townhouse. His skin smelled of soap. In the center of the room, a futon had been rolled out on the floor.

"Did you find my necklace?"

He gave a crooked smile. "It's three in the morning, Lali."

"I need a place to stay tonight."

"Won't your husband send his private army or whatever to find you?"

She sat on the futon, folded her legs to one side. "Let me stay for a while. I don't know where else to go."

"Don't you have friends?"

"They all talk."

"Wait here," he said finally. He strode out of the room, hair swinging over his shoulders.

Alone, she tried to want him. Instead she remembered Arturo on the nanny's cot, facing the wall, the muscular lines of his naked back and thighs. It's horrible, she thought, how desire attaches itself to one person. Even when I'm angry at Arturo, even when I know what he's doing to me. It's him I want.

She removed her clothes, sat on the mattress, her back against the cement wall. You're seven months pregnant, she told herself. You can't do this. She pulled a sheet over her breasts, touched her belly. The baby seemed to be sleeping.

The strangeness, the excitement, of a new man's bed. She became aware of her nakedness beneath the sheet. Her nipples tingled. She considered putting her clothes back on, hurrying to her car.

When he returned to the room, his hands were hidden behind his back. He knelt next to her and fastened a garland of white jasmine blossoms around her neck.

"You were lucky," he said. "I found it where you threw it."

She lowered the sheet, exposing her breasts.

He looked only at her eyes. "Cover yourself."

"Because I'm pregnant?"

He didn't answer. She should have felt offended. Instead she felt relieved. She pulled up the sheet. She fingered the soft, small petals on her breast. Their intensely sweet smell almost nauseated her.

Pilar's opening like a flower, her mother had said.

Arturo couldn't be in love with Pilar.

"I'll set the alarm," he said. "So you don't stay until morning."

She remembered the necklaces of garlic her grandmother had worn at night. He switched off the light. He lay on his side, away from her. She moved toward him, reached for his hair, brought some of it over her bare shoulder. Soft, thick. She thought: This is why men go crazy over long hair.

From the darkness, as she was edging into sleep, his voice came to her. "Have you ever loved?"

"Be quiet," she murmured. She turned away from him.

"It's important, Lali."

"I'm trying to sleep."

From behind, his arms encircled her belly. Minutes later, he was snoring softly. She switched on a lamp on the floor, near the mattress, then pressed her cheek against the pillow. The walls were empty. The painting of the Mahabharata had disappeared. One by one, he was cutting the strings that tied him to the city. Soon he would be gone. With a start she realized she didn't want him to.

She thought of Arturo, the cot, his hands pushing her from him.

She switched off the light, drifted in and out of sleep. The old dream came to her again, a green-eyed boy tumbling into the sea. Miguel must have been thinking of her just before he died—that was why she kept seeing him. Maybe Sister Esperanza was right. Maybe the presence that followed her, the ghost that kept appearing over her shoulder, wasn't her father after all. Maybe she needed to go south, with David, to the place where Miguel had disappeared. A pilgrimage for love, to feel a man's love again, even in memory.

She stayed awake, listening to the sounds of the night. A car's horn somewhere, dogs howling, the muffled sounds of what seemed to be lovemaking, a man's drunken shouts, a woman trying to placate him. And closer, more subtly, David's breathing and her own. It seemed to her that she had never listened with such attention. It had been a long time since she had allowed the outside world to enter into her. She felt the turnings of the baby, the softness of *sampaguita* petals on her skin, the shadows of people who had passed through these rooms. She tried to bring her attention even deeper, to the voice of the woman David said he heard, but she couldn't hear her. She nestled against him. Without waking, he tightened his arms around her. She remembered how she and Pilar had snuggled together like this when they were children, especially during typhoons, or whenever they were afraid. Perhaps what came after, the passions and love affairs and longings, were only a means back to this comfort. It wasn't Pilar's fault, or Arturo's. It wasn't anyone's fault. She couldn't follow the thought. David's warmth and her sense of his harmlessness carried her like waves into sleep.

The alarm rang. She opened her eyes, switched on the lamp. David was standing over her, one hand behind him. The other held a pair of kitchen scissors. All that remained of his hair were ragged chunks cut close to the scalp.

She pulled the sheet toward her neck. "What happened to your hair?"

He held up a plastic bag filled with reddish-brown hair. "I want to give it to you."

"Are you crazy?"

"You said you liked it. I'm trying to give everything away."

She left the bed, tied the sheet like a sarong around her. She removed the scissors from his hands, made him sit on the floor. Standing behind him, she ran her fingers through the clumps of his hair, assessing the damage. "I can't believe you did this," she said. "The one beautiful thing about you."

He tilted back his head until he could look into her eyes. "I'm told I have nice eyes."

"You'll cut them out, too, if I agree?"

"I was going to get my hair cut, anyway."

He pushed his head further back. She pressed a fingertip against his dimple. He began to laugh, as Filomena had the morning before, and again the laughter bewildered her, and again she was charmed by it. David kept his eyes on her.

She straightened his head so that he was facing forward again, away from her. She began to cut what remained of his hair, snipping the ends, trying to even out the edges and create a presentable haircut. Bits of red hair fluttered over her hands and feet, as soft as the jasmine garland around her neck.

I should be afraid of you, she thought. Instead she knew she would follow him, as far from her life as possible.

CHAPTER SEVEN

PILAR'S DREAM

A sudden external shock can dislocate the soul, leaving the body derelict and disoriented. . . . Hence, we do not startle a child for fear of dislodging the child's soul; we wake up a sleeping person gently to allow his wandering soul time to slip back into place. In more dangerous forms, "soul fright" or soul loss happens in the trauma of violence.

—RESIL B. MOJARES, "Haunting of the Filipino Writer"

PILAR

1

Who was singing outside her window? Pilar turned her face to the pillow, wanting only sleep. Wings flapped against the nipa-palm roof. Night in the province carried strange sounds. Windows opened to fireflies, mosquitoes, wandering ghosts.

Who was singing?

Hear me, hear me, it seemed to cry.

She had slept in too many beds the past weeks. Many nights she woke in panic, not knowing where she was, nor which way to turn for light.

Now she heard it distinctly—the staccato cry of a night bird. She switched on the bedside lamp and tiptoed to the window, eyes lowered, not daring to look into the night.

Keeping her gaze down, guiding herself through touch rather than vision, she felt for the wooden shutters on each side of the window, slid them toward each other. They came together with a soft thud. She wondered whether anyone could hear her. Across the corridor, Arturo and his bodyguards had taken separate rooms. Downstairs, in the darkness beneath her feet, their host had made his bed on a mattress on the living room floor.

Something banged against the window, behind the shutters. She made the sign of the cross. In Manila, she didn't believe in God or spirits or the possibility of protection, but in this dark corner of the archipelago, in the middle of this night, anything seemed possible.

She returned to bed but couldn't sleep. Sitting up in bed, cross-legged, she opened her notebook, flipped through pages of pasted newspaper clippings and her own scribbled comments.

Another banging on the window.

It's only a bird, she told herself.

The last entry, near the middle of the notebook, was handwritten in purple ink.

In the year after you died, nuns and priests led hundreds of thousands of people into the streets of Manila. There were tanks and soldiers and checkpoints all over the place, blocking their access to bridges, highways, the General's palace. Young women carried flowers to the soldiers.

Pilar picked up a pen. The tip rested on a blank line.

This whole time in the province, with Arturo, not one new entry.

She could start with one word, to see what happened. *Papa,* she wrote. Her hand began to move, across one line, then another. When it stopped, she read what she had written:

Papa, I didn't see any of this. I wasn't on the streets. Neither was Lali. We were hiding, with Arturo, with his family. We were on the wrong side.

She set the folders and notebook on the bedside table, switched off the lamp. In the darkness she tried to imagine what her father would tell her, but his warmth and words had faded.

Hear me.

She tiptoed to the window, slid open the shutters, forced herself to peer into the night. Banana trees in the garden. Beyond them, hectares of sugarcane fields rolled toward the hills. An array of brilliant stars, unlike any she had seen in Manila, pierced the sky.

Slowly, other shapes became visible. Down the road, near the fields, she saw a single thatched house. On the roof, a figure was moving, silhouetted against the sky, arms uplifted. A man. But what was he waving in the air? A stick. Perhaps a sword. He was swinging it back and forth in a wide arc over his head.

She pulled on her bathrobe, crossed the hallway, tapped on Arturo's door. No answer. She inserted the key he had given her, stepped inside his room.

He lay curled and sleeping on the bed, wearing only white underpants. Sleep had softened his face. She didn't want to think of Lali—since that afternoon at the river, she had fought away thoughts of her sister—but now she couldn't help thinking that Lali had seen him like this, almost every night, for years. Perhaps Lali had seen him so much like this that she was no longer moved by what she saw.

A furrow creased Arturo's brow as a dream or a sensation passed through him. She had never seen him like this, so shut away from her yet so vulnerable. She would never know the boy she glimpsed in his sleep, never comfort herself with memories of what he had been as a child, never see this vulnerability when he was awake.

What happens to us, she thought. What closes.

On the bedside table, under a lamp, his gun gleamed. Carefully, not wanting to wake him, afraid to touch the gun but more afraid he would reach for it before recognizing her, she picked it up and set it on the floor.

With her fingertip, she touched his shoulder.

His eyes opened. He turned toward the table.

"I put it on the floor," she whispered.

He reached over the bed. As his fingers curled around the gun, he asked, "What's wrong?"

Her nightgown was damp, sticking to her body beneath the bathrobe. She told him about the man on the roof, the sword cutting into the sky.

He set the gun on the table. Sleepily, he sat up, then stood and tightened both arms around her. She shut her eyes, feeling his strength and kindness. Thoughts slammed like a trapped bird inside her: This is wrong. No, this is contained. We're not taking anything away from Lali, and besides, Lali wanted this. And the other voice, louder: Lali would never have wanted *this*.

"It's okay," he said. "Lots of people get nightmares in places like this."

What people don't understand about Arturo, Lali had told her, laughing, at a party with too much champagne, is that he means well. You wouldn't imagine it. He would hate for strangers to imagine it. But inside he's a marshmallow.

He untied her bathrobe, cupped her waist.

"Do you want me to have a look?" he asked.

Perhaps his kindness had nothing to do with her. Perhaps she was mistaking good manners for a good heart. In the past two weeks, since the river, he had been intensely careful. Separate rooms, separate cars, few conversations. But there was a charge between them, and she was afraid everyone around them could feel it. Their rare moments alone together swung from one extreme to another: a flooding, silent passion, then these strained attempts to talk like friends.

They crossed the corridor to her bedroom. By the window, she pointed to the figure on the roof.

"It's just a man," he said.

"But what's he—"

"Nothing. Probably some kind of custom here." He gave a bright smile. "Some nights I'd like to stand on a roof and slash at the world, too."

She was intensely aware of his bare chest and arms.

How easy it was to create an exception, a separate chamber in her heart, and feel no guilt. How easily she had managed, most of this time with Arturo, to not think about what she was doing.

No wind, no cars. Just above the window screen, the night bird resumed its song.

Hear me.

He inclined his head toward the window.

"It's a bird," she said.

"Not a gecko?"

A bird. She recognized it now. She had heard it once, late at night, when she was a child. Her nanny had called the other maids, and they had gathered by her window to listen. The old washerwoman instructed them to hang garlic around the window. The *tiktik*, she whispered to Pilar—the devil's bird, it flies only at night. When you hear it sing like that, it's leading a *manananggal* to the house of a pregnant woman, to suck away her fetus. The *manananggal* was old and childless, the maids whispered, but she had once been very beautiful. And haughty—no man had ever been good enough for her. That was why she was so lonely, and loneliness made her desperate.

Now Arturo edged toward her, close enough for her to smell him. "I think it's time for you to go home," he said. "Back to Manila."

She walked to the bed, removed the bathrobe and sat down, hands clasped on her lap, on the white nightgown. Papa would be shocked if he saw me, she thought. But maybe not. Maybe something like this had happened to him. No one really knew what went on inside other people, what they were capable of, if they had the chance.

Arturo touched her shoulder. "I can't be here."

"Stay," she said.

That smile again. Arturo's number-one campaign weapon, Lali called it.

"You know I can't, Pilar."

"Just for a while?"

The smile disappeared. His gaze flicked away. It came to her that he, too, must be afraid of what was happening between them. He must have thought, when he married Lali, that their love was immutable. Lali and he had been madly in love. Pilar had seen it. Now that love had turned out to be as fragile as everything else.

She told herself: One day you'll lose him. If it could happen to Lali and him, it will happen to you.

She pulled the nightgown up over her head. He locked the door and walked toward her.

In bed, she lay on her side, eyes level with his shoulder. A large mole, dark brown and with ragged edges, protruded from his upper arm. Her lips touched it.

The bed creaked. He tensed. "I should go," he said. "People can hear everything. The walls and floors are like paper."

"We can be quiet."

He slipped an arm under her. She rested her cheek on his chest. Images came to her. The cool green water flowing over her, the sun on his skin as they lay by the rocks.

"This isn't what I want for us," he said.

Us, she repeated to herself. Her heart lifted.

"We're taking too many risks," he said.

She withdrew from him, turned to the wall. A small, sharp tightening in her belly. After her father's death, she had had terrible stomach cramps—several times a day at first, then a few times a week.

Arturo had been saying something. Now he touched her hair. She turned back to him. Hesitantly, she kissed his neck. He stopped moving. She rubbed her thumb into his shoulder, hoping she was touching him the right way.

"Talk to me," he said.

She slid down and placed a shy kiss under his navel. She told herself: Lali wouldn't hesitate, or feel awkward, or wonder what he saw in her. Lali would know what to do next.

He sat up, swung his legs over the edge of the bed.

When she looked at his face again, he was running his fingers through his hair. "I'll wait until you sleep," he said.

"Is it really because of the other people?"

"Then I'll go."

His hand cupped her cheek. She closed her eyes. She imagined Lali pressing her smooth, pale cheek into his fingers, fitting herself into his embrace.

He was shaking her, telling her to wake up. She sat up. He was wearing beige trousers and holding her bathrobe. The middle of the night. Footsteps pounded down the hallway. Doors banging, excited cries. Someone shouted his name.

He tugged her out of bed, helped her into the bathrobe. "We have to hurry," he said. "Where are your shoes?"

Without waiting for an answer, he gripped her upper arm. She broke away, gathered the folders and notebook from the bedside table, shoved them into her large black handbag. He clutched her arm again and hurried her down the stairs. The owner of the house, a small old man in red pajamas, stood at the foot of the stairs, surrounded by stunned-looking young maids in shorts and T-shirts. The old man's hand trembled on the railing. "We're very sorry, sir," he told Arturo, "but can we leave with you?"

"Take one of the jeeps," Arturo replied. To Pilar he said: "Where are your shoes?"

A bodyguard handed Arturo a pale blue shirt. He dressed quickly, buttoning the shirt as he walked out the door. In the garden, under the banana trees, the van beamed yellow headlights into the night. A dozen armed men stood around it; some held walkie-talkies against their ears. Pilar stepped barefoot into the damp earth. Pebbles pressed onto her skin.

Arturo followed her into the van. The seats were almost filled with his men. She sat beside him, just behind the driver, and tightened the belt of the white bathrobe. She set the handbag on her lap.

Arturo was leaning forward, face tense. His eyes darted from one window to another.

"What's happening?" she whispered.

"Not now." He gestured at the driver and bodyguards. "I can't talk here."

The van sped down an unlit road, dipping into potholes. Sugar fields on both sides and, in the horizon, a line of craggy mountains. She strained to see the road ahead, looking for the house she had seen from her window.

They were driving toward it. On the roof, the man was still waving his sword.

"Look," she told Arturo. "Can you ask the driver why he's doing that?"

Arturo's jaw tightened. He glanced at her, seemed about to say something, then snapped his head away. He spoke to the driver in the language she didn't understand. The man replied in cropped sentences.

"What did he say?"

"A woman's giving birth inside." Arturo swiveled his head and torso to look back at the disappearing road. She turned around, too. In the seats behind them, the bodyguards stared straight ahead. Framed by the back window, two jeeps and another van were trailing them, their deep-yellow headlights like cat-eyes in the dark. The house shrank and receded.

"But what's he doing on the roof? What did the driver say?"

Arturo faced forward again. "Fighting off some kind of spirit, to keep his baby safe, I don't know—Pilar, I don't have time for this."

The landscape rushed past them, briefly illuminated by headlights, fields metamorphosing into jungle. Trunks and branches twisted toward the sky. The driver turned into a dirt road. Coconut trees lined one side, their fronds yellow-brown in the glare of headlights. On the other side, fissures webbed the earth. She thought she saw vapors seeping out of them, small white wisps near the ground. As a schoolgirl, she had read that when the Spanish friars first came to these islands, they believed that when the rains were late, the bowels of the earth filled with hot vapors that escaped through cracks in the dry ground. Then the rains came, and mud sealed the cracks, trapping the vapors inside. Sooner or later, the vapors exploded, breaking through the ground, provoking earthquakes and eruptions, collapsing houses, flattening villages.

In the distance, near the horizon, red vapors rose toward the sky.

"Do you see that?" she asked Arturo.

Without turning his head, his eyes fixed on the road, he said, "A fire."

"How can you tell without looking?"

He glanced at her, eyes veiled. "The village is on fire."

Not vapors then, but flames.

In a casual voice, almost without inflection, he said: "Carlos C. Benedicto III—remember? The one with the lepers? Someone set his village on fire this evening. He thinks I did it."

She became aware of the damp nightgown beneath her bathrobe, her bare feet against the van's scratchy carpeting.

"Did you?" she asked softly.

"Set fire to a village?" For a moment he looked like Lali—the wide-set eyes, the cheekbones, the ruthlessness. "Really?"

She sat still, noting the shifts inside her. She could protest, ask questions, try to find out more. Instead she pressed her shoulder against him. This, too, was what it was like to be Lali—the silence, the complicity, the not-wanting-to-know. Arturo had been good to her. The violence of his world, his violence in the world, if it did exist, had nothing to do with her. Her father had taught her to believe in righteousness and honor, but Gregorio had lived in a different world, harsher and therefore simpler than her own. Other needs were at stake now, those he couldn't have imagined for her—Arturo's skin, his warmth, his presence beside her. In her mind she told her father: I never asked for much, I never expected much, I'm not like Lali, but I want this, the possibility of this, more than anything I've wanted in my life.

"Lie down!" Arturo pushed her to the floor of the van.

She squeezed into the space between two rows of seats, lying on her stomach, cheek against the coarse carpet. Grains of sand or dirt pricked her skin. He covered her with his body. "Don't move," he whispered. She felt his fear. He tried to prop himself up on his elbows, but soon gave up and allowed his body to weigh down on her.

The engine rumbled beneath her, sending vibrations through the floor and into her skin. The heat and pressure of Arturo's body constricted her chest, making it difficult to breathe. Somehow he found her hand, covered it with his. "I'm sorry," he murmured.

A long swerve, and another. The van was slowing down.

He lifted himself away from her. The door clicked open, and a warm wind blew over her. She struggled to sit up. Arturo jumped out of the van. Flashlights glowed around him.

She hurried into the night in her white bathrobe, clutching her black handbag. In front of her, flanked by men with rifles and guns, two flame trees splashed against the night. She followed Arturo down a path between the trees to a two-story wooden house. Inside, groups of people stood or squatted in the semidarkness. Heads turned to them, but no one spoke.

A tall, elderly woman in a brown dress came up to them, holding a candle. She had an angular face, thick eyebrows, skeptical eyes. She nodded at Arturo, then led Pilar up a flight of stairs and into a bedroom.

The candle spread soft light over an antique dresser and wooden bed. The woman set the candle on the dresser. "Do you need anything?" she asked Pilar.

"I didn't bring any clothes. I don't have shoes."

"I'll have something for you tomorrow." She scanned Pilar's face. "You should sleep now."

"Do you know what happened tonight?" Pilar asked.

The woman eyed her.

"There's a village on fire," Pilar said. "Not far from here."

The woman's mouth tightened. "There's no fire. I've lived here all my life. I would know if there was a fire."

Pilar was about to tell her she was wrong, but something in the woman's eyes—a condescension, or mockery—silenced her.

The sky, violet blue and cloudless, stretched high over the fields. Shadows shrouded the flame trees. Pilar gripped the window ledge, looking into the night. She imagined a child inside her, a life to nourish, something that belonged to her, something that made her belong to life.

"Pilar?" Arturo was standing at the doorway, in trousers but no shirt, his hair uncombed.

How easy it was to not ask questions. To not think, not feel, not recognize what she was doing in one part of herself. How easy to enter that separate chamber in her heart.

"Tomorrow you're going back to Manila," he said. "It's too dangerous here."

She carried the candle from the dresser to the bedside table, then reached for his hand. This time he didn't protest. He seemed shaken, in need of comfort.

They lay next to each other, facing the ceiling. As a child, in the minutes before sleep, she had imagined tiny shadows crawling in and out of the cracks above her. She couldn't see them now.

"Benedicto's men arrived ten minutes after we left that old man's house," Arturo said. His voice was hoarse, unsteady. She had never heard him sound so upset. "They rounded up every-one who was still there."

Don't tell me this, she thought.

"They set the house on fire," he said.

She covered her eyes. "And the people?"

"We don't know yet."

"The old man, the owner?"

"We don't know."

She looked at the ceiling again. She imagined the fire, the fires, the people in the village, the old man in red pajamas and the young maids in shorts and T-shirts, their sleepy, surprised faces.

His fingers grasped hers. He brought her hand to her stomach, just above her navel. Flat and smooth. He pressed her fingertips into her lower belly. The flesh was softer there, yielding.

He tugged her nightgown up over her hips.

The sex was rough, hard, almost without tenderness. He had never made love to her like that. His skin and smell and weight, the repeated impact of his hips against hers. She wished he would finish. He was hurting her. She worried that they hadn't closed the shutters. She worried someone could hear them. He was murmuring things she couldn't understand.

Minutes later, he collapsed against her. She shifted under his weight.

"Are you okay?" he asked.

She didn't answer.

He lifted himself off her. After a while, he said, "I'm sorry."

A small, sharp ache in her belly. "I'm not asking for anything." Her voice was hushed, fierce. "You know, I'm not even *asking* anything."

"Relax. I know this isn't easy for you."

"You *don't* know."

"Sometimes," he said, "I wish I could have two wives."

He might as well have struck her.

They hadn't spoken about Lali since the river. Now the muscle in his cheek twitched, as it did whenever he was upset or angry.

And *my* anger, she thought. And *my* distress?

And the village on fire? And all the other questions I'm not supposed to ask?

She twisted away from him to blow out the candle.

His hand on her belly, blocking her. "Leave it on," he said.

From behind, he cradled her against him. "Let me get through this election," he said. "After, I promise you, we'll be okay. I promise."

You promise and you're sorry, she thought, all the time. She stopped herself from saying this.

In the river she had wanted him. Now, perhaps, and this was worse, her heart felt full and quiet when she was with him. Despite everything, despite him, despite her anger, despite the village on fire and all she had seen tonight.

A gift, Lali had said. I'll want him back.

He coiled strands of her hair around his fingers. She told herself: I've never done anything so wrong.

As though he knew what she was thinking, he kissed her neck, then whispered words that seemed more radical and intimate than anything he had done to her body.

They awakened to the acrid smell of smoke. Arturo ran to the door, opened it a crack. Coughing, fingers over his mouth, he shut the door.

Somehow she found herself crawling next to him, across the room, toward the window, their heads near the floor.

At the window he slammed his fists against the screen. She helped him pry it from its frame. He told her they had to jump. She stared at the ground, about two meters below. A dozen heads thrown back, looking up at them. Shouts. She couldn't understand.

From behind, smoke and heat. Her eyes were burning. She was so afraid of burns and scars on her skin.

Her handbag, on the floor. He shouted her name. *We have to jump.*

He told her he would go first. He told her he would catch her. Then he was gone.

Her turn, now. She climbed over the ledge, pushed herself further.

Her neck and head twisted to the side. There was pain, but outside her. Later she would remember this—her surprise at how distant the pain was, then the darkness.

There were ways of forgetting. Piece by piece, she locked away the images: the night bird, the flames, the man slashing on the roof.

She asked him to help her go away.

They flew to a provincial capital. Later there was a stop in Singapore, for checkups, then a borrowed condominium in Hong Kong, where she stood by windows and watched the sea. She didn't go out alone. Once a week, a Filipina brought her groceries. Several times, Arturo flew in to see her. At night, in bed, they watched rented movies on television. She thought of the village on fire, his eyes, the old man and young girls. The first time he visited, he brought her the black handbag with her folders. The next time, a two-foot-high plant. *Mayana*. She stored the bag in a closet, set the plant on the floor, near the bay windows of the living room, where the leaves—deep red in the center, bordered by violet and green—lifted toward the light. Most days the plant was the only other living thing in the condominium, and it soothed her to touch its leaves.

Everything's okay, Arturo told her. She couldn't imagine her father's face. Arturo told her not to worry. He told her nothing irreversible had happened. She had been sick, badly bruised, perhaps in shock. Nothing was broken. No part of her body had been scarred or burned. *There was a fire. You fell. There was so much confusion. It was me they wanted. They wanted revenge. They thought I burned the village. You shouldn't have been there.* She tried not to think about the province, but her dreams trailed like shadows after his words. She started when she heard noises at night or imagined wings outside a window. She dreamed of the *tiktik* flying across the South China Sea to look for her. She dreamed of fires and unborn babies and a child running around this large apartment, full of Chinese antiques and contemporary Asian art but as quiet and sterile as a hotel suite.

When Arturo came to visit, they slept on a white bed, wide enough for six people. They didn't make love. She told him to stop coming, that soon she would be strong again, but for now she wasn't well—she couldn't make love, she had nothing to give him. He said he, too, needed quiet. He said it wasn't for her to judge what she was giving him. He held her close in bed, rested his head on her breast, stroked her hand. They didn't talk about the province, the campaign, his marriage, the village on fire. He talked about the softness of her skin. Lali didn't telephone. The air-conditioner hummed all day and night. They covered themselves with blankets. Outside, the sun pounded on concrete walls.

The *mayana* flourished. Every morning, she inspected and cared for it, wiping dust from the violet-red-green leaves, noting new growth, snapping off the largest leaves when they started to shrivel and turn pale. It had other names: Heart of Jesus, Angel Wings. Once, while pruning the plant, she accidentally broke off a healthy leaf and part of its stalk. It was too beautiful to throw away, so she stuck it into a teacup-sized pot of soil and watered it, hoping it would keep its colors a few days longer. Soon, and to her surprise, small leaves began to appear along the stem, and one day she saw that the new plant was becoming more colorful and beautiful than the old. And one day, as she fingered the leaves, she told herself that these splits she had created, these separate chambers of the heart— this stay in Hong Kong, her longing for Arturo, her love for Lali, the village on fire, the house on fire, her notebooks and faith in her father's dreams—all her selective blindnesses and absences of guilt, might at times be a good thing, might be necessary for a life. She wanted very much to believe this. And violence—the violence of Arturo's world, the violence she had allowed into her, the violence and ruthlessness of her own wanting, the violence she was certain had made her ill—she told herself violence, too, was necessary for life.

That afternoon she forced herself to go out alone, just for fifteen minutes, into the hot noisy streets of Hong Kong, the sunlight and smells and jostling crowds that spoke languages she couldn't understand. On that day she knew she would be well again. The next day she spread the folders, notebook, and some of her father's books on the dining table. She couldn't read any of them yet, but the titles and cover images began to fill her imagination—the old paintings of village life and lithographs of galleons in full sail; Stefan Zweig's *Conqueror of the Seas: The Story of Magellan*; a biography of Jose Rizal, her father's hero.

That night, she stood by the large picture window and watched small yellow lights flicker on black water. On both sides of the bay, buildings rose into the sky. This wasn't her country, with its green fields and jungles and burnt mountains, with the delicate scent of jasmine at night, birds leading lonely women to unborn babies. Fingers on her belly, she stared at the sea, waiting for the moment to tell Arturo what she had begun to understand, and what she was not yet able to accept, and imagining his shock as he listened.

CHAPTER EIGHT

THE BIRTH

Tell me, if you survive,
How many lives
You will have managed
To live, whether the brightest
Illumination comes from sporadic
lightning flashes
or the domestic yellow gleam
of the lamp
at your bedside.

—MA. LUISA A. IGLORIA,
"Petition to be Allowed to Love without Limits"

LALI

Eight days into the summer, the child was born. A hard birth, Lali said later, but at the time there was only the heat, the pulsing inside her that was not her, the violence of that wanting to be born. She wanted it to die: the pain, the pulse, the sun smashing its face against the sealed windows of the hospital room. Like a dog biting into a wounded paw, she wanted to rip out her belly to destroy the pain.

A hard birth, she said later, but in truth it was over in three hours. The doctor congratulating her. A wet creature heaving against her breasts.

She had asked not to see it. A drug, a shot in her spine, a sudden darkness to fall into, anything to keep her from seeing. She didn't want to feel it come out of her, to know without a doubt that it was hers. Now, it was too late. Fat, wrinkled, ears pressed forward, one eye swollen by the pressure of passage— this was her child. It didn't cry. Tiny fingers clawed into her skin. The newborn was trying to lift its head. Lali watched the black eyes that couldn't see her and thought: It has almost no one. She wanted to stroke it, but she was shaking so much she couldn't lift her arms from the bed to embrace her baby.

The nurse carried it away, and the doctor jabbed a needle into Lali's arm to stop the shaking. Without warning, he pressed his hands into her aching womb and forced out the placenta. When the last wave of pain had subsided, they wheeled her out of the room.

She didn't want to breastfeed, but the baby lay in a crib next to her bed and it was crying so much Lali couldn't sleep. She picked it up and pressed its mouth against her nipple. To her surprise, it began to suck, tugging at her breast. Her womb tightened.

The child was dressed in a white velvet outfit Arturo's mother had chosen. Gold embroidery across the chest, a designer sweater over pudgy arms, scraggly black hair combed to one side. It was ludicrous, Lali thought, to dress up that animality in fine clothes. She kept seeing it as it was just after birth: naked, lips parted and panting, tiny fingers like claws gripping her breasts. She didn't know what to do with that life. She watched the hunger and rage with which it sought her flesh and knew she shared its greed. She wanted to give it something, but there was almost nothing left, only the breast it sucked with such urgency she thought her heart would break.

No way out. Her passion for Arturo had taken flesh in this child. She was the mother of his daughter, inextricably bound by this infant's blood to a man who no longer wanted her.

In the last weeks of Lali's pregnancy, Pilar went abroad and Arturo began to disappear. There were excuses, of course. The trip to the province had been exhausting, Lali's mother said—Pilar needed to rest. Arturo was campaigning all over the country. And then he had business in Singapore, trips to Hong Kong, perhaps a succession of other women on the side, his fingers on bodies unscarred by the accidents of his desire.

Lali stayed in Manila and waited. At first, Arturo came back twice a week, then once a week, and, finally, not at all. He telephoned every Sunday, polite and distant. Pilar didn't call. The maids smiled at each other when they saw Lali wandering the long corridors of her home. She could no longer bear to see her friends, who were all his friends, to search their lying eyes for tracks of the conversations held without her.

What perversity it was to long for a man who hurt her.

It was her child, but as she held it in her arms, she saw the face of the man who had gone away. One arm cradling the baby, she opened the bedside drawer. She touched the objects she had brought to the hospital—a laminated novena to St. Jude, patron saint of the desperate; a Virgin Mary-shaped plastic bottle of holy water; a black-and-white photograph—her amulets against her life.

She removed the photograph from the drawer and propped it against the telephone, where she could stare at it over the head of her child.

The man in the picture wasn't her husband. It was an old photo, the only one she had of Miguel. He must have been nineteen at the time, on water skis, his arms bare and strong, his eyes narrowed into slits by his smile. Miguel. Her first lover. Who had wanted to marry her, with an insistence and innocence she would never find again. For a time, she had been happy with him, in the senseless way of the privileged, expecting only more of the same. A home like that of her parents, jewelry on her birthday, shopping trips to Hong Kong and San Francisco, dinner parties for friends who laughed and wouldn't betray her.

He had been kind to her, and generosity diminished him. In the end she couldn't bear it.

She shifted the baby to the other breast. No milk yet, only the yellow liquid that protected without nourishing.

On the photograph, her finger traced the outline of his muscled body. She didn't see him for years after the breakup, but she had kept track of him, the way one does of a life that almost happened, that might have brought happiness and calm if she had recognized at the time what she was being offered.

She was convinced now that there had been only a few moments in her life when she could have cleared the way to happiness, but she had hesitated, or stayed uncertain, waiting for something better to come along. And what followed was the tumult of years, the intractable passions and betrayals and loss, and then it was too late. What she wanted now was not happiness, but the relative absence of pain. Yet she had kept track of the boy in the photograph, who went away to study in New York, returned home to Manila, and joined the biggest company in the country, grew heavy around the waist, married a pretty woman who was often but discreetly unfaithful to him, and then disappeared, in an accident in the sea he had loved all his life. She remembered the two of them running into the South China Sea, following the red trail of a setting sun, or sailing from island to island, plunging into turquoise water so clear and tranquil they never imagined it would one day close over him.

He smiled guilelessly into the camera. Traces of some Spanish or American forebears skewed his image. She remembered the first time she had seen him—the shock of green irises on slanted eyes, the dark skin molded into Eurasian features.

The baby pulled at her nipple. She cradled it closer to her, pressing her thighs together as it sucked, her eyes on the boy's lips in the photo as the old pleasure lifted its head and uncoiled inside her.

When it was over, she leaned over the nursing child and slipped the photograph into the drawer.

The hospital room was bare, but it wouldn't stay that way. In a day or two, she would be crushed by the smell of flowers. Already the birth announcements were being engraved. Arturo's mother had prepared the list—the president, the speaker of the house, the secretary of defense, the top generals, all the allies and former allies of Arturo's family. Even those who detested him wouldn't be forgotten: a quarter of the country's ruling elite was related by blood or marriage to the infant she held in her arms.

She lowered the child into the crib. All throughout the last weeks of her pregnancy she had feared this day. Whose traits would she see in the child—Arturo's or her own? And if they were hers, would she be able to do what she had to?

She watched the curve of its cheek against the flannel sheets, dreaming of stories she had heard. Women rubbing opium on their nipples to poison their newborn daughters. Or babies smothered under pillows, abandoned in the street, thrown into waste bins, wrapped in plastic bags, deposited on doorsteps. And an Indian legend of a child suckling a beautiful woman, who suddenly turned into a fanged demon that first ripped apart and then devoured the infant at its breast.

These were the ways out.

A son might have saved her. Her duty done, Arturo's name carried and cursed for another generation, no more bitter nights with him forcing himself upon her.

The child was curled like the fetus it had been only hours before. Lali stroked its cheek, curious to see if some instinct stirred in her. Nothing. No pride, no tenderness, no warmth. Only the certainty that she couldn't be a mother to Arturo's child, and shame that it didn't know how little she could give it.

She lifted her legs over the side of the hospital bed. Tenderness in her womb. Would her body ever look the way it used to? She stood on the bed and lifted the hospital gown over her breasts, studying her reflection in the window.

It looked all right. Almost all right. She was trembling. The cold, she remembered. They had warned her she would be cold without the baby inside.

She wanted to dress up again. In short skirts and stiletto heels, in bathing suits that would make men stare at her. She wanted the sun on her body as she lay beside the pool, waiting for a lover to call and evening to come.

There had been a time when she waited only for Arturo, and the anticipation of seeing him filled her days. The ritual of the swim, the water sliding over her legs and arms, the sun browning her back. Then the clothes spread out on her bed: silk, sheer, short. She knew what he wanted.

Now, each time she imagined him, she wanted to turn away. The chiseled features, the sensual lips, those unlined hands reaching for her. Arturo had never needed to worry about pleasing a woman. The schools, the clothes, the family name gave him an assurance that most women mistook for charm.

Lali liked to watch those women's faces when she walked into a room on his arm.

The baby's head rested sideways against the pillow. It seemed to struggle in its sleep, doll fingers clenched. Did babies dream? She leaned over the crib, lips almost touching its fragrant cheek. Sweet flesh, emptied of all cruelty. She wanted to run her fingers over that furrowed brow, to smooth away the dreams or discomforts that troubled its sleep. It would be so easy to give in, to love this creature that couldn't hurt her. Her own child. She slipped her index finger into its fist; soft fingers curled around her skin. Abruptly, she lifted her face, pried out her finger, shut the crack of feeling that threatened to widen inside her.

She had never wanted anyone as much as she had wanted Arturo, and what had that brought her? Fear, the last time they made love, in those minutes after he came, not knowing how long he would stay calm inside her, nor whom he saw as he thrust himself into her.

Only a few years of tenderness and warmth, and then this— a woman turned cow with swollen breasts, his child to raise.

She had done it to herself. That was the worst thing. She

hadn't wanted a baby, only to keep him inside her, his flesh within hers for nine months. Pregnancy was erotic, not maternal. Now she was trapped.

Years ago, while she and Miguel were scuba diving, a reef shark emerged from the darkness and swam a few meters away from them. She knew it was harmless, and she refused to surface, but her heart banged against her chest for the rest of the dive. Later he told her that sharks slept like dolphins—one cerebral hemisphere at a time, a part of their brain always alert.

The baby lay on its back, so motionless that Lali was afraid. And just as suddenly, the fear was hope. She passed a finger under its nostril to see whether it was breathing. A whisper of warm air. She considered rolling it over to its belly, knowing the risks. The nurse said the child had to sleep on its back, to decrease the chances of suffocation or choking.

She wouldn't be trapped by this child. It isn't human yet, she told herself—it can't think. Consciousness would come later, but she wouldn't let it come to that.

A way out. For the baby and herself.

There were ways to do it. Accidents. A child thrown out of the window, the unforeseeable fall. Babies died. Not of hunger, not beatings, not soft bare flesh smothered by large hands. Others did that. She wouldn't. She would find a gentler way. The main thing now was to save herself. Did no one understand that? The horror other people had expressed, months ago, when that ship had sunk on its way to Manila from a southern island, and almost all the children aboard had perished. She had felt horror, too, but not surprise. Men had trampled over children in their struggle to get out. Little boys and girls wailed in the corridors and on the deck, survivors said, but there weren't enough lifeboats for all of them. Almost all the women had died, perhaps in the futile attempt to comfort the terrified children. Foolish women who gave tenderness when ruthlessness was necessary. Of the 3,000 or so people on the ship, less than 400 had survived, all but two of them young men. Life was for the strong, strength for the unsentimental.

Lali would have trampled.

And when it was done, she would be free.

The boy in the photograph had been lost years before, on another ship, but that didn't mean Miguel was dead. Survivors kept appearing, weeks and months after these accidents. His body had never been found. Those gentle arms, that guileless look when he told her he loved her. Had he trampled, too? In those final moments, did he think only of the water rising over his face? Did he pull crying children from the railing to make room for his legs and hips? Did he seek, as Lali wished she could do now, to remove everything that stood in his way?

His wife didn't believe he was dead. In the endless rounds of parties and luncheons that delimited Manila's social world, the woman had become a subject of gossip. She had dreams, people said—her husband kept coming to her at night, telling her where to look. She had spent the years since the accident traveling from island to island, seeking Miguel's traces, speaking to fishermen in hamlets that had seen no stranger in decades. And each time she was told a story—of people who knew people who had seen a green-eyed, brown-skinned Eurasian on another island, a man without memory, without past, of a gentleness and language that set him apart from any person they had seen before. And the wife abandoned her lovers to search for the man she hadn't loved. People said her family was in turmoil. They wanted her to accept that her husband was dead, but they couldn't be sure. And even if he were dead, others said, what good would it do for her to accept it? Wasn't it better for her to keep looking? There were no children to keep her busy, no children to replace him, and the lovers had taken substance only in contrast to him.

Lali kept track of his wife's searchings, as she had of the man. Was this his fate, to interest his women only when it was too late? Was he useful only as an absence that gave shape to a listless present? He had served his purpose, but Lali needed him still. She imagined him lost in one of the archipelago's thousands of islands. He would be in a home somewhere, in a simple life; he wouldn't remember her, nor his wife, nor the handful of women he had left dissatisfied by loving too freely. What was it in the human heart that despised facility? That despised a love too easily won, a man too kind, a gentleness dismissed as unworthiness. Lali needed him to stay in his island, to leave her alone with her ideas of him, her transformation of him, the photograph in a drawer she could look at whenever she wanted.

It was still dark in the room, she had no idea what time it was. The lights of the city were hazy beyond the tinted glass doors. A terrace outside. Eight floors above the ground, and the city asleep. A hope. She stood and took a few tentative steps toward the crib. She took the sleeping child into her arms. The head fell back; it almost opened its eyes. No, she thought, it has to be asleep. She couldn't do this with it watching her, even if she knew it couldn't see clearly, it couldn't know who or what she was. It can't feel, can't think, can't know, she told herself, repeating the words like an incantation, her steps getting stronger. Clutching the baby in one arm, she tried to slide open the glass doors with the other. It gave way a few millimeters. Stuck. She tried again, pushing harder. It wouldn't budge. She wanted to cry. Her shoulders, now her feet, her free arm, all strained against the edge of the glass door. It wouldn't slide open any further. The terrace, a few feet away, couldn't be reached. Eight floors from the ground, no one around, and she couldn't save herself.

She was awakened by crying.

She hadn't slept enough. Her eyes were heavy. Darkness still framed the edges of the white curtains.

He was beside her. She turned and pretended to sleep, lengthening her breaths.

"Lali," he said. "I know you're awake."

Eyes half-closed, she reached out for his hand. He didn't touch her. She sat up in bed, pulling the blanket over her breasts.

"I thought you were abroad," she said.

He bent over the crib. "She looks like you."

"You can't tell yet."

"Yes. The shape of the eyes." He paused. "I couldn't mistake your eyes."

She softened.

He stroked the child gingerly, barely touching it. The crying subsided. Lali watched him. The smooth hands, the features that had begun to lose their clarity. She imagined his kisses, his face over hers at night, a stream of lies and women in his wake.

He sat on the bed beside her. His body was stronger than it had been when she first knew him. He had pummeled it into shape with the same relentlessness he had brought to his political campaign and business deals. She felt a trace of the old excitement, unwanted and disorienting.

"It's been ages since I saw you," she said.

He looked straight at her. His eyes were a new and startling green. Contact lens, certainly. He had always been vain about his appearance. Shirts custom-made in London, suits in Paris and Milan. Who would go with him now to those cities? Pilar? Some of those women who fluttered around him at parties and meetings? She followed the line of muscle under his sleeve, imagining his arms tensed around a variety of legs and hips and breasts.

"We have to choose a name for the baby," she said.

"You haven't already?"

She reached for the child, cradled it against her.

She could make him want her again. He had always wanted her. Despite the rest, or in addition to the rest. Now she was the mother of his child. No other woman could say that.

In a low angry voice, looking at the baby, he said: "You can't control people's lives."

Pilar had told him, then. He knew she had sent Pilar to him.

She waited. When he didn't say anything else, she said, "I'm the one who should be angry."

"We're not your *puppets*."

"And in the meantime, I gave birth alone."

On his cheek, the muscle twitched. "I came as soon as I could."

"I was trying to save us," she said.

"*Save* us?"

A shadow crossed his face. Maybe he wasn't just talking about Pilar and him. Maybe he knew about David. Or that there had been someone like David. If he did, he would never forgive her. He would never come back to her. A man could do what he wanted, but a woman could not humiliate a man.

"We have to find an agreement on this," Arturo said.

She kept her eyes on the baby.

"We need to stay together until after the elections." His voice was sad and distant. "But after, I'll want custody of the baby. I want her brought up by my family."

"No one would give you custody of a baby," she said.

She felt his anger, wondered whether he would strike her. Go ahead, she thought. See what happens.

The baby opened its eyes. Lali cupped her hands under its head and buttocks and lifted it up, toward him.

He shook his head.

Her forearms trembled slightly from the weight of the child. "Hold her," she said.

Reluctantly, he took the child in his arms. It turned its head toward his shirt, searching for his breast. He smiled, embarrassed, his eyes widening.

At that moment, she wished they could still love each other, even once, even for a few hours. But all she could feel for him was a trace of the old desire, and even that was erratic and too linked to anger. The line of his naked body beside her the last time they made love. The strangeness of being with him again, the contours of his body no longer familiar, lips that pressed against her with the weight of all the other mouths he had kissed. She wanted to wipe it all away, the mouths, Pilar, the mistake of sending Pilar to him. She wanted to go back, way back, to see him again for the first time across a crowded party in San Francisco, when he had lifted his glass in greeting as she entered the room. The smell of him, the faces watching them, the rhythms of his voice as he leaned over to ask her who she was. She had been so happy. The burden of remembering that happiness. And then a dream, that first night in his arms, of fogs and darkened villages, of running for shelter from some unseen menace, waves of fear, the destroying sea behind her, always just around a corner, always just out of sight. When she awoke, she felt his eyes staring into hers. And he had lifted her in his arms and carried her to the window overlooking the lights of the city, to show her there was no sea outside, no arms like waves to take her away from him. Shadows falling against their naked bodies, and she had pressed her face against his forearm, certain he would stay beside her and watch over her, that her years of uncertainty were over.

Now she watched those arms wrapped around their child.

"I don't want to bring her up alone," she said.

"You won't have to." He lowered the baby into her arms. "I don't want to have to make things difficult for you, Lali. But it would be simplest if you agreed, without a fight, to give her to me." His eyes met hers. "Not right away. We'll wait a few months, until the election is over. We'll put things in place."

There were moments, accidents, when you wandered too far and couldn't turn back. Something irrevocable was happening, right now, and she was panicking but didn't know how to stop it.

He, too, seemed to be struggling. "It was really just to save yourself, wasn't it?" he said slowly. It wasn't a question. "Marrying me, taking your family back to Manila."

"Is that what Pilar told you?"

"Answer me," he said.

Later, she would look back and tell herself she should have reassured him. She could have brought him back to her, if she had listened to what he was really asking and calmed his fear. He needed to know she loved him. He needed love far more than she did. She needed only to tell him the truth. Because she had always loved him.

Instead she said, out of hurt and pride: "It's always about saving ourselves."

His head snapped back, as though struck. A moment later, he said: "You'll see her as much as you want. I promise you'll have everything you need. I'll never hurt you."

"I won't let you do this," she said.

He kissed her lightly on the forehead. "I'll call you tomorrow."

When he was gone, she slipped off her nightgown and removed the layers of clothing that masked her child. She held the naked baby to her, flesh against flesh. She cupped her hand over its mouth, watching the eyes that could not see her. Its gentleness moved her. Poor girl, she thought. Poor female child. What awaited her? Wouldn't it be kindness to end her life now, before she learned what it was like—the pleasures lost, the glimpses that would haunt everything that followed?

For an instant, Lali saw herself in her own arms and wished she could have destroyed the baby she had been.

She reached for the photograph in the bedside drawer and pressed it against her forehead, on the spot where Arturo's lips had touched her, an amulet against all the men she hadn't loved, or hadn't loved enough. If she could find that boy now, she would tell him she was wrong, that she was ready to live beside him, that his kindness was more important than a hundred men's passion.

But what she knew was this: her lover had disappeared in a shipwreck, by foolishness or cowardice. And his wife, unfaithful to him for years, had gone from island to island in the years that followed, convinced she would find him.

Lali feared that she, too, would live on nothing but memories and rumors from now on. Wandering from island to island in search of what she had lost, those moments of desire for the man she had married and whose blood was mingled with hers in this child.

She tucked the blanket over her baby. An epitaph to desire, perhaps, but she would nurture it, save it, bring it up to take its place beside her. This child was her undoing, but it was also her weapon against Arturo.

The baby warmed her flesh. She bent over and kissed the thin black hair on the baby's head. A name, she told herself. She had to find a name for her daughter.

CHAPTER NINE

THE CHRISTENING

We took away all their stones,
the polish of their dreams. We buried the love
that made them strong. We burned all buds and flowers.
Now there are no heroes even in their bravest songs.

—ALFRED A. YUSON, "Pillage"

PILAR

Her name was Aimee Maria Socorro Mariano y Villareal, and she had no marks on her body. Pale skin, a heart-shaped face, and wide-set black eyes, like Lali's, blinking slowly into the light.

Arturo and his mother huddled over the naked baby, examining her for birthmarks and other omens. From across the room, Pilar watched them.

"She's perfect," Marilou said triumphantly, pulling a blanket over the infant. "No moles. Not one birthmark. She looks like *us*."

Arturo laughed. Fatherhood had given him a new authority, a solidity, as though he had grown from youth to adulthood in the weeks since Aimee's birth. With slow, precise gestures, he fastened the baby's diapers, inserted her arms and legs into white pajamas. She whimpered.

"It's just me, sweetheart," he said, sounding proud and excited.

He rubbed the baby's palm. Tiny fingers grasped his thumb. She has the softest skin, he had told Pilar. If a woman had skin like that, a man would go insane.

Pilar flattened her back against the wall. Some people, like Aimee, were born lucky. This house. This family. No marks on her body. No weeks of silence and forgetting.

"She looks like Lali," Arturo told his mother.

"Are you blind?" Marilou said. "She's a Mariano, 100 percent. There is *nothing* of Lali in her."

Pilar hadn't seen Lali since that night in Nico's garden. The engraved invitation to Aimee's baptism had been delivered by messenger, three weeks earlier. On the bottom right, in small tight letters, Lali had written: *Please come. It's been long enough.* And on the back, in smaller letters: *We'll leave from the house, around ten. I'd love it if you came with us.*

But when Pilar arrived at the house that morning, Lali had already left for the cathedral. Perhaps Lali, too, was afraid to see her sister.

Arturo cradled the baby against his chest.

On the yellow and white walls of the nursery, a decorator had painted life-size nursery-rhyme characters—Little Miss Muffett, Jack and Jill, Mary and her lamb, with pastel blue and pink clothes, pale skin and faintly sinister Eurasian features.

Pilar no longer heard the devil's bird singing in the night. But sometimes, at odd moments of the day or evening, images surfaced, like goldfish cracking the surface of a pond. The fires, the flame trees, the red-green leaves of her plant, the yellow lights flickering at night on the bay of Hong Kong.

Marilou slipped her hands under the baby, adjusting its position so that its head rested firmly on the crook of Arturo's arm. "Well," Marilou said. "If she does end up looking like her mother, then she'll have moles. She's too young yet. But they'll show up later!"

Arturo laughed. To his daughter, he said, "My little girl will *always* be perfect."

"We all end up having *something* on our body, *hijo*—don't kid yourself! And thank God for that, too." Marilou unbuttoned her blouse and slipped it over one shoulder. "You see this?" She touched a large, protruding mole on her shoulder. "It's an omen. My mother told me I had to be ready to carry great burdens. And this—" She pulled back the hair from her forehead, revealing the V-shaped point at the center of her hairline. "A widow's peak. I always knew your father would die before me. Ha! In the end, that was a consolation—God works in mysterious ways."

Arturo nodded good-naturedly. "Of course, Ma."

"And that wife of yours! I've never seen a woman so vain. She wanted to try on her bikini in the *hospital*. And she refuses to breastfeed."

"You never breastfed."

"It wasn't the fashion then. They told us we were doing you a favor. American milk. That's why you got so tall. And you have muscles! I don't care what they say now."

Pilar shifted her weight from one foot to another. The room smelled. No way of hiding it. Baby cologne and baby powder and all the rest, but there was an odor beneath that sweetness—something sour, almost animal.

"A boy would have been better," Marilou said.

Arturo glanced at Pilar. They smiled at each other at the same moment. Almost immediately, his smile disappeared. He seemed embarrassed, averted his face.

Since her return to Manila, he had kept his distance. The baby, he told Pilar, whispering and uneasy on the telephone. He needed time to arrange things. Better not to see each other for the moment. It's not like Hong Kong. We don't want people to talk. The elections, you know. He couldn't leave Lali alone with the baby just now, but he would help Pilar in any way she needed. Pilar could understand that, couldn't she? No reason to worry, no reason to feel alone.

Pilar told him she did understand. She told him she was fine now. The illness—was that what it had been?—had left her feeling both fragile and intensely open, all her nerves on the outside. She walked around her house, surprised at how things really could seem transformed—the gleaming wooden floors, the tangle of bright-green plants and vines in the garden, the splinters of sunlight on mirrors and glass. She couldn't work on the folders and clippings. She couldn't think about her father, or what he would have expected her to do.

The house, her body, her days—all these seemed charged, brimming with memories and anticipation. Her doubts, the warnings she gave herself, seemed to float on the surface, unable to smother the languorous contentment inside her. Let me feel this, she thought. Let me feel happy with him, just a while longer.

As Pilar walked out the nursery door, she heard Marilou ask Arturo: "What happened to Pilar? She looks like a ghost." And: "What are you going to do with her?"

Pilar paused outside the room, waiting for his reply. Instead, his head appeared through the doorway. *You okay?* he mouthed. She nodded. His warm hand brushed against hers, then curled around the doorknob and pulled the door shut, leaving her outside.

Arturo's main opponent, Carlos C. Benedicto III, was found dead several weeks after the fires in the province. Salvaged. His eyes gouged out, his private parts mutilated. A gambling debt, the newspapers said—the man was obsessed with cockfighting. Now his wife, a distant cousin of Marilou's, was running for his seat—another housewife catapulted to politics by the death of a husband. Arturo had attended the funeral, stood next to the widow for photographers, offered his condolences. He held a televised press conference afterwards, denouncing the reign of violence in the countryside. He said a tragedy like this transcended politics—even the bitterest rivals must set aside their differences and fight for justice. He said he was offering a reward, from his own pocket, for any information leading to the arrest of Benedicto's killers. Pilar watched Arturo on television, thinking of the village on fire, the man on the roof, the van speeding through the night.

Nothing bad had happened, Arturo told her. The sun, the

fire, the winged torsos flying at night. The old man at the foot of the staircase, the sleepy-eyed young maids, the flaming village, Benedicto's death. None of that had anything to do with him.

She chose to believe him.

Let me have this.

She opened the door to Lali and Arturo's bedroom. No one inside. Pilar walked in. The room was dark, the bed unmade. She imagined indentations of bodies on the sheets and pillows.

On Lali's bedside table was a laminated novena to Saint Jude. She read the first part of the prayer:

Most holy Apostle, St. Jude, faithful servant
and friend of Jesus, the Church honors and
invokes you universally as the patron of hope.
Pray for me when I feel helpless and alone.

Her chest constricted. Was Lali praying this every night? Pilar tried to suppress the thoughts, but guilt flooded her.

In the dressing room, built-in closets lined one wall. She slid open a door. Racks of shoes, most of them imported, arranged according to color. Stiletto heels, pumps, flip-flops for the beach, pastel-colored sandals. The foreign press had written about the General's wife and her collection of shoes, but there were hundreds of women like her in Manila—the difference was a matter of means, not desire. And fear—for decades, people said, the General's wife hadn't thrown away any of her shoes or clothes. People said a shoe absorbed the imprints of a soul; a discarded blouse could slowly and from a distance poison the woman who had worn it. Perhaps Lali, too, was afraid someone might get hold of something that had touched her body and use it to perform black magic on her.

Footsteps, then more lights in the bedroom. Arturo, looking startled, entered the dressing room. He surveyed the racks of shoes, as though trying to understand what she was looking for.

"Everyone's waiting for us at the cathedral," he said uneasily. He touched her shoulder. "Are you okay?"

The pressure of his fingers radiated across her shoulder and up the back of her neck. "I'm nervous," she said. "I'm not sure I can face her. She might make a scene."

He removed his hand. "She won't make a scene. I promise you."

He hadn't told her what had happened between Lali and him when he returned to Manila. I don't want to talk about it, he had told Pilar. It's not fair to Lali. I want to be respectful toward her.

Respectful? Pilar asked.

Just know I've talked to her, he said.

Now she told him: "I love how you are with Aimee."

He lowered his head and kissed her forehead. Again there was that rush in her chest. Not happiness—the first time it happened she had thought it was happiness, but it wasn't. It was a fullness, the sense—the hope—that her life was finally happening, that at last it had content. She had told herself it was a mistake to count on him, on her longing for him, for content. She told herself she had spent too much of her life trying to avoid mistakes.

Let me have this.

From high stained-glass windows, light flowed into the cathedral. Pilar sat in a pew near the middle of the building. Guests were arriving and filling the seats. Someone began playing on the organ. Near the altar, Arturo was talking to the baby's numerous godparents—two government ministers and family friends.

Lali walked slowly down the central aisle, toward Pilar, pausing to talk with relatives and other guests. She wore a tight white dress, stiletto-heeled white sandals, a lace veil down to her shoulders.

Pilar had prepared her lines, in case she needed them. She repeated them now in her mind: *You told me to go, Lali. You said you wanted this. You said it was a gift.*

Lali was coming closer. She seemed to be looking at everyone except Pilar.

Pilar stood, stepped out to the aisle to meet her.

Lali embraced her. At first, Pilar tried to pull away, but Lali was trembling. Pilar held her close, confused and afraid. She had prepared to tell Lali many things, but she hadn't been prepared to say she was sorry, and that was the only thing she wanted to tell Lali now.

Lali stepped away. She gave a wan, brittle smile. "I'm so glad you're here," Lali said, too loudly, as though she wanted other people to hear that all was well between them. "It's been too long."

Pilar gazed at her sister's pale, inscrutable face. Be careful, she told herself. She's playing you.

The arches of Lali's eyebrows seemed like inverted smiles. She tipped back her head, neck so long and thin it seemed barely able to support the weight of her head and hair. "Don't worry," Lali said, whispering now. "I did this to myself."

Then she was gone, sauntering up the aisle, stopping to talk to friends and relatives, planting kisses on cheeks, swaying on her heels.

Pilar sat on the pew, hands clasped on her lap. She and Lali had been born in the same year, eleven months apart. They had shared the same bedroom, attended the same school, wore matching dresses and shoes, cut their hair in the same style. They had the same toys, the same books, the same high cheekbones. For years, Pilar had loved her older sister more than herself. Then one day she realized it was Lali everyone loved.

Now Pilar watched Lali and Arturo at the altar and asked herself whether she wanted Arturo only because he belonged to Lali. The line between right and wrong, her beacon in the years since her father died, had disappeared.

At the altar, after the ceremony, Arturo lifted the baby from Lali's arms and began to rock her. Lali slid her arm around his waist, turned to the photographers with her heart-stopping smile. Cameras flashed. A beautiful couple, Pilar thought. The same smile, the radiance.

Arturo tilted his head to the side, toward Lali. She looked up at him. Their lips touched.

Pilar's hands went cold. Until the baby is born, Lali had said. That was madness. The plan was madness. To save the marriage, Lali said. Well, it seemed she had saved it.

What had she, Pilar, been thinking?

She tried to comfort herself: He has to act this way. Everyone's watching.

Under the crucified Jesus, Lali and Arturo, their arms around each other's waist, beamed at the cameras.

Perhaps it was true what Lali said. Arturo couldn't make a choice. He tried to please everyone. He couldn't fire anyone. He couldn't break up with anyone. He couldn't take a stance. He pushes people, Lali said, until they're forced to make the choices he wanted all along.

From the doorway to the kitchen, Pilar watched the party. In the midst of the crowded living room, acquaintances and relatives surrounded Arturo and Lali. He didn't look at Pilar. The old sense of loneliness and exclusion waited like a shadow beside her. She told herself: He's only being cautious. He's afraid. But he looked happy. Maids brushed against her as they carried platters of appetizers into the living room. Spring rolls, cocktail sausages wrapped in flaky pastry, dips with sliced carrots and red peppers. Across the room, government officials, fashion models, and industrialists laughed around the buffet table. Cabinet ministers cried out to each other like schoolboys. Their wives stood primly beside them, with tight smiles and tight faces. Stationed near windows and entrances, bodyguards and security men surveyed the crowd. On one side of the room, Marilou sat on a leather couch, her white scarf concealing her neck.

Hand on hip, Lali was scanning the room. To avoid her, Pilar swung around, entered the yellow-tiled kitchen, hurried past the maids and cook, took the stairs to her mother's room.

A woman doctor, one of the guests, was sitting on her mother's bed, taking her blood pressure.

"She's doing well," the doctor told Pilar. She smiled kindly at Pilar's mother. "I'm trying to convince her to go out and join the party."

Pilar's mother shook her head. On the bedside table, a plastic cup held her pills—tranquilizers, blood-thinners, sleeping pills. Her mother could no longer stand up alone. When Western medicine failed to cure her, Lali had taken over. She called in an eighty-year-old woman from the mountains, the Taoist real-estate tycoon, a teenage nun from Tagaytay, psychic healers, sorcerers from southern islands. Nothing worked. Lali returned to the hospitals. Now, most doctors refused to see their mother. Get rid of her barbiturates first, they told the sisters. Pilar and Lali rummaged through the closets and threw out the pills. Lali ordered placebos, but their mother managed to bribe or intimidate the maids and drivers, and slowly rebuilt her supply.

"I'll be going now, Auntie," the doctor said, packing the stethoscope and blood-pressure cuff.

Pilar's mother gave a weak nod.

Pilar followed the doctor out the door, leaned toward her, and whispered, as she did to the few people who still visited her mother: "Isn't there something anyone can do for her?"

The doctor looked into Pilar's eyes. "You can't cure someone who doesn't want to be cured."

Pilar shut the door, sat on her mother's bed. Despite her mother's sadness, despite the musty smells and shadows, she felt safe here, away from Lali and Arturo and their baby.

Her mother's probing eyes. "You don't look well, *hija*."

"I'm fine."

"You're so thin. Why won't you tell me why you went abroad all those weeks?"

"I did tell you, Ma. I was in Hong Kong. I needed a holiday."

"Don't tell anyone about him," her mother said. "Promise me."

Pilar started. Were there no secrets in this city?

"Don't let Lali hurt you," her mother said. "You're worth more than both of them."

Under the red-pink blossoms of the frangipani tree, Lali, Arturo, and the baby were posing again for photographers. Behind them, the swimming pool was a transparent green. Further away, under a white awning, maids and caterers bustled around tables, adjusting place settings and flower arrangements.

The photographers returned their cameras to their cases. Lali removed the smile from her face and settled the baby in the nanny's arms. She climbed the stone steps to the living room, wended her way through the crowd. Men and women stopped talking and stared as she passed. Lali's long black hair swung across her back. Spaghetti straps held up the dress, exposing her creamy shoulders. Over stiletto-heeled sandals, her legs were long and pale.

Through the glass doors of the living room, Pilar watched Arturo's eyes track his wife. A thought jolted her: He'll never leave her.

Pilar glanced at her sister's nervous, drawn face and remembered Lali trembling in her arms in the cathedral. Impossible to know what Arturo had told her, what Lali wanted from her, what she was supposed to say. Even with a crowd between them, the tension between them felt so great Pilar couldn't look at Lali for more than a few moments.

At some point, Lali would turn against her, as she would against Arturo. Perhaps she already had. But there was this, too: Whatever Lali was or had been, she had always tried to protect her little sister. Lali had never set out to hurt Pilar, or to take away what she loved most, as Pilar had done to her.

Shouts, near the front door. Security men were charging toward the entrance, pistols in their hands. Arturo ran behind them.

"Everything is okay," Arturo cried. "Relax, everyone."

He stood by the doorway. Dozens of guests hurried toward him, crowded around the entrance, trying to see what had caused the commotion. Lali and Pilar squeezed through the crowd and made their way toward Arturo.

A white van was edging up the driveway. It slowed to a stop. Two soldiers jumped out and opened the back doors. A smiling man in army fatigues emerged into the sunlight. He was athletic-looking and pale, with a thin black moustache, aquiline nose, and slanted eyes.

Marilou's girlish laughter. "It's Jimbo! He's invited!"

Around Pilar, guests murmured and strained for a better look. Although officially in hiding, Jimbo had been making the rounds of Manila's social events again. Society hostesses loved him. No one dared arrest him—he was too powerful. Besides, the military and police supported him. After several Jimbo-led coup attempts and one spectacular prison escape, when his guards switched sides and ran away with him, the government increased the salaries of soldiers and policemen by 60 percent, hoping this would dissuade them from joining Jimbo's camp.

Arturo's security guards eyed the rebel leader. Jimbo shook

their hands and chatted briefly with each one, staring straight into their eyes. He seemed to electrify the air around him.

As he neared the entrance, Lali and Arturo stepped forward to meet him. "Nice to see you again," Lali said. She gave a pretty smile.

He lifted both hands in the air, in mock surrender. "I promise not to stay very long, ma'am."

"How are you?" Arturo asked, with forced heartiness.

The two men eyed each other warily.

Pilar didn't understand the intricacies of Arturo's alliances, but she knew this: Arturo and Jimbo both wanted power, and both had an enemy greater than each other, the same obstacle to their ambitions—the country's besieged, saintly president.

Marilou shepherded the guests through the living room and down the steps to the garden. Under the white awning, round tables had been set with white tablecloths, fine crystal and china, silver cutlery and centerpieces of pale pink roses. Marilou directed guests to their seats. At the far end of the garden, Pilar found her place at the table reserved for the immediate family, principal godparents, and a few government ministers and their wives. She sat and nodded at the other guests.

At the tables in front of her, people turned and looked toward the house. Arturo, Lali, and Jimbo were walking down the stone steps. As the trio passed tables, many guests stood. Men shook Jimbo's hand. At each table, one or two guests remained seated, staring at their plates. Jimbo spoke and laughed with almost everyone, even those who sat and tried to avoid his gaze. He nodded at the ministers who had ordered government troops to fire on him and his men. People whispered that funding for Jimbo's coup attempts came from the ex-dictator's seaside villa in Hawaii, but Jimbo denied this. He said the General was no longer relevant.

When they reached Pilar's table, Arturo pointed his hands,

palms flat and facing upwards, at Jimbo. "Ladies and gentlemen, our next president."

Jimbo laughed. "Only if your wife agrees to run as my vice-president." He inclined his head toward Lali. "You impressed everyone, ma'am, during that shipping incident."

"Has my husband offered you something to drink?" Lali asked smoothly, managing to sound both polite and dismissive.

She seated Jimbo between Pilar and herself, signaled at the waiters to pour champagne into the flutes. Arturo sat next to Lali. Pilar tried not to look at him.

Jimbo turned to Pilar and offered his hand. "Jaime Montenegro," he said, as though she might not know.

She pressed her palm against his. "Pilar."

"My sister-in-law," Arturo called out.

The words—her position in his life—hurt her.

The maids brought platters of stuffed crab, chicken in vinegar and soy sauce, rice, and Chinese noodles. Lali stood to help serve the guests, blocking Pilar's view of Arturo. Maternity had ripened her body, her curves barely contained by the flimsy dress. Aimee's birth seemed to have sharpened her features, accentuating her high cheekbones and the heart-shaped contour of her face.

She spooned rice and chicken onto Jimbo's plate. "You're a big hit here," she said. "Everyone loves you."

"A lot of flatterers, ma'am," he replied lightly.

"Not just flatterers." Her voice was placid, impersonal. "You have lots of friends here."

"All my friends are dead, ma'am."

The table fell silent. Lali stared at him, then set the serving spoon on the tray and sat down.

With her napkin, Marilou wiped lipstick from the rim of her champagne flute. "Did you hear that the church allows cremation now? When I was young, it was a mortal sin! When I was in school, the nuns said we had to keep our bodies intact for the Second Coming, so we can all rise from our graves and join our Lord in heaven."

"Everyone gets cremated these days," the labor minister's wife said.

Marilou flashed a coquettish smile at Jimbo. "When I die, I want to be cremated so my ashes can be placed inside my Ming antique jars and given to my son and grandchildren."

"That's a good idea," Jimbo said. His back straight, he lifted his fork until it was parallel to his mouth, then brought it toward his lips. His posture spoke of military discipline, self-restraint, moderation—qualities absent from most people in the garden, Pilar thought.

"You're much better looking in person," Marilou told him. "You shouldn't be a soldier—you should be a movie star!"

Almost everyone at the table laughed. Pilar turned away from him.

Jimbo told her: "You're always very quiet?"

Pilar folded her napkin. She became aware of heat spreading up her neck. "Actually, I was thinking about you."

"Really?" He flashed a smile at the guests. "Tell me."

Anger sparked inside her, with all the pain and confusion she had been pushing back all day. "I was thinking about how you seem so nice," she said.

Arturo and a few other guests were staring at her. Lali shot her a warning look.

"How you don't seem at all like what people say you are."

"Really? What do people say I am?"

Say it, Pilar told herself. Someone has to say it. Her father would never have sat there making small talk with Jimbo. Someone in this party has to tell the truth.

"Ruthless," she told him.

"For God's sake," Lali said.

Smiles disappeared. Government ministers held their forks in midair. Only Jimbo seemed unflustered. "Ruthless?" he repeated, as though to make sure everyone at the table heard the word. "What else do they say?"

He was staring at her. His eyes were black, feral. They helped her remember which side she was on. And that, unlike Arturo, she had to choose sides. In this world, her father had said, every honest person has to choose a side.

"They say you're brutal," she said.

Jimbo's expression remained cordial, but when he spoke his voice was icy. "Well, let me be clear," he said, addressing everyone at the table. "I detest violence. I don't want my men to hurt anyone. I've always instructed them to be polite, peaceful, and very careful."

"I can vouch for that," Marilou said cheerfully. "You know, when your men took over the buildings on Ayala Avenue during the last coup—"

"Forgive me, ma'am, but my men have never been involved in a coup."

"All right, if you want." Marilou waved her fingers in the air, brushing away his words. "Anyway. *Someone's* men took over the condominiums, and all the people there were asked, very politely, to evacuate. The rebels needed to take up their positions, so they could shoot at the government troops on the avenue."

"Ma—" Arturo cut in, his smile tense.

"Anyway, what was amazing was, this friend of mine—she was one of those asked to leave her condo—well, when her friends called from abroad to ask whether she was safe, the rebels answered the phone and took down messages for her, and all her friends were impressed by how nice they were."

"People say such nonsense," Lali said sharply, gesturing at the waiters to refill the champagne flutes.

"And they spoke good English! When my friend went back to her condo after the coup, there was a neat list of messages, with times and names and numbers all noted."

Jimbo gave a faint smile. He ignored Pilar.

"I'm sorry," Lali told him.

"There's nothing to be sorry about." To Marilou he said: "I'm flattered, ma'am. But those weren't my men."

"Well, I think it's time—" Arturo began.

Lali's slender fingers touched his shoulder. He didn't finish his sentence. Pilar watched them. He was looking at Lali. Almost at the same time, as though by agreement, Lali and Arturo turned their faces toward Jimbo. They looked like siblings. The same false smile, the same wariness in their eyes.

Pilar unfolded her napkin, set it on her lap. No one spoke to her.

Lali began chatting with the guests, her words filled with warmth and gaiety. Only someone who knew her very well, Pilar thought, would notice Lali's pallor, the feverishness in her eyes, the strain.

Who was she, Pilar, to think she could speak honestly? Who was she to think she was honorable?

The enormity, the foolishness, of what she had done came to her. The wrongness of it. She couldn't destroy her sister's family. She couldn't honor her father and carry out his work, and also love Arturo.

She was profoundly dishonest. And brutal, and ruthless.

Arturo draped his arm around the back of Lali's chair.

She would tell him it was over. It was probably already over. Perhaps Lali and Arturo already knew that. What had seemed enormous—her love for Arturo, their feelings for each other—suddenly seemed small and shameful. She would leave Manila, stay in a relative's house in the province somewhere, let all this disappear.

The band was playing the latest hits from Latin America. Guests trooped back to the living room. Men cupped their partners' hips, just above their buttocks. Swaying alone in the middle of the dance floor was a starlet best known for a spread in the Australian edition of *Playboy*. The starlet lifted her arms above her head and swayed her hips in a little circle. Men and their wives watched her.

An elderly man asked Marilou to dance. The crowd hooted as she sashayed onto the dance floor, hiked up her skirt, and stomped in rhythm to the music.

From the entrance to the kitchen, young maids peeked out at the dancers, giggling, covering their mouths with their hands. Along the walls, bodyguards and security officers swayed slightly to the music.

Pilar made her way along the edges of the crowd, crossed two rooms, descended the narrow staircase to the garage. No drivers, no houseboys. They were probably all in the servants' kitchen, at the other end of the house.

Creased playing cards on a wooden table, empty beer bottles on the floor. Just above the table, someone had taped an image of the Virgin Mary next to pin-ups of local movie stars. Inside their cages, the dogs growled. She sat down, picked up the cards, shuffled them, began to play.

Someone was rapping on the gate. The sound stopped, then started again, more insistently. After a moment, Pilar set down the cards and walked toward it.

Through a peephole, she saw a young man standing just in front of the gate. Short and scrawny, with a white cap and white jacket, several sizes too large for him. One of the guests' drivers, she thought. She unbolted the gate and opened it a few inches.

"Sorry, ma'am," he stammered. "I just went out to get cigarettes."

"I have to see your I.D."

He slipped a laminated card through the opening in the gate. She glanced at the card, returned it to him, pulled open the gate. He didn't move.

"Come inside," she said.

Uneasily, he stepped forward.

"I think all the drivers are in the kitchen," she told him. She studied his face, and began to doubt.

"Ma'am?"

"All the way down there, along the wall. Have you eaten?"

He shook his head, stared at the ground.

The dogs were agitated now, barking. He slipped his hand under his jacket and rubbed his shoulder. Pinned to his T-shirt was a black ribbon.

He saw her looking at it. "My family, ma'am."

She hesitated. "I'm sorry."

Salsa music, punctuated by laughter, drifted through the garage door. A thought flashed: He's not a driver. She gripped the edge of the gate, considered asking him to leave.

"They were coming back from my father-in-law's house," he said. "There was an accident."

He shouldn't be here, she thought. She wished she had kept his ID. Act normal, she told herself. Then go call the guards.

"You should get something to eat," she said. "Just go down that path—you see it, along the wall?—and you'll see the other drivers in the kitchen. There's food there."

"Yes, ma'am."

He shuffled down the path. She locked the gate, stood by it for several minutes. Call the guards, she told herself.

Instead she returned to the wooden table, beneath the Virgin and pin-up girls, sat down, and gathered the creased cards. The music stopped. She waited for it to start again. In that silence, the thought resurfaced: He isn't a driver. She spread the cards on the table. The band started another salsa song.

She crossed her hands over the cards.

Minutes went by, slowly. She imagined him sitting with the other drivers in the servants' kitchen, eating rice and fish, not speaking. Half an hour passed, perhaps more. The music stopped. This time it didn't start again.

She followed the cries into the living room. A jumble of images. Bodyguards and security men, shoving away dancers. Arturo swinging around. The scrawny man in the white jacket, near Arturo, his arm in the air. More cries. The images accelerated. Jimbo standing in the middle of the dance floor, feet apart. A popping, like firecrackers.

Someone pushed her to the ground.

When she looked up again, Arturo was lying on the floor. Lali, the woman doctor, and another doctor crouched over him. Pilar wanted to run to him, but her legs wouldn't move. Then she saw his head turning. His mouth was moving. He was talking.

The man in the white jacket was also on the floor. Jimbo stood over him. More popping. Now people were running— men, women, bodyguards. Several men were carrying Arturo out the front door, Lali in her white dress staggering behind them, bloodstains near her hem.

Days later, Pilar would find out who the man was. His wife and six-year-old daughter, the newspapers said, had disappeared around the time of the shipwreck. Their names weren't on the manifest. But relatives had seen them board the ship. Then the police questioned the relatives, and they changed their story. Perhaps the man's wife and daughter had boarded another ship, they said, or left another day. They were no longer sure. They didn't want to say the wrong thing. He would never have hurt anyone, his crying sister told a television reporter. He was too sad. Maybe sadness made him lose his mind. The reporter told the camera: There is a tradition of amok. The heat, the shifts in weather—these can kill moral feeling. The reporter said the young man blamed Arturo for his family's death. His sister said, No, it was all a mistake; he was working that day for one of the guests at the party. No one could find the guest or confirm the story.

But all this came later. On the day of Aimee's christening, no one knew his name.

Two hours after the shooting, the police said on the radio that the young man was dead by the time they arrived. That evening, at a press conference, the police declared he had died of his wounds on the way to the hospital.

Pilar knew he was alive when the police took him away.

In the late afternoon, caterers packed up the tables and chairs. Houseboys scrubbed the dance floor. No one spoke. In the kitchen, red-eyed maids spooned Chinese noodles, smoked salmon, and deep-pink Russian salad into plastic containers.

Bad luck—everyone knew it. A man was dead, or might soon be, on the day of Aimee's christening.

Pilar sat on the stone steps, facing the garden. Where table legs had sunk into the earth, holes now dotted the lawn. In her mind, she saw the man's nervous face, the rakish white cap.

A phone was ringing inside the house.

Footsteps. A teenage maid appeared beside her, eyes lowered. Pilar scanned her face and thought: They're all going to leave us. If that man really is dead, they'll be afraid to live here, with the ghost of a murdered man.

"It's Señorita Lali, ma'am," the girl murmured.

The phone was on a low carved table near a window overlooking the garden. Pilar stared at it, took a breath, picked it up. Lali's hoarse voice: "How's Mama? Have you seen her?"

"She's fine."

A silence. Pilar didn't dare ask about Arturo.

"He's okay," Lali said. "The doctors said he was lucky—it was just the leg." Lali began to talk quickly, as though a rush of words could displace the distrust and tensions between them: How did that man get into the house? I sent Aimee to Marilou's. Now, it's Marilou who's driving me crazy. She became hysterical in the car. They had to give her tranquilizers. She says she's having a heart attack. No one believes her, but she refuses to leave the hospital.

Pilar set the phone on the table. Outside, the sky was dimming to violet-blue. Pink blossoms floated on the pool.

When she picked up the receiver again, Lali said: "Can you imagine? Now, he owes Jimbo his life."

"I'm going back home," Pilar said.

"Don't."

"Excuse me?"

"Please don't leave. Pilar, someone has to stay with Mama."

"It's terrible here. Even the maids are crying."

A silence. Then: "Pilar, you *owe* me."

In the morning, the taxi dropped Pilar at the basement entrance of the hospital. Three flights of stairs, then another. Opaque light clouded the glass panels.

Two security men guarded his door. They recognized her, noted her name and the time in a logbook. She scribbled her initials next to her name. The guards pushed open the door.

An elderly nurse was sitting beside his bed. A white sheet over his body, tubes attached to his hand. Only his eyes turned to her. He gestured at the nurse to leave the room.

Pilar stood by the bed, remembering her father on another hospital cot.

Arturo was breathing through his mouth, lips cracked, chest rising and falling. "I know I look like hell." He gave a weak smile. "But it's just my leg."

A man was killed for your leg, she wanted to tell him. But maybe he didn't know that yet. Maybe it wasn't for her to tell him. In a soft voice, she said, "He wasn't armed."

"Who told you that?"

"The police. They came to the house. No weapon, no traces of gunpowder."

He shook his head. "I *saw* him."

"Not even a knife," Pilar said.

"That's not possible."

"Some of the guards were shooting, too. Jimbo was shooting." Anger was rising in her again. She tried to force it back. "We don't know who shot you."

"Pilar, I'm exhausted," he said.

She watched him fade into sleep. Bluish circles smudged the skin beneath his eyes. On the bedside table she saw a Virgin-shaped bottle of holy water and the laminated novena to Saint Jude, which Lali must have left here. Pilar picked up the novena.

Please make use of that particular privilege
given to you, to bring hope and comfort
and help where they are needed most
that I may receive the consolation and help
of heaven in my tribulations and sufferings

She switched off the light, lowered the shades. The room was cold. In the semidarkness, she looked at his closed eyes, his dark eyebrows and pale cheeks, remembering his kindness and skin and pleasure in her presence. It wasn't true, what she had thought at the cathedral. It wasn't true that she had wanted him only because he belonged to Lali. What she felt now, these lashings of tenderness and regret, had nothing to do with Lali.

Please let me have this.
Please let me brave enough to give this up.

She held his upper arm. The warmth of his skin entered into her. In his sleep, he seemed soft and passive. Perhaps this was what a man felt when he touched a woman. Stronger, more powerful. She stroked his hair, barely touching it so as not to wake him. There was something about violence. What she had seen in the province—the flames, the village on fire, the running into the night. She couldn't get it out of her. This is what she could never tell Arturo: She had known that man in the white jacket was dangerous, and she had let him into the house. She had wanted him to destroy the party, to hurt the people inside that house, to attack her sister and the man she loved.

It was only a feeling, she told herself. We all have violent feelings. But we don't act on them. We keep them locked away, in those separate chambers in our hearts.

That wasn't true. There were no separate chambers. The violence had permeated her, and all the rest, too. What she feared and despised most, what she wanted to be, what she fought against, what she loved, what to a large extent had given meaning to her life—all these were mixed up inside her. The best and the worst came from the same place.

CHAPTER TEN

THE JOURNEY

She doesn't see the irony of it,
how we always wind up nursing the ones
we savage the most.

—ERIC GAMALINDA, "Two Nudes"

LALI

Lali drove home. No use waiting in the hospital, with its ammonia and antiseptics and disease, with the white clothes and white rooms and white tiles unable to mask the smells of sickness and decay.

In her bathroom, she soaked a washcloth in tepid water and ran it over her thighs and the stain on her dress, scrubbing out the blood. The good wife, she told herself. The brave wife, with his blood instead of semen on her thighs.

Promise me you'll take care of Pilar, Arturo had told her in the hospital. He had been thinking of Pilar, not her, at a time like this.

Lali undressed but didn't shower, wanting to keep the day's violence on her body—the way, in other times, after making love, she spent a day and night without bathing, to keep a man's touch on her skin. From a drawer, she pulled out a black-lace garter belt, beige stockings, an almost transparent black bra. She slid the stockings over her legs, attached them to the garters. Arturo didn't like her to dress like this. Too vulgar, he said. She adjusted the cups of the bra and fastened the clasps behind her. No panties. But no possibility of sex, either. It was too soon after the birth.

She chose a grey silk coatdress, fastened the white nacre buttons in front, strapped on a pair of high-heeled sandals. She spread plum-red lipstick over her mouth.

Arturo, the family, the possibility of a life that wouldn't shatter. Where was all that now? And when he came out of the hospital, what would happen to her? And after the election, when he no longer needed her?

She reached for her hairbrush, bent over, head facing the floor, and brushed her hair from the roots to the tips, over and over again.

She was in her car, driving as fast as she could, away from the large houses and landscaped gardens. She thought of Miguel, the life she might have had with him, the people they might have become with each other. She remembered the plastic bag filled with red hair, the presence over her shoulder, and Sister Esperanza insisting it was a young man, not her father.

Go to him, Sister Esperanza had told her. Find the place where he disappeared. Ask for forgiveness. Some spirits become more desperate, more persistent, until you put them to rest.

He didn't seem surprised to see her. He crossed his arms and leaned against the doorway. Faded jeans and a red T-shirt hung loosely from his body. A pale-blue baseball cap covered his hair.

He glanced at her belly. "You're not pregnant anymore."

"And you haven't left the country."

David smiled, but his eyes darkened. "It's taking longer than I thought."

"May I come in?"

He stepped aside. The room was empty except for the mattress on the floor. Over it, where a crucifix should have been, hung a dried garland of *sampaguita* blossoms, like the one he had given her months before. She remembered how he had fastened it around her neck, how he had hunched over her and arranged jasmine petals on her breasts.

"I heard about the shooting." His eyes touched hers. "Your husband—"

"He's fine."

Across the front of his T-shirt were black inscriptions in a language she couldn't understand. She touched the brim of his baseball cap. She pulled it off. Several inches of reddish-brown hair, thick and soft-looking, streaked by the sun.

"I know," he said. "It's grown a bit."

She touched his hair, just over his neck. He didn't move. She became aware of her bare skin against the silk dress.

She sat on the mattress, under the garland of *sampaguitas*. Standing over her, he said, "Why are you here?"

"I won't stay long."

She wanted to tell him that she needed to be near a man who couldn't hurt her. She needed a man to undo the buttons on her dress, to sit with her in a bathtub and comb out her hair, to play with her and be pleasured by her, but it had been so long since she had felt for anyone what she had once felt for Arturo.

She remembered a cold night, years ago, on a trip to Europe, before Arturo. She had set out to explore the city, strange and sinister in the early hours of morning. She ended up climbing narrow stairs in Montmartre. Rows of dark houses and trees on each side, no one in sight. The silhouette of a young man, wrapped in a coat, appeared at the top of the steps. Head bent, he hurried down toward her. He stopped one step above her. She lifted her face to him. They looked at each other. He was beautiful, but not frightening. He touched her mouth. Without speaking, they moved to the shadows behind a tree. Intensity was all she wanted. No names, no emotion, no conversation. The rough bark cut into her skin. She inserted the stranger's thumb into her mouth, to silence herself. Somehow, because she had never seen the young man before and would never see him again, because she couldn't see his face clearly in the dark and would never be able to remember it, she had told herself it didn't matter.

Everyone who makes love to you leaves a mark forever, Sister Esperanza had told her.

The small, windowless room. Photographs, again, all over the walls. The Chop-Chops, the Remnants of God, their victims. In one photograph, a man wore a T-shirt exactly like David's.

"It's not the same shirt," he said, when she asked. "Look at the inscriptions."

She squinted and leaned toward the photograph. The writing on the T-shirt reminded her of the triangular amulet, inscribed with pig Latin, that her grandmother had worn between her breasts.

"They all use T-shirts like this when they go out to fight," he said. "It's supposed to protect them from bullets."

"A T-shirt against bullets?"

"The inscription, not the shirt. One of them told me there was a group of them that walked straight toward bullets. They got hit, but no one got hurt."

She started to say something, but stopped herself.

With his large-knuckled index finger, he pointed at another photograph. "You know why they call them the Chop-Chops?"

"Because that's what they do to their victims."

"Not just. They chant prayers over their machetes, to make themselves powerful. They steal kneecaps from graveyards— they hack them out of skeletons—to wear as amulets." She sensed his excitement, his efforts to control it. "They lead good lives, Lali. They pray and meditate, twice a day. They follow strict rules—no adultery, no smoking, no drinking, no dancing, no gambling, no judging others."

From some angles, and through certain expressions, she could see the Filipino in him.

"Do you pray?" he asked. "Every day."

Today the balances were fragile. She walked a tightrope, and the weaknesses no one gave her credit for—her fears for Arturo, her love for him, her anxiety for herself—waited on both sides, only a misstep away. She had to look straight ahead.

He stirred instant coffee in hot water. She cradled the chipped bowl. The garters pinched her thighs. He sat on the floor, next to her. He said he was leaving for the south, to take one last series of photos.

Steam rose from the bowl.

He talked about another massacre on an island, in another village. Reprisals, he said. He told her the name of the town closest to the village. She set the cup on the floor, made him repeat it.

It sounded like one of the places where Miguel had been seen after the shipwreck. But there had been so many places and so many sightings, and she couldn't be sure.

She sipped the coffee.

Go to him, Sister Esperanza had told her.

In the hospital, Arturo had asked for Pilar.

Sometimes she walked through a day and saw only the surfaces of people. Sometimes she saw the cracks in the surfaces, and the possibility of entering, through them, into the deeper and more radical parts of a person. The last time she saw Arturo, at the hospital, almost everything she thought she knew about him darkened.

She didn't know David. She studied his face, considering her options. She could return to her life and Arturo and baby. She could fight for them. She could not fight. She could abandon, for now, the life she had shattered.

They took a regular flight from Manila to a city in a southern island, then bounced along an unpaved road in a hired jeep for most of the afternoon. At dusk, they boarded a run-down, tilting ship for the two-day journey to the village he was seeking.

Their cabin had two single beds, a porthole, a toilet with a plastic seat. The air conditioner sputtered warm air; the walls and carpeting were stained. Lali lay in the darkness, her back to David, waiting for a sleeping pill to take effect.

In the morning, they climbed narrow metal stairs to the upper deck. Passengers sat in clusters in the open air, cradling babies and toddlers, playing guitars and singing.

David wandered through the crowds, seemingly unaware of the stares. In English and broken Tagalog, his accent fracturing the words, he tried to talk to a group of middle-aged women. They covered their mouths with their fingers, commented on his height, joked about the size of his thumb.

He smiled back at them, understanding nothing. Lali felt sorry for him. She was used to people shifting from Tagalog to English and Spanish to Ilonggo, barely noticing the transitions. Now she looked at a man who wanted to understand but couldn't communicate, and he seemed handicapped, an object of curiosity and perhaps scorn.

They leaned over the railings. The ship sailed past several small rocky islands, without trees, bushes or houses. The sun reddened his pale cheeks and nose.

"Why did you come here," she asked, "when you can't understand anything?"

He kept his eyes on the sea. His height and the solidity of his body seemed to envelop her. "I came to Asia thinking it would be liberating—not having to understand. Just watching. I spent years like that. When I finally decided to go to the Philippines, I thought, okay, now I'm ready to talk, people speak English there. It took me about a year to realize that I still had no idea what people really meant, even if I understood the words."

"Maybe you understand more than you realize?"

"No, I don't."

That face. Not beautiful, yet she was drawn to it—the intelligence and caution.

"Do I seem strange to you?" he asked.

"Well, you don't want sex," she blurted out. She stopped, embarrassed.

He laughed. "You don't know that yet."

She remembered the windowless room, the photos he had taped to the wall, the scissors in her hands.

White-crested waves chased each other over the aquamarine sea. She tried to imagine Miguel's ship, and Arturo's, disappearing into this sea.

"Sometimes I think Miguel's near." She watched David's face for signs of impatience, ready to speak of other things if he seemed uninterested or dismissive.

"Because you feel him?"

"Because I *don't* feel him, or not so much anymore. The closer we get to that town, the less I feel him." The less she felt any of the other ghosts, she wanted to add, and in truth the face over her shoulder had disappeared, but she couldn't talk about that.

Broad fingers, lightly tufted by red hair, gripped the railing. "I have a hard time believing those things," he said.

People on the top deck had snickered when he tried to talk, and now the memory of their mockery and her silence shamed her.

"Were you in love with him?" he asked.

"I need to believe that. But maybe just in retrospect."

"Lali, if it's possible," he said gently, "I'd like only good thoughts from you during this trip. Or at least, only good words."

"Those *were* good thoughts."

At the end of the second day, as a red sun dipped into the violet sea, the ship glided toward shore. A wooden pier, dim street lamps, crowds waiting, then the shouts of passengers as they hauled crates and plastic bags down the planks.

A young man stepped out of the shadows and reached for Lali's bags. He had a moon-shaped face, narrow eyes, thick eyebrows that almost met over his nose. David patted him on the back. The man stared shamelessly into Lali's eyes, then gave a bright, tight smile, like someone used to dealing with foreigners. She disliked him immediately.

He led them along the edges of the crowd toward a beer garden. Pop music pulsated from tinny speakers. Strung between bamboo poles, garlands of twinkling lights festooned the walls. At the bar, three women in short skirts and sequined halter tops glanced sideways at David. They seemed to be in their late thirties; thick black eyeliner outlined their eyes from one end to another. They tapped their high heels against the legs of their bar stools. Lali didn't sit down. "I don't want a beer," she told David. "I'll be back." She hurried away before he could stop her.

She walked along the beach to a strip of grey sand, in the shadows, away from the commotion at the pier. She looked beyond the ship to the darkening sea. All that remained of the sun was a reddish glow over the horizon.

She couldn't imagine Miguel drowning in this sea. She lowered her eyes, made the sign of the cross, tried to feel his presence. Nothing.

She told herself: His body's near. That's why I can't feel him.

David's friend guided them with a flashlight down a narrow dirt path, almost parallel to the sea. In the semidarkness, she stumbled over rocks, discarded tires, beer bottles, tangled nets. They turned into another path and began to climb a hill. Near the top, at the doorway of a sprawling cement house, a plump middle-aged woman waited for them. She led them into the living room.

They removed their shoes. Marble flooring, two televisions, an expensive stereo set, a fake-leather red couch and matching armchairs, vases of plastic roses. Everything was new. Tacked to the walls were grainy, poster-size photos of Filipinos abroad—dozens of them kneeling in front of the Eiffel Tower or Notre Dame, a man waving from the top of the Arc de Triomphe, a smiling woman and two children bundled in heavy coats in front of a bus. Overseas workers. Probably domestic help who sent money home every month. Our heroes, the president said. The country's most profitable export.

The woman led them to separate rooms. Lali's had an electric fan on the ceiling, a large bed, candles and matches by the bedside table. She locked the door and walked to the window. Darkened houses and trees, no stars. She tried to hear the sea. I don't miss Arturo, she told herself, as though saying it would make it true. He hadn't protested when she said she was going south. He had asked her only to be back for the big campaign rally with the president and her brother.

She sat on the bed. The last time she had seen Miguel, he had pushed her against the wall of the den, his hand under her skirt, telling her he would love her forever. The last time she heard him, he was crying on the phone after midnight. She had transferred the receiver from one ear to another, as though changing position would ease his discomfort. Finally, meaning to console him, she said, "You don't know what you're saying."

Another night, early in their relationship, a pretty American woman in her thirties, with short blonde hair and an unhappy marriage to a wealthy Filipino, invited Miguel and Lali and other teenage couples on a treasure hunt across Manila. One of the clues led them to a strip club, where naked girls danced on a stage, watched by overweight, yelling Australians and silent Japanese tour groups. When the girls began to kiss each other, Miguel squeezed Lali's hand and led her out to the street. Child vendors and beggars besieged them with bouquets of small red roses, *sampaguita* garlands, and outstretched hands. They bought all the roses they could hold and returned to the bar, offered them to each girl on the stage. The Australians protested drunkenly; the girls refused the flowers. When they resumed their performance, Miguel crossed his arms and watched only Lali. Years later, on a trip abroad, she had visited a nightclub where dozens of men and women were having sex in a dimly lit backroom. Arturo hadn't been with her. She had watched the shapes and shadows for a long time, then she stopped watching. This was the other life, which neither Arturo nor Miguel nor any of her lovers imagined. The Lali they loved was false, because partial. Only Miguel, among all of them, wouldn't have cared. He would have tried to understand. We need to believe we mattered to someone, she thought. We need to believe someone in the world, at some point in our lives, mattered utterly to us.

At dawn, before the heat, David and Lali hurried along the path, surrounded by deep-green bushes. Above them, pink clouds streamed across the lavender sky. The young man had disappeared. Lali didn't know where David was taking her. He navigated the winding paths with an assurance that both reassured and alarmed her.

On the outskirts of the town, the vegetation gave way to a sandy plain. They walked toward a wooden one-story schoolhouse. In the yard, a Philippine flag fluttered from a pole, its three yellow stars bleached almost white by the sun.

"This is it," David said. He removed a camera from his bag.

Inside the schoolhouse, the main hall was crammed with people sitting on the floor or sleeping on wooden crates. Mothers nursed babies; old women fingered rosaries.

David's fingers tightened around hers. He led her through the crowd. She tried to keep her eyes on the ground, but she occasionally glanced up. Slumped against a wall was a skinny girl, about ten years old, with a bloodied bandage across one eye. Next to her, a woman held a toddler whose head hung back; the woman tried to insert a nipple into its mouth.

Lali cupped a hand over her mouth. "I can't stay in here."

"It won't take long."

Head bent, she followed him across the hall.

He knocked, opened the door to a small office. Sitting behind a desk was a woman in her sixties, with sharp features and a high-collared white blouse. A wooden cross hung over her chest. David introduced the woman—a lay sister, he said, who worked for a Christian community group, organizing people in small barrios throughout the province. Lali smiled politely.

They sat on stools in front of the desk. David turned his long legs sideways, away from Lali.

The lay sister opened a folder. "What organization do you work for?"

Without hesitation, David mentioned half-a-dozen newspapers in Canada and the United States. Lali glanced at him. So he can lie, she thought, surprised.

The woman wrote down his name, telephone number, and address. She handed him a document. "You have to sign here." She watched him scratch a pen across the paper. "If these people's photographs appear in the press, there'll be reprisals. You can talk to them, but you can't use their real names. And no photos. You understand that?"

"I understand."

He slid the document across the desk. The woman studied it.

In a respectful voice, he asked, "Do you know how many people were killed?"

"No," she snapped. "We don't go into the villages and count the bodies."

"I'm sorry." He bit into his thumbnail.

"They said the villagers were feeding Communist guerillas. They said they had warned them."

"Is that true?" he asked softly.

She tapped the folder on the desk. "The villagers were Christians. We held prayer meetings. The hacenderos get very nervous about that."

"About prayer meetings?"

"They say they're a front for the Communists."

Lali stared out the window, at the sunlight. "These villages depend on the haciendas," she said. "The hacenderos give them work, take care of their families."

"What are you talking about?" he asked nervously, glancing at the lay sister.

"My husband's family has an hacienda," Lali told the woman. "But they stopped going there long ago." She didn't say: They used to have masked balls and swimming parties and picnics and friends who came to visit for months. And they were happy there—Arturo told me he was happy there, every summer when he went. She said: "Now, it's too dangerous to live there. That's not the hacenderos' fault."

David looked stricken. He leaned forward, his fingers spread wide apart on his thighs. In a meek voice, as though to distance himself from Lali, he asked the lay sister, "Do you know which vigilante group was responsible for the massacre?"

"They call themselves the Remnants of God. Don't ask me why. The biggest sugar planter here, Montemayor—his brother's the vice-governor—has a private army. He was ambushed by Communist guerillas a few months ago. He survived, but his driver and some of his bodyguards were killed. Now he arms these vigilantes. They even live in his hacienda."

"Well, with land reform—" David began.

"Land reform! You think the politicians are going to give up their haciendas?"

Don't say anything, Lali warned herself. But she said: "Land reform won't work." David grimaced and shut his eyes. He thinks I'm going to ruin his chance for interviews, she thought. He doesn't understand the situation, and all he wants to do is write about it. "Look what happened when the General gave people land," she said. "They didn't know what to do with it. A few years later, they sold their parcels back to the hacenderos. If the planters abandon their haciendas, people won't be able to eat."

The lay sister gave Lali a contemptuous look. She turned to David: "I've been working here for thirty years. Nothing's changed. Not under the General, not under President Peachy, not under anyone. Five thousand babies died on this island last year. The villages were starving, and the hacenderos were throwing costume parties in their houses in Manila. People say champagne flowed from fountains."

"That's gossip," Lali said.

"The babies?" the woman asked coldly.

David's sneaker kicked the leg of Lali's stool.

"No," Lali murmured. "I know about the babies."

The woman stood and led them to the door. "Please be respectful," she told David, ignoring Lali. "And don't take long."

The door clicked shut behind them.

"Were you trying to provoke her?" David asked.

"Don't raise your voice."

"Or were you just trying to sabotage me?"

"You talk about politics, but you don't try to understand the other points of view. You don't go deeper. It's all one-sided."

"Maybe you're right." A red blotch appeared on his neck. She had never seen him angry. "I talk about politics, and I keep forgetting that people like you, like your husband, *are* the politics of this country. Especially when you have no interest in it."

"It's not as simple as you think."

"Don't tell me you believe what you were saying in there."

"That isn't the point!"

But he was already distracted, scanning the crowded room. He walked toward an emaciated old woman. On the floor beside her, teenage boys played a board game with pebbles and ruled plywood.

"Please ask her if we can take her photograph," David said. He sounded tense, but also contrite.

Lali knelt and whispered in the local language. The old woman turned away.

"I don't think she understands me," Lali said.

He held up his camera.

"No photos," Lali said sharply.

"Ask her what happened. About the massacre."

"She won't talk."

"Lali, please, *try*."

The woman was as small as a child. Her shoulders curved toward her chest.

In the language David couldn't understand, Lali whispered:

"*Manang*, I'm so sorry to bother you. But a few years ago, there was a ship that sank near here. Do you remember?"

The woman shook her head.

Lali leaned toward her, wanting to win her trust, or at least to overcome her resistance. "Someone I know was there. The ship was the *Doña Paz*."

A teenager looked up from the board game. "The *Doña Paz*?"

Other young men began to gather around them.

"It was in the other village," the teenager said. "Not here."

"What are they saying?" David asked. "Who's Paz?"

"There were children," one of his friends added. "My uncle's children. My cousins."

"So many bodies floating."

"What are you talking about? There were no bodies. The fish ate everything."

The boys began telling stories—making them up, or embellishing them, Lali suspected. But she needed to hear more. She sat on her heels and listened. Their words bounced off each other; their expressions and gestures grew increasingly agitated.

"They found people. Weeks later, on other islands."

"Hail Mary—the captain broadcast that."

Another boy said his friends were stupid—they were talking about another ship, the one that had sunk this year. That wasn't the *Doña Paz*, and the woman was asking about the *Doña Paz*, the one that sank long ago, when they were in grade six.

"What happened to them?" David asked. "Are they telling you about the massacre?"

"There was a typhoon," said a young man with a long face and impish black eyes. "Really bad. Like God wanted to punish them."

"That's not what she wants to know!"

"They put all the children below the deck. Then they couldn't get out."

"The purser ended up here," another teenager said, smiling, trying to be helpful.

Two boys nudged the one who had just spoken. David started to speak, but Lali lifted her hand to silence him. In a firm voice, she asked the teenager, "What happened to the purser?"

The boys looked uneasy.

"What happened?" she insisted.

A silence. Then one of them, apparently the oldest in the group, said: "So many people here had family, and also friends, in the ship, ma'am. You have to understand. They were so sad. They were angry."

What did the purser say, Lali asked softly, not wanting to frighten them. The boy replied that in the end, everyone was praying on the deck. That was the last thing survivors remembered. The wind, the rain, the praying. Later the purser arrived on the island, carrying money from the ticket sales. The boy had heard his parents talking about it.

"You should be writing this down," David told her. "You won't be able to remember all this. I need to know what they're saying."

"Don't worry." She stared at the oldest boy. "Tell me what happened to the purser."

He glanced at his friends.

"The fishermen here," another boy interjected. "They attacked him. They went crazy. He left all the passengers to die and he took the money and he jumped ship. He had so much money."

"My brother was on that boat," Lali said slowly. She looked into each boy's eyes, willing them to believe her. "There are stories—and my mother has dreams—that he's still here somewhere. That he survived, but never made it back home."

The old woman shook her head.

"He had—he has—green eyes. Dark skin. Tall."

Miguel's photograph was in an envelope inside her handbag, but she couldn't bring herself to show it.

"They're dead now," the woman said. "There's nobody here with green eyes."

The young men started speaking at the same time, correcting and contradicting each other. Voices scrambled over each other, suppressing the weaker ones.

David clutched Lali's upper arm. "What are they saying? You're supposed to translate for me." He seemed frightened.

When she didn't answer, he said something under his breath, then adjusted the lens of his camera and began to photograph the teenagers. They were so busy telling stories, they didn't seem to notice.

Lali pulled away from them, trying to shut out the voices and David's insistent clicking. She watched the expressions flickering across their faces, like images without sound on a television. People could tell the stories of strangers, but not their own. Anyone who came close to their real story turned back, tried to forget what they had seen. The only way to get to someone's story was to circle it, again and again, to come close and pull away, to try to catch them off guard.

"Are they telling you anything?" David hovered over her, too white and tall and foreign. He was standing too close to her. He stood too close to everyone. The boys stepped away from him, and he, oblivious to their discomfort, moved closer each time. He pleaded, "Are you asking them about the massacre?"

"Give me a moment."

The only one who had something to say was the old woman, and that was why she wouldn't speak. David didn't understand that. You had to earn the right to question someone. But I don't want her story, Lali thought. I want to know what happened to Miguel.

The young men were still talking about typhoons and drowning. They didn't talk about the massacre in their own village, but their eyes shone with grief and excitement as they described the drowning of people they barely knew, years before. They're making most of this up, she thought, but the distress is honest. She couldn't explain this to David. He wanted his sources to be credible, his stories coherent.

His face was haggard. He looked lost in that room. Had he really hoped she could guide him through it?

He said, "You're not talking about the massacre, are you?"

"I'm coming to that. They're telling me about the shipwreck."

"You've spent all this time asking them about your boyfriend?"

"They wanted to tell me about the ship."

"I can't believe this. Are you always talking about yourself?"

"I'm doing you a *favor*. Don't forget that."

"Ask them," he said. "Please. And then translate."

"They're scared of us. Are you so blind? They think the local hacendero was behind the massacre—that lay sister said he funds the vigilantes; they live on his property. And to them we look like hacenderos. Because we're white."

"You're not white."

"I'm white to them."

"Okay, Lali. I'll ask the questions now."

He began to speak, and she translated in a deadened voice, distancing herself from both the questions and the responses. She didn't want to see or feel the stories they were describing. It was wrong to make them talk about the massacre. Either they were trying to tell the truth, the horror of what they had experienced, or they were inventing other stories to avoid those memories. She hoped they were lying.

For an hour, perhaps longer, she followed David from one crouched figure to another in the crowded room. He sat beside them on the floor. She watched his face grow calmer as he listened. The gallery of atrocities, again, but this time spoken and not seen. She managed to shut out most of the stories, but a few slipped through—children abandoned by parents who wanted to protect them, girls mutilated so they wouldn't be raped, men and boys locked into churches and burned alive.

Again and again, without David noticing, she inserted a question about a sinking ship and a man with green eyes, ferreting through their stories for traces of Miguel.

"Tell me what they said," David said, repeatedly. "Translate everything." He no longer trusted her. She watched him focus his camera on a passive face, a missing finger, a bloodied ear. A vulture, she thought, like everyone else. And she was helping him. And none of this brought her closer to the boy who slipped his hand under her skirt and worried whether she was cold when they lay on his parents' bed. Miguel's honey-brown body, beautiful, naked except for the bright purple socks he loved. He had dozens of them, all the same color. His only concession to originality, and he was so proud of them. In bed, lying next to her, he lifted his legs straight into the air and drew circles with his feet, laughing. She looked at his socks, his calves, those soccer-muscled thighs. His feet danced in the air, and she had laughed with him. Their happiness had seemed simple, foolish, discardable. It wasn't, at all.

David interrupted her thoughts, told her to ask another question, and then another. The stories awakened other stories inside her, other horrors. When the Japanese left the capital at the end of the war, her father told her, they threw babies into the air and caught them with bayonets, in front of their mothers. Now Lali heard about other children and other babies. She translated the words into English for David. There was a massacre. There were survivors. There were people from surrounding villages who fled, fearing another attack. Those who could talk didn't cry.

One person's story, her father had told her. And then another's. That's all most people can deal with. Not the suffering of the masses.

The presence over her shoulder was gone. Her father, or Miguel, or someone else—she didn't know who it was, but it had hovered over her for so long and now it did not.

Across the room, the teenage boys huddled over their board game, moving pebbles across the wood. Beside them, the old woman sat with her legs folded under her. Lali walked away from David and returned to them.

She asked, "What did they do to the purser?"

How did he die, she wanted to know. Did they beat him, did they stab him? She didn't ask: And did he know Miguel?

The boys shrugged. They didn't remember, it had happened years ago, they were children then, they were in grade six, and that was a good year. They shifted into other stories, versions of the same stories, shipwrecks and hunger and other people's pain. They glanced at the pebbles, and she knew they wanted her to go away.

David was standing beside her. Perhaps he, too, was exhausted. But he started asking questions again. She didn't tell him: No one's seen a beautiful brown-skinned boy with green eyes and purple socks; they remember the purser but not Miguel, and they would have remembered Miguel—no one could see Miguel and not remember him.

David pressed her for more words and more details. Some survivors reacted by refusing to speak, or by speaking so rapidly and in such confusion that their words meant nothing at all.

She was tired now, sickened by David's relentless probing. His eyes glittered. A scoop, she thought. He'll publish his photos and articles, and move on to other tragedies. The foreign press didn't get it. She didn't get it. *If you know something, then what?* her father had asked Pilar and her once, over dinner, eager to launch into yet another lecture on patriotism and responsibility and moral obligation. *If you know something that could help other people but would hurt you or someone you love, then what? What should you do?* Then you should forget what you know, Lali had answered silently. She had twisted her fingers under the table, trying to shut out his voice. But Pilar opened her mouth, and Lali saw from the smile on her father's face that Pilar was giving the right answer, even if it was the wrong answer, because there was always only one answer where their father was concerned, because Pilar always had to play the good daughter, because Pilar couldn't bear to imagine moral choices more nuanced than black and white, more complex than right and wrong.

Then what?

Prayers and amulets and the absence of ghosts. Lali wanted to leave the smells of this room, walk along a grey beach, watch darkness fall like a spell over the village. In this town, after dusk, almost no one seemed to switch on their lights. The previous night, as she looked out the window, the darkness had seemed almost tangible, weighted with humidity and the trilling of crickets and the iodine smell of the sea, more night than any she had seen in the city.

The last survivor, David promised her—after this one, they would leave. Another old woman, another broken face, another absence in other eyes. A dozen men and women sat in a protective circle around her. The woman's silence agitated David. "The old ones are the hardest," he told Lali, as though no one else could understand English. The elderly woman's companions turned away.

"What happened to her?" she asked.

A bony, short-legged man, perhaps in his forties, said, "They killed her family in front of her. Seven grandchildren. The youngest was ten months old. They were looking for her son." He glanced at the woman, lowered his voice. "They did things to her, then they made her stand, without anything, in front of her house for one day."

Lali scanned the old woman—the red-veined eyes, the downcast mouth, the sharp bones under her face—then focused on the small round scars on her arm.

"Cigarette burns," the man said.

The woman drew a short, wheezing breath. For a moment Lali tried to imagine her standing outside, the sagging flesh, the harsh light of noon. Had her neighbors watched her? How could anyone do those things to this woman? She forced a shift inside herself. She tried to look at the woman as those men had. The heaving chest, the folds in her neck, the wrinkled face. Lali stared at the thin arm and tried to imagine bringing a lighted cigarette to that skin. A sour taste rose up her throat. She couldn't imagine it. She couldn't imagine anything. She looked at David and with a shock realized: But he can.

That's what his photos were for. To imagine, to enter, to feel—not the pain of the victims, but the power of those who inflict it.

Go away from this, she told herself. From David, from these ideas. Anything you think you understand is wrong.

She had visited friends' haciendas, driven through the countryside in bulletproof jeeps, swam in private beaches. All her life had been an effort to shut out the faces in this room, the lives her father had fought for in his speeches. She couldn't bear that world, his world. Her father had talked. He talked while her mother cried, while her mother pawned her diamonds and peddled her jewelry to her pitying friends. Lali had watched and sworn she would never be pitied. She wasn't stupid. When the nuns took her high-school class to visit squatter communities, she thanked God she didn't live there. Her classmates splashed Johnson's baby cologne on their wrists and necks— the heat, they said, because no one wanted to talk about the stench. When she returned home, she stood under the shower for a long time. Foreigners like David didn't understand this. Distance was necessary because the squalor was so near. In your face, every time you drove down the street. The real fear was that you'd collide with it, or fall into it, or wake up one morning to see it holding a gun against your head. Poverty and desperation fascinated David because to him they were still exotic. He could fly out of the country whenever he wanted. He could decide never to return.

She longed for clean flesh, young flesh, the smell of a baby's skin. Her daughter. Aimee looked like her, Arturo said. Arturo also said that one day Lali would see it, one day she would see herself in Aimee. She remembered trying to slide open the glass doors in the hospital room, eight floors above the ground, the newborn in her arms. But the woman who wanted to kill her own baby was dead now. Blinders, she told herself. That was how people survived. Her father didn't have a chance.

"I can't take this anymore," she told David. "Let's go."

In his eyes she saw a distress that mirrored her own.

An elderly man shuffled toward them. She could no longer listen to these people. The man stood in front of them. Hooded eyes, irises clouded by cataracts. She thought she saw a few specks of green. He smiled at her, talked, but he couldn't speak any of her languages, and in the end he tottered away. Tears gathered behind her eyes. She was angry with herself. She had no right to cry. David touched her shoulder. Miguel had wanted a child with her. She had wanted to kill her baby. She would pay for that. Until the child is born, the nuns had told her, we walk in darkness. Don't think about all this. Don't think. No ghosts. The smell of flesh—old, wounded, unwashed. Men on stretchers, children in bandages, women trying to sleep on mats or crates. She didn't see the lice and scabs, the burns, the sores on a child's feet. Everywhere she turned, she saw crowds, bodies, eyes. The only thing she knew how to do was to make some men want her, but that wouldn't last and she had nothing to replace it. What lasted? Not random acts of kindness, not love, not pain. Perhaps shame.

She stood with David under the sun, on the brown-tipped grass in front of the schoolhouse.

He shaded his eyes from the sunlight. "I'm sorry if it was too much for you."

"I couldn't look at those people anymore," she said.

"You'll see them differently in the photos."

"You weren't supposed to take any."

"I'm not supposed to *publish* any."

Sunlight raked his face. Creases around his eyes. "You'll see," he said. "In the photos—in some of them, the ones I'll keep—there'll be a kind of beauty. It comes out when things are broken."

If she started thinking about Arturo again, she would have to think about Pilar, and she didn't want to think about Pilar.

David said, "I'm going to interview the men who did this."

Years ago, she had told Arturo: I don't know why, but good people always seem so porous. She had told him she needed violence, not real violence but the possibility of violence, a man making love to her so hard the pain, the sensation, became extreme.

Near the horizon, the moon hovered over volcanic peaks. Car windows opened to the night and wind. Lali felt exposed, vulnerable to attacks. In front of her, David looked out the side window. Beside him, the round-faced young man gripped the steering wheel, eyes narrowed beneath the thick eyebrows.

Without electric lights, night in the province seemed vast and ancient. The car dipped forward. Trees and bushes, briefly illuminated by headlights, flashed on each side of them. Occasionally, hamlets appeared off the main road—a few wooden shacks huddled together.

She remembered the faces of refugees in the schoolhouse, the lay sister staring out the window as they walked away.

"What will happen to them?" David had asked the woman.

"They'll go back to their villages." The lay sister had fingered the wooden cross on her chest. "What else can they do?"

She hates all of us, Lali thought now. The vigilantes and the Communists and the military, foreign journalists like David, everyone like me.

The car stopped bouncing. For several kilometers, in the middle of the deserted countryside, they drove along a stretch of smooth-concrete highway. David's friend noticed their surprise. He said the town's mayor had started the highway project here and then abandoned it, pocketing the rest of the money, as the rumor went, to build a house for one of his mistresses.

They turned a bend and drove along a road lined with trees. Another turn, and the headlights beamed upon a dozen men in army fatigues standing in the middle of the path.

David's friend stopped and opened his door. Before stepping into the night, he whispered, "Don't leave the car."

He walked cautiously down the path, toward the men, hands lifted on each side of his chest, palms facing outward. The soldiers surrounded him. A curly-haired young man pulled away from the group and ambled toward the car. A gold medallion, caught in the path of the headlight, flashed on his chest.

He stuck his head into Lali's window. "Get out," he told her amiably.

In the front seat, David turned around.

"Don't look at her," the man hissed.

David faced forward again.

Don't show fear, she told herself. She stretched her lips into a small, polite smile, reached for her purse, set it on her lap. She ran her fingers back and forth over the clasp.

He stared at her fingers. "You're not allowed here." His voice was rough. He glanced nervously at the other soldiers, who were a few yards away and arguing with David's friend. His fingers slipped over the window ledge, tapped against the inside of the door.

She unclasped the purse, felt for her wallet, removed several bills, and slid them along the door to his fingers. His hand snapped shut over the bills. He turned away from the other soldiers, glanced at the bills, stuffed them into the pocket of his pants. He sauntered back to the others. In the headlights, his white sneakers pressed down on flat reddish stones.

Lali leaned against the backrest.

David's friend was hurrying toward the car. One of the soldiers shouted: "It's all right. They have authorization."

Minutes later, they were speeding along the road.

"I thought you knew the soldiers here," David told his friend. "I thought you had arranged things."

The young man shrugged. "It's complicated."

David turned to look at Lali, raised his eyebrows. She shook her head, pressed a finger to her lips.

"The soldiers are staying with the hacendero now," his friend said quickly. "You can't blame them, *ha*? They couldn't even afford new shoes. The government sends them to fight in the jungles, and they're wearing rubber slippers."

"Government soldiers work for a sugar planter?" David asked.

"No. Some of them just live with him."

The dark road, barely wide enough for the car, curved ahead of them. It always came down to the same thing, Lali thought. Soldiers who didn't have enough, guerillas who didn't have enough, vigilantes who didn't have enough, barrio people who didn't have enough. Everyone extorting each other, levying fines on each other, seeking money from whomever they could protect or threaten.

David remained silent.

Exiles and dissidents who didn't have enough, and her mother who had to pretend she did.

She stared out the window. She remembered another night, when she was a teenager and still in Manila. She had climbed on the roof with friends, past midnight, at the end of a party. It was after the curfew—no one could go home. The city was still, the streets were empty. A convoy of army trucks appeared at one end of the highway and began to roll across it. One of Lali's friends, the son of an army general, said the trucks were carrying the dead and wounded from the war in the south. He was drunk—he shouldn't have been talking. The trucks traveled only at night, he continued, so as not to scare people in Manila, not to let them know how bad the government's losses were. You should see the military hospitals, he said, boasting—

soldiers are on the floor in the corridors, hundreds of them. Many are dying right there on the floor.

"The soldiers aren't motivated," David's friend said now. In the rearview mirror, his eyes were tense. He said soldiers saw their friends die in fights because they didn't have enough guns. They saw politicians commandeer military helicopters to fly food and actresses to their birthday parties, or to airlift cement to whatever new house they were building. "What do you expect people to do?" he asked. "What does the government expect?"

Lali didn't respond. The vehemence in his voice silenced her. She rolled up her window, leaned against the glass.

They rounded a bend marked by a large mango tree. The car dipped and rose across the dirt road, toward a group of nipa and bamboo shacks, set on pillars and clustered together. No lights. No one moving.

Lali climbed out of the car. The air was cool, the earth spongy. Her sensations felt raw, unmediated. Wind rustling leaves, a dog whimpering, her sandals scraping against stones— everything seemed magnified.

The hamlet seemed to crack open. Men in white T-shirts scrambled out of shacks, holding flashlights or machetes with red hilts. Many wore red scarves around their necks. Later she would learn that red hilts and scarves were emblems of the vigilantes who beheaded their victims, but now she straightened her back and waited for them to come to her.

Lali followed David and his friend up a bamboo ladder into one of the shacks. A low-ceilinged room without tables and chairs. David's friend told them to wait. He disappeared down the ladder. Lali and David sat on the bamboo floor, next to a hissing kerosene lamp. Near the wall, on a small altar, three candles flickered beneath an image of the Sacred Heart of Jesus. Next to it was a grainy black-and-white photo of a smiling young couple surrounded by four little boys. She knew they were dead.

"You've been here before, haven't you?" she asked.

David drew his legs toward him. "A few times."

"You think they'll let you into their secrets?"

"They know I just want to learn."

"Oh David, don't be naive."

"The rituals they use before going into battle, the amulets on their shirts—I've seen it happen. I told you. Bullets, and no one gets hurt."

"You really believe that?" she asked gently. "You're a foreigner. They'll do things for you, to impress you. Maybe to get money."

"They've never asked for money."

Voices, outside. She tiptoed to the window. A group of men with torches marched down the road. They wore jeans and red shirts, automatic pistols strapped to their waists. A stocky man strode in front of them. He was the only one not carrying a torch.

David stood beside her. "Don't let them see you," he said.

What was she doing here, with him, seeking a drowned man she hadn't loved? She couldn't sustain an attraction to David. No trace of Miguel. Arturo in the hospital, her baby at home. Pilar. Her world seemed to have shrunk to this room— an altar with images of Jesus and the smiles of a dead family, this lonely man.

She peeked out the window. The men and torch flames advanced toward the house. No women. Was she the only woman in this place? During the war, her mother said, her own father had flattened her breasts with strips of cloth, cut her hair close to her scalp, so that Japanese soldiers wouldn't notice she was a girl.

"Don't stand by the window," David whispered.

What's happening now has no meaning, she wanted to tell him. This is all a show. We shouldn't believe it.

*

David's friend appeared over the threshold. "They're waiting."

The bamboo ladder again, the spongy black earth. They wended their way through a path and climbed another ladder to another shack, which was larger than the others. The stocky man sat alone on a rattan couch, arms crossed. He turned his inquisitive, hooded eyes toward them. He exchanged pleasantries with David in good but heavily accented English. Kerosene lamps crackled around them. David began to ask questions, but the leader brushed them away and gestured at the dining table. "We'll eat first," he said.

His men sat around the table. Lali said she had already eaten, and remained on the bench. Another man brought out a platter of cassava pastries and a wicker basket filled with mangos. She listened to the low voices of the men, watched knives stabbing into mango seeds.

The leader pushed away his plate. His men stopped eating. They excused themselves, entered an adjoining room, shut the door. In the silence that followed, Lali heard the cicadas again. She pictured the darkness outside, the encroaching jungle. The air in the room was pungent with kerosene fumes.

Through the wall, a low chanting began. She imagined rites of purification, men preparing for battle.

She and David were outside, in the night, trailing silhouettes that carried torches and machetes. No one spoke. David's camera hung from a strap around his neck. He cradled it in one hand, as though to smooth its passage over bumps and holes.

They veered off the path, leaving the fields behind them, and treaded a muddy road for several kilometers. No houses, no lights, no sign of human life. Every now and then, skeletal branches stretched like arms toward the sky.

Another path, then more trees, closer and closer together, until a canopy of leaves and branches webbed over their heads. Twigs crackled under their feet. Dangling vines scratched her arms. They walked in single file. Acrid smoke from the torches drifted backwards.

A patch of violet sky appeared through the leaves. The jungle grew less dense, the night less dark. They ducked beneath low-hanging branches and emerged into a clearing.

A dozen young men were crouching on the ground or sitting on a makeshift wooden bench. The tips of their cigarettes glowed like orange dots in the night. Playfully, they waved the beams of their flashlights over each other's faces. They seemed as boyish as the teenagers at the refugee center.

When the young men saw them, they stood and lowered their flashlights, stamping golden circles into black soil. Lali sensed another presence from across the clearing. She looked at one group of trees, then another. The presence was growing stronger. Somebody was standing beneath a tree. A lanky, terrified-looking young man, his arms tied behind him.

What happened next came in staccato flashes of light and shadow, a series of frozen images succeeding each other. David's camera in midair, a moment of darkness, a camera held like a shield over his eyes. The leader of the vigilantes with his legs apart. Someone else's leg, lifted in mid-stride. A raised arm. A head half-turned.

The images gave way to movement. Two teenagers pushed and kicked the prisoner toward the bench. The man looked stunned. He stumbled but said nothing. Later, Lali would ask herself: Why didn't he fight, why didn't he ask for pity? He had nothing to lose.

Her senses seemed to function only one at a time. When she watched, she couldn't listen. When she heard, she couldn't see. Now she noticed only the clicking of a camera, then a moaning, although later she would imagine the cries of night birds, the bats, the cicadas.

The leader's mouth cut a line across his face. "You believe in God?" he asked the captive.

All her senses were functioning now.

The leader jabbed the captive's chest. The man winced. "Answer me."

The man tilted his head forward and muttered something.

"Liar," the leader said, but his voice was soothing. "Communists don't believe in God."

The captive stared nervously at him, like a child scanning the faces of adults for clues to what was expected of him.

"If you're a good Christian, we want to hear you pray to God."

A vigilante kicked the man behind the legs. His knees buckled. He knelt down.

"Start praying," the leader said calmly. "I want to hear Our Father." He raised his eyebrows at his men. "We prayed the Our Father tonight, *ha*? We all pray."

"Our Father," the captive said.

"That's all you know?"

"Our Father, who art in heaven."

Because she couldn't bear to look at him, because looking meant hearing his terror, she stared instead at the mango tree behind him, at the edge of the clearing. A beast of a tree. At least a hundred years old—five adults could join hands and still not wrap their arms around its trunk. Ten or fifteen meters high, thousands of deep green leaves masking the branches. The leaves began to ripple, almost imperceptibly at first, then gathering force.

"Hallowed be thy name." The voice was raspy and thin, fading like cigarette smoke into the darkness.

David focused his camera. Flashbulbs. The shutter clicking. The vigilantes grasped the red hilts of their machetes and planted the tips into the ground.

It seemed all the branches were shaking and breezes ripping through the leaves.

She could look, but not hear. She turned to David, so as not to see the captive. He adjusted the controls of his camera.

"If you're Christian and not a Communist," the leader said, in the same soothing voice, "how come you're not praying?" He told David: "How come you're looking at me? You're supposed to be taking pictures of him, not me."

Suddenly she understood. The vigilante leader was staging this scene for them. A show for the white-skinned foreigner and his wealthy-looking Filipina girlfriend. And David, clicking away beside her, intent on recording the scene, didn't notice. She wanted to shake him, knock the camera out of his hand. The vigilantes wouldn't go on with this if he stopped taking photos.

She focused on the kneeling man. Run, she shouted in her mind, willing him to understand her.

A teenager wrapped a red scarf around the man's eyes, knotting it so tightly that the head snapped backward. The bound wrists lifted a few inches into the air. Someone coughed, then stopped.

A part of her wanted to see it happen.

The Japanese had buried her grand-uncle alive during the war. Near the end of the war, her mother's aunt knelt in a town square, arms tied behind her, cheek pressed against a bloody cement slab. Japanese soldiers pulled her long hair over her head to expose her neck. She knelt there for hours, not daring to move, waiting to be beheaded, long after the Japanese soldiers heard the orders to retreat and ran away.

Now she thought: They're doing this for us.

She glanced sideways at David. Without speaking, using only her eyes, she tried to tell him: If we walk away, they won't do anything. If we stop watching, they won't kill him.

She wanted to see it happen.

The captive on his knees, head lowered.

The leaves were hissing now. The camera clicked.

Shouts. From behind, someone pulled her away. She twisted her torso, trying to pry the arms away from her waist. In the moonlight, the leaves of the mango tree were rattling.

A cry. Dozens of leaves lifted into the air, hovering like small birds over the branches, then took flight into the violet sky.

She heard a woman scream, but that wasn't possible, that wasn't possible, there was no woman here but herself.

Later David would tell her: The Tibetans say demons guard the gates of feeling, we can take in only so much, and that's what saves us. Later he would say: I was taking photographs. I couldn't take in everything that was happening. I didn't understand until it was too late.

The brain makes choices, her father had told her, when she was a little girl and had a terrible toothache. One side of her face, from the chin to the temple, throbbed with pain. He told her to pinch her inner arm as hard as she could, until she felt only the pain in her arm, not the toothache. A small pain can fool a big one, he said. The brain can process only one strong feeling at a time.

David's friend drove them to a wooden house by the sea. The faint curve of a darkened beach behind the house. No trees, no other buildings. As they pulled up, a heavyset woman stepped out the front door. She walked to the car. "I'm Sister Connie," she whispered. "Come inside. Don't let anyone see you."

In the living room, David, his friend, and Sister Connie sat around a table. They spoke in hushed tones. Lali sat on the sofa, ankles crossed like a schoolgirl's. She couldn't talk. She kept seeing the young man's face, his terror. She knew there were deaths like this, she knew there was savagery—her own father had been murdered, but she had never felt so close to horror.

David and she had done nothing to help the man cowering on his knees.

Red-hilted machetes, raised in the air. Teenage boys, eyes bright. Had they been terrified, too?

At the table, David asked, "What did he do?"

"They said he was a Communist guerilla," his friend said.

Sister Connie grimaced. "Communist! He was helping us organize prayer meetings in his barrio. He was a lay brother. A Christian."

"We met another lay sister—in the schoolhouse," David said.

"With the refugees from the massacre?"

David nodded. After a moment, he asked, "Aren't you afraid?"

"They won't come for me," she replied brusquely. Lali noticed that she couldn't meet his eyes. "I've been here too long."

"Did he have a family?" David's voice was soft, respectful.

"Six or seven children, mostly girls. There's an Irish priest in the next town—he took in the family."

Don't believe her, Lali told him silently.

"We started this years ago," Sister Connie said. "It's the only way. There's a network now of Christian communities all over the island—lay priests and sisters trying to help the people in the barrios. We teach them livelihood projects."

Livelihood projects, Lali repeated to herself. Suddenly, unreasonably, she was angry. In Manila, this was a favorite pastime of Chanel No. 5-scented socialites who had never worked for a living but prided themselves on their social conscience and constructive use of their free time.

"The hacenderos think we're subversives," Sister Connie was saying. "Every once in a while, when they get too drunk or one of their people gets hurt in some skirmish, they set their paramilitary goons on a village."

Sister Connie sipped water. She set the glass on the table. In a small, pained voice, she asked, "Did he suffer?"

David glanced at Lali. They both heard the other, unspeakable questions. What was it like, the moment of death? Was he brave? Did he betray us?

"No." David's response was almost inaudible.

Lali uncrossed her ankles, crossed them again. Perhaps she was wrong about Sister Connie. Sometimes it was hard to distinguish heartlessness from pain.

"I'd like to go to the funeral," David said.

"There's no funeral," Sister Connie pressed both hands into her belly. "They have to bury him right away, as quickly as they can."

"I'd like to be a witness to that, if I may," David told her.

"I don't know if you can go."

"And the body?" Lali asked quietly. She hadn't seen what had happened. She told herself she hadn't seen him, after. In her memory, she saw not his death, but leaves, lifting like birds into the sky.

"We sent someone to get it." Sister Connie gave David a calculating look. "Even if you go, you can't publish anything about it."

A man beheaded in front of her, and she hadn't seen it.

"You can ask the priest, if you really want to go," Sister Connie said doubtfully. "But there won't be anyone. The villagers are all in the refugee center, or in hiding. Even his family is terrified. They won't have a wake. They're scared the vigilantes will attack them."

Lali wanted to say: David ate with the vigilantes. He knows them.

Sister Connie tipped her chair forward. "I'll have to get you I.D. cards. It's the system here. The mayor gives them out, but they're issued by the private armies or the vigilantes, and that depends where you are. If you don't have the right I.D., you can't enter or leave the village."

She called out to someone in the kitchen. A young girl,

about fourteen, in shorts and rubber thongs, slipped into the living room.

"Bring some sandwiches for our guests," Sister Connie told her gently. The girl lowered her head, nodded. She fled the room. "The vigilantes ration the rice," Sister Connie said. "We're allowed only two *gantas* of rice per week. Any more, they say, and we're feeding the guerillas."

Lali studied Sister Connie's face as she talked. Slowly she placed her: educated, middle class, no real money. A trace of Spanish blood. Perhaps she still had cousins in local politics, or aunts with money. They would protect her.

"The army and the vigilantes guard the *haciendas* around here," Sister Connie said. "They divide the barrios up between them. And the big planters pay off all of them."

The girl returned with a platter of crustless white-bread sandwiches, cut diagonally in half and filled with orange processed cheese.

Sister Connie picked up a sandwich. "Last time they did something like this, the vigilantes presented the man's head to the army. The army refused it." She brought the triangle to her mouth, parted her lips. A moment later, without looking at it, she returned the half-eaten sandwich to the platter.

Lali rubbed her knees. They wouldn't stop trembling. Sister Connie looked at her and said: "It's late. They've prepared your rooms upstairs."

Sitting on the bed, Lali watched David undress. His large, pale body in the unlit room. Outside, waves lapped an invisible shore. She wondered whether she could ever return to the sea without remembering this night.

Her knees were still shaking. She held them. They seemed to belong to someone else.

"Sister Connie won't like it if she finds out we're sleeping in the same room," he said.

Another death, but no ghosts. A bad sign.

"They killed him for us," she said. He didn't seem to hear her.

How to go on after a night like this, how to erase the memory of that face?

David sat on the bed. His body, so near, consoled her.

Had he seen other deaths like this?

"We should pray for him," she said, though at this moment God seemed as dark and unreachable as the night sky outside the window.

"We'll pray if you want," he said.

"I didn't see what they did to him. I didn't see what he was like, afterwards."

She kept imagining a terrified face, severed from a thin body. She understood why people needed to see and even touch their dead. The reality of a corpse, to replace these imaginings.

"I didn't see anything. I saw leaves flying into the air."

"You need to calm down," he said.

He stood and walked to the window. She went to him, looked out. Sister Connie in a white nightgown, among the shadows in the garden, was watering the grass with a rubber hose. The rush of water.

"We should sleep," he said. "Tomorrow will be difficult." He placed an arm around her.

Perhaps there was nothing beyond this comfort. No passion, no pleasure, no lover tracing invisible words over her skin.

The sun outside the window shone with such brilliance that for a moment Lali thought the death had been a dream. She reached for David across the bed but touched only his pillow.

She found him in the dining room, stooped over the table, stirring powdered coffee in a bowl of hot water. Next to the bowl were large platters of garlic rice and fried eggs.

"It's late," he said. He couldn't meet her eyes. "I was going to wake you up. Everyone's gone."

They ate in silence. She thought she heard a radio somewhere, the faint lilt of girls' voices, the murmurs of the sea. She served herself twice, forced cold eggs and rice into her mouth. She ate until the heaviness in her stomach anchored her to her body again.

He wiped his mouth with the back of his hand. Shadows under his eyes.

"Where's your friend?" she asked, not knowing what else to say.

"I can't find him." He sounded tense, as though the question, or his answer, upset him.

She followed him outside. The garden, so luxuriant the night before, had grown parched and scraggly under the morning sun. Dust mixed with sand beneath her sandals. On each side of the safe house were wooden shacks she hadn't noticed in the darkness. Behind the shacks, an unruly landscape of coconut and papaya trees, giant ferns, flowering bushes. And beyond, still hidden, the keening sea.

*

Inside the car, she asked, "You know how to get there?"

He glanced at her. "You bet."

He drove slowly down the bumpy road. She stared straight ahead, the sun in her eyes, willing him to talk to her. She would listen to anything he said now, all that maddening talk about politics, history, her life, those opinions and certainties about things he would never understand, anything to distract her from the sunlight outside and the darkness in her own mind.

On the outskirts of the village, a dozen government soldiers sat on a bench in front of a hut, under the shade of a mango tree. As the car approached, the soldiers lined up in the middle of the road. David eased the car to a stop.

A soldier swaggered toward them. "Where you going?" he asked roughly, his voice twisted into an approximation of an American accent, as if this were the way to make the white man understand him.

David handed him the forged I.D. cards and some papers.

The soldier studied the documents. He looked into the car, craning his neck to see Lali. "Okay. Fine. Where you going?"

"To a burial," David said carefully. "We have permission."

"No one allowed."

"Please go and ask your superiors. They know we're going."

"Wait there." He pointed a roughened finger at David. His fingernail was sliced down the middle into two thick, yellowed segments.

He walked away, almost insolently, in the sunlight, dust clouds rising over his rubber sandals. He entered the wooden shack. Minutes later, another man, older than the first, strode toward the car. His face was thin and angular. He said, "There's a fee for leaving the village."

"That isn't what we were told." David's voice was strained.

"Listen. You want to go to your funeral? You go to your funeral. But there's a fee."

"They told me I.D. cards and a letter of permission would be enough."

Lali touched his shoulder, to calm him. Don't provoke, she thought. In this country, people get killed for a look.

"You want photos?" the soldier asked. A gold-plated medallion of the Virgin Mary dangled from his neck. "You a journalist? We have photos."

David looked at him. Finally he said, "Show them to me."

The soldier reached into his vest and removed a creased brown envelope. He slipped it over the window. David set the envelope on his lap and carefully removed a stack of photos. Lali glanced at the one on top. Polaroid, dark, grainy. But the images were visible: two teenagers, kneeling, holding up a man's head.

"How much?" David asked.

Lali looked at his profile, remembering the machetes. "You can't," she said.

David slipped the top photo under the pile. She couldn't look at the next photo.

"You like the pictures?" the soldier asked.

"How much?"

"Whatever you like, sir. You decide."

You can't do this, she thought, yet already she imagined him taping the photos to the wall of his windowless room. She stared at the sky. No clouds. The dead man would become a photo now. And ordinary men with medallions and machetes and soothing voices would pose beside whatever remained of him.

Lali looked at the scrawny girls and little boy on the path ahead of her. They scampered to keep up with a frail young woman walking resolutely forward. The children stretched their tiny arms, trying to hold on to their mother's hands or her dress. From behind, the woman and her children looked like a giant, many-legged insect. A few paces ahead of them, David, two plantation workers, and an old Irish priest carried a wooden casket. The sun beat down on them; the wind rustled the stalks on each side of the path.

The children skittered on their short legs, trying to stay close to their mother. How many were they? Six girls, all skinny and probably older than they looked, and a boy of about two. He stumbled, lost hold of his mother, turned around in confusion. To Lali's surprise, he smiled at her. A wide-eyed child, his face round and good-natured. She smiled back. Frightened, he scrambled back to his mother.

They trudged up a hill, away from the fields. A small wooden chapel stood on the mound, surrounded by weeds and bushes, grass growing on the roof. She kept her eyes on David. Even as he stooped to carry the casket, he towered above the others. She followed the casket through ankle-high grass to an abandoned cemetery behind the chapel. Several dozen wooden crosses, bleached almost white by the sun, leaned to the right, as though pushed there by years of wind. Clucking brown chickens and chicks scuttled in the grass between the crosses.

The men set the casket on the ground and wiped their foreheads. David and the Irish priest stood close to each other, whispering. The priest smiled uncertainly. The workers smoked cigarettes. The younger children began to chase the chickens. From the corner of her eyes, Lali studied the young widow. Emaciated, with high cheekbones and shifty eyes. She was watching her son. When he stumbled into a cluster of brown stalks, she ran and scooped him into her arms.

The men lifted the casket again and staggered through the cemetery. The little girls skipped behind their mother, thumbs and forefingers pinching her dress.

The dead man couldn't be buried in his village, David had told her. The family didn't have enough money. They were also afraid that a wake with many people would attract attention, that the vigilantes would return.

In a field beyond the cemetery, over a shallow grave, the old priest muttered prayers. Cane stalks swayed in the distance. The woman stared into space. The children clung to her; she spread her thin arms and tried to hold all of them. No one spoke or cried.

The priest sprinkled earth over the coffin. The workers shoveled soil, broken branches, and small rocks over the grave.

When it was over, the widow turned hesitantly to the priest. "How will I find him, Father?"

The priest's blue eyes, sad and protruding, focused on her. "My dear?"

"When the bodies are resurrected, at the end of the world." She pushed her children away. They took a few steps forward, stopped, clustered together, not looking at their mother. "I won't be able to find him."

Understanding, then distress, flickered across the priest's face. "You don't have to worry, my dear. Our Lord promised us that the bodies will be made whole again."

The widow lowered her voice. "I'm afraid, Father."

That's why they do it, Lali realized with a start. They cut him up so he can't be resurrected. They terrorize the family, even after death.

"You must trust your faith," the priest murmured. "God takes care of those who believe in him."

David crouched on the grass, a few feet in front of the children. The boy glanced at him. David smiled encouragingly. The toddler looked away but began to walk toward David, sideways, pretending to ignore him. As he came closer, David stretched out his arms. The boy bounded forward, and David lifted him onto his lap. The child seemed shocked, about to cry. David bounced him up and down. Soon the toddler was smiling. His mother swung around, tense and alert. David sat still, arms around the child.

The mother gave David a hollow smile. "Take him with you, sir," she said, using the local dialect. "I give him to you."

"My dear," the priest protested.

David looked quizzically at Lali. In a monotone, avoiding his eyes, she translated the woman's words.

"Your son needs you now," the priest said soothingly.

The woman knelt next to David. "Help me, sir." Her voice was cajoling, but her eyes were fierce. "He's a boy. When he grows up, they'll kill him also. He loves you already, sir."

The six girls huddled together, as though to shield themselves from their mother's words. The toddler struggled out of David's lap. His mother pushed him back toward David. The child looked terrified but didn't cry.

"I'll take him," Lali said suddenly. She turned to the priest. "I can take care of him, Father. I know someone who can prepare a new birth certificate."

The mother stared at her.

"Are you mad?" David asked.

Lali smiled at the woman, inclined her head. The boy hooked his arm around his mother's leg. David stood and strode away, head bent, shoulders hunched.

Later Lali told him: Babies can be borrowed or given away. Very poor women sometimes offer their babies to strangers, hoping someone will take care of them. One of her uncles, sitting in the backseat of his Mercedes as his chauffeur drove him home from the office, had accepted a baby from a beggar at a stoplight. If you don't take her, she'll die, the woman had told him. By the time the lights turned green, her uncle, who was gay, found himself a father, a baby in his arms. Lali knew several people who had been raised by childless relatives—their real parents had seven or eight children and had offered the youngest to a barren sister or cousin.

"That's heartless," David said.

"No. It's kind."

They were sitting in bed, in a dark room in Sister Connie's house, wearing only their underwear. His warm hand pressed against hers. Her legs didn't shake. Outside the open window, a few stars punctured the sky. Near the bed, balanced on an empty Coke bottle, a red-tipped coil of mosquito repellent burned slowly.

The little boy had clung to David without speaking during the long ride back to the safe house. Later he fell asleep, exhausted, curled next to a maid in a cot.

Lali shut her eyes, trying to feel the presence over her shoulder.

"What will you do with him?" David asked.

"He'll grow up in the house. My father was always bringing up other people's kids."

"He'll live with the maids?"

"I don't know yet."

He gave a low, disapproving whistle. "You can't just take over someone's life like that." He turned to her. "Is there anything you think you can't do?"

Perhaps the presences were gone forever. Papa, Miguel, that poor man kneeling in the jungle.

"He needs to be with his mother," David said. "You should bring him back to her."

"His mother begged you to take him. And the priest said I could."

"You don't have the right," he said.

"No one has the *right*. You can't keep talking about rights. They didn't have the right to kill his father."

"Or to kill yours."

She caught her breath. She forced herself to consider the

connection, then dismissed it. Her father was dead, not killed. He had been so careless with his life, with their lives, that she cringed whenever people called him a martyr.

"Vigilantes didn't kill my father," she said.

She didn't say: My father killed my father. My father almost killed *us*.

"They're not bad men, Lali. They pray for guidance."

"What happened in the jungle, last night, in the clearing—"

"I can't talk about it."

"That's why I took the boy." Her throat was hurting. "I won't harm him."

"Children need to be loved. They need to be with their parents."

"Children need to be cared for." She imagined the boy asleep in a maid's cot and, a sea away, a baby girl in a white crib and Arturo in her sister's arms.

Calm down, she told herself. Look around you. Listen. This room, the sky, the stars. David's breathing. Your breathing. The sea. She told herself: This will pass.

Stop lying to yourself.

She would accept any lie now.

The deepest spiritual law is to love, a psychic had told her. But there was another law, deeper and more insidious, and that was to survive.

What else could she do? Skin against skin, feeling herself only through contact with another.

His bare legs and arms, so close to hers. Touch him, she told herself. Just this once. They had never made love. But if she did touch him, she might find her father or her sister or the body in the clearing. She moved her legs away.

Touch him. You need to feel yourself again.

She couldn't live a life without wanting.

Something banged and rattled in the garden. From beneath

the door, the strip of light disappeared. Watching her confusion, David said: "They've turned off the generator."

She waited for her eyes to adjust to the new, deeper darkness. "Tell me a story," she said. "One true thing. Something you've never told anyone."

He was silent for a long time. Then he said: "They thought I was Mexican. In school. Later I learned about all those centuries of trade between Manila and Acapulco, but in school they just said—Mexican, with weird eyes and a weird nose. I don't think any of them had ever seen a Mexican."

Some bloods don't mix, her mother had said. Filipinos blend very well with Spanish or Chinese or French—the children usually are beautiful, even if the parents aren't—but Filipinos and white Americans can have strange-looking babies. *Mestisong bangus*, her mother called them—half-human, half-fish.

"There weren't any other Filipinos in our town. Just me and my mother."

He wanted so badly to be recognized as Filipino, when his accent was so American, when he walked and gestured and took up space like an American. She wished she could make him feel at home here.

"One true thing," she said gently.

"You start."

She pressed her back against the headboard. "Last night, what happened . . ." She stopped, checking inside herself for confirmation. One true thing, she told herself, but it was hard to know the difference between honesty and provocation. It was hard to remember what truth felt like.

He stretched his legs, hooked his right foot behind his left ankle.

She closed her eyes, not wanting to adjust her words to his discomfort. "I think they beheaded him for us."

"That's not true," he said.

"And a part of me wanted it. I wanted to know, from inside myself, what it was, what I would feel."

She wanted to say: I feel it when the dead are near. But David wouldn't believe her.

He lit an Indonesian cigarette. The smell of cloves mingled with the chemical fumes of the mosquito coil.

"We could have saved him," she said.

"No, Lali."

They sat in darkness without speaking.

A faint rumbling in the distance, perhaps a car on the road, or thunder from the mountains.

The rumbling grew louder.

Yellow lights swept through the window and over the bed. Car doors banged. Men were speaking. A lizard scurried across the wall, tail swinging, running from the light.

David and she dressed in the dark, hurried down the stairs.

Sister Connie stood near the middle of the living room, holding a candle. "Be calm," she said.

Young girls huddled together, roused from sleep, their faces puffy and languid. One of them carried the little boy. His head rested on her shoulder.

"Turn on the generator," Sister Connie told the houseboys. "Use the kitchen door. Then come back, right away, and lock the door."

The young men rushed away. Minutes later, Lali heard a rattling sound. Sister Connie switched on a lamp next to the couch and blew out the candle flame. She lowered an album onto the record player and set the needle in place. A scratchy recording of the Rolling Stones, *Brown Sugar*.

"Everyone dance," she said.

They looked at her.

"Dance!" She reached for David's hands and, holding him at arms' length, began shifting her weight from foot to foot.

Someone pounded on the door.

"One moment!" she called out. "We're coming!"

Lali swayed slightly, unable to follow the rhythms of the music. Her knees were shaking again. Above the refrains, she heard pounding and shouts. The young maids held hands and tried to dance with each other, gestures strained, faces frightened. The boy whimpered. Lali lifted him into her arms. His coarse black hair was under her nose.

"Don't stop dancing!" Sister Connie turned up the volume of the music. She told Lali: "They think we're Communists, but if we were Communists, we wouldn't be dancing to rock music."

Sister Connie strode across the room, unbolted the door, and walked outside. In the garden, a dozen men in army fatigues stood next to two trucks, the headlights on.

Sister Connie ambled toward the men. Lali stepped forward, but David held her back. The weight of the boy made her arms ache. She handed him to David. The men clustered around Sister Connie. Lali heard the purring engines, the music pulsating inside the house.

Sister Connie was walking back to the verandah, flanked by two soldiers. She gave David a tense smile. "I've told these gentlemen we were having a little party."

Lali tried to look into the men's eyes, but saw only shadows. It was hard to breathe.

"I explained to them that you're visiting from Manila," Sister Connie said, staring meaningfully at Lali.

Try to understand, Lali admonished herself. She's trying to tell you something. "We're visiting from Manila," Lali said at last, her voice flat. She glanced at Sister Connie, hoping for instructions, some sign, but the woman's face was immobile. "We came to use the beach," Lali ventured.

"No one comes here for vacation," one of the soldiers said. He was a short, muscled man. He looked at the soldiers next to the trucks. "These people came here to use the beach," he shouted. Someone snickered. Turning to the two women, he said: "Go use the beach, then. Go swimming. We'll talk when you finish."

Lali and David followed Sister Connie into the house.

"We can't do that," Lali said. "We can't go into the water. In front of those men. We're making ourselves completely vulnerable."

"We do *exactly* what they say," Sister Connie replied. "If we say no to anything, if we even act like we're not sure, they'll use it against us." She began to call out orders. The maids flurried about, running up and down the stairs and from room to room. "Do you understand me?"

Lali nodded. The assurance in Sister Connie's voice convinced but did not calm her.

One of the girls returned, her arms full of swimsuits. She set them on the floor. Lali, David, and Sister Connie squatted beside her, the boy on David's knees, his face pressed against David's chest. The women sifted through the pile of swimsuits; most of them were black or navy blue one-piece suits with foam-padded bra cups. Strewn among them like discarded flowers were the tops and bottoms of bikinis—flimsy synthetic tissues in bright pink, green, and yellow. Lali selected several one-piece swimsuits. She reached for the boy. With a gentleness that touched her, David settled him into her arms. The child didn't protest; only a slight stiffening in his body betrayed his fear. Poor baby, she thought. Her own fear had blinded her. Holding him over her hip, pressing the swimsuits against his buttocks, she carried him up the stairs.

She settled him on her bed and closed the shutters. Without switching on the lights, she turned away from him, undressed, tried on a bathing suit. The bra cups were too large, but otherwise the suit seemed to fit.

She turned around. He was sitting up, legs stretched in front of him, hands on his knees. He's beautiful, she thought.

And his eyes are intelligent. All the rest, she could add later. Schools, books, travel, culture. The accent. Maybe he would become her son, closer to her than her own daughter. She knelt beside him, lifted his chin, smiled at him. She wanted him to smile back. Instead he lowered his head. She glimpsed the enormity of what had happened to him.

She sat on the bed, lifted him sideways onto her lap, wrapped her arms around him. He wouldn't look at her, but he didn't resist her. Perhaps he was too afraid to resist anyone. Perhaps he wouldn't let himself be surprised by anything anymore. She rubbed his back, not knowing how else to comfort him. Almost imperceptibly, he softened against her. She kissed his head.

Minutes later, carrying the boy, she walked behind David and Sister Connie down the darkened beach toward the sea. She watched David's long, gaunt body, clad only in white boxer shorts, and Sister Connie's huge thighs swelling beneath her black swimsuit.

They waded into shallow water. Thousands of tiny stars, scattered across the dark dome of the sky. She looked over her shoulder. Fifty meters away, the house stood like a cardboard cutout against the night sky. She heard the faint strains of "Honky Tonk Woman." The silhouettes of armed men appeared on one side of the house.

David hoisted the boy onto his shoulders, and they walked deeper into the cool sea. Lali's lower legs disappeared into black water.

"Act like we're enjoying," Sister Connie whispered. She splashed the surface of the water. "Act natural."

Lali knew the men were watching them. Were they government soldiers, or part of a private army? Or vigilantes dressing up like soldiers? No way of knowing. David kicked up water. She surveyed the cove. On the far end, kilometers away, stood the mountains that had given the island its name—stripped of trees but filled with spirits, people said. On the other end of the cove, a cliff rose over the water. Sister Connie followed her gaze. Something seemed to catch her eye.

"Do you see it?" Sister Connie asked. "That light? Like a torch?"

Holding the boy's ankles over his chest, David turned toward the cliff. "That's bizarre. What makes it shine like that?"

Lali couldn't see a light. "Don't talk so loud. They can hear us."

"It's better to talk." Sister Connie's solid body seemed planted like a mangrove into the sea. "Don't stare at it. It's bad luck. It appears there sometimes."

Lali searched again. She couldn't see anything. That wasn't right. She could usually sense things.

"Does anyone live there?" David asked. "Is it a house?"

Lali scanned the cliff. Only darkness. "What is it?"

"We should go back," David said edgily. "They're waiting."

Sister Connie was staring at the cliff. "It's been there forever."

We can't be doing this, Lali thought. We can't be talking about a light I don't see when armed men are waiting for us next to the house, and no one will tell me what they want from us.

"Fishermen use it," Sister Connie said. "They've always been using that light, to guide their position. Spanish priests wrote about it. They couldn't figure it out."

David squinted. "It could just be a white rock."

"It isn't a rock," Sister Connie replied. "Otherwise it wouldn't be so bright—we're too far away."

The men on the hill were squatting now, guns upright, stick figures in the night. No more music. Lali reached for the boy's foot. His skin was cold. She rubbed her fingers over it.

"Some people say it's an enormous, precious stone," Sister Connie said.

She's acting like nothing's happening, Lali thought.

"They say some people stole it, centuries ago, from the king of Ceylon, then sailed up here on pirate winds and placed it up on the cliff for safekeeping."

Maybe there was no light up there. Maybe they were pretending.

"They put a spell on it—anyone who tries to climb that cliff, to reach the light, becomes blind, or dies."

Lali stroked the boy's calves. A strong body—compact, solid. In her fingers, she sensed the man he would become. David, she thought suddenly—that would be a good name for the boy.

"We should go back," Sister Connie said.

Lali tugged jeans over her damp legs. The nuns had told her: Men don't rape women who wear pants. It's too much effort.

David's voice, through the door, urgent: "Are you ready? They're waiting for us."

She picked up the child David, opened the door, followed the man down the stairs. Sister Connie was standing at the bottom, her large-cheeked face lifted toward them. "They're asking for you," she said smugly.

In that instant Lali knew that Sister Connie had made a deal with the soldiers. She had called them in. The elaborate ritual of dancing and running into the ocean was fake, staged, a game Sister Connie had to play before delivering her guests to the soldiers.

Betrayal, everywhere. Arturo had tried to warn her: You don't know your enemies.

Lali and David followed the lay sister into the night and heat. No one spoke. A few meters away, the men watched her. She walked toward them, clutching the boy.

They formed a circle around her but didn't touch her, then led David and her to the military truck. She pressed the boy's head against her shoulder, carried him into the back of the truck. She sat on rough planks, her back against David's, the boy on her lap. Eight men crouched around her. She wanted to talk to them, but their guns silenced her.

David's spine rubbed against hers. She felt his fear.

The truck bounced and rattled. She stroked the boy's arm.

Shouting, outside the truck. Then she was being jostled outside. The boy clung to her. She glimpsed David's face. Panic.

The boy straddled her hip. She tightened one arm around him. With the other, she reached out for David. The vigilantes kept a distance around them.

They walked through the darkness, toward a one-story, cement building on a deserted stretch of road. A flag drooped from a pole in the courtyard.

The men pushed David into the building, then stepped back as Lali walked in. The fluorescent lights hurt her eyes. A filing cabinet, cement floors, a poster of the president, with her toothy smile and white square eyeglasses. Two military men sat behind large desks. One soldier was in his mid-fifties, the other in his twenties. Both were small, sharp-featured, and wiry.

She looked at them and thought: No one can touch me.

David leaned against the wall. The middle-aged soldier ambled toward him. He touched the scapular around David's neck.

Lali straightened her shoulders and stared at the soldier. "Where's your supervising officer?" she asked coldly.

The soldier stepped away from David. "We need to write a report, ma'am. We need your names."

"I need *your* name. Both your names."

The soldiers exchanged glances. The older one said, "Please take a seat, ma'am."

She tipped back her head, exaggerated her convent-school accent. "Anything happens here, and you'll be sorry. The governor is my uncle." That wasn't strictly true. He was her mother's third cousin. But he came to family reunions, and he knew who she was.

"Have patience, ma'am," the younger soldier said.

"Please have a seat," the other said, glancing at the boy.

He knows the child isn't mine, she thought. She pressed the boy against her. She didn't want to look at him. She couldn't deal with pity or tenderness now.

"These boys, ma'am—they don't mean harm. We're here to protect you."

"Where's your phone?" she asked.

The older man picked up the receiver, wiped the mouth-piece with his handkerchief before handing it to her. "Please understand, ma'am. We have to do our duty. They thought you were guerillas."

"I look like a guerilla?"

"We're very sorry, ma'am."

Through the window, she saw the soldiers leaning against the military truck. They looked about seventeen or eighteen years old, with delicate, almost feminine features.

Lali flipped through the pages of her phonebook, dialed a number, spoke in a low voice. She passed the receiver to the middle-aged soldier. His eyes narrowed as he listened, his silence broken only by "Yes, sir," "No, sir," "Of course, sir." The younger man watched him warily and, Lali thought, with growing anger. David stared at the ceiling.

When he hung up, the older man said: "Sorry, ma'am. It was a big misunderstanding. These boys, they get carried away. We've had so many hostilities this week. They were trying to help."

Lali lifted the child higher on her hip. "You should be arresting them, not us. Are you aware of what happened last night?"

He gave a tense, mirthless smile. "They help us, ma'am. We can't do everything ourselves."

A few minutes after midnight, the governor's male secretary appeared at the military outpost. He accompanied David, Lali, and the boy outside. The young men and the military truck had disappeared. The secretary opened the back door of the governor's SUV, and they climbed into it.

Lali made the boy lie down on the back seat, his head on her lap. She reached for his hand. He tried to pull it away, but she tightened her grip. She was beginning to understand him. In the beginning, when she saw he was exhausted, she had urged him to shut his eyes—she told him sleep would come more easily that way. He had obeyed her, but his eyes opened a moment later. Finally, she realized that to fall asleep, he needed to stare into space. He kept his eyes open as long as he could, and closed them only in the instant before sleep. Now he fixed a point on the ceiling of the SUV.

Next to her, David leaned against the window. It seemed like years since she had seen him across the crowded mall, years since he had seemed a stranger.

She stroked the boy's hair.

"We should never have come here," David said.

Be kind to him, she told herself. Maybe you should try to make love with him, just once, even without passion. She told herself she had already broken, with Arturo, the last taboo of desire, which was to simulate desire. She wondered if she could ever love someone again.

They spent the night in the governor's vacation house by the sea. In a four-poster bed, she lay between David and the toddler, listening to their breathing. They were both asleep. David spooned Lali, his arms around her waist. Next to her, the boy murmured in his dreams. Even in sleep, he stiffened when she tried to embrace him.

Sandwiched between them, unable to sleep, she stared out the window. The moon cast troubling shadows across the room. Gently, she pushed the boy away from her, removed herself from David's embrace. In his sleep, David tried to hold on to her.

She walked to a table by the window. No lights on the sea, no sounds from the road.

A sheet of paper on the table, a pen in her hand. It had been years since she had written anyone a letter. She wasn't sure she could do it now.

David and the boy curled toward each other on the white sheets.

Dear Arturo, she wrote, in the flowery handwriting she had learned in convent school. She ran her fingertip over the letters, imagining they could open a passage to him.

Dear Arturo.

She had never asked herself who he was. Even after all these years. She had measured what he could give her, weighing every sexual favor against the possible benefits, preparing herself for every imagined betrayal.

Dear Arturo.

The first time she had seen him. He had been young and not cynical. A smooth-skinned boy who smelled of cognac and aftershave. The money in his smile, the symmetry in his features. Generations of carefully chosen wives and husbands had led to this—a pretty boy with exquisite manners, perfect teeth, and a disconcerting blend of entitlement, sensuality, and kindness.

Dear Arturo.

She folded the paper in half.

I've never written you a letter. Seeing words on paper makes me afraid. Only the pressure of fingers protects them from—

He had believed the world was simple. He had wanted their marriage, their love, to be simple.

Arturo.

She didn't know him. She had never wanted to. She had spent their life together trying not to be known. Evading his desire, his real desire, which was to enter into her. His desire, his real desire, which was to be loved by her.

She wished she had been able to. But something in her had always distrusted love. She wanted sensation, not sentiment. His violence was sensation. Strapping her to a bed, making her stand naked on high heels in front of a full-length mirror.

In bed, he seemed to avoid sentiment as much as she did. Or perhaps he had only pretended to, perhaps he hadn't wanted to frighten her with his feelings. He was a skilled lover, pleased by her pleasure, but he had never looked into her eyes and kissed her while he made love to her. Miguel had done this. She didn't know, even now, whether she could risk tenderness in a lover.

Dear Arturo. I'm sitting here at night, and I wish I were with you. Do you think—

She pushed away the paper and looked out the window. Flame trees in shadow, the yellow moon. The savage beauty of this countryside, so still in the moonlight. She was safe here, in her uncle's home, but the night felt dense with violence. She wished she had never come to this island, never seen a man kneeling in a jungle or little girls scrambling behind a wooden casket, mango leaves flying into the air or tiny fingertips pinching a mother's skirt. This journey was supposed to make sense. People were supposed to do one thing after another and believe it all made sense. What was one more death among so many? She couldn't destroy the images of other nights, a dead man's son sleeping in her bed, David's gaunt features, the dark-eyed whores tapping their heels against the legs of barstools. She couldn't enter into any of them, would never know what they felt or loved or longed for.

Dear Arturo. I understand, for the first time, what Papa was talking about. Not all of it, I could never understand all of it. But why he let himself die. I think that's what I couldn't forgive—he knew if he continued what he was doing, he would have to die, and he went straight toward it, like a madman, like a suicide. But now I understand a little, I think. Why some lives are worth a death. Why some people decide their lives are dispensable. Why life can feel like death, why life gets confused with death. Why death can justify a life. You loved life, I couldn't resist that. I've been wrong, Arturo—

She picked up another sheet of paper.

Arturo, do you think that—do you think, after all this time—

She scratched out the sentence.

Dear Arturo, do you think, after everything that's happened to us, between us, that we could try—

Dear Arturo, you seemed so sure of life, you didn't ask questions, I could forgive you everything because of that, I knew I could marry you because—

She crumpled the paper, started again.

The night here is beautiful, Arturo, so much horror—

It's quiet tonight, the night is beautiful, I've seen terrible things. I'm afraid, Arturo. I want to come home.

They traveled most of the next day. First in the governor's helicopter, then in his Mercedes-Benz. Just before nightfall, they reached the governor's mansion in the provincial capital. High walls, armed men by the gates, two swimming pools, a tennis court, uniformed maids standing by the front door. Months ago, a life ago, none of this would have upset her. The governor and his family were in Manila, but the maids had prepared separate rooms for David and her. White satin sheets, monogrammed pillowcases, orchids in a vase by the bed, air-conditioners running. In perfect and melodic English, the housekeeper told them the governor's plane would take them to Manila the next morning.

Two young maids in white uniforms and rubber thongs led the boy upstairs for a bath. David disappeared into his room. Lali wandered restlessly around the ground floor. In the living room, expensive art lined the walls, and locked glass cases held an extensive collection of Oriental antiques. She stared at the blue and white wares. In Manila, people whispered that the governor had been involved in the discovery of a sunken galleon off a nearby island. The French and Philippine governments had financed the search, but the best antiques, people said, disappeared into private collections. The old Acapulco-Manila route, Lali thought. Seven thousand islands, pirate winds, boats sailing in and out at night—who could secure the borders of an archipelago?

A clock chimed six o'clock. It was dark outside.

She walked into a yellow Provençal-style kitchen. "Is there Mass tonight?" she asked the startled cook.

"Not tonight, ma'am."

Lali felt the boy before she saw him. He was sitting on a stool in a corner of the kitchen, hands on his lap, eyes lowered. Freshly bathed, damp hair combed away from his forehead. His khaki shorts and Lacoste T-shirt probably belonged to one of the governor's grandsons. He sat very still, as though hoping not to be noticed. His feet dangled a few inches over the floor. Her heart went out to him.

What would she say, if anyone asked her what had happened?

Dear Arturo, I've seen so many deaths I thought another wouldn't matter—

She had to be careful—the boy mustn't know the details of his father's death. Otherwise, he'd be obliged to seek revenge. This knowledge was a weapon, too.

Arturo, if I can't write you, it's because I don't know how to talk about what happened.

Arturo, I saw a man killed. I took his son.

Now it was past midnight, and she was standing in the governor's garden. The delicate fragrance of *sampaguitas*. When she was young, a gardener had told her that the *sampaguita's* roots had two opposite properties: the roots growing toward the east were extremely poisonous, but those reaching to the west were beneficial and, at times, miraculous. Carefully, she felt for the roots that snaked to the east and tugged them out of the earth.

She remembered a summer visit to this house, years ago, when she was a child. On her first morning, in a corner of this garden, she had seen a small white flower with dozens of petals, alone on the grass. Watch it, the maids told her—it changes color every few hours. She spent a day running to look at it. The petals remained white until about ten in the morning, then slowly began to turn pink. At two in the afternoon, the white flower had become deep pink. By the time the sun had set, the petals were red against the deep-green grass. At night, its color faded until it became almost as pale as the moon. The next morning, the petals were white again, damp with dew. The maids called it the Holy Rosary—its strange changes of color, they said, represented the three mysteries of the rosary.

Why did I want to kill my daughter, and why do I want this son?

Now she imagined herself back in Manila, in David's townhouse. In the small windowless room, he slid a knife around the edges of his photos, coaxed them from the wall, and piled them on the floor.

She remembered what Sister Esperanza had told her. *I'm not saying the family is the solution to anything. No family helps any of us. But you can't just escape yours because you don't like who you become when you're with them.*

She needed to forget this violence, this darkness, everything she had seen.

Arturo, I need to go home.

Chapter Eleven

Scales

On the seventh day, my love, I surrendered

—Barbara Jane Reyes, "A Genesis of We, Cleaved"

ARTURO

The president, people said, was growing scales like a lizard. She hadn't been seen in weeks. No photos in the newspapers, no speeches on television, no ribbon-cutting or state dinners, no sirens escorting her to fortune-tellers or to the archbishop's dinner parties. Spirits possessed her, people whispered. Her scales were a curse. And they were contagious—people said scales were appearing on those close to her. And now, children were beginning to disappear. From slums to mansions, women heard the rumors: children were being kidnapped, the president's brother had given the order—at night his men threw babies from bridges to pacify the spirits that were punishing his sister.

Arturo glanced at the alarm clock. Almost 5:30 P.M. Five more hours until the meeting at the palace. He hated this time of day—the grey light slanting across the city, the passage into night.

He poured a glass of Bordeaux from the bottle on the bedside table.

Get back to the campaign, his mother kept telling him. After all the money we've spent, after all the people counting on us. We can't let things slip now. Arturo was determined to let them slip. For the first time in years, he ate as much as he wanted. Lechon, garlic-fried rice, several desserts after each meal—*sans rival* and *brazo de Mercedes* and, the day before yesterday, ten *yemas* in one sitting, cracking the caramel crust to reach the thick custard balls in the center. You're beginning to look like your father, Marilou said. You have to lose weight.

He set the wineglass on the table and lit a cigarette.

We can't continue, Pilar had told him.

Her face and voice were earnest, so different from her soft, beckoning body.

Pilar thought people should be good, and that made her weak. Lali thought most people were unreliable or dangerous or at least self-absorbed, so they never surprised her.

He didn't want to know where Lali was.

After the war, his father told him, church bells rang across Manila at noon and every evening at 6 P.M. to announce the angelus. The whole city came to a standstill, as if by enchantment. Jeepneys and buses and horse-drawn carriages stopped in the middle of the road, pedestrians leaned against walls and lowered their heads. Manila, the Distinguished and Ever Loyal City, Pearl of the Orient, burned by its occupiers and bombed by its saviors, remembered the men, women, and children who had died in the final weeks of war. Two hundred thousand killed, Arturo's father told him. Sons, brothers, and fathers beheaded or stabbed with bayonets, girls sequestered and raped in bayside hotels.

Marilou told her husband: The war's over. Stop talking.

The old walled city, the Spanish homes—most of the city damaged or destroyed. The Japanese, retreating, burned everything in their path. The Americans bombed the rest. During liberation, women spat into the faces of American soldiers.

His father said: The Japanese ordered families to gather at dawn, in a square in Malate, and the Japanese officers chose the girls we were all in love with. They took the prettiest first, then the whitest, then the youngest.

Thank God, his mother said. Can you imagine how good God was to us? We are the only country in the world, the only country in history, where no babies were born from rapes. No half-Japanese children after the war. It was a miracle.

Forty years after the war, when groups of Japanese tourists entered a restaurant or a store, Marilou turned pale and fled the room.

A breeze blew through the open windows of his mother's long dining room. The room was dark. At the far end, near the river, small candles flickered on the floor. Shadows knelt in a half circle around the lights.

One foot at a time, trying to steady himself so that no one would suspect he had been drinking, Arturo walked across the marble floor, wearing only shorts. He focused on his bare feet.

The shadows became people. His mother, her suspicious eyes. Aimee's nanny. The cook Filomena—she had gained so much weight—and five teenage maids, as fine-boned and agitated as sparrows.

Marilou bent over something on the floor. He stepped closer. It was Aimee, wrapped in blankets, lying on a pillow. Marilou's eyes darted toward him. She picked up the baby.

Forming his words carefully, trying not to slur, he asked, "What are you doing?"

"You should get dressed," Marilou said sharply. "Put on a shirt."

"Give her to me, Ma."

Marilou hesitated. She settled the baby in his arms. His thumb touched Aimee's warm cheek. Black hair, a pink blotch on her forehead, Lali's large eyes. His chest tightened with love and apprehension.

Marilou pressed her hand on his shoulder. "Sit down, *hijo*."

She helped him sit on the floor, next to the candles.

He held Aimee against his bare chest, pretending to soothe

her but in truth trying to center himself around her, to anchor himself in her. Aimee felt solid and compact, the only real thing in that room.

Marilou told the nanny and maids to leave them alone. When they were gone, she asked Arturo, "Are you going to make it to your meeting tonight?"

He nodded.

For a few moments, she didn't speak. Then: "One week, two weeks after the hospital—I can understand. But it's been long enough! Your leg's almost okay. I can't believe you'd let yourself get drunk the night you're meeting Ricky!"

"I'm not drunk."

"You asked what I was doing? I was praying over Aimee. I'm taking care of your daughter! Someone has to, don't you think? No one knows where her mother is, and her father sits in his room from morning to night, drinking and eating."

He lifted himself from the floor. One step, then another, until he was leaning against the balcony, over the black river. His mind felt clear, even if his voice had slurred. Aimee was calm in his arms. Her trust in him, her contentment, frightened him.

The breeze carried a faint odor of the chemical fumes from factories on the other bank. How long could his mother keep living here? One by one, the neighbors had moved away to the gated subdivisions in Makati, their colonial homes sold and razed to the ground, replaced by factories and warehouses.

Without turning to his mother, he said, "I'll take Aimee to the beach this weekend. She needs fresh air."

"She's not leaving the house! Babies are disappearing."

"You can't believe that."

"Listen, *hijo*," she said, from behind him. "I'm sorry I have to be the one to tell you, but you need to know something. Just so you're not surprised tonight. I know what Ricky's like."

He tightened his arms around Aimee.

"Lali was arrested in Negros," she said.

He didn't speak.

"With some American so-called journalist."

"I know," he said, still facing the river, speaking softly to hide his emotion.

"Well. Of course you know. That's very good." She paused. "And she's okay now. You know that, too, don't you? She's been back a few weeks."

"You know, Mama, Lali reminds me of you."

He turned to her. She stood with her legs apart, plump feet tucked into pink high-heeled slippers.

"The willfulness," he said.

"I'm sorry to upset you. But you need to know."

"The faith in herself."

He had loved the skin on Lali's thighs, and how easily they bruised.

"I never wanted you to marry her."

"My marriage is none of your business, Ma."

"Until you win, everything is my business! You think things just take care of themselves? You think it's been easy for me?"

She was right, of course. He had let her take over everything, since the hospital. Even before the hospital. She did her best. It wasn't the life she had expected, either.

"I'm doing everything you want," he said.

"Have you thought about what you're going to tell Ricky tonight? There is not one mayor in one godforsaken town who's going to support you, unless Ricky's sister gives the word!" She gave a wide, fake smile. He tensed, bracing himself for a change in tactics. "Darling," she said, cajoling, "we can *win*. But we need President Peachy's support. We need Ricky."

In the semidarkness, illuminated only by candlelight and the faint light at the other end of the dining room, his mother's face seemed softer. He remembered the young woman he had seen in photographs—pouting lips, arched eyebrows, mid-calf dresses cinched at the waist. She had been beautiful, in the contrived way of the 1950s. Not his kind of beauty—her skin would never bruise under anyone's touch—but ripe and alluring all the same. He considered how life had transformed the girl in the photographs into the woman before him now.

He turned back to the river. Aimee was sleeping in his arms. He held her closer. She sighed, turned her face to his skin. On the other bank, close to the ground, yellow lights glowed.

Lali's pale face, black hair in disarray on a pillow, head tilted upward, the sensuality and hunger on her face. The thought of another man seeing her like that made him nauseous.

He imagined Pilar. The thick eyebrows, those fearful eyes. Pilar was so much braver than she knew, precisely because she was so afraid.

He didn't want a false life.

Maybe a false life was the only honorable choice. They were all counting on him. All of them, even Pilar. Whatever they told him, whatever they told themselves, they all needed money, safety, everything he could give them. They expected him to do what no one else wanted to, what on some level they would look down on him for doing. The violence, the campaign, the ambition.

He settled the baby in his mother's arms, touched her shoulder. "Don't worry, Ma. I'll deal with Ricky."

His mother seemed shaken. She lowered her head, kissed Aimee's forehead. There was something in the way she held Aimee, a protectiveness and kindness. Even Marilou became maternal with a baby.

No babies were born from rapes, she had told him. No half-Japanese children after the war. Suddenly he understood. They had all been killed at birth.

Enough, he told himself. Starting tomorrow, he would pummel his body and mind back into shape.

Just before 11 P.M., he passed a security checkpoint, parked his car near the presidential palace. He walked to another checkpoint. Soldiers inspected his I.D. and searched him. Other soldiers escorted him into the building. Before the revolution, he had visited the palace regularly for the General's parties, enjoying the champagne, the actors and musicians the General's wife flew in from America, the caviar and vodka, the young socialites and fashion models who feigned disinterest but would, he knew, be happy to go to a borrowed apartment with him that night.

A presidential guard accompanied him through the foyer and into a hallway. The palace had the hushed, musty feel of a museum. The president refused to live or work there. Too ostentatious, she said. A monument to the General's corruption and the First Lady's greed. For a few months after her inauguration, she opened the palace to the public, displaying the excesses of her predecessors—the elevated gold-plated thrones where the General and his wife received visitors, the five-gallon bottle of Chanel No. 5 in the First Lady's bathroom, the basement filled with hundreds of French and Italian couture gowns.

Arturo followed the guard up an ornate, winding staircase and into a high-ceilinged room that was decorated with pillars, gold moldings, and red-velvet chairs. Guards stood along the walls.

Across from him hung a massive oil painting of the First

Lady, seated, surrounded by her four daughters. The women all had diamond tiaras pinned to their black hair. There had been a twin portrait with the General and his two sons, years ago.

Arturo had spent a night with the youngest daughter. The wild one, people said. She had just broken up with her Swiss banker boyfriend. For months after that, she called Arturo at odd hours of the night. He tried to soothe her, but she wanted to see him again and he said it was impossible, the General would never allow it, the General had bigger plans for her. In reality he was afraid of her. She was married now and safe in Hawaii, living in the villa with the extended family and the General's embalmed corpse. The family wanted a hero's burial for him in Manila, and refused to bury him anywhere else.

Arturo scrutinized her face in the portrait. A bland prettiness had replaced her edgy, push-it-to-the-limit attractiveness. Only the First Lady remained interesting. The artist's brush softened but couldn't disguise the set of her mouth, that peculiar blend of naiveté and ruthlessness in her eyes. She and her husband had stolen and bullied and perhaps killed, but their extravagance continued to fascinate the country. They had always been kind to him.

In the basement, a guard opened the door to a large, brightly lit room. Groups of men, most of them in long sleeves, sat around square tables. Young women in miniskirts served drinks. On the other end, Ricky and his men slouched around a long oval table.

As Arturo approached the table, the president's brother stood to meet him. Ricky was tall and overweight, with curly black hair and a boyish smile. He pumped Arturo's hand. A psychopath, Arturo thought, but charming. People loved Ricky much more than his sister. President Peachy had studied comparative literature at Radcliffe and spoke French and

German. Ricky had been kicked out of two universities in
Manila, but he sang and danced at fiestas, spoke and swore in
several local languages. He distributed 500-peso bills during
campaign trips or while visiting injured soldiers at the military
hospital. He had tears in his eyes when he praised the soldiers
on television. It's fascinating, Lali said, how someone without
morals can be so caring.

Arturo followed the president's brother around the room.
Hiding his distaste, he shook hands with the so-called midnight cabinet—a group of Ricky's classmates, relatives, and
business associates who came to the palace every night, advis-
ing Ricky on state matters and negotiating business deals.

Ricky led Arturo back to the oval table. "Have something
to eat."

"I've had dinner," Arturo said politely. From the corner of his
eye, he watched a well-known Chinese tycoon enter the room.

"Have another dinner!"

The men at the table laughed, with false heartiness.

A uniformed waiter set several bottles of Château Petrus on
the table. Each bottle cost more than the president's monthly
salary, but Ricky was generous. His mistresses and fifteen children had million-dollar homes in Forbes Park and Dasmariñas
Village; their neighbors, most of them from Manila's old elite,
complained quietly among themselves. One mistress displayed
three dozen garden gnomes on her front lawn. Another had
installed an Olympic-size pool with wave machines and covered her garden with white sand and coconut trees. Mistress
number three built a home cinema that seated up to 100 people, while number four, an aspiring chef, constructed a mansion with four kitchens and four dining rooms, each with a different color theme.

"Come with me," Ricky told him abruptly, as though talking to a houseboy.

Heat spread across Arturo's neck. He told himself: Don't

say anything. You need him. You need his sister. Get through
this.

Adjoining the main room was a much smaller one. A low
ceiling, bare white walls, no windows. Under a fluorescent
lamp, four men sat around a table. Their eyes flicked nervously
toward Ricky, then focused again on their cards. Arturo recognized two of them—a provincial governor and a Chinese-
Filipino businessman who ran the duty-free business. Other
men were drinking and talking at a small bar. Standing behind
the bar was a teenage waitress in a skimpy lime-green halter
dress.

"Last time, we played from midnight to noon," Ricky told
Arturo. "You don't like my food?"

"I'll have some in a while, sir," Arturo said.

"How is the lovely wife?" Ricky asked, with a disingenuous
smile.

"She's fine."

"I hear she's traveling."

Arturo took a sip of water, moistened his lips.

"Sorry we missed your daughter's baptism," Ricky said.

"No problem."

"We were up late that night. All night, if I remember."

Swaying on her heels, the teenage waitress carried a tray of
wine and Scotch to the table. She bent over to pour the drinks.
Arturo watched her. He remembered the young waitress in
that remote island, in the bar by the pier—the mole over her
lip and the sweet smell, the way she had blushed when he
spoke to her. He wished he had talked to her more. He considered taking this teenager aside, asking her questions.
Women always had something interesting to say, even someone
this young. She was the only lightness in this room.

She noticed him watching her, lowered her eyes. She
seemed worried, uncertain. She had impossibly small bones.
Her hair was long and black, her face heart-shaped. Almost the

same shape as Lali's. Where did Ricky find girls like her? Soft-featured and hesitant, not vulgar.

Ricky turned to him. "Your father-in-law was a big poker player, wasn't he? Do you play?"

"No."

"You MBA types. Study, study, study." He grabbed the girl from behind and pressed her hips against his. Arturo flinched. The girl closed her eyes and stretched her lips, trying to smile, and failing. The poker players stared at their cards.

Arturo sipped water. It was difficult to swallow. Ricky had seen him watching the girl. He had mistaken Arturo's interest for desire and was groping the girl now to humiliate him.

Ricky released the girl, wrapped his arm around her waist, and steered her out of the room. As she passed Arturo, her gentle, frightened eyes touched his. He was startled by the pity he felt. She lifted a tiny hand, pushed her thick hair away from her face. On her wrist were small round scars, pale against her brown skin. With a start he understood. Cigarette burns.

He couldn't save her. She needed Ricky's money more than she needed to be saved.

Twelve million dollars in bribes. That was the talk at dinner parties and coffee shops. The week before, Ricky had given interviews to the leading newspapers. He denied the allegations. Yes, he had received money, but these were honest commissions. He had given most of it back to the poor, set up foundations to help them, solicited donations from the country's wealthiest families. He had appointed family members to the foundations' board of directors only to keep an eye on accounts.

Arturo returned to the main room. He sat on a white leather couch and watched television with a group of drowsy men. Each time a young woman offered him wine or Scotch, he shook his head and didn't look in her eyes. Hours passed. No sign of Ricky. No sign of the girl with the green halter dress and the scars on her wrist. No one left the room.

At about 2 A.M., some of Ricky's friends began to sing. *Hey Jude, don't be afraid.* At some point, a slender man sauntered toward Arturo, his long black hair swinging, a large folder under his arm. Arturo knew who he was—Manila's most celebrated interior decorator. "You're here, too?" he asked Arturo. He offered his graceful fingers. Arturo held them briefly. The decorator wiped the seat of the chair with a tissue and sat down with a sigh. "Ricky tells me to come here. A business meeting at 1 A.M. Of course he's late."

"My appointment was for midnight. He's always late."

The decorator tucked his hair behind his ears. "He wants me to decorate his girlfriend's bedroom, but you cannot imagine his *taste*."

Arturo gave a genuine smile, for the first time that night. He liked this man.

"He tells me he wants the room to be red," the decorator continued. His features were chiseled and delicate. "Red! 'What kind of red, sir?' I ask him. 'Red,' he says again. I bring him patterns. Every shade of red you can imagine. No, no, no, he says. For two hours, we look. Finally, I say: 'Sir, I don't know any other kind of red. You have to explain to me.' He tells me: 'I want menstruation red.' Can you imagine? What am I supposed to do? Whatever people say, at least the General and the First Lady treated me with respect. They paid on time. They trusted my judgment."

A pale, slender girl appeared at the doorway. Everyone awake turned to her. Her face a perfect oval, her eyes feline. Straight black hair, to her waist. A white dress outlined her body.

The decorator winked at Arturo. "That's a new one. She's only sixteen. But he's got a newer one." He whispered the name of a former child star. "She's pregnant—and she just turned fifteen!"

The girl stepped forward and surveyed the room cautiously, like a child. Arturo felt a stirring. "She's very pretty," he said.

"Gorgeous," the decorator replied distractedly. "But she'll age badly."

Arturo watched the girl. He wanted to despise Ricky for being with someone so young and vulnerable. Instead, to his discomfort, he envied him.

He turned away.

"And President Peachy," the decorator said. "Do you think it's true, about the scales? Ricky should be the one changing into a frog, not her."

Arturo looked back at the girl. "A lizard," he said. "They say."

"Anyway," the decorator said. "Frogs, lizards, fish. What difference does it make? If something happens to her, *he* takes over."

Just before dawn, Ricky tapped Arturo's shoulder. "No one can keep up with us," he said, gesturing at the men slumped and sleeping on couches and armchairs. "Come on."

Narrow hallways led to a back door, then to an enclosed garden and oval swimming pool. Armed guards stood along high walls. Yellow-tinged footlights, hidden in the grass, illuminated the paths. The air smelled of chlorine.

Ricky stripped to his underpants and jumped feet first into the pool. He popped up with a whoop, his hair slicked back. Underwater lights deepened the sockets of his eyes. He dog-paddled across the pool and back again, head out of the water. After three laps, he hoisted himself out of the pool. An aide brought him a towel and an orange bathrobe. He patted the towel over his body and put on the robe.

"Look at this," he told Arturo, gesturing at the cloudy sky. "Sometimes, I stare at the sky at night, and I tell myself that life really is a mystery. I should have been a musician, not a statesman. I was really good—I could have been a star." He removed a pack of cigarettes from the pocket of his robe, lit a cigarette.

He didn't offer one to Arturo. "But my sister couldn't handle this country on her own. She asked me to sacrifice my dreams. One day I'll get back to my music—you mark my words. Always stay true to your dreams—that's my motto."

Arturo clamped a smile on his face. He had to stay focused.

Ricky asked, "Have you been back here since the General got kicked out?"

"Not to the palace," Arturo replied carefully. "But I met your sister a few times at the guest house."

Ricky drew on the cigarette. "She doesn't want to endorse you. I've tried. No way, she says. Hard for her to forgive and forget. She's too educated and not smart enough, if you know what I mean. But I'm working on her. Forgiveness and compassion, all that."

"I appreciate it."

"Let's not bullshit each other," Ricky snapped.

Arturo crossed his arms.

"I'm good to my friends," Ricky said. "I help them when they need it. But it has to be win-win."

"Of course." Trying to sound casual, Arturo asked, "And what can your friends do for you in return?"

"I ask them to remember. That's all."

"I know that."

"You know that? You think you're a hot shot, don't you? With your stateside MBA and half-baked American accent. You're like my sister. All theory, no results. You know what's my management technique? Friendship. Loyalty. Vision. Did you learn that at Wharton?"

"I didn't go to Wharton, sir."

"If you're such a hot shot, how come I'm the one running the country?"

"I believe your sister is running the country, sir."

Ricky laughed. "You're not afraid, are you?"

Arturo waited.

"We have to find a way of making you palatable," Ricky said. "Otherwise, my sister can't back you."

"I'm ready to do whatever's necessary, sir."

Ricky loosened the belt of his bathrobe. The orange cloth parted over his hairless chest. "Your wife—she can be useful."

Arturo tensed. "I'm afraid we can't count on her."

"I know." Ricky rolled his eyes. "Women. What do you expect? That's why I have several of them—they cancel each other out. Divide and conquer—that's my motto. Come on. We'll talk later. I'll show you around. You'll see what you've been missing."

Bodyguards accompanied them back into the building. Inside the elevator, harsh light revealed a few faded acne scars on Ricky's cheeks. His curly black hair glistened.

The elevator doors opened. Ricky led him down a corridor and into the palace's old discotheque. Red carpets and couches, a dance floor in the middle, mirrors on the ceiling and walls. Without windows, like a bunker. The General had built the discotheque so that his wife and children wouldn't have to leave the palace to go dancing. Manila was too dangerous, even under martial law. Gunfights erupted in elegant nightclubs; sons of wealthy families had been killed for overtaking their classmates on the highway.

Arturo scanned the room, remembering other evenings. Drugs, pulsating music, strobe lights, smoke from dry ice blowing across the dance floor. Ravishing girls from Manila's best families emerging from the mist with red lips, stiletto heels, and skimpy dresses they had bought in Paris or New York. The dictator's daughters glided from table to table, heavily made up and generous with the friends and drugs they had flown in from abroad. The low tables and red-velvet armchairs were gone, as were the cushions embroidered with the First Lady's favorite sayings. *Nice girls go to heaven; bad girls go everywhere else.*

"What a waste," Ricky said. "My sister refuses to use it for parties."

Over the zinc bar, a fresco depicted the General's wife and four daughters in a forest, yellow roses in their hands and hair.

"I used to ask myself how they could live like this, without windows," Arturo said.

"They thought everybody was trying to get them."

"A lot of people were."

"My sister didn't want me to set up office here, but I told her: What do you expect me to do? Hold office in our house in Greenhills? She was the one who begged me to head the anti-crime commission."

Arturo nodded. "We've backed your projects, sir."

"I don't forget."

"And we'll continue."

How many attempted coups d'état would it take to drive this buffoon out of power?

The last time Arturo had seen Jimbo, at Aimee's christening, the rebel-chief had told him: *Don't get caught in their game, Arturo. You have to save yourself.* Even at the time, Arturo wasn't sure he had heard correctly.

"I'm going to be honest," Ricky said. "It's going to be hard for my sister to endorse you. Too many things against you. That shipping disaster, for example."

"All charges were dropped. We helped every single family."

"Maybe, but the public hasn't forgotten. And Jimbo came out the big hero, which doesn't look good for us. But your wife made a big impression." An insinuating smile. "She looked like a movie star, standing there with Jimbo. And that speech. She has guts, that woman. You like strong women, no? Everyone was talking about her. And you were nowhere."

Arturo tried to swallow. He had expected the night to be difficult, but something else was going on. Ricky was taunting him, preparing him for something.

"And that arson charge," Ricky said. "You shouldn't set fire to villages."

On Arturo's cheek, the muscle tightened. He covered it with his hand. "My men never set fire to a village."

"And then your number-one opponent—what was his name? Benedicto?—found dead."

"I'm going home."

"No need to get angry. I'm not interested in what really happened. I'm talking about what people perceive. Let's face it—you're seen as the General's crony who's been involved in some very bad stuff since you got back. How can my sister endorse you? You're the opposite of everything she stands for. Come on—don't look at me like that. I'll show you something else."

At the far end of the discotheque, Ricky slid open a door and gestured at Arturo to enter. A shooting gallery, with racks of handguns and rifles on one wall and a dozen life-size cardboard bodies lined up across the room. The room smelled like burned popcorn.

"Want to try it?" Ricky asked.

Arturo shook his head, glanced at the closed door. A small room, probably soundproof, full of guns. He didn't want to be alone here with Ricky. One of the rooms in the palace, according to Manila rumor, had been used as a torture chamber during Ricky's notorious but short-lived reign as head of the anti-crime commission. In a widely reported incident, he had shot and killed a captured drug dealer while speaking on the telephone to a newspaper columnist. Ricky, the columnist later wrote, was angry because she had barraged him with questions about his links to organized smuggling. He had asked her to hold for a moment, then she heard the gunshots.

Now Ricky said: "I used to practice with bull's-eyes, but I missed all the time. Then I discovered human figures."

Arturo glanced at his watch. Almost 6 A.M. Outside these walls, the sky was turning light.

Ricky opened a cupboard and poured Scotch into two glasses. He clinked his glass against Arturo's. Arturo lifted his glass in a toast and returned it to the table without drinking from it.

"We'll figure something out," Ricky said. "We'll have to use your wife—the memory of her father, all that. Millions of votes right there. She'll be your saving grace. We can say you had a political and moral awakening when you married her. She helped you turn against the General, you joined the opposition because of her."

"We did support your sister."

"Ha. Only at the very end."

An aide entered the room, set plates of fried rice, scrambled eggs, and sausages on a table. Ricky sat, gestured at Arturo to sit across from him. He told the aide to wait outside. "We have the rally coming up," Ricky said. "I want you and your wife on stage. She makes a big speech. I want to hear her praising *me*, too. For a change."

"I don't think she'll do that," Arturo said. He didn't say: Unlike me, Lali doesn't make deals with people she despises.

"That's your problem. You want our endorsement? We have to rehabilitate you. There are conditions." Ricky patted his mouth with a linen napkin, folded the napkin, and set it on the table. "You know, we can help you persuade her."

Arturo cut into the sausage and, with the tip of his knife, pushed the piece to the side of the plate.

"No heroes in this country." Ricky seemed pensive now, less brash. "How do you think your wife's father got out of the country?"

Arturo tried to cut another slice of sausage. He fumbled.

"You think the General just let him escape?" Ricky asked.

Arturo set his knife and fork on the plate.

"He switched sides," Ricky said. "He made a deal with the General."

Ricky kept talking. Gregorio betrayed us, he said. He

betrayed his friends, my sister. Here's the truth about your father-in-law, Arturo. He was a coward, a traitor. He was no hero.

"Gregorio despised the General," Arturo said at last. "He would never have switched sides."

Ricky shrugged. "And yet he did."

"I *knew* Gregorio."

Ricky looked at Arturo with what seemed like compassion. Arturo wanted to smash his fist into Ricky's face. Instead he reached for the Scotch.

"We can produce very convincing evidence," Ricky said. "Even proof, if you want. Documents, a recording."

Arturo ferreted through his thoughts for some counter-argument or defense, or at least a way out of this room and this night. "I don't believe it," he said finally. Even to his ears, the words sounded hollow.

"I know it's hard." Ricky sounded regretful. "But everyone has a weak spot. That's what makes people interesting. Your father-in-law, for example. A good man—no one's denying that—but he loved his family." He bit into a piece of toast. "Come on. You believe a sixty-five-year-old man climbed over a prison wall, ran across a field, and just happened to find a helicopter waiting for him? He made a deal with the General, in return for safe exile. And all that time, in San Francisco—pretending to be with us and working against us."

Arturo wished Lali were with him. She had always interpreted people for him. She would know how to silence Ricky.

"It doesn't make sense." Arturo tried to sound cool and dismissive. "If Gregorio was on the General's side, the General wouldn't have had him killed."

A pitying smile. "You still think it was the General?" Ricky began to speak, between bites of sausage and eggs. One faction of the opposition—not *me*, he said—had to stop Gregorio, so he wouldn't betray anyone else.

The Scotch stung Arturo's throat, spread its warmth inside his chest. Ricky was a liar. But Arturo began calculating what this might mean, if it were true. Why was Ricky telling him this? What did Ricky want him to do with it? Gregorio had betrayed the opposition? The opposition—the new president, Ricky's men—had been behind Gregorio's murder? How could this be possible? Yet it felt true. He could denounce them, but that would mean denouncing Gregorio, explaining why his own side had turned against him. He couldn't do that to Lali and Pilar. He couldn't do that to himself. It would end his political career. He had everything to lose, and Ricky knew it.

"It's not true," Arturo said coldly. "People would have heard about it."

"We knew he could be useful—"

"I would have heard *something*."

"Especially as a martyr."

Arturo pushed the glass away from him. "What do you want from me?"

"Calm down. Let me say one thing. Don't think you can go talk about this. One, you have no proof. And two, if you tried, we would release what *we* know, with proof, and you would regret it."

"Your sister declared him a national hero. She wouldn't have done that if he had betrayed her."

"He's a very good national hero, isn't he? All those things he wrote. Prison, exile, martyrdom. The revolution."

"And you come into power."

"My sister comes into power," Ricky said good-naturedly. "And the press likes it."

Arturo could never tell this to Lali and Pilar: The General didn't kill your father—your father's friends did.

It would shatter Pilar.

"What do you want?" Arturo asked.

"I'm trying to give you what *you* want. You want my sister

to endorse you? Then get ready for the rally. With your wife. I told you, she's useful for us. People worship her father."

"My wife has no illusions about her father."

"You figure it out." Ricky's eyes were distant, as though he had already detached himself from the conversation. He stood and turned his back to Arturo while he rummaged in the cupboard. A room full of guns, and Ricky knew he was safe, even with his back turned. Arturo wasn't even a threat.

Save yourself.

Ricky asked, "You know where your wife is?"

"Of course."

"Why are you getting so hostile again?"

"How much do you want?" Arturo asked. He had an image of the girl with the scar on her wrist, her worried eyes and heart-shaped face. Everyone became a whore around Ricky.

Ricky turned to him. "You think this is about money?"

"A contribution, then." Arturo wanted to punch Ricky's thick lips. Anything to make him stop talking.

"I'm sorry to be the bearer of bad news." Ricky's expression was warm, his voice compassionate. "But don't kill the messenger. It's Gregorio who's the problem, not me. We're trying to make the best of a bad situation."

Arturo rubbed the cuff of his shirt. He sensed he had reached some boundary, that everything that happened from now on would be tainted by what he did or did not do this night. The cuff felt stiff and starched beneath his fingers.

Several aides and bodyguards strode into the room. One held up a hanger with olive-green military fatigues.

Ricky stood. "We need men like you, Arturo." He slipped off his bathrobe. "Men who can sacrifice their personal lives for the good of their country."

The greatest threat to this country, Jimbo had said, is a leader with education, integrity, and no social status.

Jimbo was a threat. Arturo would never be one.

Save yourself—when Jimbo had told him this, at Aimee's christening, Arturo had shaken his head. He wasn't willing to join forces again with a renegade and get dragged into another round of coups d'état. We may have the same enemy, he had told Jimbo, but we're not fighting for the same thing.

Save yourself.

Arturo didn't know what or whom to save. But he knew that at some point, even someone like him had to take a stance.

Take her, Ricky said.

And Arturo did. In the passenger's seat beside him, the girl with the lime-green dress and scars on her wrist clasped her hands over her lap. A gift, Ricky had said. Her long, thick hair seemed too heavy for her fragile neck and shoulders. Lali's hair was like that, too.

The girl was looking out the windshield, not at him. In a soothing voice, trying not to frighten her, he asked where her family was from, how many brothers and sisters she had, when she had moved to Manila. She answered with a nervous smile, in faltering English. He learned where she came from. He started to speak to her in her own language. Her face relaxed.

He drove past the neighborhood where his parents had lived before the war. Images of bombed buildings and fires appeared in his mind, interspersed with the sepia-colored photos he had seen in books and photo albums, the wooden colonial homes and lush vegetation. He felt the fatigue in his hands, in his head. With one hand he rubbed his eyes. The girl leaned against the window.

Dawn. The car advanced through empty streets. A gray sky covered the city.

Condensation filmed the windshield, obscuring the city and houses. With a fingertip, he traced a line down the misted glass, wiped clear a space in front of him. As a boy, during the long drive to school, he had sat in the back and written his name on the windows, waiting for condensation to efface the letters before tracing them out again.

Now he opened the windows a crack. Slowly, the glass became clear again.

Ricky was right. Everyone had a weak spot. Those activists who had been imprisoned and tortured under the General—many of them, too, had reached their breaking point, not always when expected. When Peachy came to power, she released the General's opponents and other dissidents from prison, appointed some of them to public office, acclaimed them as heroes. On the day the political prisoners were freed, Manila rejoiced; thousands of people threw yellow confetti from the high-rise office buildings along Ayala Avenue, exhilarated by the promise of a new era and clean government. Within a year, some of the revolution's heroes had taken over the wards and businesses of the General's cronies, added their relatives to the public payroll, accepted commissions from the kidnapping and smuggling syndicates. At the same time, the left-wing movement began to turn against itself, with excommunications, infighting, assassinations. People watched all this, saddened but not surprised. What do you expect, people said. Poverty and loss were always just a misstep away. Everyone had to take care of their families.

"Where do you live?" he asked the girl.

She sat up straight, crossed her legs toward him. He sensed her tension.

"With my sister, sir."

It took more questions and reassurance to find out the address. He drove her there, to a dilapidated neighborhood. She pointed at the house. He stopped the car. She uncrossed her legs, parted them slightly, arched her back. One last, half-hearted effort to seduce him. He pretended not to notice. He gave her money, more than he should have. Eyes lowered, she thanked him, hurried out of the car. She ran in her heels past the house, down another block, disappeared into a side street. She had given him the wrong address.

He sat there, staring at his hands on the steering wheel. He told himself he was still a good person, like the schoolboy he had been. Or at least a decent person, despite the violence around him, despite the deals he had made and would continue to make with people like Ricky, despite what would soon become the rest of his life.

He started the car. He needed one clean good thing, right now, after this night.

A military checkpoint blocked the entrance to Epifanio de los Santos Avenue. Soldiers waved the car through. Along the pothole-ridden highway, he passed high cement walls that protected the enclaves of the wealthy and, further down, the low whitewashed walls the First Lady had constructed to hide the squatter colonies. Beneath a bridge, rainwater stagnated in opaque brown puddles. He shut the windows, then accelerated. On each side, water rose like a fan, splattered against the glass.

The subdivision was built on a ridge several hundred meters above the lake and volcano. The road curved past multimillion-peso weekend houses, partly visible through fences and iron grilles, surrounded by giant ferns, fruit trees, orchid plantations. He switched off the air-conditioner, rolled down the windows. Cool air washed through the car. At the vacation house of one of Lali and Pilar's cousins, an hour from Manila, he parked the car in the garage. A maid unlocked the front door. Across the vast living room, floor-to-ceiling windows opened to a teak-floored terrace. Beyond it, the sky dissolved into a gray lake.

A woman was sitting at the far end of the terrace, her back to him, hair twisted into a chignon. Her neck was bare. He removed his shoes and walked toward her.

Without turning her head, Pilar asked, "What are you doing here?"

He walked past her to the edge of the terrace and grasped the railing. The air was crisp. Beneath him, in the middle of the lake, the volcano looked small and forlorn. He thought: There's a point when I can't even justify myself to myself.

Her footsteps behind him, coming closer.

Now she was beside him. Lali's perfume again. Rive Gauche. He didn't turn to her.

They looked out at the lake, the mansions lining the ridge. "My great-grandparents had a home here," he said. "Before I was born. It was already in ruins when I was a kid."

"You shouldn't be here," she said softly. "It's over. Please don't make it difficult."

In his mind he told her: Try dealing with Ricky, Pilar. Try selling yourself to him. It's easy to be righteous when you live in a bubble.

Her fingers touched the railing. Her nails were cut close to the skin. A pianist's fingers, he had told her, the first time he held them. Long, slender, strong-knuckled. He wanted her to keep believing in her father, in everything she thought he stood for. That saved a part of himself, too.

"My parents and I used to stay in the lodge," he said. "I had nightmares about the volcano erupting."

He would make sure she never learned about her father's treachery. Not treachery, he corrected himself. Love. Gregorio had loved his family more than his country. Gregorio, at least, had taken a stance.

"Are you okay?" she asked. "I didn't sleep last night."

Let's run away, he thought. Take the car, a plane.

Near the banks of the lake, dark branches floated in opaque green water. This volcano was dormant, a black cone in muddy water. "Have you ever seen an eruption?" he asked.

"Arturo," she said, tense. "You can't stay. We can't see each other."

He turned to her, examining her for the first time. A loose-fitting white blouse and dark slacks. No makeup, no jewelry. She had never had much use for vanity or seduction. Her hips and cheeks seemed fuller. This pleased him, though he had always preferred very thin, small-boned women.

"I'm not going back to Lali," he said. "It's not a question of you or her."

She seemed startled. After a moment, she said: "You have to. You can't break up your family."

"I'm with her until the election."

"Don't make things worse."

"We don't have to keep doing what people expect," he said.

She fingered her neckline. "I'm asking you to leave. I told you: it's finished."

He heard the doubt in her voice. He should kiss her now. That's what they both wanted. Instead he told himself: Don't be weak. His father, grandfather, great-grandfather—they had held on to power, increased or at least maintained it during their lifetimes. He owed that much to his family, whether or not he stayed with Lali. Nothing changes in this country, Lali had told him. Not in the past hundred years, not in the hundred to come. Nothing except the increasing weakness of men like himself. The sons of sons, weaker and more sentimental and more spoiled, with each generation. Only the women they married kept the family strong.

He edged toward Pilar. She tensed, but didn't move away.

Take a stance. Was that what Jimbo meant? Do something, for once in your life, that's bigger than yourself. Gregorio had taken a stance. For a man of honor, betrayal was the hardest choice.

"I need to sleep, a few hours," he said. "Then, please, let me show you one thing."

Her eyes met his. He saw what he wanted.

"One afternoon, Pilar. A few hours. That's all. Then I'll leave."

"Promise me," she said.

In the rearview mirror, he watched her hurry from the house toward the car. Her loose, white blouse billowed around her. Her hair was partially undone. So many things about her—the long neck and limbs and thick, black hair—reminded him of Lali.

He leaned across the seat and opened the passenger door.

She stepped in. "Let's go," she said uneasily.

He turned the key in the ignition. The floor vibrated. He

sped out of the property and into the winding roads. After a few minutes, slowing down, he turned into an unpaved road. They didn't speak. Trees on all sides, light falling like rain from the gaps between leaves. The road narrowed, then ended. Boulders in front of them, then the forest. He switched off the engine and stepped out. He inhaled deeply, taking in the clean cool air.

"Arturo?" Pilar was standing on the other side of the car. She walked around and stood beside him. She lifted herself on her heels, her hair so near his face he could smell the strawberry scent of her shampoo.

"Tell me now where we're going?" she asked. Her hair had come completely undone, falling over her shoulders.

"There's an underground pool," he said. "In a cave. It's a place I loved as a kid."

Her eyes brightened. He remembered the river, that afternoon in the jungle.

He touched her cheek. "You'll love it there."

She took a step back, away from his hand. He didn't know what to say. He wanted to make her happy, take her to the place where he had been happy. It had been decades since he had gone to the cave. He hoped he could find it now.

He led her into the forest, improvising a path between tree trunks and bushes. Above them, branches and leaves weaved a canopy that almost obscured the sky. Everything looked different from what he remembered. He tried to let his body, his instincts, guide him.

Finally, after wandering around in silence and retracing their steps, they reached the edge of the forest. The ground dropped off sharply. "I think this is it," he said. "Can you follow me down?"

"Of course," she said doubtfully.

They descended the slope, slipping on fallen twigs and patches of loose earth, holding on to branches and rocks. He tried to help her, but she refused. Several meters down, a wide, flat rock jutted out of the slope.

"It's here!" He showed her an opening, almost hidden by vegetation, barely large enough for one person to crawl into. His heart thumped with pleasure. "Let's go inside?"

She nodded.

He entered first, on his hands and knees. A dark, narrow tunnel, about four feet high. The air was dank. Beneath his hands and on either side, rocks pressed against him. A drop of water fell on his face. How triumphant he had felt, as a boy, when he had found this place. How brave he had been to enter it.

Behind him, Pilar's ragged breathing.

The tunnel narrowed. The craggy ceiling almost touched his head. He lay on his belly and dragged himself over damp stone and earth. The light faded as he slid deeper into the cave. He began to feel anxious, the old fear of the dark returning. It won't turn completely dark, he repeated to himself, soothing himself. There'll be some light, later. Your eyes will adjust.

It wasn't the dark he feared, but not being able to see.

"Arturo? Why aren't you moving?" Her voice was small and tough, as though she, too, were fighting her fear. "I want to go back."

"We can't turn around." He dragged himself forward. "It gets better. We're almost there."

The tunnel widened. Space now, several feet over his head. On his hands and knees, he crawled forward, patting the earth in front of him until he came to the end of flat ground. He examined the rocks and compact soil over the edge. Another steep slope. He remembered this. From below, the slosh of water.

"It's down there! Can you hear it?"

She didn't answer.

He pushed himself over the edge, feet first. He slid and forced his way down the slope. At the bottom, in near-darkness, he groped the ground in front of him, trying to define contours and boundaries. His eyes began to adjust to the darkness. A few meters away, in the shadows, he saw the small pool, the flat rocks around it. The fine hairs stood on his arm. It was smaller than he remembered, but just as mysterious and beautiful.

Another drop of water fell on his face. The ceiling of the cave soared above him, about fifteen meters high. Pinpricks of light, at the very top. Impossible to know what lived up there, among the rocks and crevices. Bats, maybe. The smell was pungent here, almost fetid.

"Arturo?"

He stood, turned around. At the top of the slope, her silhouette appeared.

"Slide down," he said. "I'll help you."

She pushed herself down the slope, heels digging into the earth. When she was near enough, he grasped her legs and guided her down. Her blouse had bunched up over her waist. She stood and brushed her pants.

"How will we get back up?" she asked.

"Don't worry. I've done this so many times." He wanted her to see what he had loved here, to feel the magic of the place, not be distracted by her worries or even by him.

She scanned the walls of jagged rock, the dark pool. For a while, she didn't speak. "It's like something from a fairy tale," she whispered. "I've never seen anything like it."

He felt a rush of gratitude. He was right to have come here with her. She was simpler than Lali, kinder. Hesitantly, he told her what he had never told anyone before: that this place had seemed alive for him, when he was a boy. The cave had been his friend, his protector, taking him in and soothing him each time he came here. It was dark and full of shadows, but not pitch-black—he could see, and he hadn't been afraid. He told her he had never brought anyone else here.

"Do you still feel those things?" she asked, looking into his eyes. "Now?"

He shook his head. There was no protection now, only the memory of a child's imagination, his loneliness. Whenever his parents brought him here for a weekend, he hid here to stay as far away from them and their fights as possible. He told her he no longer felt protected, but he remembered how strong the feeling had been.

A shadow crossed her face. He didn't want to ask her what was wrong. He wanted to reassure her, to tell her he wanted only to show her this place, nothing more, and after that, he would leave, but he was afraid that would start a long discussion, and he didn't want trouble now.

He walked to the pool, crouched beside it. The water was dark, its smell musty and strong. When he was a boy, he had heard stories of hot springs forming after eruptions. Some were so potent that no one dared bathe in them; instead, people leaned over the edges and inhaled their vapors. The family cook told him she had once plumed a chicken by plunging it into a hot spring, then cooked it by keeping it under the water for a few minutes. Another time she had dipped a crab into a spring just to see what would happen. The part underwater immediately turned black while the top half stayed red.

"There are lots of mineral springs around here," he said, without turning to her. "My mother would make me take a bath in one every time we were up here." Marilou had never found out about this one. He sat beside the pool. A thin layer of mist spread over the surface.

Pilar knelt, not far from him, and sat on the back of her heels, torso arched, emphasizing her breasts and buttocks. He looked sideways at her. She had no idea how beautiful she was.

He held his hands a few inches above the water. Slowly, he brought them closer.

"Is it safe to touch it?" she asked.

His fingertips brushed the water. Warm, slightly fizzy. He lowered his hands into the pool. The old sensations flooded through him, the pleasure of swimming in this place, the plunging and warmth.

"The water's good," he said.

"Then I'm going in." She sounded excited.

She unzipped her pants and briskly tugged them down over her legs. Her white blouse barely covered her hips.

She sat on the edge of the pool, slid into the water. She floated on her back, the blouse ballooning on the surface. Shyly, she asked, "Are you coming in?"

He stripped to his underwear and lowered himself into the water, holding onto the edge of the pool. His feet touched bottom, which was smooth and hard. For a moment he couldn't see her among the vapors and shadows.

Her voice seemed to float across the darkness. "I'm here. You can stand. It's not deep."

"I *am* standing."

She swam toward him, stood up. "It's like a dream, this place."

Her black hair, wet and long. He imagined his arms encircling her waist, the softness of her.

He wouldn't touch her. One clean, good thing, he reminded himself. Not more confusion, after last night. And he had promised her.

She lowered herself until her chin touched the water. He wanted to give her something, even a promise of something. He didn't want to think about Lali or Ricky or what waited for him outside this cave. He wished he could find his old friend again, that dark amorphous being who didn't just live in the cave but *was* the cave, all of it, the water and the air and the smells. When had he lost it? When had he stopped believing in it? Why had it abandoned him?

Pilar swam into the shadows. He had a flash of Lali's pale

face and neck and bare shoulders. He remembered the first time he had seen Lali, swaying across the room on stiletto heels, and the exhilaration he had felt and tried to hide. You don't deserve me, Lali had told him once, laughing, standing on the bed and wrapping a braided black-satin whip like a bracelet around her wrist. A nun had made the whip, in a convent, she told him. Someone had figured out that whips and handcuffs were more profitable than strawberry jam, and the nuns were told that those strange-looking accessories were just belts and bracelets.

Pilar had disappeared into the shadows.

You have everything, he told himself. People admire you. You have houses, cars, a political career, good businesses.

He grasped the edge of the pool.

"What's wrong?" Pilar asked.

The sudden vertiginous drop, which he often felt just before sleep.

The car rushed past grassy slopes. No houses, no villages. In the distance, a light fell from a clearing in the grey sky. He squinted at the darkening landscape. Somewhere up ahead, a dirt road led to his great-grandparents' home. Trees growing inside, vines clawing on the walls, rats nesting under floorboards. His father had taken him there when he was a boy, describing the elegance of a life Arturo hadn't known.

The first fat raindrops struck the glass. Without turning her head, Pilar said, "What would you do if I became pregnant?"

He switched on the wipers, rolled up the windows.

"Did you hear me?" she asked. "If I—"

He cut her off. "Are you?"

"I'm asking what you would do."

His throat tightened. "You can't keep it."

A brittle laugh. "Well, I'm not. Thanks a lot, anyway."

"Have you seen Dr. Magsino?"

"How do you know about him?"

"Everyone knows about him." Not this, he thought. I didn't come here for this. He said gently, "I thought you were on the pill." He became aware of the pounding of his heart. He drove without speaking for several minutes, rehearsing lines in his head. "Pilar," he said at last, trying to sound reasonable. "I already have a baby. I don't want another one."

"I saw you when Lali found out she was pregnant. I'd never seen you so happy."

"Lali's my *wife*."

For a long while she was silent. Then, in a strained voice, as though battling the question even as she asked it: "You never loved me, did you?"

"For God's sake." He squeezed the wheel. They were all the same. Most women, after a while. The same demands, the same accusations. He didn't want her to be pregnant. He wouldn't allow it. He remembered Ricky's leering smile, the insinuations, the threats. He couldn't deal with this, too. Why was she doing this to him? They had just come from a place he loved. She had loved it, too.

He pulled away from his thoughts, reproached himself for them. He touched the back of her hand, tried to summon the compassion he knew was in him. "You need to have a blood test," he said, as kindly as he could.

She removed her hand. "I'm *not* pregnant. I was asking you a question. You can't just come and see me whenever you feel like it—"

In his mind he told her: We didn't make love, Pilar. We didn't even kiss. I didn't touch you. I'm doing everything you wanted.

Waves of rain rolled toward the car. The headlights barely penetrated the darkness. He said: "My father's family used to live near here. Do you want to see the house?"

"I'm *talking* to you."

In a quiet tone, almost lost in the crash of water against glass and metal, he told her he had never been attracted to pregnant women. He told her he didn't understand why some of his girlfriends had let themselves get pregnant. In a part of himself, he felt each one had betrayed him. They had wanted something from him—marriage, his name, his money, his love. I can decide about having a baby, too, he said. It's not just you women who decide. He explained to her that he had helped three women get abortions, stayed beside them, paid for everything, took them home, comforted them. He told her he had never seen any of them again.

"That's horrible," she said.

"It isn't."

She didn't reply. He couldn't bring himself to look at her.

It wasn't true, what he had told her. He had kept track of those women, watched them from afar with their husbands and children and the darkness in their eyes. He hadn't wanted the babies, but it wounded him to hurt women he had loved. He wanted to stay close to them, but he couldn't take them out—they were married now, and married women couldn't dine alone with ex-lovers and other women's husbands. But those lost babies remained like invisible chains between them.

He peered out the windshield. Rain for miles ahead, but to the left of the road, near the horizon, a clearing in the clouds. A sign. He forced himself to look away from the light and focus on the road ahead. There were no signs. A man saw light on top of the mountain, and called it God. Every single thing had to be infused with meaning, because people were scared that nothing meant anything in itself. Sometimes light breaking through clouds was just light. No signs. No God. No significance.

Save yourself.

"I don't believe in abortions," she was saying. There was an edge in her voice, a defiance. He shouldn't have come. He was upsetting her too much. He was upsetting himself.

"I believe there's life from the very beginning," she said.

At a fork in the road, he swerved to the right. "That's just our Catholic upbringing." If he looked at her, he might stop the car, take her in his arms and tell her she could do anything she wanted, if that would make her happy again.

"I truly believe it," she told him.

"We can believe whatever we want." He tried to respond only to her words and not to the soft, distressed woman beside him. He wondered whether he could find the house again. His great-grandfather, people said, had been a frail man, barely five feet two, but cunning and brave. We're not far, he told himself. He imagined the abandoned mansion, half-eaten by insects and vegetation.

She said, "I don't understand how any woman could kill her own baby."

He heard the insistence in her voice, the fragility. He wouldn't answer. She would only become more upset.

"I think it's horrible what happens in the States, for example," she said, "when women say they have a right to choose what happens to their bodies."

He gripped the wheel. "Men have a right to choose, too."

"Why choose only when the baby's in your stomach? Why not kill a newborn if it becomes a problem? If it wasn't the newborn you *planned*?"

"Are you sure you're not pregnant?"

"Are you listening to me?" she asked.

"I can repeat everything you've said."

"I'm asking if you *understand* me."

"I understand," he said automatically. Stop talking, he wanted to tell her. That's not why I came here. You don't know about last night. You don't know about Ricky, or your father, or all I'm doing for you. I'm protecting you. I'm protecting you, Lali, everyone. Why can't you try, even a little, to protect me, too?

He turned right again and began to climb a narrow dirt road. The rain eased into a light strumming. He could no longer see the shaft of sunlight.

She didn't speak. Maybe she had expected him to make love to her in the pool. Maybe she felt rejected. How could he know what she wanted, when she kept telling him different things?

He glanced at her. "My great-grandfather lived to one hundred and three. Three wives, twenty-one children—and those are just the legitimate ones."

"Stop it."

He wanted to tell her other things about his great-grandfather, the half-Chinese peasant who had built the family's fortune in one generation, but she seemed on the verge of tears. He considered driving to the main road and taking her back to her cousin's home, but he wanted her to see the house, or what remained of it, if he could find it. That house, even in ruins, had been his protector, too.

At ninety-six, his great-grandfather had brandished a machete and led his sons, daughters, and grandchildren into battle against angry tenants attacking the family home. You have his blood, Arturo told himself. Ricky can't hurt you.

"I don't understand you," she said. "Sometimes I think I do. Then there's this, I don't know—this coldness in you. This hardness. What happened in the province, the fires—"

"I had nothing to do with that."

"It's in your eyes. You're not the same—"

"I'm exactly the same."

"You don't see yourself, Arturo." She sounded close to tears. She paused. "I don't want to visit your great-grandfather's home. Please take me back."

He pulled over, stopped the car, turned to her. "Ricky's

blackmailing me," he said. "I saw him last night. That's why I'm here."

She stared at the windshield.

"He wants Lali involved. He wants her to speak at his rally. You know how she feels about Ricky. She'll never do it." He warned himself: Don't say anything about Gregorio. She needs to believe in something good.

"This doesn't concern me," she said. But she looked stricken.

"He wants money. A lot. He's calling it a donation. It won't end there."

She clasped her hands over her lap, like the girl in the lime-green dress. He should have taken that girl home, instead of coming here. He needed a break after Ricky, not this.

"But that's what you expected from him, isn't it?" she asked.

"He wants to hurt me. Humiliate all of us."

The province, Pilar. The fires. *Nothing,* he told himself. The scars on that teenager's wrist. *Nothing.*

It was a mistake to have gone looking for Pilar. It was a mistake to think he could find refuge here, with her, or anywhere, with anyone. Everyone you think you love, Lali told him, is a mask or a mirror.

He started the car. They drove through wet, empty roads. The rain had stopped. He told her he had come here because he needed to find something good, simple, and she was the kindest person he knew.

"I'm not kind," she said. Without looking at him, her voice both soft and harsh, she told him the violence was beginning to enter into her, too. "It scared me. That's why I left. It wasn't about saving your marriage."

"I don't believe that." In the distance, a small bridge appeared, its metal structure pale in the moonlight, spanning a dry riverbed.

"What we felt," she said, "in the beginning—"

"Don't say it." He didn't want to talk about love. She was unfair.

From the corner of his eye, he saw her head turn toward him.

"One good thing," he said. "That's all I want today."

Switching gears, he eased the car up a mound and onto the bridge. He stopped, walked out of the car. The wind carried grains of sand. She remained inside the car, staring at the windshield.

He walked halfway across the bridge, held the railing with both hands. Warmth in his fingers. There was some kind of energy here. Perhaps this was what people called a place of power. He had never felt one before, except perhaps as a child in that cave. Lali said the country was full of these places—waterfalls, bends in the river, churches, shrines built on busy sidewalks. In places like this, Lali said, people experienced accidents, visions, miracles.

He remembered the rumors: the president covered in scales, babies kidnapped and sacrificed from bridges. He began to make out shapes on the riverbed—branches, discarded tires, gallon-sized plastic jugs half-buried in the sand.

Of course he had choices—he could go back and find the girl with the lime-green dress and scars on her wrist, he could tell Pilar what he knew about her father, he could refuse Ricky's demands.

He had no choice. He was entering the narrowing tunnel of the rest of his life, and he couldn't turn back.

The car door slammed. She was walking across the bridge, toward him. Her blouse was still wet. Her hair, damp and slightly wavy, framed her face. He tensed as she approached. On the floor of the bridge, crevices and tiny cracks shimmered with rainwater.

He had loved Lali. Touched her, caressed her, made love to

her so many times and for so many years that she seemed part of his own flesh, at times more real than himself. A single word or smell conjured her. He glimpsed her in strange places, sensed her in empty rooms. He felt her on this bridge. Lali said you never lose those you lose violently. Their ghosts linger. He had never believed in those things.

Pilar touched his arm. "I'm sorry we fought."

He wasn't being fair to her. He draped an arm around her shoulders. This, too, could be the rest of his life—standing on a bridge over a dead river, beside a woman who would never understand him, who may or may not be carrying his baby, who would never know the truth about her father. Perhaps Pilar was right. Something in him had hardened, or closed.

How many lives were decided by indecision?

They returned to the car. He fastened the seatbelt, glanced at her. "Don't worry," he said. "We'll deal with whatever happens."

He reached for her hand, pressed it against his thigh, covered it with his fingers. They all had the same skin, impossibly soft—Pilar, Lali, Aimee.

She wasn't pregnant. Suddenly, he was certain.

"I don't want a baby," he told her, "but it's your choice. I'll support you in whatever you choose."

He faced the road, switched on the engine. Her fingers rested on his thigh. Making someone happy could count as love. It was fair to make her feel she had a choice.

The fires, the violence, Benedicto's death. He hadn't chosen all that. He hadn't done any of that. He had only, at worst, let things happen.

Eyes fixed on the road, he brought Pilar's hand to his lips. He knew what had to be done. Things get broken, Lali said. Not everything can be put back together again.

Chapter Twelve

Home

The simplest acts, also the most
extravagant: what we take
into our bodies, the small
gestures of ordinary life—
that knocking at the door of a deeper
hunger; how, after we have entered the foyer,
we want to know what it is that shines
so warmly from behind
the other closed doors.

—Luisa A. Igloria, "Chinatown, Moon Festival"

LALI

1

On the day Lali hoped to return to Arturo, she washed herself in David's bathroom. There was no sink and no shower stall, only a faucet protruding from the cement wall, and a long-handled bucket beneath it. She poured cold water into the bucket and emptied it over her head, scrubbed shampoo into her hair and soap onto her skin, trying to rub out the jasmine-scented oils David had massaged onto her back and arms the night before. When she was done, she dried herself and mopped the floor with her towel.

David and the boy waited outside, in the almost empty room. Together she and David washed the child, shampooed his black hair, brushed it until it gleamed. With a damp cloth she wiped his eyes and imagined what Arturo would see. Faces change, she would tell him. She would say she knew a white man who was born and grew up in China, among the Chinese, and ended up looking part Chinese. Facial expressions and gestures transformed traits. Culture was stronger than blood. In thirty years, people would think he was their son.

Arturo would never believe her.

On the street in front of his townhouse, next to a scraggly tree, David waved down a taxi. His red hair had started to grow again over his sunburned neck. He loaded her backpack into the trunk, crouched on the muddy pavement, and hugged the boy. David closed his eyes and whispered into the boy's ear. For a moment she saw David's Filipino side, the tenderness in his expression, his eyes. But when he stood, he became American again, tall and lanky and conspicuous in that run-down neighborhood.

His skin was softer than she had expected. An Asian soft-ness, she had told him the night before, as they lay in each other's arms, on his mattress on the floor. They had talked about everything except the journey south, the clearing in the jungle, the blindfolded man on his knees. In the half-darkness, whispering so as not to awaken the boy, David had asked: "Are you sure you want to do this? He won't try to punish you?" She said, "I'll be fine." She was breathing through her mouth. David stroked her hair. His arm circled her bare waist. "You can come back here whenever you want," he told her. "I'll give you the keys." Her lips touched the hollow in the center of his chest, between his nipples. They held each other with such ten-derness and regret it seemed indecent to even try to make love.

Now, in the sunlight, David opened the back door of the taxi and helped her inside. He lifted the boy and sat him on her lap. The child lowered his head, crossed his ankles. Lali clutched the handbag beside her and looked up at David. His jeans hung loosely around his hips, and his features were gaunt. They had both lost a great deal of weight these past weeks. Neither of them had noticed it, until they returned to Manila.

"You're sure?" David asked.

She nodded. She didn't want to talk about her sadness at leaving him, nor about her fear of what might happen if Arturo refused to take her back.

David leaned into the taxi, cupped the boy's cheek, touched her shoulder. He seemed lost and alone again, as he had been when she first met him at the mall. He shut the door. As the taxi drove away, she turned her head to look at him, a stick fig-ure shrinking on the sidewalk. Tears gathered behind her eyes.

The boy's heels tapped against her calves. She wrapped her

arms around his plump, warm body, trying to comfort him. Softly, in a language he understood, she told him why they were leaving and where she was taking him, and why there was no reason to be afraid.

When she saw her home, she wanted to run away. Instead she held the boy's hand and guided him up the bougainvillea-lined driveway. At the top of the driveway, three-foot-high burial jars flanked mahogany doors. The security guard was asleep on his chair, a pistol strapped to his waist. A logbook lay open on his lap.

"Ma'am?" The guard staggered to his feet, eyes wide. He was a head taller than her, and twice as wide. He apologized for napping. She wasn't supposed to know he had two jobs, night and day. He unlocked the front door, his smile bright and anxious. "Don't worry," she said.

Sunlight streamed into the living room, refracted on glass cases filled with antique vases and figurines. Across the room, sliding doors opened to the garden, the kalachuchi tree in blossom, the blue-tiled swimming pool. She straddled the boy on her hip, grasped his waist. His thighs tightened against her. She tried to imagine what another strange house must feel like for him.

Balancing him on her hip, arm hooked around his waist to secure and reassure him, she crossed the living room. Nothing seemed familiar. Even her footsteps sounded harsh on the stone floor.

Voices drifted from another room, punctuated by the faint clicks of glasses and silverware. Her pulse raced. She strained to listen. It wasn't Arturo. She walked through a side door and into a hallway lined with his model ships. The boy straightened, suddenly curious. He extended an arm, trying to touch them. Galleons, she whispered. Magellan's ships. He had no idea what they were. She pressed the child's fingers against the sails, ran the pad of his index finger across the stitches and the minuscule nail heads hammered into varnished planks. She remembered Arturo's fingers holding these nails and threads and sails.

She had thought it was easy to give Arturo what he wanted. She had spent years learning to make love to him, responding to his reactions, soliciting confidences and fantasies, and mirroring them back to him, offering none of her own. His wanting, always. She had shown him only the surfaces of her own. Tell me what you want, she had told him. Ask me what you've never asked any other woman. She had always been willing. She wanted him to go further with her than he ever had before. She had never imagined he would one day stop wanting her.

At the far end of the garden, Arturo sat at a wrought-iron table. A maid held a tray with mangoes and finger-sized bananas. From inside the house, hidden in the shadows next to the arched doorway, Lali watched him. She felt a rush of longing, darkened by shame. She held the boy like a shield against her.

Late-afternoon sunlight encased Arturo. He poured wine into his glass.

He raised his head but didn't see her. On the walls of the swimming pool, small patches of forest-green algae stained the blue tiles.

The boy fidgeted in her arms. She stroked his cheek. In her mind she said: Please, dear God. She tried to walk into the garden, but her knees were shaking. She couldn't let Arturo see her like this. No one wanted someone weak, or humbled, or desperate to be with them.

She waited until the trembling stopped, then walked deeper into the house.

Her mother lay in bed, head and torso propped up by pillows, watching a variety show on television. When she saw Lali and the boy, she switched off the television and told the nurse to leave the room.

"Bring him closer," she told Lali.

With a start, Lali realized her mother had been expecting the boy. Information traveled along secret, efficient channels, constructed during the long years of dictatorship. If her mother knew about the boy, then Arturo did as well.

Lali sat on the bed, the boy on her lap.

"Poor thing," her mother said. "Does he speak English?"

Lali shook her head.

Her mother touched his chin and lifted his face. He shut his eyes and pulled away, an inch or two out of her reach. In English, her mother said, "You can't keep him."

"He has nowhere to go. I need your help, Ma."

"You can't impose him on Arturo. What's going on with you? You can't leave your husband and baby and just come back with someone else's child!"

"Arturo's the one who left *me*, Ma."

"Nonsense. Men do things like that. It doesn't mean they're gone. You have to act like it never happened." Her mother tucked a blanket around the boy's legs. "Look, he's cold. Poor baby. Have you spoken to Arturo? Does he know you're here?"

Lali shook her head.

"You have to talk to him. Leave the boy with me. Arturo's still your husband. Sit down with him. Charm him. You have to play the woman. You know how to do that." Her mother sounded afraid. She would never be on Lali's side. No one in this house would choose Lali over Arturo.

"You can't destroy our lives for some man you found in the streets," her mother said.

On the terrace, the wrought-iron table was empty. Lali wanted to talk to Arturo outdoors, where people could hear them, restrain him if he became angry. She scanned the garden.

He was kneeling by the edge of the swimming pool, bending over the water and skimming the surface with a large leaf. She knew what he was doing—scooping out butterflies, ants, bees. He often checked the pool before leaving the garden, rescued whatever creatures he found floating there.

She walked toward him. He didn't turn to her. The pale skin on his neck, his arms. Arturo leaned forward and extended his hand toward a yellow butterfly in the water, just out of his reach. He ran the leaf over the surface, creating waves to move the butterfly closer. It floated further away.

She stood next to him.

"Are you planning to stay?" he asked abruptly, still on his knees.

"I'd like to."

He skimmed the surface of the water, concentrating on the leaf and insects. In a low, hostile voice, he talked about the rally and the schedule leading up to it. She couldn't absorb most of what he was saying. In her mind she told him: You were with Pilar. Don't punish me for what you did yourself.

"Ricky expects us to say certain things," he said. "He wants you to give a speech."

"Ricky?"

For the first time that afternoon, he faced her. "We have to say whatever Ricky wants," he said. "We don't have a choice."

Listen to him, she told herself. Placate him. You didn't come here to fight. If he wants to talk about the campaign, then talk about the campaign. Carefully, she said: "I want you to win, just as much as you do. But there are limits."

He lifted the leaf from the pool, tapped it gently against the cement. A large red ant, encased in water, slid out of it. The ant didn't move.

She tensed, waiting for him to accuse her or attack her. But when he spoke again, his voice was kind. "I don't want to hurt you, Lali."

She wanted to touch his mouth.

"So don't force me to put pressure on you," he said. "That's Ricky's deal, in exchange for the president's support."

She thought: You were the one who pulled away, Arturo. I couldn't understand why. After the eclipse, all that had happened, your distance. You can't make it all my fault.

He would make it her fault. Her absence, her trip to the south, the visible betrayal. And she was a woman. That made it unforgiveable.

He blew at the red ant, trying to dry it and free it from the water.

"I'll go to the rally," she said at last. "I'll do whatever you want."

"Good." He paused. "I'm moving to my mother's house, for now. You can stay here. I'm taking Aimee with me." He set the leaf on the cement. The pool's surface was clear now. Even the yellow butterfly was gone. "She can visit you here whenever you want."

He was standing now, facing her. The sadness between them was almost palpable. She wanted to take him in her arms, tell him they could throw away everything that had happened, forget everything, go back to what they had been. Their love—the way they had loved, their happiness, that madness—was worth so much more than all this. They both knew they would never find someone else like each other. They would never love someone else the way they had loved each other.

"You can't keep that boy here," Arturo said.

It was dangerous to talk about the boy now. She searched Arturo's face, trying to find a crack, something that would allow her to reach him. She couldn't afford a mistake. "Vigilantes killed his father," she said. It would be an error to talk about the beheading. "His mother was afraid they'd come for him, too."

"You can't have the son of a murdered man here. He'll grow up and want revenge."

"He doesn't have anyone else."

His eyes held hers. She saw the crack. "He'll hate every-thing we stand for," he said. "He's a time bomb."

"If you take Aimee with you—"

"I can't think about this now," he said.

"Then let me have him. At least until I find a better solu-tion."

They didn't speak. Dogs were barking in the garage and in the neighbors' houses. Somewhere, a radio was playing.

"You're making it impossible for us," he said.

She tended to the boy, played with him on her mother's bed, let him sleep in her room. For the first time in more than a year, her mother allowed her to draw the curtains and let light into the room. The boy smiled more often these days, but timidly, turning his head away. Lali's heart lifted whenever she saw him. Almost every day, Arturo's driver brought Aimee and her nanny to visit. Lali held her daughter, fed her. She felt closest to Aimee when the boy was with her.

One week passed. Another began. Pilar didn't call. Marilou had left for a retreat in the mountains. Arturo stayed away. Lali told herself: Things will settle, he needs his space. I won't worry yet.

On the ninth day, he called her. "You have to come here," he said, with the clipped, brusque tone he used to hide distress. "Filomena's sick. She's asking for you."

"What's wrong?"

"She won't tell us. She says she'll talk only to you."

A houseboy opened the high gates of Marilou's house. Lali parked the car and entered into the house with apprehension, worried about Filomena and reluctant to see Arturo without preparation.

Three girls were sweeping the downstairs living room.

"Where's Señorito Arturo?" Lali asked.

They seemed startled to see her. A bad sign. "In the dining room, ma'am," one girl said.

She hurried up the stairs and down the long corridor to the main kitchen. Arturo was waiting for her. "Thanks for coming so quickly," he said, without warmth.

"Where's Filomena?"

"Downstairs, in her room."

"What happened?"

"She won't tell anyone. She was bleeding. I called the doctor." His gaze shifted away from her, toward the balcony at the far end of the room.

Lali followed his gaze. It was Pilar walking toward them. That was why the maids had been nervous to see her. Lali became intensely aware of Arturo beside her, the tension in him as he watched Pilar. High-heeled sandals, a short skirt, bare legs, her blouse loose but with a low neckline. Pilar's hair, usually tied into a ponytail, fell over her shoulders. There was something inexpert in her appearance, a self-consciousness and lack of ease in those clothes that seemed both childlike and erotic.

Lali fixed a smile. She tried to reassure herself. Arturo must be tired of Pilar by now. Her grateful, timid sister, shutting the windows, the lights, her eyes.

Awkwardly, the sisters faced each other. "Take me to Filomena," Lali told Arturo.

Pilar glanced nervously at him.

"You can stay here," Lali told Pilar. "I'll go with Arturo." With her thumb and index finger, Lali tried to circle her own wrist. It had been Arturo's way of comforting her, years ago, whenever she was upset. Her fingers, unlike his, didn't close the circle.

He led her past the dirty kitchen to the servants' quarters. They walked along low-ceilinged corridors. She glanced into tiny rooms with bunk beds and no windows. On the walls hung posters of the Sacred Heart and taped photos of the children left behind in the provinces.

In her room, Filomena lay on a single bed, eyes shut, a towel under her hips. Crumpled on the floor, near the bed, was a bloody sheet. Three young women knelt beside her, fanning her face and neck. Taped to the wall along the bed were the smiling faces of local movie actresses, cut out from magazines.

A woman, barely five feet tall and skinny, tiptoed into the room. Her black hair was cut in a blunt line under her ears. Her eyes were round, her lips frosted pink. It was the woman doctor from the public clinic down the street, where the maids and houseboys went for shots and minor treatments. "She won't tell me anything," the doctor said. "She won't let me examine her."

Filomena turned her head toward Lali. "Señorita," she told her.

"Do you want us to leave?" Arturo asked.

Lali nodded, not trusting herself to look at him. When everyone had left the room, she crouched by the bed and held Filomena's hand. "*Manang*, what's happening to you? You have to answer now."

"Promise me they won't fire me, ma'am. Señorito Arturo listens to you."

"*Manang*, you have to let the *doktora* examine you, if you want me to help you."

"Promise me, Señorita. I have nowhere to go. You're the only one he listens to."

"I promise." Filomena had lived with Arturo's family for more than 20 years. She had no other home. Lali touched the cook's flushed cheek, pressed her palm against her forehead. No fever. "Tell me what happened."

"Nothing," Filomena said, and shut her eyes.

While the doctor examined Filomena, Arturo and Lali waited outside the servants' quarters, on the pavement near the river. The smell of frying fish drifted from the kitchen. He looked out toward the Pasig. His arms were crossed tightly in front of him, his shoulders hunched. She didn't know how to comfort him. Filomena was like his mother.

At last the doctor came to them, swaying on her high heels. "She's okay," she said. "It's normal."

Arturo uncrossed his arms. "Bleeding like that is normal?"

"She just had a baby."

Arturo stared at her. "She wasn't pregnant."

The doctor rubbed her earlobe. "I guess she was, or she wouldn't have given birth."

In the silence that followed, images came to Lali—the garlands of garlic hanging from windows, Filomena's shapeless dresses, the thickening belly. She had read about things like this, in newspapers and magazines. Women who didn't know they were pregnant, until they gave birth.

"So where's the baby?" Arturo asked. His eyes seemed to recede into himself, as though he wanted to stop seeing, to make all this disappear.

"She won't tell us."

Footsteps on the pavement. Pilar was walking toward them. "They told me—" Her voice caught. "It's not possible."

Arturo looked back at the river.

"Did she tell you anything?" Lali asked the doctor.

Pilar said, "We would have heard it cry!"

"Did she say where the baby is?" Lali insisted.

"She said it's a miscarriage," the doctor replied. "She said it happened in the toilet. She said she had no period for four months. But all the signs are normal."

"Normal for what?" Lali asked.

"A nine-month pregnancy."

"We have to find the baby," Lali said, beginning to panic.

Pilar said, "She wouldn't have—"

"Go inside," Lali told Pilar and the doctor. "Tell everyone to look. Everyone! Tell the maids to look inside—every room, every corner, every closet. The houseboys, outside. Let them check *everything*. I'll talk to Filomena."

A red blotch appeared on Arturo's neck. Pilar didn't move. "She told me she never had a boyfriend," the doctor said.

Filomena was still on the cot, hands flat on her stomach. Arturo and Lali stood over her.

"Where is it?" Lali asked. "Please answer me."

Filomena's chest rose and fell. She didn't look at them.

"You tell us the truth, *manang*," Lali said, "or you're leaving this house."

Filomena's eyes widened.

Lali knelt by the bed, whispered into her ear: "Tell me where it is. Otherwise, you leave tomorrow."

Filomena turned to the wall, toward the photos of movie stars taped to the wall. When Filomena's mother had been pregnant with her, Lali remembered now, she had tacked up photos of Hollywood stars, hoping their beauty would enter her eyes and transform the fetus inside her. Filomena, too, had wanted a pretty baby. She had known she was pregnant. She had had dreams for her baby. What had she done with it?

A maid popped her head into the room. "Ma'am! Sir!"

They hurried out of the room. Another maid was standing at the end of the corridor, surrounded by many others. Pilar was there, too, half-hidden by the crowd.

The maids stepped aside as Lali and Arturo approached, making way for them. Wrapped in a pale blue sheet, the baby lay in a teenager's arms. Lali glimpsed a tiny face. "We have to go to the hospital," she told Arturo.

"I'm not sure—"

"We have to go!" Lali reached for the baby.

It was almost weightless in her arms, and still. Lali held the baby tentatively, not wanting to hurt it, afraid to look at it.

"How could she do this?" Pilar asked, raising her voice.

"How could she? She could have given it to me. I would have *kept* it."

No one answered her.

Arturo shot Pilar a look of exasperation and distaste. Lali noted the expression, stored it away.

He told Lali, "I'll get the car."

A slight pressure, on Lali's forearm. She looked at the baby. The tiny lips parted. It gave a soft cry.

Arturo drove the car himself, accelerating at yellow lights, taking the side streets and cutting through gated communities to avoid traffic. In the back seat, Lali held the silent baby. Filomena leaned heavily against her. The car jolted forward. With one hand Lali braced herself against the seat in front of her.

She began to pray, a silent bargaining.

The car rushed not to the public hospital where the maids usually went, but toward Manila's most expensive private hospital. In the emergency room, Arturo ordered the nurse to page a doctor he knew, one of his old schoolmates.

Nurses took the baby, and orderlies wheeled Filomena away. Lali and Arturo climbed the stairs to the cement terrace, which overlooked the smoggy skyline of Manila. Smokers lined the wall, seeking the few inches of shade that protected them from the sun. Arturo smoked one cigarette, then another. He squinted into the sunlight. She wanted to say something, to soothe him, but she couldn't find the words.

When they returned to the emergency room, the doctor told them: "She'll be okay. The baby, too." Arturo tilted his head back, facing the ceiling. Lali was certain he was praying.

They returned to Marilou's house. Pilar was gone. In his mother's garden, in the late afternoon, Lali and Arturo stood by the wrought-iron grille that bordered the gray river. He seemed too shaken to be left alone.

"I can't even begin to imagine why Filomena did that," he said.

Lali thought of Aimee in her arms in the hospital and the window that wouldn't open, the accident that separated her from Filomena.

"Don't judge her too harshly," she said.

"You know what Filomena used to tell me, when I was a child? God put pain and evil in the world to teach us how to love other people."

He removed a pack of cigarettes from his pocket, fished one out. He hunched over and lit it, cupping his hands around the flame. "She's a good person," he said. "The kindest I've known."

"She must have been desperate," Lali said.

She didn't tell him: The young men with machetes and amulets were good people, too. Like the man they had beheaded, and the children that clutched their mother's skirt, and the widow who had shoved her young son into David's arms.

"You know someone for years," he said, "then suddenly everything you know about them evaporates. Suddenly you *see* them." He drew on the cigarette. "I've never seen Filomena like that. I've never seen Pilar like that. Did you see Pilar's face? It didn't even look like her face."

Lali remained silent, considering this. How could you do this, Pilar had kept saying. How could you?

It wasn't fair for Arturo to judge Pilar, either.

"I've spent my whole life trying to accept things," he said.

"Let it go."

"Blinders," he said. "Selective vision. Isn't that how everyone survives in this country? That's what I liked about you—you never pretended."

"Of course I do. We all pretend."

"I *trusted* Filomena."

He had always needed Lali when things were difficult. She had been calm with the baby. She had stayed beside him, without showing emotion. That coldness in her, that efficiency in times of crisis, had always been attractive to him. Inside, he was afraid.

"Now, Filomena has to leave," he said. "How can we keep her after this?"

"Give her a chance."

She sat on the narrow ledge, at the base of the wrought-iron grille. He sat beside her. Their thighs almost touched. The nearness of him unsettled her.

"She tried to kill her own baby," he said. "She can't stay."

A mosquito buzzed around Lali's ear.

"You know what I think?" she asked. "I think Filomena didn't even look at the baby. I think she wrapped it up and put it wherever she put it—I don't want to know—and she made herself forget it." His fingers rested on his thigh. She imagined them touching Pilar. Stop it, she told herself. Don't be ridiculous. Whatever you think you know, you're wrong. You can't begin to know what they were like together. She said: "I think Filomena just wanted to forget. So it doesn't matter if you let her stay. It would have been different if she had been angry, or full of hate. But she just wanted to make everything disappear." She thought of the hospital room again, and Aimee in her arms.

He moved his thigh away, crossed one leg over the other, away from her. "I saw her almost every week," he said. "For nine months. I didn't even notice she was pregnant."

"No one did," she said gently. "Don't blame yourself."

There were more serious things, far worse than this, and he had erased them, as Filomena had erased her baby. The village on fire, Benedicto's murder. We can't face the darkest things about ourselves, she thought. We grieve the small things, we feel guilty for the lesser wrongs.

Perhaps this was love, too—to see the worst parts of him and embrace them, to help him hide them from himself.

It might be possible, she thought. Marriages could survive infidelities, sadness, the loss of passion. She could give him a part of herself, just enough to make him happy, while the other self—the hungry, dangerous, prowling self—stayed apart.

"I want to meet him," Arturo said quietly. "That man you were seeing."

She took the cigarette, inhaled, blew out the smoke. "You told me the marriage was over." Her voice was calm, though her pulse raced. "It was your decision. Don't do this to me."

"Take me to him."

After a moment, she said: "You can keep everything, you know, if you want to. Aimee, Pilar, the house, everything."

"And what would you want in return?"

"I don't need your money."

"You'll need someone's."

"Arturo, I don't want to spend the rest of my life fighting you."

How could they have loved each other so much and come to this?

"Take me to him."

She considered the risk. He needed to see what he feared most. She needed to put his fears to rest. In David's home, they might have a chance.

"Take me," he said.

No car in front of David's townhouse, no lights inside.

With the keys David had given her, she unlocked the front door and stepped inside. The white room, the mattress. Nothing else. Plastic venetian blinds fell crookedly over the front window.

The air smelled of David. He had been there recently, perhaps even that afternoon.

Arturo strode past her to the small, windowless room, as though he needed to escape the main room and the sight of the mattress on the floor. She followed him. No more photographs on the walls. Half-attached pieces of tape remained, where the photos had been pulled out. In patches across the wall, paint was peeling, or stained by the outlines of missing photographs.

Arturo didn't speak. She wanted to tell him: David and I never made love. It was the truth. Arturo would never believe her. In the deepest sense, he was right. David and she had crossed other boundaries.

He took a step toward her. She was afraid he would hit her. But when she looked at his face, he seemed lost, heartbroken. He walked out of the room and toward the front door.

"I'll drive you," she said.

"No. I'll find a taxi."

He shut the front door behind him. From a gap in the blinds, she watched him hurry down the darkened street.

She sat on the mattress, waiting for enough time to pass before driving home. She didn't want to risk seeing him on the street, to make him feel she was following him. She lay down and shut her eyes.

A rumbling awakened her. A car's engine, just outside the house, then men's voices, arguing. She couldn't make out the words. She tiptoed to the front window and peered through the gap in the blinds. In front of the house, young men were scrambling into a jeep.

Headlights turned low, the jeep started to pull away. At the back of the vehicle, one shadowed head rose high above the others. She recognized the awkwardness in the posture, the shape of the head. David. He must have recognized her car, known she was inside, found an excuse not to enter the house and to prevent the others from entering it.

She realized she had no idea what David did, what the rest of his life might be. She thought of the young man who had met them at the pier, the strangers who opened their houses to him, the vigilantes who offered them dinner and took them to the execution—so many people knew him. Even the rebels at the checkpoint had waved him through.

The jeep was shrinking into the darkness. Her heart went out to him, as it had to Arturo. She wished she could tell him to be careful. He had tried to be good to her. He had shown her a life she hadn't realized was possible, a life with almost nothing to prop it up. Just intensity, and that seductive, futile righteousness.

She waited a long time, lying on the mattress in the unlit room, until she was certain they wouldn't come back. She drifted into a half sleep, awoke with a start, sickened, sensing that Arturo was with Pilar at that moment, that he hadn't returned to Marilou's house. She felt their presence on the mattress, as though they were beside her.

Stop it, she told herself. Don't be a coward. You have to face this. Arturo had faced coming here, to David's house. They had to go all the way to the end, to what they feared most. She curled up on David's mattress. Occasionally, headlights from a passing car sent lights and shadows across the walls. Everything will be all right, she told herself. Arturo will talk to you again. He'll love you again. He'll tire of Pilar. From now on, she would show him that she was on his side. She would do whatever he wanted. She would speak at the rally, say what Ricky told her to say. She would do whatever was necessary to come home.

CHAPTER THIRTEEN

THE BLACKOUT

Manila is full of the black ruins of my life.
The beggars beg for mercy and the children die
in war or peace. It has spoken nothing to me
these thirty years. I have found in it
neither love nor solitude

—ERIC GAMALINDA,
"Lament Beginning w/a Line after Cavafy"

1

Another coup alert, always another. The city lived on rumors. No one took any chances. The government announced a 6 P.M. curfew. That morning, Arturo drove across town, transporting his mother, Aimee, her nanny, Filomena, and her baby from Marilou's house to the relative safety of his home in the gated community. The president, people whispered, had taken a private plane to seek refuge in a Carmelite convent in a southern island. People said Jimbo was planning the attack. Others said no, Jimbo wasn't the threat—all this was a diversion orchestrated by Ricky to create confusion.

Those were the rumors. Some of them, Arturo thought, had to be true. Kilometers away from his house, workers were hammering a wooden stage, fastening posters, testing lights and microphones for the rally. At 8 P.M. the next evening, if all went well, signs with the president's image would bob over the crowd. *President Peachy, we love you.* People hadn't seen her in weeks, they wouldn't see her at the rally, but they believed in her.

It didn't matter what he said on that stage. No one came to a rally to hear speeches. Most of the candidates around him would be movie stars or television personalities. No one would notice when he bartered a part of Lali's past, her father's conscience, any remaining belief in courage or honor, in exchange for Ricky's crude smile and the president's support. It was no longer possible to save himself.

In the late afternoon, rumors spread that rebels were marching toward Manila and government soldiers were setting up checkpoints at every entrance to the city. Marilou bathed in a sunken tub, surrounded by flickering candles, in the middle of the teak-paneled guest bathroom. Shadows hid her body. The lights were off, the shutters drawn. At the far end of the room, glass doors revealed a softly lit bamboo garden. Two maids sat on the floor around her, their legs tucked modestly under them.

"Thirty minutes in a milk bath, at least once a week," she told Arturo through the open doorway that separated the bathroom from the guest bedroom. "You should try it, *hijo*. My dermatologist says it's the best thing for your skin."

Sitting on the bed, Arturo turned his gaze to the news on television. "One day, Ma." He considered shutting the door, but she would feel upset, probably insulted.

An army general was talking on the screen, surrounded by reporters. The scene shifted to a boy soldier who was smoking a cigarette in a jungle. How old was he? Thirteen? Nine? Impossible to tell from that hollowed stare.

A faint whirring, outside, beyond the sounds of air-conditioning and the television. Arturo strode across the room, opened a window, stared at the sky. Nothing. The whirring grew louder, then faded. Another one began, intensified. Only military helicopters would be flying at this hour, so close to curfew. But were they defending the government, or deserting it? Soldiers had switched sides before, near the end of the General's reign, jumping from their tanks to join the crowds, landing helicopters near the protestors, and walking out with their hands up, waving white flags, while the crowd cheered.

"*Hijo?*" his mother called out from the bathroom. "You know her, my dermatologist? *Doktora* Macasaet? The one whose husband left her for his assistant?"

He heard the nervousness beneath her words. "I know her

husband," he said. He shut the window, twisted the handle to secure it.

Jimbo was a military man. The soldiers respected him. And more—Jimbo inspired them. He made them believe they could make the world a better place. That was where Ricky was vulnerable. Jimbo, like Gregorio, made people dream.

"Talk to me, *hijo*," his mother said plaintively. "How come you're not talking to me? I want to hear *exactly* what you're going to say at the rally tomorrow. Come here where I can see you."

"In a moment, Ma."

For the longest time, into adulthood, he had believed the world was good. He had believed that people, except for his father, were basically good.

"Remember, when you were in grade five, how you won the oratory contest thanks to me? I taught you how to perform every single line. 'O Captain! My Captain!' I was so proud of you. Are you going to tell me what you're going to say?"

"I haven't decided," he said gently, though he and his aides had discussed exactly what he and Lali had to do and say on that stage.

"Do you think we'll still have a rally?" she asked.

"I'm certain, Ma."

More whirring, muffled by glass and distance. He wasn't certain of anything. He sat on the edge of the bed. An image of Lali, in this room, a year ago. She had pulled him away from their own crowded party, hurried him here, to the guest bedroom, locked the door. Tangled black hair, a yellow bruise on her inner thigh, that wicked, inviting smile.

"And what about that wife of yours?" his mother called out, startling him. Most of the time, Marilou seemed absorbed in herself, but at times a shrewd animal intelligence surfaced, and she responded to his thoughts as though he had spoken them out loud.

"And who's that boy from the province she brought back? I don't say anything, you know. I bite my tongue. A hundred times a day, I bite my tongue." She sounded childlike, despite her words. Compassion stirred inside him. He wondered at what point she, too, had stopped believing in the person she had hoped to be.

"What does she want?" Marilou asked. "For you to act like he's your son? He's not your son. And she spends all that money on him. And his haircut! She thinks that now he looks like the other kids in the park? All the nannies know he's not."

The young maids sat quietly around the bathtub, eyes lowered, pretending not to be there. The muscle twitched on his cheek. There were layers of invisibility in this country. The revolution had failed almost everyone. He felt both angry and ashamed. He told himself he hadn't created the system. He told himself he couldn't change it. Whatever he did tomorrow, whatever that cost him, he would at least be protecting his family's future. And giving them a chance, even the slightest chance, even if it was too late for him, to save themselves.

Pilar held the telephone, pressing Arturo's voice against her. She hadn't heard from him since Filomena gave birth.

"I'm sending my driver to pick you up," he said. "It's not safe there. You need to come here."

"I'm fine," she replied. She was sitting at the dining table in her parents' home, her notebooks and folders spread in front of her, next to a pile of newspapers. She had been sitting there most of the afternoon, trying to read the papers or open the folders, her gaze returning again and again to the patches of sunlight on the floor.

"It isn't safe," he insisted.

"Nothing's going to happen."

He was whispering something. The sounds were muffled, as though he had clamped his hand over the speaker and was talking to someone beside him. Then he said, clearly now, "I'm sending the driver."

"There's no need." Her fingers slid back and forth along the edge of the table. "No one's going to stage a coup when everyone's expecting it."

She thought she could hear his breathing. She wondered whether he thought of her, whether he lay alone in bed at night and imagined her against him, as she imagined him.

"I don't want you to take a risk," he said.

She hoped he would say something else, apologize perhaps, or speak to her as he had in the province, in the river, all those times he had let her see the kind, complex man behind the surfaces life had imposed on him. She realized she had never loved anyone before him. Perhaps she would never love anyone else. To her surprise, she felt relief. There would be no need for other men. No emptiness, no searching. But then, there would be no children.

"I'm okay," she told him, smiling so he would hear only lightness in her voice.

Lali squeezed through an upstairs window and stepped out to the galvanized iron roof. Night had fallen, the sky unrelieved by a moon or stars. In front of her stretched the grey roofs and shadowed walls of mansions, broken in places by gardens or yellow lights. In the distance, on one of the high walls that enclosed the subdivision, dark figures walked back and forth. Guards, certainly. Armed. Beyond them, a scattering of red headlights on the highway, the illuminated signs on the roofs of five-star hotels.

We knew the Japanese were coming, her mother had said, even before we saw them. There was a stillness, an excitement in the air, like just before a typhoon.

Only a handful of headlights now on the highway. Lali imagined soldiers manning the checkpoints and waving cars away.

Tomorrow, on a stage, she would stand with Arturo and Ricky, betray everything her father stood for.

Her father would have understood.

She wasn't betraying her country. You couldn't betray what you had never promised or pretended to be loyal to.

Something was moving, on the far end of the highway, to the left. Small shadows, growing larger as they advanced. She began to see what they were. A military convoy, one dark-green truck after another, rolling across the highway. Government troops. She remembered the young men in the south, who had been huddled inside a truck and fingering amulets and crosses. And David's back, in the darkness, against hers, the smell of his fear.

She told herself David didn't matter. She told herself it was Arturo she wanted. She needed to believe this.

The highway cut across the city like a black river. Hundreds of small, star-like lights glimmered across Manila.

Suddenly, everything went black.

Lali shut her eyes, opened them again. Blackout. No lights anywhere—not in the streets, the houses, the gardens. She stood and scanned the horizon. The city, as far as she could see, had plunged into darkness.

A light flickered beneath her, in a neighbor's garden. A minute or two later, the beam of a flashlight swept over a wall. Slowly, in one window after another, feeble yellow lights appeared. Candles, perhaps, or kerosene lanterns.

She thought she heard Arturo calling out for her. She swung around, almost losing her balance.

Arturo gathered the family in the bedroom of Lali's mother. Two kerosene lanterns hissed on a counter. The windows were closed, curtains drawn, to keep the air cool. Lali's mother and Marilou lay on opposite sides of the bed, as far from each other as possible. On one armchair, the nanny cradled Aimee. Lali sat on the other armchair, the boy David squeezed in next to her. He was hunched over a coloring book, face close to the page, rubbing a red crayon up and down inside a balloon. She wrapped an arm around him. He pressed his crayon harder onto the page.

Lali watched Arturo fiddle with the radio. He hadn't told her he was coming back home, with Aimee and his mother.

A young man's voice on the radio: "Make sure that all your appliances are unplugged right now. Otherwise they'll short-circuit when the electricity comes back on!"

Arturo's shoulders tensed.

"We are getting reports that there was an explosion in a big power station south of Manila," the radio announcer said. "We have no confirmation yet. It seems there are thousands of homes, maybe hundreds of thousands, in Manila, all over Luzon, without light and electricity."

It's probably the government, Lali thought—Ricky ordering a blackout to frighten people, so he can justify whatever he's planning to announce at the rally.

"And that's our latest news update! Welcome now to the Tito Junior show. My guest tonight is Uncle James, beauty consultant to the Miss Philippines pageant. Uncle James, can you tell us what advice you give to women who want to join a beauty contest?"

The nanny stopped rocking Aimee. She stared at the radio.

On the radio, an older male voice said: "Well, aside from watching your figure, Tito Junior, you have to watch the news so you can answer questions intelligently. Poise also. And pastels— that's very important. No dark colors. They make you sweat, especially under the bright lights. Pastels reflect the heat."

"Thank you, Uncle James," the radio announcer said. "Any other advice for all the aspiring beauty queens who are listening to us right now?"

The smell of kerosene in the room. Lali wondered whether the fumes were bad for Aimee and David.

"Well, it's very important to develop yourself—to become outgoing, to meet people, to act sociable. Otherwise, how can anyone discover you? And once you enter a contest, never ever think of yourself as a loser. Always have a fighting attitude!"

Arturo tilted back his head, as he had done in the emergency room.

"We've just received a message from the president's office," the announcer said. "The technical issues at the power plants are being addressed. The rally tomorrow will go through as scheduled. Generators will be ready in case power isn't back. And all the stars scheduled to perform have confirmed their appearance!"

No one spoke, not even Marilou. On the bed, Lali's mother seemed small and frail, shrunken by Marilou's presence.

"And here's another announcement, from the Catholic Bishops' office. At precisely ten o'clock tonight, everyone is asked to go outside and make lots of noise, to show their support for all those who are trying to save the country. Who are determined to fight corruption even at the risk of their own lives."

"Good God," Arturo said.

"What did he just say?" Marilou asked.

"A protest, Ma."

"Ten o'clock tonight," the announcer continued calmly, as though he were reading a weather report. "As much noise as you can."

"A protest?" Marilou asked.

"A noise barrage," Arturo said.

A crackling from the radio, then static. The voices disappeared.

Lali tried to meet Arturo's eyes. He didn't look at her. A noise barrage, in the middle of the blackout. And the announcement came from the Catholic Bishops' office? That meant the archbishop himself must have given the order. To support Jimbo, perhaps, the rebels, whoever wanted to bring the government down. Or maybe not to support anyone, but just to protest—against Ricky, the government, the corruption, the rally, the people in that rally. That was crazy. Ricky would go ballistic.

The boy pressed closer to her. He rubbed the red crayon hard against the page, filling the balloon and shoving the tip beyond the outline.

Just before 10 P.M., she and Arturo climbed out on the roof. The city still in darkness. She stood next to him, her back against the wall. He was so close to her, yet remained so distant. The air was warm, humid. On other roofs, neighbors sat in clusters, shadows against the grey sky.

A spattering at first, like firecrackers. A car honked. Another honk, then another, several now, overlapping. Brief honks followed by long pauses, as though the people pressing on their horns were testing what would happen, waiting to see whether others would join in. A few isolated shouts from the neighbors' homes. Some kind of metallic banging. Dogs began barking.

The noises intensified. Honking cars, dozens of them, then perhaps hundreds.

Without turning his head, Arturo said, "They're doing it."

He sounded too emotional. She didn't know what to say.

All across Manila, it seemed, in driveways and garages, people were sitting in parked cars and pressing on horns, answering the bishops' call. The sounds gathered force, weakened slightly, rose again. In the house just across from theirs, the neighbors' teenage daughters stood by an open window, striking saucepans together. But the subdivision was relatively quiet, with too many people linked to the government or afraid to antagonize it. The noise, almost a roar now, was coming from further away.

Helicopters flew over them.

An explosion, in the distance, far more intense than the other noises. To the left, near the horizon, smoke covered part of the city.

Another explosion, closer to them. The horns and shouts and other noises stopped.

"We should go inside," he said, but he didn't move. He seemed mesmerized, as she was, as the neighbors on the rooftops seemed to be.

He returned with the radio, sat beside her on the roof. Helicopters continued to fly over them, the whirring stronger. He balanced the radio on his thigh. Scattered voices, some static. Then a young woman's voice: "We are hearing that many people have been arrested. We need to show them you're all behind us. We need your support. We need more noise. Please go out of your homes and help us."

"The last time there was something like this," Arturo said, "it was to kick out the General."

Lali waited. The noise barrage was starting up again, horns honking off and on.

He stared at the horizon. "How can I show up tomorrow? How can I stand next to Ricky and act like nothing happened?"

Suddenly, she understood. He wanted to be part of it—the protests, the clamor, the upheaval in the streets. He couldn't be part of it. She couldn't let him. She hadn't come this far, and at such cost to herself, to have him falter now.

"We have to think of Aimee," she said. "We have to think of the family." She thought: This is my life, too, Arturo.

He didn't answer. He was looking for a way out. He had never wanted to run for office. All that was Marilou's plan. He had tried only to do his duty.

More explosions, far away, then smoke in various areas of the city. The horns and banging stopped again. Ricky would be merciless. There would be tear gas and helicopters and maybe troops searching homes, making arrests, or threatening people, until the protest ended.

In a soft voice, he said, "The whole country's rising up against the government."

"Manila's not the whole country! You don't need a lot of people to make a lot of noise."

"I don't want to go on."

"You can't just back out." He couldn't do this to her. "We have everything to lose."

He began to speak. He said he was sorry for what he was about to say, but she had to understand. He told her about Ricky, the night at the palace. He told her there were other reasons to hate Ricky. He said: Your father switched sides, Lali. All that time, in San Francisco—

She listened calmly, as though from far away. This was the shock: she wasn't surprised. On some level, she had always known.

It wasn't the General who had him killed, Arturo said. It may have been Ricky, Peachy's people, his friends.

For a long while, she remained silent. At last she asked, "How could you know this and agree to be Ricky's candidate?"

"Ricky was threatening us."

"Don't talk to me about threats."

"You *know* the reasons," he said. "Everyone wants this from me. Everyone expects me to do everything."

"You should have told me!"

He shook his head. He ran his fingers over his eyes. She remembered her father's hands shaking, too, as he knotted his tie and put on his one good suit, the first time she had brought Arturo home for dinner.

"How long have you known this?" she asked.

He looked at her with compassion. "I didn't, until Ricky told me."

She turned away. The city was quiet now. The neighbors had disappeared from the roofs. The planes, the explosions—they had frightened whoever was out there.

It was difficult to breathe.

"Are you okay?" he asked.

It came to her that Arturo had probably seen through everything—her father's suit, her secondhand clothes, the false elegance of the dinner, her mother's efforts to please him. He must have seen, from the beginning, how desperate their situation was, how much they needed him. Why had she never seen it? Her parents needed her to marry him. To protect Pilar and her. To save her father and mother. In his heart, her father had wanted a good marriage for her. And Arturo had known this, and never mentioned it to Lali, never thrown it in her face, even in their most difficult moments. He told people he couldn't believe his luck when she had agreed to marry him. And he had made her feel that way, for so many years—that she was cherished, loved, his prize, undeserved, that he was the lucky one. And all the while, he had kept his secrets, and her family's self-deceptions, to himself. Arturo, with all his flaws, had tried in his own way to be honorable, perhaps far more so than her father, and herself. She hadn't seen it. How could she have been so negligent, and so proud? How had she allowed that love to flounder, thinking it would withstand everything? She thought of the underground rivers again, flowing between people, connecting them to each other. There was so much more to her and Arturo than this wreckage they had created on the surface.

She would never find her way back to him.

She couldn't ask him to run now, with Ricky, after what he had told her. There were certain lines even she could not cross.

"If I back out of the campaign," Arturo said carefully, "Ricky will try to hurt us. He'll probably reveal everything he knows about your father. He'll say your father was a traitor. Do you understand? He'll turn this against you, me, Pilar, your mother. Your reputation, mine. Our credibility."

He was whispering, yet he seemed more animated than he had been in a long time.

Her poor father.

Arturo rubbed his cheek. "Ricky will do all he can to hurt us," he said. "You realize that? We might have to leave the country."

"So we'll do it first," she said.

"Do what first?"

"We'll say what we know, before he does. About Papa. About Ricky's role in what happened to Papa. So it comes from us, not him. Then it isn't his weapon."

He lifted some strands of hair from her cheek and tucked them behind her ear. "You'll denounce your own father?"

"We'll still go to the rally," she said, more decisively than she felt. "We can say all this there. We have to plan it."

"No. It'll be safer to talk after the rally."

"I'm not scared."

He told her he hoped he would be able to say everything

she wanted to: expose Ricky, the government, the corruption, her father's killing. "You shouldn't have to do it," he said. "I can. But after we say it, we can't go back."

Her dream of a safe life, broken. But there was clarity, too. The choice, like all choices born of desperation, was simple.

"We have to tell Pilar," she said. "We have to warn her. She can't find out on TV."

The lost came to Lali only in dreams now. David, tall and gaunt, trudging through dirt paths in the night, under a yellow moon.

Lali lay alone in bed and tried to hold on to these images of him. David, the moon, the paths—all of them receding.

She switched on the bedside lamp. Light filled the room. Electricity was back. On the radio, the news about the rally. Soon thousands of people would be heading there. Manila was still on red alert, the entrances to the city were closed, but roads leading to the rally were open. Ricky had commandeered the city's public buses to transport supporters to the rally. She turned the dial, back and forth. The renegade station was no longer broadcasting. No one talked about the noise barrage.

After breakfast, as the sun began to heat the city, Lali drove through a highway and side streets to Pilar's home.

She rang the doorbell, pressed her palm against the wooden door. How long had it been since she had entered this house? Years. She hadn't been inside since they left for San Francisco.

The door opened a crack. Pilar's voice. "Who is it?"

"Can I come in?" Lali asked.

Pilar pulled the door wide open. "Is everything okay?"

"Everyone's fine."

Pilar stepped aside. Hesitantly, Lali walked past her. The old mirror in the hallway, the tiles on the floor, the threadbare couch, the verandah and tangled garden. Nothing had changed. A hollowing inside her, as though everything she had tried to feel or not feel since her father's death suddenly collapsed. In their place rushed in an almost unbearable sense of loss. Even the smells—the mustiness, that faint odor of mold, the wet earth—carried memories of him. It was difficult to step forward. He was everywhere. Their old selves, too, were here—Pilar and her as children, with their braids and starched, convent-school uniforms, skipping after each other through these rooms.

But there were no ghosts. She thought of the presence that had hovered over her shoulder for so long, the glimpses of a shattered face. Her father, she presumed, or Miguel. She hadn't sensed the presence in a long time. She couldn't feel it now. Perhaps it *was* Miguel—Sister Esperanza had said it was a young man—and the trip to the south had appeased him. It was good when ghosts disappeared. That meant they had moved on. Often, it was the living who kept ghosts in the world, binding them with their grief and attachment. Often, it was the living who tormented the dead.

She sat across from Pilar at the dining table. Between them, closer to Pilar, were two neat piles of folders, a stack of newspapers, several scattered papers, a spiral notebook.

"Arturo's leaving the campaign," Lali said, "after the rally."

Pilar reached for the notebook, opened it, tore out a corner from the last page. She tore the scrap of paper in half, then in half again.

"He's going to denounce Ricky," Lali said, speaking more loudly, as though this would make Pilar respond to her.

"You're not making sense," Pilar said.

Looking at Pilar's slender fingers on the table and at the scrap of paper in her hand, Lali talked about the noise barrage and the tear gas and what Arturo had told her, on the roof, about leaving the campaign. She was aware that she was rambling. She watched Pilar fold another corner of the paper, tear it out, shred it into pieces. She told herself she shouldn't be talking about Arturo to Pilar. She was here to talk about her father.

Finally, faltering, she told Pilar about what Ricky had said about their father. Pilar tore out another sheet of paper.

"Stop it," Lali said.

Pilar stood and began to arrange all the folders and papers into a single pile. In a low voice, she said, "If you or Arturo say anything—anything—against Papa, anything to hurt him—"

"We can't hurt him," Lali said. "But we can hurt ourselves."

"If you say anything at all, I will fight you. I'll deny everything. I'll say you're using this for political ends. I know a lot about Arturo and you."

Pilar wasn't denying anything, Lali thought. She just didn't want other people to find out. There was a difference. Had Pilar, too, sensed, on some level, what had really been happening in San Francisco? How many people had sensed something? Did their mother know? How many people had refused to see, or hidden what they did see from Pilar and her?

"Why do you believe what Arturo tells you?" Pilar asked. "Or what Ricky told him?"

"Because I *know*."

"I think Arturo's just shifting sides again, because the country is shifting." Pilar's voice was tight and pained. "As soon as the General lost control of the country, Arturo abandoned him. Arturo always abandons the losing side."

"Pilar, I'm sorry."

"How can you even consider—"

"We need to tell the truth."

"Since when do you or Arturo care about the truth?"

We're switching roles, Lali thought, as Arturo had done, as the whole world seemed to be doing. It was Pilar who believed

that people had to tell the truth, that honor and ideals mattered.

Stay focused, Lali told herself. You can't stay here all day.
You have to get to the rally.

Pilar kept rearranging folders in the pile, her hands moving
with nervous efficiency. Lali wished she could hold her sister's
hands until the nervousness stopped. Pilar was fragile. But
there was violence, an anger, in that fragility that had always
made Lali wary. She told Pilar, "We have to be good to each
other."

Pilar lowered her head and rubbed her forehead, as she had
as a child.

Lali couldn't remember a life without Pilar. She had hurt
Pilar, damaged her, in so many ways. She should never have
sent her to Arturo. She hadn't measured the consequences.

That wasn't true: she had measured the consequences for
herself, for Arturo, for her marriage. Not for Pilar.

So much to undo. So much of life couldn't be undone. Her
father must have felt that, too.

She remembered a rainy night in San Francisco, when he
had slumped into his armchair and told her: "Everything I
fought for—the best years of my life—was a mistake." She had
protested then. She told him he shouldn't speak that way. He
had done good things, great things. He shook his head.
"Everything was misconceived," he said.

How could she not have understood? Had her mother?
Was that why she refused to leave her room?

Pilar said: "How can you even think of saying anything
about him, after everything he did, for us, for the country?"

"He would want us to tell the truth," Lali said. She told
herself: This is how we can really honor him. This is how to be
like him, or like he wanted to be. Tell the truth about him,
even if it destroys him. He would have told the truth about
someone like him. Out loud she said: "You always blamed me

for marrying Arturo. But Papa *wanted* me to marry him. He wanted us to be safe."

"Then let's be safe. Let's keep *him* safe."

"It's strange to hear you—"

"We have to get rid of his papers," Pilar said.

Lali didn't speak.

"There can't be anything left," Pilar continued. "There mustn't be anything to find. Nothing anyone can use against him."

Lali remained silent, weighing what this meant, afraid to say something that would upset Pilar even more. She considered her options. She could tell Pilar they had to face the truth about their father, that they couldn't hide or destroy his papers. Or she could help Pilar destroy anything that might give them a better idea of who he was, and why he had done what he did.

The choice, again, was clear. Never mind her father's papers, his words, the secrets there. Pilar was in distress. Their father was dead.

"Tell me what you want me to do," Lali said.

Pilar looked at her with surprise and gratitude. "Throw them out. The books. We can put them out in the garbage. But the papers we'll burn."

Lali followed her sister into their parents' room. Her throat tightened. The crocheted bedspread, his desk, the bookshelf, the filing cabinet, the closet—these hadn't changed, either. By his desk were the cartons they had shipped back from San Francisco, unopened. Pilar had never looked through his papers. Perhaps, without admitting it to herself, Pilar had been afraid of what she might find there. Lali was certain now. On some level, Pilar, too, had known.

"Help me," Pilar said. "We have to do this quickly. Can you get the garbage bags?"

When Lali returned with the bags, Pilar was on her knees, with a pair of scissors, slicing open the tape that sealed the cartons. She stood and lifted the flaps, folded them outwards. Inside were folders, envelopes, books. The sisters flipped through the pages of each book to make sure nothing was hidden there, then placed the books in garbage bags. Next they removed all the folders and papers from the cartons and, without examining them, stuffed them into another bag. When that bag filled up, they began another. They opened their father's filing cabinet, pulled out all the folders, dumped them into the bag.

Lali's movements were swift and determined, but she felt shocked, and inside she was thinking: We can't destroy this. This is Papa's life.

She had to protect Pilar.

They tugged the bags of papers and folders across the floor of the bedroom, then the living room. They carried them into the garden. Pilar dragged a large metal drum, about three feet high and two feet wide, across the grass and set it in the middle of the garden. There were ashes inside, moist with rainwater, and a few leaves that hadn't burned completely.

Working quickly, without speaking, and without looking at each other, they emptied bags of papers, folders, letters, and photos into the drum. Pilar struck a match, held it to a sheet of paper, dropped the flaming sheet into the drum. She did it again, and again, until the fire began to catch. Lali peered over the edge of the drum. Flames spreading inside, rising up the walls of the barrel. Smoke. They backed away.

"Anything you say about Papa," Pilar said, "I'll fight you until there's nothing left."

Lali heard the doubt in her sister's voice. "I still have to say what I know, Pilar."

With the back of her hand, Pilar wiped her eyes. "Even if it were true, what you say about Papa, does it take away all the rest? Does it make everything else a lie? One mistake. He did so much that was good. He made one wrong choice."

"It changes everything," Lali said.

"One wrong choice. For the right reasons."

"Should we throw away his clothes, too?" Lali asked, looking for an excuse to leave the garden, this conversation, the smoke, the sight of her father's papers turning into ash.

"I can't touch his clothes," Pilar whispered. Then: "I'm scared."

Lali's eyes stung from the smoke. She, too, was afraid. But she told Pilar what she used to tell her when they were children: *As long as I'm here, I promise, nothing will ever happen to you.*

They wanted it to be true. They knew it wasn't. No one was there for anyone, in the deepest sense. People, even those you loved most and those who loved you most, could disappear, turn against you, hurt you more than anyone else, precisely because you had loved them.

Perhaps this was the strongest bond Lali would ever have—her love for Pilar, her attachment to her. With all its complications, it was deeper and would probably be more durable than what she felt for Arturo, Miguel, perhaps even the children.

She was wrong. Children were the only permanence. All the rest—the friendships, the passions, the loves—ended.

She had never known a life without Pilar.

Carefully, a few folders at a time, Pilar emptied another garbage bag into the metal drum. The sisters stood by the drum, watching the flame and smoke.

"I didn't think you'd come back to him," Pilar said.

Lali waited.

"I never meant it to go so far, La."

She was talking about Arturo.

"It's okay," Lali said sharply. "I don't want to talk about it."

"I'm sorry."

"Don't say that." Lali was determined to make Pilar stop speaking. "I'm the one who always lets everything go too far."

Pilar reached for her hand. "Don't go to the rally, La. It's dangerous. Don't antagonize Ricky. You saw how it was last night."

"If anything ever happens to me," Lali replied, "promise me you'll take the children."

I should have protected Papa, Pilar thought. I should have understood what was happening.

She was sitting alone in the verandah, after Lali left, staring at the drum, the smoke, the empty bags on the grass. Some of the folders and papers hadn't burned completely. She had to douse them with water.

Her father had changed during those last years in San Francisco. He spent most mornings and afternoons at home, watching game shows on television. He stopped lecturing them over dinner. He stopped asking Pilar's mother where she went during the day. Their lives were hard. No one wanted to make him feel responsible. Even Lali took a part-time job that she never talked about, as though to spare their father's feelings. Pilar couldn't remember what the job was. There were so many things she hadn't paid enough attention to. And the lights switched off in corridors, the pawnshops in districts where they thought no Filipino would see them.

What had kept the family alive all those years? Where had the money, little as it was, come from?

And every night, Lali sat by her father's armchair, leaned against him, while Pilar watched. He was wheezing then, his breathing so obstructed he couldn't lie down.

You have to stop smoking, Lali told him. You're killing yourself.

Everyone said Lali knew how to handle him.

You should have been a boy, he told Lali, with warmth and pride.

And once, speaking to someone on the phone, he said: I was wrong about Lali. People surprise you.

Her mother gave up on him. She needed her daughters to give her what Gregorio no longer could. When Lali brought Arturo home the first time, her father wore a suit and tie. Her mother brushed Lali's hair, fussed over her makeup, fastened her own mother's diamond earrings to her eldest daughter's ears.

One night in San Francisco, Lali told Pilar: Mama and Papa are both dying here. Can't you see that?

Lali had tried to save them. Lali had always been the good daughter.

On the stage, a line of wooden chairs faced the crowd. Arturo shifted uneasily in his seat, next to the other candidates—actors, actresses, television stars, the grandson of a former president, and heirs to political dynasties, several of them his neighbors. He could smell the barbecued pork from food vendors along the edges of the crowd.

Thousands of people jammed into the square, under floodlights. Old men and women, clusters of teenagers, middle-aged couples, young families with children. Had any of them been protesting last night? How many people had Ricky arrested? For now, at least, Ricky had erased all traces of the noise barrage and all other expressions of dissent. He had paid supporters to be here. Many others, Arturo was certain, came without payment, holding banners and posters with Gregorio's face. Many displayed Peachy's face, too. Ricky had sent word he would be arriving late. He was held up at a birthday dinner, his aides said. More likely he was in a parked van somewhere, the air-conditioner running while he drank or napped, waiting for a dramatic moment to enter the rally.

One of the country's most popular singers, a statuesque Spanish-Filipina in her fifties, swept onto the stage. She was wearing a sequined white and gold evening gown, her blonde-streaked hair tied in a chignon. The crowd cheered. She waved, gestured at them to be silent. The lights dimmed over the crowd. She began a heartbreaking rendition of a Tagalog love song. Her pure, clear voice, the haunting melody, the emotion in the words—all these contrasted with the humidity and heat of the night, the crowd, the agitation in Arturo's mind. He was aware that everything he was doing now, on this stage, would be for the last time. No sense of purpose or meaning could calm his fears. He had hated politics, the deals he had to make, the monotony of speeches and rallies, the islands flattened by poverty and terror, the corpses in funeral homes or living rooms. But it came to him, as he stared out at the faces and listened to the song, that he would miss some of it, the novelty and strangeness, those stunning landscapes, these faces.

The song ended. The crowd applauded. Manila's mayor strode across the stage, thanked the singer and the people for being there. In a rousing tone, he introduced the candidates, pointing at them as he mentioned their names. Speaking into the microphone, he asked the candidates' spouses to join them on the stage. Cameras flashed. Lali, wearing a white dress and a white flower in her black hair, squeezed in next to Arturo. She gave her bright, tight smile, the one she used for strangers. Her eyes were distant. He held her hand, which was soft and cool, unresisting but unresponsive. He told himself she, too, was anxious. The band started playing. The candidates and their spouses held hands and, in a line, stepped forward together, raising their arms in a V sign. The crowd's applause was restrained.

After several candidates had spoken, Lali and Arturo walked up to the microphone. She surveyed the square. Thousands of faces looking up at them. And everywhere, bobbing above the crowd, her father's face. She remembered arriving at the airport from San Francisco, after her father's death, and the crowds that had met them, many of them waving these same images of her father, and the band playing the songs he had loved.

Beside her, Arturo began speaking into the microphone. The usual campaign pitch, short and well-practiced. They would reveal nothing now. They had agreed on that. After the rally, when the children were out of Manila and just before they themselves left, they would meet a few journalists Arturo knew well, explain why Arturo was withdrawing from the campaign, denounce Ricky and her father.

She forced herself to smile and nod as he spoke. When he finished, she stood close to the microphone and thanked everyone for being there. She thanked them from her heart, she said. She said what she was supposed to say, with more warmth and fervor than the words deserved.

The mayor returned to the stage. At the microphone, he asked for a round of applause for the candidates and their spouses. When the clapping faded, he said it was time for the spouses to the leave the stage. "They'll be back soon!" he said. Arturo touched Lali's shoulder. She knew he wanted to tell her something, but this wasn't the time.

She followed the other spouses off the stage. Four of Arturo's bodyguards escorted her to the van a few blocks away. She entered it, settled into a leather seat. Two bodyguards sat in front of her, two in the back. The driver switched on the air-conditioning. She asked him to find a radio station covering the rally. They all had to wait now, for an hour or longer, while the candidates gave their speeches and entertainers performed, until it was time for Arturo and her to talk to the crowd again. She leaned back and closed her eyes, not wanting to think about what lay ahead.

On the stage, as other candidates spoke, Arturo searched the shadowed areas beyond the square, hoping for a glimpse of the van. He remembered Lali beside him, her scent and that sensuality she radiated even when she wasn't aware of it. He scanned the crowd, imagining the white dress and white orchid in her black hair, that cold and dazzling smile. She, too, was so much braver than she knew.

The news came over the radio. An explosion at the rally. The announcer sounded confused. Lali opened the window of the van. A siren wailing in the distance. Some horns. Then people running toward the van, away from the square. She couldn't see their faces. She told the driver to take her to the square.

The van tried to advance. Cars and jeepneys jammed the road in front of them, their headlights puncturing the night. The road was packed with people and tricycles and motorcycles, all moving away from the square. An attack, the radio announcer said. No one knew how many were hurt. More voices on the radio. Grenades, the announcer said. An army spokesman blamed the Communists. Government officials blamed the military, or Jimbo, or the guerillas. Journalists blamed the government.

Sirens and horns, audible even inside the van. In front of them, many people abandoned their vehicles and ran, squeezing into the dark narrow spaces between vehicles.

The van started to sway, rocked by the crowd. A blur of heads and dark hair, near the windows. The bodyguards jumped out, tried to keep people away. As soon as the rocking stopped, Lali opened the door. She plunged alone into the oncoming crowd, pushing against them.

As in a dream, disconnected from her body and the chaos around her, she forced her way through the dark streets. A crush of people, moving toward her.

She reached the edge of the square. Floodlights, as though for a movie, hurt her eyes. Fragments everywhere—pieces of wood, metal, paper. Smoke. At the far end of the square, the stage. Only about a third of it was still standing, wooden beams jutting out. The rest of the stage had collapsed. People were scrambling over the rubble. She couldn't see well. Bright lights but so many shadows. A poster of her father, near her feet. She became aware of sirens—ambulances, she thought, or police cars. A television crew. Stretchers. Now, she saw people on the ground. She saw people crouching over other people on the ground. That smell. Somehow, she was making her way across the square.

Up ahead, the stage. She sidestepped wood, metal, trampled posters, people. Where were all those lights coming from? She tried to look only at her feet. She wanted to walk more quickly, but her legs wouldn't obey her. A pounding in her ears. Maybe this was what it was like to be a ghost—you saw everything, but no one could see you, and nothing you did had any effect on what you saw.

She lifted her head. Now she saw too much. Hundreds of people in the square, the rescuers and the wounded, people like her wandering through the wreckage, distraught. And ghosts, too, suddenly, all over the square. She needed to reach the stage. She had to be logical. She had to plan a path through this chaos, to the stage. Where was he? Where would he be? She scraped her nails across her forearm, to make herself feel something so her mind would wake up and she would think clearly.

Now a man with a bony face was standing in front of her. "I am under the employ of the government, ma'am," he said in an odd voice, without inflection. "I can show you my I.D. I prayed very hard, up to this morning." He seemed to be in shock. She nodded, took a step away.

She started to run, awkward, stumbling.

Now she found an ambulance worker, who was kneeling. She knelt next to him, told him Arturo's name. He's a candidate, she said. He was on the stage. The man shook his head.

She stood, lowered her face to her hands. She prayed to God, Mother Mary, the Holy Spirit, Saint Jude, the presence over her shoulder, her father. She asked all of them to forgive her for all she had done in the past, for all she had not done. She asked them to save Arturo. She promised to try, with all her heart, to be good. No answer, no guidance. Only the smell of smoke, the cries of the wounded and the frantic.

Lali recognized the pale pink shirt first, then the curve of his shoulders, his hair. He was on the ground, not moving, head turned away from her. A large plank, near his feet. Other people, on the ground near him.

She forced herself toward him, her heart and mind pulling back. Now she was beside him. One side of his face was bloodied and damaged. She could only glance at it. A few meters away, ambulance workers leaned over someone. She rushed to them, would not leave them alone until they came back with her. Now they were crouching beside Arturo, tending to him. She covered his hand with hers. She forced herself to look at his face. So much blood. He looked like someone else, someone she knew. She couldn't remember whom.

She began to whisper to him, without knowing what she was saying.

"I can't see anything," he murmured.

He could speak. Elation.

"Everything's black," he said, panicked. She knew he was terrified of the dark. Very gently, barely touching him, she caressed his hand, told him she was there.

One of the ambulance workers told him not to worry, he would be all right, he had probably been blinded temporarily by the explosion.

Other people surrounded them now. They were lifting him onto a stretcher. They asked her to step back. They told her she couldn't come with them in the ambulance. They needed all the space. She told them she was coming anyway. She followed the stretcher through the crowd and wreckage, barely seeing anything around her. She asked them the name of the hospital. They told her to let go of his hand. Just before they loaded him into the ambulance, she leaned over to whisper to him again. At that moment, with horror, she recognized his face. It was the presence she had glimpsed over her shoulder, the shadow with the shattered face. She had thought it was her father, or Miguel, someone from the past. She was wrong. It was the face Arturo had today. She had been seeing the future, not the past.

Everything she knew about Arturo, about herself with Arturo, their marriage, their love—all that seemed to rush in front of her. For a few moments, she felt she was really seeing him. That vulnerable, uncertain, well-meaning boy. She hadn't known how to save him. The presence over her shoulder had been a warning. She should have tried to understand. She should have asked it questions. She had desperately failed Arturo, as she had failed her father.

She had to do something. If she did the right thing now, then everything would change and he would be all right again.

You have to give up what is most dear to you, Sister Esperanza had said, to receive what you want most in the world.

Lali prayed. She tried to make a deal.

She had been wrong to think he was hers. She had been wrong to think that if she tried hard enough, if she convinced him to try hard enough, they could be together again. They were finished. They had hurt each other too much. It would be a violence to hold him to her. She had to remove herself from him. That was the only way to save him.

She stood until the ambulance wasn't there anymore. She was shaking again. When it subsided, she walked back to the square. The lights stung her eyes. She wandered through the crowd.

Another explosion. It seemed far away. Then another, closer. The smell was terrible. A huge noise, deafening, her whole body jolted. Then the darkness.

*

Arturo could see again, with one eye. Bandages covered the other eye and most of his face. Pilar and his mother visited him every day in the hospital. They leaned over the narrow bed. Sometimes, in his delirium, he couldn't tell them apart. His mother brought him *lengua de gato*, *sans rival*, and baskets of fruit. A crucifix to hang over the bed and a Virgin filled with holy water for the bedside table. She hired three private nurses and bought a small refrigerator for the hospital room.

In the beginning, in his pain, he called out for Lali. She's in another hospital, his mother told him. There were more bombings, after they took you. She's okay, you'll see her soon. When the pain subsided, he asked for Aimee. She's only a baby, his mother said. She can't see you like this. You'll scare her.

When he was alone with a nurse, he watched the television mounted on the wall across from his bed. The same clip of Ricky, over and over again. Tanned and relaxed, wearing military fatigues and surrounded by supporters and journalists. "We've lost four of our top candidates," he spoke into a microphone. "Six more are still in the hospital. I was lucky. God was watching over me, but my heart bleeds for my friends and their loved ones."

There was a state of emergency, a newscaster said. Curfew had been imposed, all public gatherings banned. Newspapers were being raided. Jimbo's face flashed across the screen. Idealistic young soldiers had barricaded themselves in Fort Bonifacio and were calling on other troops to join them. The elections were postponed.

Arturo asked to see Lali. It won't be long, his mother said. They removed some of the bandages. He lost an eye. We'll replace it, his mother said. No one will know the difference. The doctors saved the other. That was a miracle.

He didn't want to see what had happened to his face.

He wanted to know what had happened to Lali.

"You'll look normal again," his mother said. "You won't go blind. You're not going to stop fighting. In my family, we're all fighters."

"Lali was there," he said, "at the square, after the explosion, after everything happened. I heard her speak to me."

"You were alone when the ambulance workers found you. You were unconscious. You couldn't *see*."

"She was there," he said. "Ma, I can still feel her."

Chapter Fourteen
Their Lives

Today I let light have its way.

—Angela Narciso Torres, "Recuerdo a mi madre"

They never found Lali.

And she had been the most alive.

She would never have left the children, Pilar and Arturo told each other. She would never have left *us*.

This was the story they could live with.

Pilar took care of the children, as Lali had asked her to. Pilar never had a child. After the bombing, after the hospital, she and Arturo moved with the children to a house on an island, by the beach. Arturo said he wanted a peaceful life, for all of them, with no space for violence. It didn't last very long. He said he missed Manila. Pilar knew he missed Lali most of all, but he was too kind to tell her this. She knew he looked at her and saw Lali. But Pilar saw Lali everywhere, too.

Pilar and Arturo tried, for a time, to be together. They told themselves it was good for the children. They hoped it would also be good for them. But she had seen his face, in the hospital, when he understood Lali wasn't coming back. You couldn't stay with a man when you had seen him weep like that for someone else. Pilar didn't hold this against him. We have one great love in a life, she told herself. His was Lali. He was hers. These were accidents. We don't choose our passions.

When it ended with Arturo, she took the children to San Francisco, far from the kidnappings and violence of Manila, and far away from him, too. He wanted them to leave Manila. He said they would have a better life in the States, a better chance at a life. He said he wanted them to save themselves, and he would do everything he could to help them.

Pilar brought up the children in a house outside San Francisco. It was the first place she had ever felt a gentle, sustained happiness. She sensed Lali there, almost every day, especially in the beginning. It was true, what Lali said: you never lose those you lose violently. It was strange, Pilar thought, how you ended up finding your life, but not where you thought it would be. She had never expected children. She had never expected or imagined the happiness that came with children. It seemed to her there were times in a life when things just came together, and it didn't necessarily have anything to do with you. There were the hard years, the years of uncertainty and panic, which could last a long time, no matter what you did. There were the plateau years, when nothing really happened, when you waited for something to happen. Then there were the happy years, when everything just seemed to flow. The happy years, we get once in a lifetime, Pilar thought, but we realize that only when they're gone. And those were her happy years, in that house outside San Francisco, with Aimee and David.

With Arturo, too. He often came from Manila to visit them. He was a very good father. He adopted David and came to love him as his own son. He saw Lali in David, too. Every Valentine's Day, he sent roses to Aimee, Pilar, Filomena, his mother, and Pilar's mother. He took care of all of them. Filomena and her daughter lived with him. He sent Filomena's daughter to university and found her a good job. As he grew older, he sponsored other scholars, all young women, and he visited them regularly in the province and paid for their schooling and expenses in exchange for their company and affection. He never married again.

People didn't notice his fake eye, or hardly. Sometimes he wore an eye patch. That made people remember what had happened to him. Some people thought he was a hero. He said all he had done was survive a bombing.

Pilar never wrote a book about her father. She collected newspaper clippings about Arturo. He went back to politics. He never denounced Ricky. He never revealed what he knew about Gregorio. It was too late to say anything, he said, after the bombing, after what happened to his eye, after Lali wasn't there anymore. He had to build his life again. He had to make the family safe again. In twenty years, he never lost an election. When he was campaigning, he visited as many as ten wakes a day. He learned to look without distress at the dead.

Ricky was elected president, and Arturo backed him. Arturo became almost as corrupt as Ricky, but there was goodness in him, too, which Ricky never had. Arturo still brightened a room when he entered it. People loved him. Men and women touched his shoulder when he talked to them.

He adored Aimee. She went to business school in Boston and worked for the Philippine National Bank in New York. She looked like Lali—the eyes, the heart-shaped face, that dazzling smile—but she reminded people of Arturo, the way he used to be, in her tenderness, in her belief that people were basically good, in the way she made everyone feel special and seen. She married a golden-skinned, green-eyed banker from New York who loved to sail almost as much as he loved her. She expected to be happy. She expected to be loved. And so she was. She had no interest in the General, in Gregorio's death, in Gregorio's life, in Arturo's politics, in the past. She had no memories of Lali. She knew Lali from photographs and Pilar's stories. It hurt Arturo to speak about Lali, and when Aimee was old enough to understand this, she stopped asking. She loved Arturo and Pilar. She spoke on the phone to her older brother, David, almost every week.

David remembered Lali. People who didn't know his story said he looked like Arturo. A darker version of Arturo. Lali was right. Faces changed. Upbringing was stronger than blood. David was the toughest of them all. He went back to Manila, worked for Arturo's campaigns. Much later, he ran for office himself. People said he had politics in his blood. Like father, like son, people said. Pilar did everything she could to convince him to stay in the States. He wouldn't listen. She told him it would break her heart if he moved back to Manila, if he entered politics. Only bad can come from this, she told Arturo. One day he'll go back to the province and look for the men who beheaded his father. And his own cycle of violence will begin.

Pilar no longer feared birds singing at night. She was afraid of water. The Pacific, the Atlantic, the Pasig, the South China Sea, ponds, and rivers. She worried when she heard that Aimee and her husband and Arturo were sailing. She had images of water rising and taking them in. At times she couldn't breathe, imagining this.

The General's children returned to the Philippines. Two sons were popular congressmen, and the youngest daughter became governor of her father's home province. Jimbo went to prison and was released, and he was elected senator the next year.

There was much Arturo and Pilar wished they had understood. How years of good acts and good intentions could turn or break in an instant. How life could break in an instant. What they might have done, what they might have said, how they could have saved Lali.

We did what we could, Pilar told him. They both needed to believe this. We tried our best, Pilar said. They were flawed people, in flawed lives, but they had wanted to be honorable, or at least kind, in a world where it was often difficult to be either. They needed to believe this, too.

Lali had told them she loved them. Arturo and Pilar carried her words inside them, whether or not they were true, with the children's love and their affection for each other. On Lali's birthday, in different parts of the world, Arturo, Pilar, Aimee, the young David, and an older David entered churches and lit candles for her. In the end, Pilar and Arturo told each other, life gave more than it took away. The family lived far apart but never lost each other. When they were together, they found in each other's eyes and words traces of what they had loved most in Lali, and, at times, when they needed it most, glimpses of what she had loved in them.

ACKNOWLEDGMENTS

With gratitude especially to Karina Bolasco, Thomas
O'Brien, Greg Brillantes, Ray Else, Eric Gamalinda, Marie
Houzelle, Laure Millet, Georgia Smith, Hannah Davis Taieb,
Jessica Zafra, and the DWG writers: Albert Alla, Mia Bailey,
Kirk Butler, Peter Brown, Mary Ellen Gallagher, Rafael
Herrero, Helen Cusack O'Keeffe, Sophie McVeigh, and Tasha
Ong (extra thanks to Tasha for that invaluable final reading). I
am grateful to the Warren Wilson MFA faculty and alumna,
especially Aneesha Capur, Chris Causey, Nick Fox, Shadab
Zeest Hashmi, Murad Kalam, Victor LaValle, Krys Lee, Karen
Llagas, Kai Maristed, Kevin McIlvoy, Allison Paige, Robert
Rorke, Kimberly Jean Smith, Irene Svete, and Ellen Bryant
Voigt, with special thanks to David Haynes. In perhaps more
ways than they know, I am indebted to Peachy Avanceña, Dina
and Babsie Chuidian, Nathalie Cunnington, Tina Cuyugan,
Ron Day, Karla Delgado, Marisa Grassi, Luisa Igloria, Miriam
de Vera Lacaba, Pete Lacaba, Marra Lanot, Anthea Linklater,
Em Lombos, Ed and Diego Maranan, Fidel Nemenzo, Arnel
Patawaran, Tata Poblador, Dodi Quimpo, Marivic Raquiza,
Barbara Jane Reyes, Ramon Sunico, Asanka Suraweera, Eileen
R. Tabios, Angela Narciso Torres, Ricky de Ungria, Marianne
Villanueva, and Alfred Yuson. Kassia Aleksic and Oona
Viguerie, thank you, again and always. And finally, to my

friends, loves and companions in Paris, Manila, and else-where—including the Pinay sisterhood in Paris, Assumption and Ateneo friends, the PSI group and others—you know who you are, and how much your stories, love, and friendship have meant over the years.

Excerpts on each chapter page are used with permission from the following authors: Eric Gamalinda, "Lament Beginning w/a Line after Cavafy" in *Returning a Borrowed Tongue*, edited by Nick Carbó, Minneapolis: Coffee House Press, 1995; "Two Nudes" in *Amigo Warfare*, Ohio: Cherry Grove Collection, 2007; Maria Luisa Igloria, "Riversong" in *Blood Sacrifice*, Quezon City: University of the Philippines Press, 1997; "Petition to be Allowed to Love without Limits" in *Blood Sacrifice*, Quezon City: University of the Philippines Press, 1997; "Chinatown, Moon Festival" in *Going Home to a Landscape*, edited by Marianne Villanueva and Virginia Cerenio, Oregon: Calyx Books, 2003; Nick Joaquin, "May Day Eve" in *Nick Joaquin: Prose and Poems*, Manila: Bookmark Inc., 1991; Emmanuel Lacaba, "Il Principe" in *Salvaged Poems*, edited by Jose F. Lacaba, Manila: Salinlahi Publishing House, 1986, second printing: Quezon City, Office of Research and Publications, Ateneo de Manila University, 2001; Resil B. Mojares, "Catechisms of the Body" in *Waiting for Maria Makiling: Essays in Philippine Cultural History*, Quezon City: Ateneo de Manila University Press, 2002; "Haunting of the Filipino Writer" in *Waiting for Maria Makiling: Essays in Philippine Cultural History*, Quezon City: Ateneo de Manila University Press, 2002; Barbara Jane Reyes, "A Genesis of We, Cleaved" in *Diwata*, BOA Editions Ltd., 2010; Eileen R. Tabios, "Pilipinx," from the MDR Poetry Generator; *Puñeta: Political Pilipinx Poetry*, edited by Eileen R. Tabios, Chicago: Locofo Chaps, Moria Poetry Press, 2017; Angela Narciso Torres, "Postcards from Bohol" in *Rattle* #24 (Winter 2005); "Recuerdo a mi madre" in Jet Fuel Review (jetfuelreview.com/angela-narciso-torres-fall-2017.html), Fall 2017; Ricardo M. de Ungria, "Continuing Love," written for the Agnes Locsin dance "A Love Story," in honor of Carmen D. Locsin, *Cordite Poetry Review* (two-poems-by-ricardo-m-de-ungria/), October 31, 2012; Alfred A. Yuson, "Pillage" in *Our Own Voice* (poems2002c-10.shtml), October 2002.